First,
Do No Harm

First,
Do No Harm

Larry Karp

First Trade Paperback Edition 2004

10 9 8 7 6 5 4 3 2 1

Library of Congress Catalog Card Number: 2004117190

ISBN: 1-59058-166-0   Trade Paperback

Poisoned Pen Press
6962 E. First Ave., Ste. 103
Scottsdale, AZ 85251
www.poisonedpenpress.com
info@poisonedpenpress.com

Printed in the United States of America

For Myra
The Song Is You

Know then thyself, presume not God to scan;
The proper study of mankind is man.
Placed on this isthmus of a middle state,
A being darkly wise and rudely great...
Created half to rise, and half to fall
Great lord of all things, yet a prey to all;
Sole judge of truth, in endless error hurled;
The glory, jest and riddle of the world!
Alexander Pope
An Essay On Man

Chapter 1

In the light of blue moons, certain doctors appear and blaze into legend, medical sports of nature with diagnostic acumen beyond uncanny, healing powers just this side of miraculous. I'm not talking about the likes of Pasteur, Semmelweis, Walter Reed, healers whose heroic campaigns against the double-headed dragons of disease and human stupidity won them seats as Knights of the Hippocratic Round Table. Legendary docs are not knights, but Merlins, watching over fiercely bubbling cauldrons full of dark ingredients. Dark ingredients, strong magic. Darker ingredients, stronger magic, but greater risk of the pot boiling over—disaster. Unspeakable ingredients...

My grandfather was one of those Merlins, though I didn't know it until just a couple of days ago. I didn't know anything about my grandfather until a couple of days ago, and I'm twenty-eight years old. Dad never would talk about his father, strange, but Dad is Leo Firestone...yes, *that* Leo Firestone. The painter. Refusing to mention his own father's name is way down on the list of Leo Firestone's oddities.

Way up on that list is Dad's art. Nightmarish, bizarre. A teddy bear with barbed-wire fur next to a small disembodied hand, fingers gouged, bleeding. Couples embracing through jagged shards of glass. Doorknobs shaped like grenades. Spring-loaded knives poised to fly up through the seat of a well-used armchair. A mother putting her baby to her breast, the nipple a minefield of tiny blades. Worst are the faces, never shown directly, features shadowed and indistinct, a compelling ambiguity that never fails to pull me, resisting, into the damn paintings, to be slashed and stuck and gouged.

Dad first caught notice in the Fifties, one of those stormy young postwar artists in New York who somehow managed to find time to work despite a full schedule of brawling and carousing. Some of Dad's early companions flamed out in alcohol; some went out on the wrong end of a hypodermic needle. Others gave up, bought a suit and tie. But Dad prospered. Critics pronounced his work as brilliant as it was troubling. Gallery owners fought to feature his canvases. The more Dad called them leeches and vultures, the more they pursued him. Brilliant timing, the perfect Sixties *artiste*, he left a legacy of angry insults and bloodied faces that may never be matched by any painter, sculptor, writer, or musician.

By the early Seventies, Dad could call any shot he wanted. He sold his little place in the Village, bought a piece of property on Peconic Bay, way out on Long Island, and built a house and studio for himself and his pianist-friend, Tanya Rudolph. Maybe music really does soothe savage breasts, but more likely Tanya just had what it took to stand up to my father. Early on, their fights were the stuff of tabloid headlines, but the only people who ever came away injured were those who tried to get between them. A year after they moved to Peconic, Tanya became Mrs. Firestone, and two years after that—following some loud and serious discussions—I made my appearance. Mother wanted two children. Dad finally agreed to start with one and see what happened. The fact I remained an only child speaks for itself. That, Dad would talk about. My grandparents, never.

Our house was a white stucco-coated Chinese puzzle, all intersecting acute angles, lots of glass. Inside, teak and mahogany-paneled walls covered with paintings, Dad's, his friends'. My favorite was a five-by-four canvas of Mother, hung directly above her Steinway grand in the living room. Typically cryptic face, but Mother, no doubt. Dad really caught that particular way she angled her hip when she stood, the familiar tilt of her head, her flowing platinum hair. Mother went white in her twenties, had the great good smarts to never dye it.

Personality encounters were frequent at our house, artistic skirmishes routine. But space wars, never. Mother's kitchen was immense, bright with copper and steel. Her Steinway seemed dwarfed in its corner of the massive living room. I had both bedroom and private playroom. At one extreme of the house stood Dad's airy painting studio, at the other, his den, a small room with no windows. Dad kept that room locked whether he was inside or not, and Do Not Disturb was understood. No one but Dad went in there, ever. Not Mother, not the cleaning lady, not me.

Wild...first word to mind for my childhood memories. Winter nights, wind-whipped sheets of water against floor-to-ceiling windows, heavy percussive beat of waves slamming into the shore. One weekend when I was seven or eight, Norman Mailer came to visit. Picture me under the round glass coffee table, watching two men with dark raging eyes, beefy faces, crowns of wild black curls, going nose-to-nose, at least half-crocked, over some artistic particular I couldn't begin to understand. Mailer was no pygmy, but Dad was three or four inches taller, with more muscle and less fat. Mother sat at her piano, hands gliding over the keys, white hair dancing around her face. Every now and then she stopped playing long enough to sip at a drink and study the combatants over the rim of the glass. Laugh lines traveled from the corners of her light blue eyes, then she tossed out a line that stopped Dad and Mailer cold. They all laughed, laughed, laughed.

I was no honor-roll student, worked only at what interested me, responded with equal indifference to carrots and sticks. I refused to learn anything by rote, accepted no givens—a pesty kid, always with a "Why?" or a "How?" Dad called me Professor Skeptikos, used to tell Mother they should've used birth control on that trip to Greece the year before I was born. "He drives me nuts. Asks a question, I give him an answer, here come ten more questions."

One Saturday when I was eleven, Dad came back from a day in New York carrying a carton and wearing a smile straight off the Sphinx. He set the carton on the kitchen table, kissed Mother, then turned to me. "Well? Aren't you going to open it?"

Christmas in March? I tore into that carton, and when a thick manual fell out I thought I'd burst. "A *computer*. For me?" I ran over, hugged my father.

"Atari-ST," he growled. "Supposed to have the best color graphics. And some new system where you can compose music, then hook up a synthesizer—"

"MIDI," I hooted. "Oh, wow!" I scanned the room, a little man trying to spot a cab in a downpour. Dad jerked a thumb toward the front door. "Rest is in the car, you can help me schlep it in. Monitor, printer, bagful of books. It's a kind of kit. You've got to put it together."

I drew in a breath. I'd been a model-builder since the age of four, when I got a Lego set. At eight I built a model car that ran, at nine, an airplane that flew.

"Maybe *that*'ll keep him out of my hair for a little while," Dad muttered at Mother.

Mother smiled, slipped me a wink.

Dad got me out of his hair, all right. He clearly knew nothing about computers, no point asking him questions. But if he was trying to nudge me toward a career in the arts with that Atari, he failed miserably. Color graphics and

MIDI ports were fun, but the computer itself was a whole new world. I found out about bulletin boards, spent a chunk of my savings on a 1200-baud modem, tied up our phone for hours, equal parts software and smut. Not long 'til I began to tinker with the software, putting together programs that by all rights should've blown higher than Everest, and sometimes did. But more and more often, they performed as I intended, usually pointing the way to a new challenge. Add, upgrade, *ad infinitum*. My childhood playroom became a jungle of wires connecting components set on shelves among books, floppies, tapes, CDs. I worked after school, weekends, and summers to support my habit. When I finished college, I signed on as program designer with Custom Softies, a company in a little office on the tenth floor of an old office building on East Fifteenth, near Union Square. Took a week to move all my stuff into my new apartment in Manhattan.

Five years, no problems, but then my bosses overextended. A couple of weeks after employees voted to accept an across-the-board pay cut, Dad came in to New York to supervise an exhibit setup. Afterward, he took me to dinner. When he asked what was new, I told him about the salary cut. He shrugged. "You'll get by."

"I suspect," I said. "But just in case, I took a night job."

Dad looked amused. "What kind of night job?"

"At Bellevue..." I paused as Dad's face settled into a scowl, clay hardening. "Bellevue's Cardiology Department is one of Custom Softie's biggest accounts, so I spend a lot of time there. Last week, I saw an ad on a bulletin board for part-time nurse's aides. O.J.T.—"

Dad sprang to his feet roaring. "Jesus *Christ*. A nurse's aide? At *Bellevue*? Most ridiculous goddamn thing I ever heard." He reached into his pocket. "How much do you need?" Wallet out, open, fingers pulling at bills. "Shit, Martin, I've got more money than I can ever spend." He held out five hundreds. "Here. Quit that fucking job."

People around us turned to look. I brushed the money away. "Thanks, Dad, but I'd rather try to do it on my own."

The rest of the meal was a disaster. I don't think Dad spoke ten words. After that, I always took care to avoid mentioning my second job, and Dad never brought it up. I worked three partial shifts a week at Bellevue, and a full shift on Sunday. I checked vital signs, gave medications, made sure charts were up to date, emptied bedpans. I even met a girl at Bellevue, married her last year. When I introduced her to Dad and Mother, I told them we'd met at a party.

I watched the Bellevue doctors carefully, listened just as hard. Sometimes they took me aside to explain points. Dr. Charles Donovan, an internist, kept encouraging me to apply to medical school. I talked it over with my wife. Helene gave me that soft smile, the one that had sent me out to buy an engagement ring. "I think that's wonderful, Martin. I do. We'll have no trouble managing on my income."

"But we've talked about children—"

"We'll just keep talking for a while. Do it, Martin."

So I took the M.C.A.T., had an interview at N.Y.U. Med School, and got accepted. Helene was thrilled. "Let's go to Palais Royal. It's Friday, but maybe we can get a late table...oh, wait. Your parents?"

"I never told them I applied," I said. "If I didn't get in, easier to not have to explain why."

Funny look. Helene handed me the phone. "Well, now you don't need to explain. Just call them. See if they'd like to come in and join us."

No way around it. Three tries before I punched the right numbers into the phone. Dad answered. "Firestone."

"Dad? Martin. I've got something to tell you."

"Somebody's a little late this month?"

"Not that, no. Dad, I applied to medical schools this year, and I've just been accepted. N.Y.U."

Silence...well, not quite. Better, no words. I heard a choking sound, almost strangling. "You *what?*" Dad finally said.

I wished time into rewind. "Got accepted to medical school. I'm going to be a doctor. Start the day after Labor—"

Dad cut me off with a volley of language as foul as I've ever heard, made steelworkers sound like sixty-year-old schoolmarms. I tried a couple of times to break in, but it was like holding a sheet of cellophane up to the stream from a firehose. Finally, Dad barked, "You know where Manny's is? Restaurant."

"Well, sure. You've taken me there a lot. Second, near Fifty-fourth."

"Meet you there tomorrow, one-thirty. Lunch." Not a question, not even a statement. "I...I've..."

First sign of weakness, but I knew better than to take advantage. Just waited.

"Got a story to tell you." Slam.

Helene looked up, brows together, as I set down the phone. "Martin, what on earth happened?"

"I walked into an ambush, that's what. For some reason, Dad's more than unhappy. Sounds like I'll get the score tomorrow. Lunch, command performance."

"Your father's very strange, Martin. Sometimes he scares me."

The words were out of my mouth before I completed the thought. "The scariest people are scared people."

This was not like Dad, not at all. A story to tell, barely able to contain it? Dad never told me stories, not about birds and bees, not about anything. Aphorisms were more his style, one-line zingers, right to the heart of the matter and the gut of the listener. As I waited outside Manny's, I couldn't imagine what was coming.

One-thirty sharp, there was Dad in his favorite gray work shirt, splotch of bright green paint above the pocket. He nodded, motioned me inside, not a word.

Lunch hour waning, several highbacked mahogany booths empty. Dad motioned to one all the way in back. "We're going to be here a while," he told the headwaiter. "We'll order, then I don't want anyone bothering us." He pulled a fifty from his wallet, handed it to the *maitre d'*, who slipped it in one smooth motion into his shirt pocket. "I understand, sir. I'll let your waiter know."

As we slid into opposite seats I snuck a look at Dad. Cheeks finished with rough sandpaper, skin slack over the bones. Fatigue lines etched at the corners of his eyes. Dark eyes bloodshot, muddy. Hair tumbling over his forehead and ears. How much sleep did he get last night? How much did he drink? Seventy-six years old, still knocking down the sauce from dark to dawn, then going all-out the next day. He flipped the menu open, scanned it, set it down, looked around.

The waiter, a slim young man in white shirt and snappy plaid tie, caught Dad's eye, scurried over. "Yes, sir? You want to order already?"

Nod. "New York steak sandwich, rare. And a Manhattan, heavy on bitters. Martin?"

I tried not to think about Dad's liver. "Same sandwich," I said. "And iced tea."

The waiter scribbled. "Got it." He slipped his order pad inside his cummerbund. "Headwaiter talked to me. I'll bring your orders soon's they're ready. Then, you want something else, *you* call *me*. Right?"

Dad allowed himself the tiniest trace of smile, not pleasant. "Right."

The waiter left quickly. Dad drummed fingers on the table top, looked one way, then the other. Slowly, those black eyes turned toward me, focused, locked into place.

"All right, Martin. What's with this crap about medical school?"

I learned as a young boy, flinch and I was a goner. "No crap," I said. "I applied, I got accepted, I'm going. If there's crap, it's coming from your side of the table, and I don't understand. I'm not asking you to pay my way. I'm not asking you for anything. What the hell's your problem?"

"What's my *problem*? I'll *tell* you what's my problem." Head cocked, left eye half-closed, mouth twisted like a badly healed scar. "I ask my son a simple fucking question and he won't give me an answer. Martin, why...the...hell... do...you...want...to...go...to...medical school?" Every word punctuated with a sharp nod of his head. Then the ultimate shrug, hands extended toward me, palms up.

Where was he going, my crazy father? I cleared my throat. "All right. Computers are exploding in medical use. Horizon's endless. In ten years doctors will use them every day. Diagnosis, treatment, consultation. Research, devising new paradigms—"

Dad's huge fist hit the table so hard I jumped. "God-damn, Martin, you're not at an interview and I'm not a dean, so spare me the bullshit. First, you take a lousy night job for peanuts to work at a hospital. Now, all of a sudden, at twenty-eight, you're going to medical school. I'm asking you why, and I want an honest answer. Is that too much to expect?"

Dad watched me like a hawk taking aim at a poor salmon, flopping its way upstream in shallow water. "Dad... I'm not sure I *can* tell you exactly why. All those years I played with computers, I thought I was making science fiction real, and then I started working with the cardiac team at Bellevue. I saw them put new valves into hearts. Dad, I watched a *heart transplant*—they put a new heart into a man's body, he was dying. Three weeks later he walked out of the hospital. What could I ever do with a computer to match that? If a computer crashes, no big deal, just start over, but a doctor gets just one chance, and he'd better do it right...no, he's *got* to do it right. I felt hollow, Dad, trivial. Like the big game's going on, people pitching, batting, catching, throwing, the crowd's cheering...and there I am on the bench in the dugout, a lousy batboy. When I saw that ad on the bulletin board, I had to take it. And you were right. Nothing to do with my pay cut."

All of a sudden, Dad looked like a man just told the governor had declined to issue a last-minute stay. "I'm going to tell you a story, Martin." Voice like a ghost's. "Should've long ago, maybe, but I thought...hoped... June, 1943, I was sixteen. Finishing my junior year of high school. Summer before, I worked as a soda jerk, Ransome's Confectionery, a few blocks from our house. But Mr. Ransome enlisted in the Navy that spring, closed the store, sold the property."

Dad, a teenaged soda jerk? I must've smiled, because he stopped talking, stared at me. "Hell's so funny, Martin?"

"Sorry, Dad. I just can't picture you behind a soda counter with a little white cap on your head."

Lines around his mouth softened. He seemed to be looking at something far away. "Neither could Samuel."

"Samuel?"

"My father."

"You called your father by his first name?"

"My mother too. Part of your grandfather's way of teaching me self-reliance. As far back as I can remember, it was 'Count on your*self*. Trust your*self*.'"

Dad's eyes, black ice. His story hardly begun, already enlightening. "Didn't people think that was strange?" I asked. "Especially in those days?"

"If it were anyone else...but your grandfather was Samuel Firestone, and Samuel Firestone's son calling his parents by their first names was the least..." Again, that massive fist, bang, on the table top. Silverware clattered. "Martin,

God *damn* it. Would you kindly shut up for a minute and listen to me?"

The waiter set down our drinks, glanced at Dad, left in a hurry.

"Sorry, Dad. I'm all ears." I gave him the go-ahead.

He glared just a bit too long, almost smiled, managed not to. He coughed, knocked down half his Manhattan in a swallow, then turned back to me.

All right, then. One evening at dinner, a week before school was out, Samuel asked whether I'd found a summer job. I told him no, but I had a couple of leads.

He jumped in, both feet. "You can use this summer to see what being a doctor is really about. I'll make you my extern. Take you to the office, to the hospital on rounds, into surgery. House calls, emergencies. Where I go, you'll go."

I couldn't answer. Sixty years ago, doctors were revered, trusted without reservation. People cracked jokes about lawyers, bankers, politicians, even ministers, but never about doctors. But even more than that, there was something about my father…when he walked into a room, people stopped talking, stopped whatever they were doing, turned to him. He defined center stage. Where he'd go, I'd go? I might still be sitting there wordless at the dinner table if my mother hadn't said, "Samuel, do you think that kind of work would be good for him—staying up all hours, going to some of the places you go? He's only sixteen, still a growing boy. And with all the men who've been drafted, he shouldn't have any trouble finding a job."

Samuel laughed, pointed at me. "He's six-four, a hundred-eighty. If he grows any more… All right, Ramona, I won't overwork the lad, promise. If I keep him out at night, he can sleep late the next day. But it's time for him to stop being a soda jerk. Next year, he'll be going to college, and the sooner a college student declares for premed, the better his chances of getting into a medical school. Or, if Leo's drafted, he could choose the medical corps."

"If that's what he wants." Ramona tried to keep her voice even, didn't come close. The thought of her son, her only child, being drafted and going off to Asia or Europe to be shot at, was her special nightmare. "Do you want to be a doctor, Leo?"

"I don't know," I said. "Maybe, if I'm good enough. But I also like to paint."

Samuel leaned toward me across the edge of the table, then started to smile. When your grandfather smiled, the room lit. Tanned face, perfect white teeth, black wavy hair, neatly trimmed. The most alert blue eyes imaginable. I could never read *The Great Gatsby* without seeing my father. Now he turned that smile on me full blast. "You can still paint, Leo. Painting's a great hobby, good relaxation, but you need to live your life in the world. I say you're plenty good enough to be a doctor, and this summer you can learn firsthand what being a doctor is all about. What do you say? Think you can handle it?"

He was some piece of work, my father. Not "Do you want to?" or "Would you like to try it?" "Yes, I can handle it," I said to Samuel, with all the offended dignity a sixteen-year-old could muster.

Samuel stuck out his hand. "Shake, Extern."

Ramona, pale, silent, watched me shake.

"You start first day after school's out," Samuel said. "Hospital rounds, eight o'clock." That was it. All employment formalities taken care of. In 1943, a doctor didn't need anyone's permission to give a student a summer externship. Especially if the extern was his son. Especially if the doctor was Samuel Firestone. He was a legend in Hobart.

Hobart, New Jersey, where Dad grew up. One of those metropolitan Jersey cities still struggling to recover from the disasters of the Sixties, but in Dad's youth, Hobart was a textile town with a busy central business district surrounded by vibrant ethnic neighborhoods, families going back three, four generations under the same roof.

So that summer I carried my father's big black bag. It took me no time to see he was a great doctor, an outstanding diagnostician, but there was something else. The minute your grandfather walked into a room and caught the patient's eye, that patient knew he was going to get better. You could read it all over his face. I watched Samuel treat sore throats, heart disease, diabetes, learned how to set broken bones. I assisted at gall bladder surgery, went along on post-op visits. Then one night, after I'd been on the job for almost a month, Samuel shook me awake just a little after twelve. "Come on, Leo, up, move it. Sick kid Down-river."

I threw on clothes, charged after Samuel, outside. He had the 'thirty-nine Plymouth started before I was onto the passenger seat. We backed out of the driveway, Samuel's face glowing in streetlamp light. Gasoline rationing stickers on the rear windows flashed into view, a black-and-white A, good for three gallons a week, for ordinary persons to make do. But Samuel Firestone was not an ordinary person, and he never just made do. Next to the A was his C sticker, doctor's guarantee of fill-up on demand. The day I watched him put on that sticker he winked at me and said, "Every job's got bennies."

Not much traffic at twelve-thirty in the morning. We shot down Roosevelt Avenue at fifty-five, never mind the wartime thirty-five-mile-an-hour speed limit. No cop in town would've stopped Samuel Firestone's car, not even for an air-raid drill, not for any reason. Windows wide open, mid-July, a real Jersey summer night, temperature about eighty, humidity in the nineties. Samuel wheeled a sharp right off Roosevelt onto Straight Street, then across to Fulton, finally a right onto River Street. A couple of blocks up, he pulled to the curb, killed the motor, set the brake.

I grabbed the emergency bag off the back seat where Samuel always kept it, jumped out, paused long enough to lock the doors. Not many people in Hobart locked cars in 1943, but in that neighborhood you did. Down-river was Hobart's equal-opportunity neighborhood, big fat zero for everyone. Mazes of crooked little streets squished between the shopping district and the Passaic River, tumble-down coldwater shacks only real estate agents would call houses and no one would call homes. Bars, brothels, dollar-a-night hotels. Down-river was jagged bottle-edges, knives, guns. You tried not to let the sun set on you Down-river.

Not easy to keep pace with Samuel. We ran past Marvin's Bar, music blasting into the street over drunken shouting and laughter. Artie Shaw, "Perfidia." Samuel danced along, double-time. He motioned me past a couple of sorry little houses into a narrow open doorway, then up a flight of stairs to a small landing. Air like a blanket soaked in piss, sweat, and months-old cabbage stew. Wall plaster yellowed, chipped. Samuel motioned toward an iron handrail, lower end hanging loose. "Careful, Leo." Then he took off up the steps, three at a pace. By the time I hit the second-story landing, he was knocking at the door. "Lou, Lena," he called. "Samuel Firestone."

The door flew open. Samuel strode in, me on his heels, trying to look a hell of a lot surer than I felt. Just one room, curtain pulled across the back to make a bedroom, tiny kitchen off to the left. From behind the curtain came loud sobs, now and then a whimper. Couple of windows up, but not a stir of a breeze off the river. I could taste the stench of rancid cooking fat, shit, human secretions. A short chunky man in an undershirt and boxer shorts stood near the curtain, bloodshot eyes glaring at me. The man swiped the back of his hand across his nostrils. Samuel smiled. "Lou Westcott, my son Leo. He's learning to be a doctor."

Lou raked stringy black hair back off his forehead, then nodded at me, almost a bow. "Welcome." One word, couched in respect. No argument if Dr. Samuel Firestone wanted to bring his son along to learn the trade.

Samuel flipped his Panama onto the post of a ratty stuffed green chair, then turned to a stocky, coarse-featured redhead in a nightgown that barely covered her breasts above and her crotch below. "Lena, you're looking good. Little guy's in back?"

Lena pointed toward the curtain. "He's got pain, Doc, don't know what's the matter." I heard generations of hardscrabble Appalachian farmers in Lena's twang. "Just rolls around, pullin' at his shoulder. I wanted to do a mustard plaster before I called you, but he wouldn't let me put it on."

Samuel glanced toward the curtain, where the sobs were slowly developing into howls. "How long's he been hurting, Lena?"

She glanced at Lou, who let out a low growl like a threatened animal. "Just about an hour, Doc. Not even."

Samuel looked at his watch. "Little before midnight, then. Was he asleep? Woke up with pain?"

Again Lena looked at Lou, but before she could say anything, Samuel moved toward the curtain. "Let's have a look." He pulled the curtain aside, and there on a filthy uncovered mattress sat a two-year-old version of Lou, pasty face mottled from crying, making frantic grabs at his right shoulder. I could've painted him onto velvet, straight from life. "Hey, Bub," Samuel said. "Shoulder bothering you, is it? We'll take care of that."

He walked to the low bed, sat on the edge, talking all the while, eye to eye. He had that little boy mesmerized, only an occasional snuffle. But when he reached for the injured shoulder, Bub pulled away.

Lena said, "Bub, now you let Doc Firestone look at your shoulder," but Samuel didn't seem to hear her. He took the doctor's bag from me, snapped it open, fumbled around inside, came out with a New Year's noisemaker, one of those little blat-horns where you blow paper out, then it rolls back. He blew. Bub jumped six inches. Samuel blew again. The kid started to laugh, reached for the noisemaker, then screamed and clutched at his shoulder. Samuel nodded, put the mouthpiece between Bub's lips. "Blow," he said. The boy just stared at him. "Blow!" The kid blew a short blast, laughed again, then blew harder. Lena let out a sloppy giggle.

"Keep blowing, Bub, that's right," said Samuel, all the while fiddling gently with the boy's shoulder and upper arm.

"Dislocation," he mumbled in my direction. "Subcoracoid, most common kind. Elbow's displaced out from his side, see? And that bump in his armpit—head of the humerus. No crepitus, so probably no fracture." Samuel stood up, took us all in with a look. "I'll need your help," he said. "The three of you."

"What's wrong?" Lena, anxious.

"Shoulder's dislocated. Must've happened when he fell out of bed."

Lena went white. I thought Lou might hit the deck. Samuel didn't seem to notice, just kept talking. "We've got to get the bones back into place, then keep them there. Only take a few seconds but it'll be painful. We'll put him on the floor, on his back. Leo, you kneel across him, right below his stomach, rest your hands on his chest. Lena, sit above his head, hold it down. Lou, keep his left shoulder on the ground. None of you let him move, not a muscle. That's important. Understand?"

One yes and two yeahs. Samuel smiled. "Boy'll be fine, don't worry." He shrugged out of his jacket, slung it onto the chair, sat on the edge of the bed, winked at Bub. Then he unlaced his right shoe, slipped it off, dropped it. Bub started whimpering again.

"Come on, Lena," Samuel said, very gently, then stood up. "Sooner we get started, easier it's going to be on everyone."

As Lena bent, I could see all the way to China down the front of her nightgown. She picked up the boy as if he were made of eggshell, lowered him to the floor.

"Now," Samuel said. "Everyone in place, fast."

Lena cradled the boy's head between her hands. Lou fell onto the boy's left shoulder. I flopped across his belly. The kid started to howl, legs kicked wildly under me. Samuel scampered to the floor at my left, shot his stockinged right foot into the boy's armpit. "Look at the shoulders," Samuel whispered to me. "See the difference?"

"Right one's sunken on top," I said.

"Sure is." Samuel grabbed the boy's flailing hand. Slowly, firmly, he pulled downward, then pressed the arm against the boy's body. "Watch the shoulders," Samuel whispered again.

The kid let out a screech that could've shattered glass, as the lump in his right armpit slid up and out of sight. The shoulders looked symmetrical.

"Okay, done." Carefully, Samuel laid the boy's arm across his chest. "Leo, go get some gauze strips out of my bag. Lena, Lou, relax, just a little. Let him sit up."

By the time I got back with my hands full of rolled gauze, the war zone had pretty well cleared. Bub was snuffling but calm. "Start unrolling," Samuel said, not letting go of the boy's hand. "Still hurt, Bub?" The boy shook his head. The way Lena looked at my father made my cheeks flame.

Calmly, slowly, Samuel wrapped gauze around Bub's arm and shoulder. When the boy started to cry again, Samuel picked up the noisemaker, stuck it into his mouth and blew. He kept blowing, loud, then soft, long and short, as he worked gauze round and round, splinting the boy's arm against his chest. "Dislocation means you've torn a ligament," he muttered to me between noisemaker blasts. "Move the arm before the ligament heals, it dislocates again."

Finally Samuel stood up, stretched. "Sit in a chair with him, Lena. Hold his arm just like we've got it. He'll need a little medicine." Samuel grabbed his jacket, slapped the Panama into place on his head. "Back in a few minutes."

I could hardly contain myself. Soon as we got into the car I asked Samuel how he knew the boy had hurt himself by falling out of bed. Samuel smiled, this time not pleasantly. "Most common cause of shoulder dislocation is a fall on the outstretched hand or elbow. Did you look around that place? Where does the little boy sleep?"

"I didn't see any—"

"Other bed? No, there isn't one. The kid sleeps with his parents. Did you smell the booze on them?"

"I smelled something. But there were so many smells in there—"

"All right. Here's what happened. Lou and Lena left the kid in the bed asleep, went down to the bar, had a few shots, came back ready for some business people usually like to conduct in private. But they've got no privacy. Probably they woke the kid, he got in the way, and one of them gave him a shove or just out and pitched him off the bed."

"Are you going to call the police?"

"The *police*?" Samuel sounded weary. "Leo, think. Those poor red-earth southerners came up here looking for jobs in the silk mills, didn't know silk's been on its uppers for the last ten years. If they can squeeze out a couple bucks a week they're doing well. Look where they live, for Christ's sake, look how they live. Children are the last thing they want or need, but their creator gave them an irresistible urge, and their priest tells them contraception's a mortal sin." Samuel was shouting now, any momentary fatigue blown away. "They have a few drinks to take the edge off their pain, then go home to do just about the only thing two people in their situation can do to forget it all, if only for a while. Kid wakes up, starts crying. A little impatience, little thoughtlessness, and there's your dislocated shoulder. Next week they'll go to confession, be forgiven, and drop money they can't spare onto a plate so the Pope can buy another gold cup for a cathedral. You want me to call the cops, Leo? Who for?"

Samuel wheeled onto East Sixteenth, pulled to the curb near the corner of Seventh Avenue, snapped off the ignition as if he were angry at the car. "Suppose I call the cops," he said. "Suppose they lock Lou and Lena up. You think that kid'd be better off at the county orphanage?"

He threw the car door open, jumped out, slammed it shut. I did the same, then followed him to the door of a pharmacy. Dark inside. Samuel rang the buzzer, once, twice. A man's head poked out the second story window. "We're closed," the man bellowed. He jabbed a finger at his watch. "It's nearly two in the goddamn morning... Samuel?"

"Get your fat ass down here, Jack," Samuel shouted back. "Emergency."

A couple of minutes later, a light went on inside the drugstore, then the door opened. A big man wearing only green and white striped pajama bottoms stood in the entryway, peppering Samuel with silent anger. He ran fingers through a meager crop of greasy reddish hair, as if that might stimulate it to grow. "You and your fucking emergencies," he growled at Samuel. "What is it this time? Some nigger got watermelon withdrawal?"

My father didn't say a word, just stared. When the man began to shuffle in place, Samuel started talking. "Few things, Jack. I need a pediatric sedative, phenobarb elixir. A tonic, yeast, B-C vitamins, iron. Cod-liver oil. Oh, and roller gauze. Ten packs." He nodded toward Jack's black woolly chest. "Don't get any hair in the medicines."

Jack stomped off behind the counter, muttering. He pulled bottles from shelves, measured, mixed solutions through funnels into small brown bottles, all very meticulous. That impressed me. Never mind his nasty talk, no matter how he really felt, if he had to do that job he was going to do it right. Samuel strolled through the pharmacy, aisle by aisle, hands behind his back. Finally Jack waddled up to him, a bag full of bottles in one arm, bag of gauze rolls in the other. "Be six eighty-five, Samuel."

"That's with the doctor discount?"

Samuel's voice was calm and level, not so Jack's. "Doctor discount?" the fat man bellowed. "Shit, Samuel, this isn't for your own use. Or your family's."

"That sick baby with no watermelon is my nephew," Samuel said, and now there was an edge to his voice that put me on ready alert. "You can extend my courtesy that far, considering…"

"Aw right, aw *right*." Jack waved a hand of surrender back and forth in front of Samuel's face, then stormed to the cash register and rang up five dollars and forty-eight cents. "Christ Almighty," he grumbled. "Get waked up middle of the night to lose money."

"When you start with a sixty percent markup you don't lose by giving twenty," Samuel said. "If your brain were half as smart as your mouth, you'd say thank you and mean it."

Jack gave Samuel a sour look with his change. Samuel tipped his hat as we left. I felt like the invisible boy—all the time we were inside no one said a word to me. I wondered what Samuel meant for Jack to consider, but didn't dare ask.

As we pulled away from the curb Samuel said, "She's going to have to keep that shoulder immobilized a while." "She," I noticed, not "They." "Kids heal faster than adults, but if he moves his arm before the ligament's had a chance to grow together, his shoulder'll come apart again. And a kid like that needs tonics and vitamins because he doesn't get anything like proper food."

Back at Lou and Lena's, the little boy didn't even whimper while Samuel and I wrapped his chest and arm into a sling. As we put him into bed, Samuel's hand slid under the dirty pillow, a fast out-and-back like a lizard's tongue. Lena looked at the bottles and gauze, then at Lou. She worked a button at the top of her nightgown. Finally she said, "Doc, how much's all this gonna—"

"Part of the call," Samuel said. "I'll put it on the tab." He pointed to the bottles of tonics. "Teaspoon of each with breakfast and supper every day. And he can't move his shoulder at all for a couple of weeks. Don't take off that gauze, not for anything. Bring him to my office in the morning, ten o'clock. We'll see how he's doing, take a couple of X-rays. Write it down if you have to, Lena, because if you aren't there—"

Lou, all this time slumped against the far wall like a prisoner waiting for sentence to be passed, suddenly went stiff. Lena jumped forward. "I'll be there, Doc."

The two of them nodded like Oriental windup toys. Samuel smiled. "Good."

"I'll be there," Lena repeated. "And I promise I'll give him his medicines, just exactly like you said. I won't let him out of my sight, not for a minute."

Lou came forward, grabbed Samuel's hand. "Hey Doc, thanks. You're the only—"

He was going to say my father was the only doctor who'd come Down-river at one in the morning to see an injured kid with stone-broke parents. Who'd not only come, but would make sure the kid had all the medicines he needed. Who'd know the parents had caused the disaster but would treat the kid anyway, and not call the cops. Samuel cut him off with a handshake and a quick pat on the arm.

Right then the wall phone in the kitchen rang. Lena picked off the receiver, listened, then held it out toward Samuel. "For you, Doc."

Samuel said hello, then, "Go ahead, I'm listening." Could've been anything from a stroke to the sniffles, no clue from my father's face. After about a half-minute, he said, "They think it looks like a *heart attack?* Call them back, Ramona, tell them I'll be right over."

"Another patient." Lena's tone suggested she herself was being put upon. Samuel smiled as he gave her back the phone.

We were away from the curb, flying up River Street, before I'd slammed my door. I shouted above the wind whipping through the open car windows, "What'd you do right before we left? Your hand, under the pillow?"

Quick glance sideways, little smile. "You don't miss much, good. Five-dollar bill. Lena'll find it soon as she goes to look after the boy. Maybe she'll buy a little decent food."

"You don't think she and Lou'll just spend it on liquor?"

Street lamps made a strobe show of Samuel's widening smile. "No, I don't. At least until that kid's shoulder is healed, every time the two of them turn around they're going to see my face. And Leo… Sometimes it won't be their imagination."

Chapter 2

Dad stopped talking as the waiter set plates in front of us. The young man looked at Dad's empty glass. "Another drink, sir?"

"Yes."

Heavy grease for vocal cords. Dad watched the waiter walk away, then snapped off nearly a quarter of the sandwich, chewed, spoke between bites.

Where was I...oh yeah. My shoulder whacked against the car door as Samuel peeled a hard right onto Fifth. Cross streets flew by. At Twenty-second, he turned left, braked with a squeal, pulled up in front of a small house behind a chain-link fence. I reached for the door handle.

"Wait in the car, Leo. Be back in a few minutes."

"Wait in the *car?*" I didn't stop to think, just fired two barrels of teenage guff into my father's face. "That's the way you're going to show me what it is to be a doctor? By making me sit in a car at two in the morning?"

Samuel moved his head so the brim of his Panama shaded his eyes. Once, when I was five, he took me to the circus; we watched a juggler throw one ball into the air, then two, three, four, five, six, seven. That man was keeping seven balls going, and all the while the crowd cheered, my father just muttered, "Go for eight. *Go for eight.*"

"You said where you went I'd go," I barked. "What's in that house you don't want me to see?"

Samuel's smile said both "You win," and "You asked for it." He nodded. "Come on."

I grabbed his black bag and trotted after him. He was already at the gate, pushing it open. We walked along a concrete path, then up six swaybacked wooden steps. The porch sagged inward and to the right, where three windows were set into a tricornered bay, cheap white lacy curtains behind them. To the left of the bay, the front door, open behind a battered screen panel. Samuel rang the bell, called out, "Murray? Lily?"

The waiter put Dad's second Manhattan on the table next to his plate. Without looking away, Dad grabbed the glass, gulped a swallow.

A light went on over our heads. A few seconds later, a barrel of a man in an undershirt and a pair of grimy work pants lumbered to the door. "Samuel, jeez, what took you so—" He stopped cold when he saw me, then stared at my father. Not quite the reception I'd gotten from Lou.

"It's all right, Murray." Samuel sounded as if he were soothing a kid awakening from a nightmare. "Leo's working with me this summer, wants to see what doctor-business is really like. We were on a call Down-river, sick little boy. Ramona caught up with me there."

I thought my father's voice changed just a bit on the last two sentences. Little more emphasis on each word, little more time between words? Murray's eyes told me nothing. He opened the screen door. "Murray Fleischmann, my son Leo," Samuel said. "Murray and his father and brother run Fleischmann Scrap, up Fifth at Wait Street."

Like shaking with a ham. My hand vanished. Murray was a round, bulky man with thick, hairy arms and the neck of an ox. Not someone to ever take lightly. He released my hand; I rubbed my tingling fingers. Then he pointed at the wall to his left. "In the living room, Samuel." Voice like a file on hard wood. "Lily's in there with him."

We followed Murray through an archway into the room behind the angled bay. Furniture straight from the junkyard. Old ugly overstuffed chairs, a sagging couch, nothing matched. At the middle of the floor, a woman stood wringing her hands over a man who was lying on his side, twisted, body bent like a Hallowe'en cat. Relief spread across the woman's face when she saw Samuel, but as she noticed me her eyes widened and her hand flew up to cover her mouth.

At the sight of the man's face I dropped Samuel's bag. A wide-eyed corpse grinning like a diabolical spirit makes an impression on a sixteen-year-old boy. "He's...dead?" I blurted, then felt ridiculous.

Samuel crouched over the body, took the man's right wrist between thumb and forefinger, dropped it, then looked up at Murray and the woman. "Lily, this is my son, Leo," Samuel said, just as matter-of-factly as he'd told Murray a minute before. "He came along on a call Down-river. First time for him, seeing a dead person." He looked me up and down, smiled. "At least as far as I know."

I nodded. Everyone in that room knew the man on the floor was dead, but only Samuel could *pronounce* death. I couldn't pronounce anything, just extended a shaky hand toward Lily.

Boiling summer night or not, Lily's hand was icy. She was tall, slender as Murray was round, with features as delicate as his were coarse. She wore a light blue summer bathrobe, obviously nothing underneath. Shining black hair, dark eyes, eyebrows plucked. I heard my mother's voice, "A cheap woman."

Samuel straightened, which drew my attention back to the man on the floor. Eyes bulging, skin bluish, purple lips twisted into an expression of anguish nearly a laugh. A froth of saliva ran from the lower corner of his mouth. Dead, but he looked still in agony. "What happened?" Samuel asked.

Murray looked at Lily. She returned the look. "Tell him."

"No, *you* tell him."

"No, *you*."

"Aw *right*," Murray growled, then pointed at Lily. "She was upstairs sleeping, which I couldn't do—too goddamn hot and humid. I was sitting down here, looking at the paper." He pointed toward a brown leather chair in the far corner, next to a cardboard-shaded floor lamp; pages of newspaper lay scattered in front of the chair. ALLIED AIR FORCES BLAST RUHR. "I hear someone on the steps outside and think to myself, what, past one in the morning, who's coming? Screen door opens, then I hear a shuffly noise. I'm up on my feet, going through the room, when something goes thump in the front hallway. I run on in and there's Jonas, down on the floor, holding his chest, groaning something terrible. 'Murray, help me, I can't breathe.'"

The big man snorted, covered his eyes. His shoulders heaved. Lily put a hand on his arm. He cried harder. "*Christ*, Samuel." Murray pulled a crumpled handkerchief out of his pocket, swiped his face, then extended both arms, a silent plea for help. "There's my brother on the floor, he can't breathe, terrible pain in his chest. I tell him don't worry, I'll get you comfortable and call Samuel Firestone. So I lift him up, walk him into the living room, I'm gonna put him on the couch. But all of a sudden he falls down, right where he is now."

"Murray hollered, woke me up. I ran down, thought maybe we should try giving him mouth-to-mouth..." Lily's small voice petered out. She looked about to cry too.

"It wouldn't have mattered," Samuel said. "He was probably dead before he hit the floor, massive heart attack. Nothing would've brought him back. Last time I checked him, couple of weeks ago—" Samuel stopped just long enough to take in Murray's and Lily's astonished faces. "You didn't know? He didn't say anything to you?"

"About?" Murray looked at sea.

"His heart condition."

Murray and Lily gawked at each other, dumb-struck twins.

"He was in the office once or twice a week the past few months," Samuel said. "Shortness of breath, chest pain. I put him on medication, nitro and digitalis, told him to take things a little easier, cut down on cigarettes—"

"Cut down on…?" Murray wailed. "Guy smoked two packs a day since forever. And he didn't let up at work, never for a second. Always schlepping that heavy crap around the yard. If I'd'a known, I wouldn'a ever let him—"

"Like you could've stopped him." Lily patted Murray's hand. "What your brother wanted to do, he did. He only knew one way to live."

"And now he's dead. Thirty-six years old."

Samuel took Murray by the shoulders, propelled him into the hall. "Go in the kitchen with Lily, drink a cup of tea. Your family have a preference in funeral homes?"

Another silent exchange between Murray and Lily. Lot of lines to read between in this house. Finally, Lily said, "Most of the Jewish families around here use Rappaport."

"No family besides you and Oscar?"

Murray shook his head. "Nope. Just me an' Pop."

"Jonas never got married, did he?"

Murray chuckled. "No way. Jonas loved the ladies all right, but never the same one for long enough to get any knots tied."

"Okay, I'll take it from here. Go on, both of you, get a load off your feet. I'll call Rappaport."

Samuel dialed, talked, hung up the phone. "They'll be here in a few minutes to pick up the body," he said to me. "I'll sign the death certificate, and that should do it."

I'd been staring at the dead man on the floor. "Samuel, how did you diagnose a massive heart attack?"

He smiled, then pointed at the body as if it were an exhibit in a grand museum of death where he was curator. "Medical history of a man with severe coronary artery disease who won't admit to it, won't slow down. A bomb waiting to go off. Tonight it went. Murray said Jonas clutched his chest, complained of severe pain. The pain of a heart deprived of blood is terrible.

You cut off blood to the heart, the heart can't pump nearly as well, so less and less oxygen gets circulated to the body. Skin goes from pink to blue, patient dies."

"Why couldn't it have been a stroke?"

"With chest pain? A stroke, he'd have grabbed his head, complained of headache."

"How about a…what do you call it? When the aorta blows out in the chest?"

"Aneurysm?"

"That's it."

He clapped my shoulder. "Good thinking, Leo. Symptoms might be similar with an aneurysm, but that's where probabilities come in. If you're out in the street and hear hoofbeats, more likely you'll see a horse than a zebra. Aortic aneurysm blowouts are very rare, but severe heart attacks happen every day. On top of that, Jonas was a hard worker and a heavy smoker. All adds up."

"But you still can't tell for sure without an autopsy," I said.

Samuel shrugged dismissal. "Seems clear to me Jonas had heart disease, but all right—just for a minute, suppose I'm wrong. Let's say he *did* rupture an aneurysm. Think, Leo. Would that matter to Murray and Lily? Or Pop Fleischmann? What'd be the point of doing an autopsy? Why should we inflict more pain on the family, never mind the cost?"

Samuel never scored intimidation points in arguments, didn't have to. He nailed you on reason. Still, I wasn't satisfied. I stared at the body. Jonas Fleischmann's eyes stared back at me. I knelt beside him, brought myself by short degrees to touch his hand. Warm. But when I lifted it, his entire upper body came along. Like moving a deformed wooden statue.

"Rigor mortis," Samuel said from behind me. "After death, muscle proteins coagulate, make the body stiff. Lasts several hours."

"It must come on pretty fast."

Samuel nodded agreement. "Yes."

"All right." Then I asked if he knew where the bathroom was. He looked me up and down. "You're…"

"I'm fine," I said, trying to sound manful. "Just have to pee."

Samuel led me out of the living room into the hall, past a flight of stairs, into the kitchen. Lily and Murray, each with a teacup, sat at a small white table in front of a stove. Samuel pointed to a doorway at the back of the room. As I walked off, Samuel said, "Murray, did you call Oscar?"

Murray looked like a sixth grader who forgot the big assignment 'til teacher called for the papers. "I wasn't sure if I oughta wake him up to tell him a thing like that."

I wanted to hear more, but was already at the bathroom. Inside, I pressed my ear to the wooden panel, no good. Voices, but I couldn't make out words. Finally I did what I went in there to do. When I came out, Murray, Lily and Samuel were on their way into the hall. I ran after them. They let in the Rappaport Funeral Home attendants, led them into the living room. While Samuel filled out the death certificate, the two attendants worked Jonas Fleischmann's body into a canvas bag. Samuel wrote quickly. Cause of death, massive coronary thrombosis. Underlying conditions, severe arteriosclerotic coronary artery disease. Then he signed his name, and we all followed the attendants outside, to the open rear of the hearse. The two men slung the bag, thud, then slammed the door, hustled up front, got in, drove off. Samuel saw the expression on my face. "All in a night's work for them," he said. "Too easy to get used to some things we never should take for granted."

Lily walked over, rested both hands on my father's forearms. "Samuel, thank you. I just don't know what we'd've done—"

"My job," he said casually. "Sorry, Lily." He took Murray's hand. The big man looked ill at ease. "Hey, Samuel, you're sure you don't mind...I mean about telling Pop? What with the way him and you—"

"No sweat," Samuel said, sharply I thought. "We'll stop on our way home."

As Samuel started the Plymouth, he looked my way. "Tough for a parent to lose a child, tough for another child to break the news. Murray couldn't bring himself to tell his father, so I'll do it." Samuel hung a quick midstreet U, then drove to Fifth and turned left.

"I was wondering…" I said.

Samuel half-turned his head.

"Mr. Fleischmann—Jonas. His hand was so warm. I thought you didn't get rigor mortis until the body cools off."

"Good point, Leo. Usually you don't. But when a person's in excruciating pain right at the moment his heart stops, all his muscles are clenched, and that's how they stay. Terrible way to go."

I said the okay that means this is as far as I can go right now. Come morning, I'd do some reading.

Samuel stopped in front of a small frame house up a hill behind a crumbling waist-high concrete wall. The wooden steps groaned under our feet. Samuel motioned toward a hole in the porch flooring, nudged me gently to the side. He rang the bell, waited, rang it again. From inside I heard, "Yeah, yeah, I'm comin'. Hold your pants." Then a man opened the door.

Talk about being created in a father's image. A forty-years-older edition of Murray Fleischmann filled the doorway. Light from a bulb in the porch ceiling reflected off Oscar Fleischmann's oily brow; behind his high forehead a gray thicket ran rampant. An unlit cigar dangled from beefy lips. Black grease all over his undershirt, chest hair grease-caked into whorls and tangles. Dirty khaki pants held at the waist by a string, a ragged hole at the left knee. I counted five buttons in his open fly. Piggy eyes moved slowly from Samuel to me, then back to my father. Oscar pulled the cigar from his mouth with two sausage-fingers, then rumbled, "The *fuck* you doin' here, Sammy?"

Never in my life had I heard anyone speak to my father in anything like those words and that tone. And "Sammy"? I'd never heard anyone even call him Sam, not his friends, not my mother. But he didn't seem to notice, just said lightly, "How're you doing, Oscar?"

Oscar laughed disparagingly. "How'm I doin', he wants to know. At two in the mornin' how *should* I be doin? An' why's he all of a sudden give a hoot in hell about how I'm doin'?"

By the time I realized he was talking to me, Samuel said, "I've just come from Murray's, Os. Sorry, but I've got bad news for you."

"What, Murray ain't dead, is he?"

"Not Murray," Samuel said quietly. "Jonas. I'm sorry."

A laugh, more disparaging than the last. Oscar turned around, then waddled back inside the house. Samuel followed. I kept at a safe distance behind him.

When we reached the living room, Oscar stopped, shoved his cigar back into the corner of his mouth, looked both of us up and down. The room was a pigsty. Few lumpy chairs, a sofa with springs protruding through the seat. All over, dust. Papers and odd chunks of metal here, there, everywhere. A half-eaten plate of food sat on a battered three-legged table to my left. Oscar shot a stream of brown saliva, ping, into a grimy steel spittoon. "Jonas, Christ! Thank God it was him, not Murray." He peered at Samuel, trying to make contact beneath the brim of my father's Panama, which he hadn't removed. "Hell'd he die from?"

"Massive coronary artery occlusion."

"Fuck's *that* supposed to be?"

"Heart attack. And I thought you just might be sorry to hear it."

Oscar cackled, poked Samuel in the chest with his cigarless hand. "Ol' Os never was one for big fancy words," he said. "Plain fact, Jonas was a cunt first-class. Talk, he was good at, but I hadda kick his ass 'least once an hour to get a decent day's work outa him." Oscar launched another missile into the spittoon, then squinted at Samuel. "Now, if you're all done here, kindly get your cheesy ass outa my house and keep it out. Tomorrow, while you're gettin' paid for finger-fuckin' the mayor's wife, you can think about me havin' to go find some half-wit nigger or spic or dago who ain't been drafted, who might just put in maybe half a day's work for two days' pay."

"I'll think of you limping up to the poorhouse, Oscar." Samuel's voice was surprisingly soft. "You old reptile! You'll hire some poor southern kid at fifteen a week, then put twelve in his pay envelope and if he has enough balls to complain, you'll tell him there was fifteen when you gave it to him. And you'll take home half of what would've been Jonas' share."

Oscar fired a wad onto the floor, squarely between Samuel's shoes. "Jonas, that goldbrick! I don't even want to hear his name no more. Now take your kid an' get the hell out." The fat cigar stump wiggled between Oscar's lips. "Maybe I can get a few hours' sleep before the goddamn night's over." He stamped to the front doorway, motioned with his hand. "This's called a door. You know how to use it or do I gotta show you?"

Samuel tipped his Panama lightly. "If I can help, give me a call."

Oscar snatched his cigar from his mouth; I thought he was going to throw it into Samuel's face. "Give *you* a call? Shit! Willkie'd be president before *that* ever happens. I don't care if every schmuck in this stupid town thinks you're one-up on Jesus Christ, or if Murray an' that floozie-wife of his think you're the swellest Joe ever came down the pike."

Samuel took my elbow, led me to the creaky front steps.

"You and me both know you're a goddamn wooden nickel," Oscar shouted after us. "You already done to me all you're ever gonna. Be fuckin' snowballs in hell before I'd ever call you."

Samuel's face was tight, deep lines etched at the corners of his mouth. "How about you drive me home," he said. "Let's see if you've learned anything the last six months." He opened the passenger door, slid in.

I fumbled in my pocket for the key. "I've been wondering—when I turn seventeen, how're you going to explain to Ramona that I don't need driving lessons?"

He smiled, fatigue lines vanished. "Probably just tell her you've already had them. What do you think, something magical happens on a kid's seventeenth birthday, and bingo, it's all right for him to drive a car? *I* figured you were ready six months ago, so that's when I started teaching you. Now, let's go. I wouldn't mind getting a few hours' sleep myself before it's time for morning rounds."

I trotted around the car, sat in the driver's seat, slipped the key into the ignition. As I reached for the choke, Samuel said, "Don't need that—motor's still warm, remember?" I nodded, turned the ignition switch, then pushed the ball of my foot against the starter button. The motor caught. I brought my heel down on the accelerator, pulled away from the curb in first, moved nicely into second, then third. "Good, Leo," Samuel said. "Looks like you've got the hang of shifting."

"How could you manage to be so polite to him?" I asked. "Old Mr. Fleischmann."

Samuel smiled. "Were you listening to what he told us?"

"Sure. He actually sounded *glad* Jonas died. How can a father talk like that about his son?"

I pulled up neatly at a stop sign, then turned the steering wheel and leaned on the accelerator. We putted up Roosevelt, past darkened shops and houses. "That's what Oscar said, Leo. But what he told us is he's nearly seventy years old, his two wives died young, he works like a horse every day in that junkyard, lives in squalor, and now he loses a child. All that considered, he's still a son of a bitch, but that's not a medical diagnosis. You're a doctor, you always need to do whatever you can to help someone. And you start by trying to hear what the son of a bitch is trying to tell you."

I said, "All right," and kept driving. But I had more on my mind than being careful to keep the accelerator coordinated with the clutch pedal, thoughts I couldn't bring myself to turn into speech.

Back home, I slept fitfully, finally woke about ten o'clock, still thinking. Samuel was long gone, and when I went down to the kitchen I found a note from Ramona, "Going to the hairdresser's." All through a slow breakfast an idea disturbed me, danced around my edge of consciousness.

Chapter 3

Dad drained his glass. The waiter snatched it up practically before it hit the table top. Dad sat silent, motionless, staring into his past. Pain and determination battled across his face. Finally, determination took over the field.

I realized I'd been hearing music, a saxophone...Harmony—her *name*, Harmony Belmont. Girl next door...we were friends...no, more than friends...but not just...you know...

I'd never seen Dad rattled, hinges about to come off. He looked on the verge of aborting his mission. When the waiter gingerly set another Manhattan in front of him, he snatched the glass, took a gulp, sighed, then cleared his throat.

We were born within days of each other, grew up together...we were always together. Told each other everything. She was nuts for saxophones, adored Tony Parenti, worshiped Coleman Hawkins. All that summer she entertained the neighborhood, blew hell out of her horn, every chance she got. Her parents made her practice in the basement, right across their driveway from our kitchen, so that morning at breakfast I had a front-row seat. "Blues My Naughty Sweetie Gave to Me," loud, brassy, a little raggedy but no apologies. Harmony. I swallowed my last mouthful of cornflakes, ran water over the bowl and spoon, then charged out the back door, across the driveway, down through Belmonts' wooden cellar door. Harmony didn't hear, went right on honking, peering at the music on the stand in front of her, trying to make out notes in the crummy light from an unshaded overhead bulb. I coughed.

She turned, saw me, blinked, then slowly lowered her sax.

Deja-vuey feeling. I'd seen that girl, where?

"You're not at the Red Cross," I said.

She blew a disgusted razz with her tongue against her upper lip. "I'm going in at one today. Gauze shipments were late, so no bandages to roll 'til afternoon. But why aren't *you* out with your father?"

"I was," I said. "Until three A.M. So I slept late."

She turned her eyes on me, full power. Oh, Martin, her eyes…wonderful nearsighted green eyes, shining like emeralds through huge round glasses. Those eyes could be beacons or guideposts, alert signals, warning flares. Right then they were searchlights. "What'd you see?"

I told her about the little boy with the dislocated shoulder, then hesitated. She picked right up. "And?"

I recited the story of our stop at the Fleischmanns'. "Keeps bothering me," I said. "Rigor mortis, while the body was still warm? I didn't think—"

"If Samuel said, it must be."

"If Samuel said." Harmony wanted to go to drama school, write plays and act, which her parents thought was ridiculous. But Samuel encouraged her. "You've got talent," he once told her over dinner at our house. "Get yourself into drama school. If your father won't pay, I will." Ramona dropped a dish of mashed potatoes. Samuel chuckled. Later, in the living room, after Harmony went home, Ramona really gave it to Samuel.

"That girl's full of crazy ideas, and you egg her on. Telling her you'll pay her way through school? Never mind where the money would come from, it's none of your business."

"Helping people *is* my business," Samuel said. "She's going to end up in trouble," Ramona snapped. Samuel shrugged. "Let it be *her* trouble."

Harmony ducked through the leather neck strap, set her sax on a little wooden table, then stood. She was tall for a girl, five-nine, almost gangling. Long sandy hair flew around her face, first hiding freckles, then revealing them. "You don't think Samuel was right? Let's go look it up in his books."

This girl—where the hell had I seen her?

Back across the driveway, into my house, to my father's study, a large room with floor-to-ceiling shelves interrupted only by twin windows on the front wall, looking out onto Roosevelt Avenue. Samuel read everything—medicine, history, economics, philosophy, psychology, auto repair, novels. I went to the medical section, pulled down the heavy *Textbook of Medicine* by Dr. Edgar Grant, set it on Samuel's desk, flipped through the index. "Rigor mortis, page 47." Harmony peered at the book over my shoulder; her hair tickled my cheek. "Rigor mortis," I read. "Muscles initially relax after death. The body is limp. Coagulation of muscle protein begins in four to ten hours after death."

I stopped reading, turned to Harmony. "Murray said his brother walked into the house and died on the way into the living room. Samuel and I got there less than fifteen minutes after Murray called, so Jonas couldn't have been dead more than half an hour, and he was literally stiff as a board. *And* his hand was warm." I looked back at the book. "See algor mortis, cooling of the body after death, page 51." I zipped four pages ahead, read aloud. "After death, the body cools at about three degrees per hour."

"So?" Harmony still sounded defiant.

"So if rigor mortis doesn't kick in until at least four hours after death, the body should be down to about eighty-six degrees by then. I'd have noticed that when I picked up Jonas' hand."

Harmony leaned forward, turned back to Rigor Mortis, pointed at a list titled EXCEPTIONS. "Let's see if heart attack's there."

It wasn't. Strychnine Poisoning headed the short column. I got up, walked to the shelves, grabbed Wentworth's *Handbook of Toxicology*, opened to Strychnine. "Strychnine," I read, "is used primarily as rat poison, but in extremely small measures can be prescribed as a stimulant. A poisonous dose in humans produces muscle stiffness, then spasms, finally terrible tonic convulsions, all the muscles contracting until the victim is pulled into arch-back posture. The slightest stimulation—a sound, a motion, a light being switched on—worsens the convulsion. Finally the victim dies of asphyxiation, eyes bulging, face in ghastly contortion. Because the poison keeps muscles contracted after death, rigor mortis sets in immediately."

By the time I finished reading, my hands were shaking so badly I could hardly hold the book. I lowered it to my father's desk, then looked at Harmony. "That was Jonas Fleischmann—arched back, eyes bulging, face contorted."

She rested a hand on mine. "Samuel said it was a heart attack." Defiance still in her voice, but now tempered by a little defensiveness. Harmony didn't back down easily. She never...well, behaved like a girl. In school, they made her wear a skirt and blouse, but the minute she got home she was into a man's shirt and dungarees. Didn't wear makeup, unusual in those days. Boys liked to tease her, see how riled they could get her. They called her Harmful, or Harmless, or Hearty-har-har. Once, right in front of me, a boy called her Harlotry. I threw a punch, pure reflex; the boy's nose exploded in claret. When the principal called me on the carpet Samuel went storming in, told the principal if I hadn't hit that kid, *he'd* have broken *my* nose.

Dad ran a finger slowly across the bridge of his nose. I'd've bet every cent in my pocket he had no idea he did it. He looked at his drink as if his next line might've been inscribed on the cherry.

"Samuel wants me to think for myself," I said to Harmony. "And I think Jonas Fleischmann looked exactly like Wentworth's description of strychnine poisoning. But Samuel signed him out as a heart attack. Samuel's the best diagnostician in town, maybe in the state, maybe the whole country. Why did he insist it could only be a heart attack?"

She focused those green torches on me, didn't say a word. I picked up the books, reshelved them, checked my watch. "Eleven-thirty—got an hour?"

"What for?"

"Get your bike."

In those days, doctors' offices were usually right in their own houses, but Samuel said he didn't want patients bothering Ramona, so he rented office space six blocks down Roosevelt, in an older one-story house with a big wraparound porch. Harmony and I left our bikes against the side of the building and walked into my father's office. The door was always open. No nurse, no receptionist, no appointments. When Samuel finished afternoon rounds at the hospital he drove or walked to the office, said hello to the people waiting, then went through a door into the back. A few minutes later the door opened, and there stood Samuel, sleeves rolled up, looking around the waiting room. "Who's first?" Then somebody got up and walked back into the exam room. Never an argument over who was before whom.

But Samuel wouldn't come for another three or four hours, so the waiting room was empty when Harmony and I got there. We went back to the consultation room, to the four-drawer file cabinet that held patients' records. I opened the second drawer from the top, looked through the Fs, found Fleischmann, Lily and Murray, but no Oscar or Jonas. My throat felt dry, bad taste in my mouth. I flipped a few charts forward, a few back, no luck. Samuel's charting was as meticulous as the way he dressed. If he'd ever treated Jonas Fleischmann, there'd be a chart, and it would be right there.

"Let's check the desk," Harmony said.

I closed the file drawer, walked to the paper-strewn desk, looked at every sheet, careful not to disturb any of them. No file labeled Fleischmann, Jonas. Nothing in any way to do with Fleischmann, Jonas. My mind tried to invent reasons for the missing chart, but only one held water. Samuel simply didn't have a chart for Fleischmann, Jonas. Samuel wasn't treating him for a heart condition or anything else.

"Samuel lied to me," I said to Harmony.

She looked away for a moment, then put a hand on my arm. "Let's go back." She flashed an up-to-something grin. "I'm thinking."

Riding home, my pedal mechanism made a rhythmic sound somewhere between a swish and a click, *strych-nine, strych-nine, strych-nine*. I tried to ignore it by counting silver and gold stars in windows along the way, taking my usual hard look at the big white house between Twenty-fourth and Twenty-fifth. All three Vermeulen brothers enlisted right after Pearl Harbor. Bill's silver star went gold at Guadalcanal, Harold's at El Alamein. Arnie was somewhere in the E.T.O. His star was still silver, good. Would the war go on long enough for Ramona to put a star in our window? I stopped counting, rode the rest of the way home to *strych-nine, strych-nine, strych-nine*. Harmony waved back at me as she turned off on Twenty-seventh Street to go to the Red Cross. Rolling bandages every day with a bunch of old ladies—I felt sad for her, and a little guilty. Would Samuel have gotten me to extern for him if I'd been a girl? And if he had, would Ramona have let me do it?

When I walked into the house I heard Ramona call, "Leo?" from the living room. I went in, found her behind a card table, working a jigsaw puzzle. "Nice hairdo," I said.

Dance music from the big Philco waterfall-front radio at her right shoulder, "They're Either Too Old or Too Young." Ramona smiled, put down the puzzle piece in her hand, gave the back of her hair a pat upward, the way women do. "You like it, Leo? I'm glad."

Even when my mother smiled she looked sad. In her wedding photo she stood with Samuel in that early Twenties pose, she in her white gown, he in a tuxedo, heads close, his hand resting lightly on her arm. Samuel's eyes were vibrant, lips slightly parted, ready to leap into action the instant the photographer snapped the lens. My mother's face was calm, but her eyes projected a melancholy resignation, rather than serenity. The entire forty-four years the couple had aged since 1921 seemed to have been done by my mother alone.

"It suits you, Ramona," I said.

Her smile broadened, but the more she smiled, the sadder her expression became. "You're so serious, Leo. Even when you were still in short pants, you were fifty years old."

What you both wanted, what you got, I thought. Count on your*self.* Trust your*self.* But I just smiled back at her.

Sinatra burst through the Philco, "Oh, What a Beautiful Morning." Ramona crinkled her nose. "That little draft-dodger. I can't understand why all those girls go crazy over him." She snapped the dial to silence Frankie, then turned to face me. "Where've you been?"

"Down to Samuel's office. I wanted to learn more about last night's case. His books here didn't have all the information."

"Did you find what you were looking for?"

"Not altogether. I'll have to do some more work."

Ramona shook her head, laughed. "The way you're going, you may be able to skip medical school. Why don't you talk to Reuben Goldberg, the orthopedic surgeon. You know him, don't you?"

I nodded.

"He should be able to tell you whatever you want to know about a dislocated shoulder."

"Not that case," I said. "The other one. Afterward."

She looked me a question.

"At Fleischmann's. *After* the dislocated shoulder. After you called."

Now she looked thoroughly confused. "*I* called, dear?"

I thought back to the phone call at Lou and Lena's. Lena said, "For you, Doc," as she gave the phone to Samuel. He said, "They think it looks like a *heart attack?* Call them back, Ramona, tell them I'll be right over." Talking slowly, loud. "Didn't you call Lou and Lena's about a quarter after one?" I asked. "To tell Samuel to go to Murray and Lily Fleischmann's?"

Before I finished talking she was shaking her head slowly, twisting her gold wedding band. Once, that ring was engraved all around with wavy lines; over the years I'd watched her burnish it smooth. "I didn't make any phone call, dear. After you and your father left to go see that little boy, I fell back asleep and didn't wake up 'til almost eight this morning."

"I guess I misunderstood," I said, but knew I hadn't. I *knew* my father said, "Call them back, Ramona." As if she were speaking through a tunnel I heard my mother offer me lunch. I shook my head. "Maybe in a while. I slept really late, had a late breakfast."

"All right, dear. I picked up some fresh Jewish rye bread at the Tenth Avenue bakery, and a few slices of corned beef from Harry the butcher. I stopped there at just the right time."

I thanked her, then went upstairs, past the bedrooms to the attic. That was my cave, where I went to be alone. Dusty, crammed with old stuff going back at least to the previous owner of the house. Big steamer trunks, boxes of china, barbells, a moth-eaten raccoon coat. I plopped between the wall and a trunk, leaned back, pulled up my knees, thought. Samuel said he'd been treating Jonas Fleischmann for severe coronary artery disease, but his office files said he hadn't treated Jonas at all. Jonas dead on the living room floor looked like a textbook case of strychnine poisoning, but Samuel diagnosed it as a heart attack. Now, that phone call. Either my mother was lying or my father was. Smart money on Samuel, heavy odds.

I looked around the attic, idly, I thought, but curiosity's never idle. Woman's clothing mannequin, bowling ball, croquet set, child's bow and arrow, an old music box... I lifted the lid, pulled on the crank lever. But instead of winding the spring, the cylinder went round and round, and notes played very fast. Then I noticed two empty screw holes at the right of the base-plate—something missing in front of the cylinder. Gave me an idea. I closed the lid, grabbed a cloth, threw it around the music box, tucked the package under my arm, ran downstairs. "See you later, Ramona," I shouted as I charged outside. I squeezed the music box into the wire basket in front of my bike handlebars, then started pedaling down Roosevelt, back in the direction I'd gone with Samuel the night before.

My bike was one of those great big old Schwinns; between it and the music box, I was moving a good sixty pounds. Hot afternoon breezes blew my hair into my face. By the time I got to Wait Street I was drenched in sweat. I pedaled past rows of dingy two-family houses, only an occasional window-star, all silver. An old woman, Polish or Russian, sat stonefaced on a porch next to a radio. I caught a few bars of Bunny Berigan's trumpet, "I Can't Get Started. "

Coming up on Fifth Avenue, I saw a corrugated iron wall with a dented, chipped porcelain-metal sign, FLEISCHMANN SCRAP. I walked my bike through the open gate and up to a dilapidated little building, leaned the bike against the shack, took the music box, carried it through the open doorway. No one there. Few chairs, couple of file cabinets, a wooden desk holding a battered Smith-Corona typewriter. An old Atwater-Kent metal radio sat precariously on the window sill, tuned to the Giants' ballgame. Cliff Melton, the Giants' pitcher, threw a fastball to Stan Musial, who hammered it into right-center field for a double. Marty Marion came around to score, six-nothing, Cardinals.

Back outside the shabby office, I looked around, still didn't see anyone; just piles of *stuff* everywhere, all the way down to the river bank. But the longer I scanned the yard, the more I saw order, like sorted with like. A mound of old automobile

tires and inner tubes. Wheels and axles heaped next to gears
and pulleys, across from a stretch of auto parts. Kitchen appliances. Clawfoot bathroom tubs, sinks, toilets. Mattresses, old
beds. At the farthest reach of the yard, just this side of the river,
something was burning, spewing thick black smoke. I took off
in that direction, walked past stacked tables and chairs, suitcases
and old steamer trunks, a hill of organ pipes next to a stack
of wood. I passed a small mountain of battered soda fountain
equipment, tripped over the protruding leg of an ice cream parlor
chair, nearly went sprawling.

As I came closer to the source of the smoke I saw it was
garbage. Fabric scraps, torn pillows, chunks of wood, a sofa in
pieces. Those days, junkmen stripped what might be useful and
burned the rest. Fleischmann Scrap did its burning at the far
end of the yard, so smoke would drift away, across the Passaic
River into Emerson Township. Even so, the stink was intense.
I started to cough.

I turned to go back, found myself looking into the eyes of a
gigantic black man. "He'p you, boy?" he asked.

Big as he was, his voice was gentle. I held out the music box,
lifted the lid, pointed. "I came to see if Murray could help," I
said. "Part's missing, see?"

The black man looked where I pointed. "Mmmmm. Gov'nor."
He scratched his chin. "Fleischmanns ain't workin' today." He
leaned forward; a drop of sweat fell from his brow into the
music box. "Murray's brother, Jonas…" The man's voice became
a hoarse conspiratorial whisper, as if someone else in that wide-
open scrapyard might be listening. "…had a heart attack. Passed
last night."

I felt like a mooncalf. Did I think Murray would be in the
yard the day after his brother died? I didn't think, period.

The man held out a grimy, greasy hand. "I'm George Templeton, I work here. You be?"

I balanced the music box on my left hip, shook his hand.
"Leo Firestone."

I thought his eyes might blow right out of his head. "Doctor Samuel Firestone's boy?"

"You know my father?"

George let go of my hand, laughed, then looked at me as if I might be giving his leg a hard pull. "Ain't *nobody* in Hobart don't know your daddy. He come when my li'l girl was sufferin' wit' stomachache and fever and di'rrhea. He give her testses, then say, 'She got stomach worms, could make her sick enough to die—but you give her these-here med'cines just 'xactly like I tell you, she go'n get better.' We do it. Afterwards, I look in the toilet and there's these skinny white worms, wigglin' all around in that mess, one of 'em, I swear, a foot long. My wife scream and run. I ask your daddy, can I pay you so much a week 'cause we ain't got much money? An' he look at me with that smile a his, and say, 'George, my big radio's on the blink. Fix it for me, we be close enough to even.' So next day I go on over, fix his radio, and that be that."

I wondered why Samuel didn't put George's bill on the tab the way he did with Lou and Lena. Then it hit me. The dignity of that black man, his bearing, his speech. He'd've never accepted charity, would've been offended. So Samuel let him pay in trade, not unusual in those days.

"But I'll bet Samuel filed an IOU on Lou and Lena," I said. "Bet he was holding papers on half the population of Hobart, and knew exactly which one to pull and when."

For an instant Dad was the school principal, and I was the kid who snuck up behind and gave him a hotfoot. Then his gaze softened, and he came dangerously close to smiling. "You and he..." Dad grabbed his glass with both hands, knocked down a mouthful of Manhattan, sighed.

George's story about his daughter and her roundworms turned on a light in my head. "My father treated Jonas, too," I said. "For his heart condition."

"Noooo! Jonas never said no word." George's mouth flew open; his eyes filled with anger. "It's a *shame*," he blurted. "How the good're always dyin' young. Jonas, the onliest one wouldn't do no business with Mr. Black. Mr. *Red-Dexter* Black. When Red come by, Jonas wouldn't talk to him. Wouldn't even look at him."

I thought I knew what George was talking about, but wanted to be sure. "Mr. Red-Dexter Black?"

"Mmmm." George looked all around, then leaned forward to whisper again. "Scrap metal—we suppose' to sell every bit to the gov'mint. But Red Dexter pay more, whole lot more. Murray and Oscar take his money. But never Jonas. And never *me.*"

So Murray and his father were selling scrap metal on the black market, and Jonas wouldn't go along. Bad situation. Yes, Samuel held IOUs all over the city, but people who hold IOUs also give them, and now I felt pretty sure of why my father signed Jonas out as a heart attack. George saved me from saying something very stupid by pointing at the music box. "Let's go see if we cain't find a right gov'nor."

Back to the office shed, around to the far side of the building, where dead entertainment machines, music boxes, phonographs, radios, were stacked under the rough eaves. We tore into the music-box pile, but no luck. Every governor was either too large or too small. George looked apologetic. "Tell you what—come back day after tomorra. Murray be here then, Oscar too. Jonas' funeral's tomorra, won't nobody be here. I tol' Murray if I ain't a pallbearer, him and me go'n fight."

I pictured Joe Louis in one corner, Jack Dempsey in the other.

"You want, you can leave your music box." George held out a massive hand. "Be safe here. I'll make sure."

Joe Louis watching my music box? Any time. I thanked George, handed him my project, then bicycled out through the gate and home.

Chapter 4

Dad looked at his empty Manhattan glass. His food was gone as well, sandwich long since gobbled down in four or five monster bites. He signaled the waiter, who came right over, took the glass. "Another," Dad said, then turned back to me, settled himself in his seat, cleared his throat.

As I pulled into the driveway, I heard Harmony's saxophone, "Body and Soul." I was barely through the cellar door when she jumped from her chair, dropped the sax on the table. I glanced past her, toward my easel at the far side of the room, below the little window. My hideout-studio, safe from critics. "Leo, you *can't* go painting now," she shouted. "I've got to talk to you. I've been thinking about this business with your father—"

I held out a hand, stop. "You want to talk about that, sit down. There's more." I told her what I'd heard from George, then said, "I'm going to have a talk with Samuel tonight."

"No, don't—*don't* do that." When she laughed or got angry she had beautiful dimples, which she hated. "Leo, don't be a dumbo. Do you just want to fight with Samuel, or do you want to find out what really happened?"

"How else am I going to find—"

"I *said* I was thinking. Why don't *you?* Bet we can dope it, you and me, but if you go blab to Samuel now, all you'll do is blow our cover."

Spitting words out of the corner of her mouth like Bogart, writing a real-life play with a co-starring role for herself. I worked hard not to smile.

"Well?" Quick one-two from those green eyes. "I'm right, aren't I?"

"Okay," I said quietly. "I won't spill the beans."

She wasn't sure whether or not I was teasing. I wish you could've seen her face. "No, really," I said. "I promise."

"All right, then. Come back after dinner, sleep over. Maybe we can figure it out between us."

We did that often, sat talking in the Belmonts' living room, or outside on a warm summer night. We'd talk about anything and everything, sometimes 'til one or two in the morning. Ramona didn't like it, said she stayed awake listening for me, couldn't fall asleep until she knew I was home. Finally, one evening, I told her if I wasn't home by eleven I'd just stay in the Belmonts' guest bedroom. She didn't like that any better, but Samuel told her to back off, I was being considerate and reasonable.

The waiter set Manhattan IV at Dad's elbow. He grabbed the glass by the stem, swigged a mouthful, then picked up his story through a gargle.

That evening, Harmony and I sat outdoors, swung back and forth, thought, talked, argued. Dr. and Mrs. Belmont came out around ten-thirty to say they were turning in. What a god-damn pair. Dr. Fielding J. Belmont, a snowman with legs, black mustache, gold-rimmed spectacles, and a Durante-nose hanging above overdeveloped incisor teeth. Mrs. Doctor Belmont, a skinny little woman with big eyes, pointy nose, and hands that couldn't seem to stop massaging each other. "Look how they sit, Fielding," Mrs. Belmont said, and I swear I heard Harmony's teeth grind. "On opposite ends of the swing. Like an old married couple."

Dr. Belmont harrumphed. "What do you expect, Lissa? She dresses like a boy, talks like a boy, behaves like a boy, and I don't guess Leo *likes* boys. At least not that way."

"I don't think Betty Grable's got a lot to worry about," Mrs. Belmont chirped.

"She sure doesn't from my sister," said Harmony. "Laura's got a darker mustache than Dad."

Dr. Belmont shook a finger at her. "Young lady, watch your tongue. Let's see whether *you* can get into Wellesley and be on the Dean's List. *And* get your M-A-N." Quick glance in my direction. "And a teaching certificate, a girl can always count on getting a job teaching school. Your sister—"

"Has a Dean's List Certificate for her entire first year." Harmony mimicked her father's speech. "And a very nice boy friend at Harvard, not fighting in the war because of a physical disability. No guts."

After Dr. and Mrs. Belmont finally went inside, Harmony looked at her shoes and muttered, "Jerks! Leo, do you know how lucky you are to have Samuel for a father? I'd give anything…" I edged over, put my arms around her, let her snuffle on my shoulder for a while. Couple of times I made a move toward her shirt buttons, but didn't have the nerve. 1943.

We swung and talked 'til after midnight, but couldn't come up with anything besides what I was already doing, snooping around the junkyard. When I told her my excuse for being there she surprised me—bounced on the seat, clapped her hands. "An old music box? I heard one years ago, in a museum exhibit in New York, *so* pretty. After you fix it, would you give it to me? Please?"

I felt as if I might disappear into those green eyes, just a couple of inches from mine. "Sure. If you want it."

"I do, I do." Harmony planted a tiny kiss on the end of my nose, then quickly backed away. Her eyes went sad. "Boys're so damn lucky. You go out on calls with Samuel, go to the junkyard to do detective work, you're even learning how to fix a music box. All I ever get to do is wrap bandages with a bunch of old fossils."

Next day I went with Samuel on hospital rounds, then house calls, then to the office. Whichever sickroom we walked into, I saw the same expression on patients' faces. *It's going to be all right*. Even old Yetta Aronowitz, riddled with cancer, propped up in bed and down to eighty pounds, brightened the instant she saw Samuel. He peered at her jaundiced eyes, listened to her lungs, tapped her swollen abdomen, then gave her a wicked look. "Another month, you're on your way to Atlantic City." Pause, just long enough for the old woman to shoot him a sharp side-squint. "Miss America Contest," Samuel said. "With you in it, they'll never cancel, war or no war." Mrs. Aronowitz tried to laugh, coughed. Her round little husband smiled. Samuel played people like Heifetz played fiddles.

But away from his instrument, the fiddler went grim. A step outside Mrs. Aronowitz's room, Samuel's face was a storm cloud, ready to blow. Routine after visiting a terminal patient. I learned early—get him thinking about the next case. "Going to send Mr. Wilson home today?" I asked, and as usual, it worked. Samuel smiled, bright sunshine, storm passed. "I think so. Looks like we've got that ulcer licked. Just have to make sure he sticks to his diet this time."

After office visits, Samuel went home. I made for the Steinberg Hospital Library, looked up arteriosclerotic heart disease and strychnine poisoning in book after book after book. Nothing to change my opinion about Jonas Fleischmann's cause of death. I did read that symptoms of tetanus are similar to those of strychnine poisoning, but a good dose of strychnine can be fatal within twenty minutes, while tetanus comes on much more slowly. If Jonas had scratched his finger on a contaminated piece of metal he'd've had plenty of time to call Samuel for help.

Halfway through dinner that evening, the phone rang. Samuel jumped up, snatched the receiver, nodded as he listened. "Yes...yes... Sounds for real. Be right over." He dropped the receiver back into the cradle. "Lily Fleischmann. Her niece is in labor."

Just hearing the name Fleischmann was flint to my tinder. I nearly went over backward, pushing away from the table. Samuel chuckled. Ramona clicked her tongue. "Today, of all days. Jonas' funeral."

"Take it up with You-Know-Who," Samuel said lightly. "Old He-Who-Taketh-and-Giveth-on-the-Same-Day." He squeezed Ramona's shoulder, danced past us into the living room.

I kissed Ramona. She looked up at me, sad smile. "That man—I don't know where he gets his energy."

I ran down the porch stairs to the car. To Samuel, no call was ever routine. He took off down Roosevelt like a bat out of hell. We zipped past Steinberg Hospital, odd. I pointed. "Samuel…?"

"Home delivery." Eyes straight ahead, watching the road.

"Why?"

"Hospital beds've gotten tight, war injuries. And with so many nurses gone overseas, the ones still here are on roller skates twenty-four hours a day. Besides, hospitals cost money that some people don't have."

Muggy night air swirled through the car. Samuel rested an elbow on the window edge. "After the war, maybe I'll get a little money together, buy a convertible." He switched on the radio. Benny Goodman, "A Smoo-o-o-th One." Samuel started whistling along, note-perfect, right on with every nuance of those clarinet whinnies. All the way to the Fleischmanns', Samuel whistled. "Oh Look At Me Now," "Throwin' Stones at the Sun," "More Than You Know," not a dropped note. Then he whistled solo from the car up to the front door.

Murray let us in, dark blue shirt open halfway down the front, sleeves rolled. Sweat streamed down his cheeks. My shirt was plastered to my back, but Samuel, as always, looked cool and comfortable. Murray bounced a glance from Samuel to me, then back. "Hey, it's Dr. Firestone and Doc F, Junior again. Givin' twofers this week, Samuel?"

No malice in his voice, nothing offensive. Just his way. A junkman's heavy-handed humor. But I heard my mother's voice. "A coarse man."

"For you, special," Samuel said, then his tone softened. "Doing all right, Murray?"

Murray looked blank, then recognition lit his eyes. "Oh yeah, sure. Thanks, Samuel. Funeral's done, Jonas is under ground. Finished."

As Murray talked, a heavy man in a three-piece woolen suit walked into the hall from the living room. Full beard, thinning black hair, impressive bay window. On his head he wore a black *yarmulke*. He shook an angry finger at Murray. "I heard that. 'Finished'! You put your brother in the earth, turn around, go right back to work. That's not—"

Murray cut him off with an upraised hand and a sharp "Sha! Hey, Ez, let the doctors go upstairs, okay? Maybe I gotta listen to this stuff but they don't."

The fat man nodded at Samuel, mumbled, "G'd evening, Dr. Firestone," then ran eyes over me as if I were a worm. "This pisher's a doctor? He don't look old enough to tie his shoes."

Samuel laughed out loud, said, "Top o' the evening to you, Ez," then turned around. I followed him to the foot of the stairs. He stopped long enough to whisper back at me, "Lesson for today—don't get into pissing contests with skunks." Then he tore upstairs, three at a time. With the heavy bag, I could do only two.

From the top of the stairs I heard soft cries. Four closed doors and one open, that obviously a bathroom. Samuel clearly knew where to go. We trotted single-file through the atrium, into the farthest room.

A girl lay writhing and moaning in a double bed facing the door. Lily Fleischmann sat on her left, holding her hand. On the girl's right sat a well-dressed woman, stiff, almost prim in a white silk blouse and plaid skirt. Lily smiled at Samuel but the other woman took one look at me, threw her hand to her chest and half-rose from her chair.

Samuel returned Lily's smile, then said, "Okay, Shannon," to the girl in the bed. "This's what we've been waiting for." He half-turned toward me. "Shannon Herlihy, my son, Leo. He's learning to be a doctor. Leo, that's Shannon's Aunt Nancy." As if we were at a cocktail party.

Aunt Nancy didn't seem overly reassured. Shannon quieted, tried to smile, couldn't quite make it. She wasn't much older than I. Would've been pretty, except her face was swollen, lips thick, eyelids bloated. Long blonde hair, matted in sweat. The man downstairs, Ez? Couldn't be her father, could he? Her *husband?*

Samuel rested a hand on Shannon's round abdomen, raised an eyebrow as she began to squirm. The girl cried out, threw her head back and forth on the pillow. "Good contraction," Samuel said, then, "Face, fingers're a little puffy, aren't they, Leo? Toxemia, a high blood pressure condition, happens only in pregnancy. Soon's the baby's out, she'll be fine." Talking to both Shannon and me.

Lily gave him a rubber glove. As he slipped it on, he said to the girl, "Going to see how far along you are. Anything bothers you, tell me." Never for an instant letting go of her eyes. He reached under the sheet covering her, and as he bent forward, Shannon's face scrunched up. "Hurt?" Samuel asked.

"No, just feels funny. I'm scared."

Samuel pulled off the glove, said quickly to Lily, "Fully effaced, four centimeters dilated, water bag intact, head's right down there." Then he looked back to Shannon. "Sure you're scared. Everybody's scared when they're doing something new and big and important. But it's going great. Nancy, Lily, Leo and I'll be with you the whole way."

"But Doctor Firestone, I'm afraid it's gonna hurt, like with those contraptions."

I struggled to keep my face straight, but Samuel smiled openly. "Yes, it will hurt some. When it gets worse than the cramps you're having now, we'll give you medicine, twilight sleep. Afterward, you won't remember anything bad at all. Promise."

Twilight sleep, gold-standard labor painkiller then, a combination of morphine and scopolamine. Shannon started another contraction, screamed, thrashed. Lily said, softly, "Breathe, honey, deep, like I told you. In....out....in....out. Breathe with me, that's right. Good." When the pain let up, Lily took a washcloth, dipped it into a bowl of water on a nightstand, washed the girl's face. Shannon managed a wan smile. I glanced at Aunt Nancy, sitting there holding Shannon's right hand loosely, now and then smiling at the girl and nodding her head, yes-yes, like a mechanical doll. I wondered why she didn't just wait downstairs.

A couple of hours later, Shannon started thrashing with every contraction, pulled her hands away from Lily and Aunt Nancy, beat fists on the pillow. Samuel examined her, looked pleased. "Six centimeters, baby's head oriented just right. You're doing great, Shannon—now for that twilight sleep. Then I can break your water and we'll be off to the races. Next thing you know, you'll have had your baby."

He took vials of morphine and scopolamine from his bag, drew the contents into a syringe, then plunged the needle into Shannon's hip. A few minutes later, the girl's eyes closed and her body relaxed. Samuel gently worked a long needle inside her vagina. Light-green fluid burst onto the sheet. My father looked at Lily, eyes twinkling with mischief. "Passaic Falls."

Lily rolled her eyes and walked toward the door. "I'll get fresh linen."

Clean bedsheets or not, that odd labor-room odor of sweat and raw flesh got stronger and stronger as hours dragged. I wondered what races we were off to. Twilight sleep, I learned, was not exactly sleep. Shannon screamed, flung her limbs wildly, shouted the vilest words. Lily, Aunt Nancy and I took turns standing guard at the bedside so Shannon couldn't throw herself to the floor.

About one in the morning, Samuel said she was fully dilated and the head just needed to come down, probably another hour. Lily looked at me. "I could use a Pepsi. We got that and ginger ale down in the fridge. How about you go have a bottle, then bring us one. What d' you want, Nancy? Samuel?"

Aunt Nancy shook her head. My father thought for a moment. "Ginger ale."

As I went down the stairs I heard loud voices from the living room. "Listen, Ezra, I hate being rude to a guest. But I been telling you for almost an hour now, I had a big day, and I'm tired. I want to go to bed, I got to go to work today."

"And that is why I am not leaving." Ezra sounded like a puffed-up schoolmaster. "You're afraid maybe those gangsters you sell your scrap to'll go someplace else if you ain't at work today? A week, you should stay home, say morning *kaddish*, then sit *shiva* all the day. It's the law."

"For Christ sake, I'm talking to a wall. Yeah, fine, it's the law. So is sellin' scrap to Uncle. Which by the way is none of your damn business if I do or I don't."

I tiptoed from the bottom step to the edge of the living room doorway. "I make it my business," Ezra roared. "Suppose I go drop a word to the right person. What do you think would happen then?"

I knew what would happen. In 1943, a junkyard selling scrap to the enemy? Especially a junkyard run by Jews? Let word get out, and that yard would go up in smoke one night. People would be beaten, maybe killed.

Strangely, Murray didn't sound concerned. "Sure, Ez," he said. "You just go and drop that word. Go ahead. Then one day you can explain to God why you turned the *goyim* loose on me."

Ez's comeback was so savage I flinched against the wall. "A Jew who disobeys the laws of his people *and* the laws of his country is not just a bad Jew," the big man bellowed. "He's a bad man."

Silence, just for a moment, like the premonition of a whirlwind. Then as if he were talking to a dog he was whipping, Ezra shouted, "In Poland alone, Hitler kills six thousand Jews every day. Which is no secret to nobody no more, except maybe Mr. Roosevelt. The Nazis pack Jews with their yellow stars into trains like cattle, off to the concentration camps, the gas chambers, and they ain't going to stop 'til every Jew in Europe is dead. You're a Jew, Murray. You think maybe those Nazi *momsers* would tell you you're not?"

I stretched my neck to peer around the corner of the doorway and peek with my right eye. Ezra was choleric, crimson-faced, arms up and out like a round buzzard ready to swoop down onto Murray and tear him to bits. But Murray just looked at that furious fat man and laughed. Then he said, "Tell me I'm whatever you want, Ez. There's people tell me I'm a schmuck, but I don't think on accounta that I gotta *be* a schmuck."

Ezra looked like a tire that had just caught a nail. He staggered back a step, lowered his arms, dropped his chin to his chest. Murray took him by the elbow, guided him toward the hall. I turned, trotted across the hall into the kitchen. "I appreciate you want to help me, Ez," I heard Murray say. "But when you offer a man help and he says no, you gotta leave him be. All them mumbo-jumbo prayers, they don't make the least bit a sense to me. Jonas is dead, gone. He's in the ground, that's that, and I got a business to run. Person's gotta eat. G'night."

The screen door slammed. I ran to the refrigerator, grabbed two Pepsis and a ginger ale, flipped all three caps on an opener, then started back through the hallway. Murray stood in the living room doorway. A smile of crafty amusement ran up the left side of his face. "Well, if it ain't Young Doc Firestone. How's it going up there, Dockie?"

"Dockie." I liked that. All of a sudden, I felt energized. "Samuel says she's doing well, fully dilated, just has to push a while." I held up the bottles. "Hot up there. We got thirsty." Murray didn't say anything, so I went on. "That girl, Shannon? She's your niece?"

Murray wasn't quite quick enough to keep an instant of surprise from flashing over his face. "Yeah, my niece," he said. "And what you're really asking is, where's her husband, right? And why she comes to her auntie's house to have her baby."

The junkman's voice was like ice creaking under my feet. I took a step backward, glanced over my shoulder at the stairs. "Lemme give you a little bit of advice, Dockie, okay?"

I looked Murray in the eye, good move. He smiled. "You're all right, Dockie. Ain't many guys your age'd go along with their old man and sit for a whole night watching something come out of a girl 'steada going off someplace with a girl they could put something *in*. It's important a doc should ask the right questions, but it's also important he shouldn't ask the wrong ones. Kapeesh?"

"Yes," I said. "I'm sorry."

"Nah." With a wave, Murray sent my apology flying past him into the living room. "You were born smart, but ain't nobody was ever born knowing anything. You gotta learn." Crafty smile back over his face. "Like you gotta learn how to listen to people from behind a wall without having them see you. Or know you're there. Like when I hear stairs creaking, but afterwards I don't hear no creaking floorboards going into the kitchen."

He saw my embarrassment, started to laugh again. "Hey, don't worry, Dockie." Disparaging headshake. "That Ezra Shnayerson, he's the rabbi in the orthodox synagogue over on Ellison. Whatever stick he's got up his ass, he ain't gonna drop no word, at least not to anybody but me. See, Orthodox Jews don't bother Christian people, but they think God told them it's their job to straighten out a Jew who knows crap when he smells it. So on accounta me, Ez is scared his soul's gonna be S.O.L. on Judgment Day. There's another lesson, Dockie, and I bet your old man'd tell you the same. Don't ever depend on nobody else, not in this world. All that ever gets you is scared or in trouble. Or both."

I liked Murray. He was rough, but his eyes and voice were kind. I asked would he really be at work later that day. He looked at his watch. "Christ, after one o'clock—that's two nights outa three. Yeah, I'll be there. Why?"

"I went to see you yesterday," I said. "Forgot about the funeral. I've got a music box missing its governor. George couldn't find one that'd fit. He said to come back today and see you."

Murray smiled. "Music box, huh? Governor? Sure, Dockie, can do. But you gotta excuse me for now. If I don't get my beauty sleep I ain't gonna be worth a fly's fart at that yard to you or anybody else." He motioned me to the stairs; I went up, heard him clopping behind me.

Chapter 5

The waiter picked up my empty sandwich plate, pointed at my iced-tea glass. "Another?" I shook my head. As he walked off, I said to Dad, "Bet you didn't look back down those stairs."

Dad chuckled, lifted his glass, took a quick swallow.

I got up to that labor room as fast as I could move with those three open soda bottles. About an hour later, the baby was ready to come. Samuel put on forceps, pulled. The crown of the head, all dark curly hair, stretched that poor girl to what looked like the breaking point. I held my breath as she let loose a sound like an engine revving out of control. Samuel slid off the forceps, took hold of the baby's head, guided it out. The face was like a plum. Samuel pulled downward. Shannon screamed, and out came shoulders, then the body, in a gush of dark greenish fluid full of clumps that looked like olive-colored blood clots. "God damn," Samuel muttered. "Meconium." He threw two clamps across the cord, cut between them, laid the baby on the mother's belly, head downward. Then he picked up a red rubber bulb and sucked at the baby's nose and throat. No response.

Shannon, free of pain, lay still in her twilight sleep, but Aunt Nancy leaped off her chair, clutched at her temples, and screamed, "My baby!"

Her baby? I thought. Samuel didn't seem to notice. He pinched the baby's nose, put his lips to the baby's mouth. Samuel's chest expanded, once, twice, a third time. Then he straightened, lifted the baby's legs, gave it a couple of light taps on the bottom. The baby's face contorted. It flexed its arms and legs, let out a howl, turned pink. Samuel smiled at Aunt Nancy. "Baby's fine, don't worry. Had a little something stuck in its throat but that's gone now." Aunt Nancy clutched him with both hands, yelled, "You saved his life," then turned toward Lily and screeched, *"He breathed life into my baby."*

After we cleaned Shannon up, Samuel and I went down to the kitchen, took bottles of Pepsi from the refrigerator, sat at the table. Sweat and body oil gave Samuel's face a golden glow. "That green stuff," he said. "Meconium. If a baby doesn't get enough oxygen, its anal sphincter relaxes and releases meconium into the fluid. Baby inhales it on the way out, clumps get stuck in the trachea, baby can't breathe. I sucked out the plug."

I thought of Aunt Nancy, grabbing at him, screaming he'd breathed life into her baby. Why didn't he tell *her* he'd only released an obstruction? "Where did it go?" I asked. "The meconium plug."

Samuel laughed. "Where do you think?" He laughed harder, must've been the look on my face. "Won't do me any harm—there're no bacteria inside the uterus." Then a sudden change in the weather. Samuel cocked his head, gave me a hard look. "All right, no, it wasn't pleasant. But by the time I went and dug a suction tube out of my bag, that baby might've been damaged or dead. A mouthful of baby shit might not taste good, but it beats sending a kid out brain-damaged." He wiped his hands on a towel. "Come on. Let's say good-bye."

Samuel let me drive again. All the way home, I had to fight the whole way to keep my mind on the road. Blonde, blue-eyed Shannon looked as much like Lily's niece as I did. And what about Aunt Nancy? From the beginning of labor 'til the end, you'd have thought *she* was having the baby. And what was it Samuel told Shannon when he injected the morphine and

scopolamine? "Next thing you know you'll have *had* your baby."
Not "you'll *have* your baby."

"Leo, you're going to give me whiplash, going from first to
second. What's with you?"

I should've answered his question with mine, but couldn't,
not after my little encounter with Murray. "Sorry," I mumbled.
"Guess I'm a little tired."

Not tired enough to fall asleep, though. Between the terrible
humidity and those questions barreling around in my head, I
tossed, turned the other way, stuck to the sheet, didn't drop off
'til after dawn. Past ten when I woke. As I stumbled into the
kitchen in my pajama bottoms, hair over my eyes, Ramona
looked around from the sink where she was peeling potatoes.
"I can't keep up with him," I muttered.

"Sunday, Monday, or Always?" Crosby crooned his question
through the boxy little Crosley on the cupboard next to the
refrigerator. Ramona dropped a half-peeled potato, came over to
put an arm around me. "No one can keep up with your father,"
she said. "And Leo…" Twisting, tugging at her wedding ring.
"You don't have to. In fact, I wish you wouldn't try." A weak
smile painted itself across her face. "Well, maybe in a few years
you'll have a fighting chance, but right now you need more sleep
than he does. You're still growing." She pushed me into a chair.
"Sit. I'll make you an omelet."

Less than an hour later, I was on my way to the junkyard.
As I rode in, I saw George and Oscar Fleischmann across the
yard, working at a pile of scrap. I parked my bike next to the
office shack, went inside. Murray grinned at me from behind
the desk. "Hey, Dockie, you keep banker's hours. Nice work if
you can get it."

Behind him, the Atwater-Kent on the window sill played "All
Through the Night." My music box sat on the desk, a small brass
object next to it. A man slouched in a chair across the desk from
Murray swiveled to take me in. Skinny little character, thin face
under a wide snap-brim. Dark blue suit with white pinstripes,
straight off a Brooks Brothers hanger. "This here's young Doc

Firestone," Murray said to the man. "Samuel's kid, he's already learning the racket. Leo, Mr. Dexter."

Mr. Dexter stretched his thin red mustache into a pencil line. His teeth were dark, deeply tobacco-stained. "Nice to meetcha, Leo." He flicked the tip of his tongue over his lower lip.

"Just be a couple minutes, Red," Murray said. "Gotta take care of the Dockie."

Red Dexter leaned back dangerously in his chair. "No rush, Murray. Too damn hot to hurry."

"C'mere." Murray plucked the small brass piece off the table. It looked like a butterfly inside a horseshoe. Behind us, Red Dexter sang in a high-pitched, wheezy voice, "Dirty Gertie from Bizerte, hid a mousetrap 'neath her skirtie."

Murray tried not to laugh as he waved the caged butterfly in my face. "Lookit, Dockie, here's what's missing—the governor. Only you need one just a little bigger. Gotta fit exactly a hundred percent with that gear at the end of the cylinder. Now—"

"Filthy Annie from Trapani, stashed a razor up her fanny."

Murray chuckled, shook his head. "See, Dockie, power from the spring's what makes the cylinder turn, and this little governor's gotta let down that spring power so the music plays just right. Not too slow, not too fast."

"Speed control," I said.

"Bingo, Dockie." Murray gave me a solid clap on the shoulder. "You're learning."

"Hey, Leo, lemme ask you a question." Red Dexter waggled a finger. "Why're you so interested in fixin' this thing from outa the last century that nobody cares about no more? Lookit all that metal inside. Uncle Sam could make a lotta bullets, blow a bunch of krauts into pieces."

It suddenly occurred to me I might've picked a flimsy excuse to play spy in a junkyard. On billboards, on the radio, in newspapers and magazines, everywhere, the question was, "What can *I* do to help win the war?" Two answers. "Buy bonds." "Turn in scrap metal." Downtown, in front of City Hall, a huge banner hung across Market Street, big block letters telling us to SLAP THE JAP RIGHT OFF THE MAP BY SALVAGING SCRAP. Men brought old tools, women lugged frying pans, little kids gave their electric trains, then scrounged empty cigarette packages on the sidewalk. Less than an hour before, as I sat in the kitchen, eating my omelet, I heard a radio group sing, "Scrap, scrap, turn in your scrap. Mash a Nazi, zap a Jap." Now here I was, telling Murray and Red Dexter I wanted to put together two heavy handfuls of brass and iron so they'd play music. "I…I found it in our attic," I stammered, then added, "It used to be my grandmother's."

Fortunately, Murray misread the cause of my distress. "Leave the kid alone, huh, Red? He wants to fix up his grandma's music box, that's okay. Unk'll just have to manage with a few less bullets. He don't exactly get every single chunka metal comes around, now, does he?"

Red Dexter's jaw dropped, then he started to laugh. He reached inside his jacket, pulled a pack of Lucky Strikes from his shirt pocket, tapped the bottom of the pack, stuck a cigarette into the corner of his mouth. Then he flicked a fingernail across the head of a match, lit up, inhaled, blew a long cloud of smoke toward Murray's face. "You're a card, Murray," he said. "But maybe you should watch out just a little bit. Most games, the joker don't get to play."

I kept my eyes on the music box and butterfly-governor.

"Hey, Red, long's I put up, you know what you can do." Murray rested a hand on my shoulder. "You want to fix Granny's music box, Dockie, you come to the right place. Me and your old man, we're more alike than you prob'ly think. He patches up broken-down people, I fix broken-down machines. And when the person's too sick for your old man or the machine's too sick for me…" Murray swept his arm toward the window, at the heaps of rusting scrap outside.

"You're a fuckin' philosopher, Murray." Red snickered, then shot Murray another cloud of smoke.

"First I'm a card, now I'm a philosopher." Murray's tone was light. "Keep your pants on, Red. Hey, whyn'cha take a couple minutes, go give *your* kid a few lessons in the business. He's what, two already? Old enough to start making some scratch."

Dexter looked like a man who'd been pointing a gun at an adversary, then suddenly realized his weapon was somehow no longer in his hand. He shook his head, turned away, took a deep drag on the cigarette. Murray handed me the music box. "Go on downtown, Washington Street just offa Roosevelt. Hogue's Clocks and Anti-cues. Chester Hogue fixes clocks and music boxes, got a ton of parts. He'll have the right governor, guaranteed. Come on back with it, and I'll show you how to make that music box like new."

I thanked Murray, then told Red Dexter I was pleased to meet him.

"Likewise, Dockie."

I turned to go but before I could take a step, a brown river rat shot through a crack in the wall, zipped right in front of my shoes, then disappeared through a floorboard knothole. I yelped. Murray laughed. "More a the bastards every day," he said. "And every day they look fatter and fatter."

"Oughta set traps," Red said.

Murray waved him off. "Y' think I don't? But every rat I nail, seems like there's two more the next day. Maybe I oughta just live and let live, huh?"

Red gave him a strange look. I ran out, squeezed the music box into my bike basket, hopped aboard, pedaled crosstown toward Washington Street. I was nearly there when a line from Wentworth's *Toxicology* hit me between the eyes: "Strychnine is used primarily as rat poison."

I pulled up under a weathered gold-lettered sign, HOGUE'S CLOCKS AND ANTIQUES, leaned my bike against the storefront. When I opened the front door, a little bell tinkled. One step inside, I was swimming in a river of mildew, mold and stale cigarette smoke. Glass showcases head-high on both sides of the aisle, so dirty I could barely make out the merchandise. A few yards inside the door on the left, a woman sat behind a gouged, scratched wooden counter that looked like a swaybacked butcher's block. Scraggly gray hair, a look on her face like she'd been sucking lemons. Tacked onto the wall behind her was a huge photograph of FDR with his creased gray fedora, big smile, cigarette holder at a jaunty forty-five degree angle. Without looking, the woman tapped a cigarette out of a pack of Camels—the President's brand—set it into the corner of her mouth, and lit up as if she were performing a patriotic duty. "Whaddaya want, kid?" she snarled.

"I'm looking for Chester Hogue," I said, then added, "Murray Fleischmann sent me."

The woman blew smoke from the far corner of her lips, then took the cigarette between two fingers and bellowed toward the rear of the shop, "Hey, *Chet*—someone comin' back."

I thanked the woman and started along the aisle toward Chet. On my left, old tables and chairs, stacked to the ceiling. On my right, display cabinets crammed with glass and pottery. At the rear of the shop, behind a long wooden counter, I saw a hunched figure at a worktable. Around him everywhere, clocks. Clocks hung on walls, heaped on wooden shelves, piled on the floor. As I came up to the counter, the figure turned toward me, pulled a loupe from his eye, blinked, then croaked, "Whatcha got there, Sonny?"

He stood up slowly. I thought of a turtle trying to extend its head out of foul water to breathe a bit of pure air. White shirt, dark blue vest, trousers held up by blue suspenders. Face like a hatchet, just a few strands of sandy hair running across the top of his head, watery light blue eyes and a disconcerting blinking tic. He looked like a character out of Dickens, some bookkeeper who'd sat fifty years on a high stool, bent over a ledger. On his worktable was a medium-sized clock carcass.

I laid my music box on the counter. Mr. Hogue lifted the lid, peered inside, blink-blink-blink. Then he shook his head sadly and said, "Tut, tut." First time I'd ever heard a real person say tut-tut, and I came awfully close to laughing. "Oh, I'm sorry, Sonny. Very sorry. Couldn't give you much for this, maybe a nickel. Governor's missing, see?"

The old bastard. In those days antique music boxes really weren't worth a lot of money, but a nickel? "I'm not here to sell it, Mr. Hogue," I said. "I'm fixing it and I need a governor."

"Oho, you need a governor, do you? Well, they're very hard to come by, you see, and—"

"Murray Fleischmann sent me," I said, as if I were invoking protection by a patron saint. "He's helping me fix it, and he said you'll have a governor to fit." I paused, then decided to go ahead. "And if the whole box isn't worth more than a nickel, I guess the governor won't cost more than a penny."

Mr. Hogue looked me up, down and sideways, blink-blink-blink. Then he started to snicker. "Got a mouth on you, Sonny, that's okay. You're gonna do all right for yourself." He waved me to the end of the counter. "Come on back, bring your music box. We'll go find you a governor."

I cradled the music box under my arm, pushed past the wooden gate at the end of the counter, followed Mr. Hogue through a door into a back room bursting with clocks. Battered, broken grandfather clocks, table clocks, wall clocks. Piles of parts on the floor, a waist-high mound of keys to my left. Mr. Hogue motioned me along. "Music box stuff's in the back."

Was it ever. Like walking through some kind of Fort Knox for antiques. Music boxes, all sizes and shapes, practically floor-to-ceiling. Piles of parts, literally tons of metal. Mr. Hogue sure wasn't making many trips to the salvage center. He pointed at a heap of governors, dead brass butterflies a foot high. "Let's see your box."

I held out the music box. Mr. Hogue opened the lid, whipped a pair of calipers out of his pocket, measured the distance between those two small holes in the bedplate. Then he crouched over the pile, put calipers to governors, occasionally handed one up to me. When I had six or seven, he motioned me back toward his workbench. Go-go-go, blink-blink-blink.

At his bench, he took the mechanism out of the case, then screwed one governor after another into place on the bedplate and tried to turn the big gear on the end of the cylinder, the one that mates with the governor wheel. The first three governors wouldn't work. Mr. Hogue shook his head, pointed. "Gears bind, see?" But when he tried the fourth governor, he smiled. Little butterfly wings turned, then the cylinder began to rotate. "That oughta do it. You said Murray's helpin' you with the work?"

"More than helping. He's showing me how."

"Good man, Murray," Hogue said. "You'll learn a lot from him."

"What do I owe you for the governor?" I asked, very businesslike, I thought.

That set Mr. Hogue cackling. "Guess a penny." He held out his hand. I pulled a penny out of my pocket, dropped it into his grease-stained palm. He flipped it into the air, caught it. "You're gonna do awright, Sonny," he wheezed. "You're polite, but at the same time you don't let people push you around. If you'n' Murray need any more help, just come on back. Now…" He gestured with his head toward his bench. "I need to get on back to work. See you."

Murray laughed when I got back to the yard and told him about Mr. Hogue and the governor. "Christ on a crutch, that Chester. He'd pay his mother a nickel for her solid silver soup tureen if he could get away with it. Glad you didn't let him jew you…hey, what's the matter?"

"Just surprised," I said. "I mean, especially since you're Jewish." Then I remembered what he'd said to Ezra the night before, tried to backtrack. "I mean—"

Murray waved a hand, no sweat. "Don't make no nevermind. Just a way of talking, is all. Come on, let's get you started fixing this thing."

I followed him behind the shed to a wooden table, faded, rickety, covered with junk. Murray swept his huge hand across the tabletop; scrap clattered to the ground. He put the music box in the clearing, pulled a screwdriver from a tool belt on his waist, waved it at the music box like a magic wand. Then he looked at me with mock gravity. "Watch close, Dockie. Ain't just anybody gets to learn my secrets."

After we took the mechanism apart, Murray left, and I started scrubbing with a brush and brass polish. I dripped sweat onto my work. My T-shirt stuck to my neck and back. But I saw Harmony's face as she begged me to give her the music box… thought about Jonas Fleischmann, heart attack, strychnine. Rat poison, junkyard rats, black market scrap metal. I was trying to make some sense when a shadow dropped across my work. "Fuck you doin', kid?" A growl.

I put down the piece of brass I was cleaning, and there in all his glory was Oscar Fleischmann. Blue and white bib overalls with no shirt, red neckerchief over nut-brown shoulders, gray chest hairs running riot. His belly shook, biceps bulged. When he bent to see what was on the table in front of me, the stink of cigarettes and garlic nearly knocked me off my chair. "Hell's this?" he grunted.

"I'm fixing a music box," I said, then for the second time invoked the name of my patron saint. "Murray's helping me."

"You get it here?"

I took the Hogue approach—be polite but don't let anyone push you around. "It was my grandmother's," I said. "I brought it from home and got a governor for it from Chester Hogue. Now Murray is showing me how to fix it."

"Huh!" Oscar spat on the ground. His gob curled at the edges, raised a little dust cloud in the light brown dirt. I decided to edge into the real reason I was spending time in that junkyard, see what I might learn. "Sorry about Jonas, Mr. Fleischmann," I said.

Oscar gave me a long look. Light flashed in his eyes. "God *damn*, I thought I seen you before. You're Samuel Firestone's kid."

I nodded.

Oscar shook his head, spat again. "What're you doin' here, then? Why ain't you out wipin' your old man's ass for him, like the other night?"

No way to answer that without being either inflammatory or candy-assed, so I picked up the part I'd been working on, went back to brushing. But Oscar gave me a slap to the cheek that set my teeth rattling. "Hey, shitface—when I'm talkin' to you, *listen*. Don't go pretendin' like I ain't here."

I dropped my work, looked up slowly. With fists balled, Oscar put me in mind of a double bazooka, rockets loaded, ready to fire. I jumped and wheeled around, my own fists up and ready. I was a good five inches taller than Oscar, at least fifty years younger, had a longer reach. After a moment's faceoff, he lowered his hands, then flipped me a derisive laugh. "You're lucky, kid, I hope y' know that. You oughta be goin' home with most of your teeth missin' an' blood pourin' outa your mouth. This here's *my* yard." He pointed at the dismembered music box on the table. "So pick up your shit and get outa here. Murray's got better to do than waste his time with you. He don't wise up and do his work, he can go lay down next to his putz brother."

Oscar's back was to the office, so he didn't see Murray come around the corner. Murray stood listening, his face growing darker with every word. By the time Oscar wound up his speech, Murray was near-black. A blood vessel on his left temple bulged below his thinning hairline. He stomped forward, grabbed Oscar by the shoulder, spun him around. "You ever call Jonas a putz again—"

"You'll do what? He *was* a putz. A solid brass, gold-plated idiot. An' you're gettin' to be one too, suckin' up to Sammy Firestone. You think you're in business with Sammy? Well, I got news for you. Wait'll some shit hits the fan. You'll be standin' there with it all over your face, and Sammy Firestone'll walk away in his white Panama hat, not a spot on him."

I jumped forward but Murray waved me back. He was furious. "I say shut it, Pop, I *mean* shut it. I want to show this kid how to fix a machine, I'll show him. He don't need no permission from you to be here. *Your* junkyard?" Murray turned around, bent from the waist and blasted a loud, long fart at Oscar. "Wasn't for Mom, you wouldn't've ever set your smelly feet in this yard."

Oscar blew Murray a Bronx cheer. "Like if birds didn't have wings they wouldn't fly. Well, I got papers to *show* it's my yard. You don't like the way I run it, go work someplace else." Oscar glared at me. "I knew your ol' man when he didn't have a pot to pee in, went around in patched shirts, sewed-together pants, holes in his shoes. Go on home and ask him where a pisher like him got money to go to medical school. Tell him Ol' Os Fleischmann said *he* paid his way." Oscar thumped his hairy chest like King Kong. "With the dough I put down to buy his business, that he stole and sold the fuckin' place out from under me."

Murray raised a warning finger in Oscar's direction, then put a hand on my shoulder. "Cover up your work, Dockie." Oscar snorted at "Dockie." "Get a tarp outa the office, write your name on a piece a paper, put the paper on top a the work, lay the tarp over it all. Then come on back tomorra. Every one a them pieces is gonna be right where you left them, I guarantee. Now go on."

I took off around the corner toward the office. From behind me I heard Oscar say, "You and what army guarantees?" By the time I got back with the tarp and paper, Murray and Oscar were gone. I covered my work, got on my bike, headed home.

Halfway down the last block I heard the sax, "Somebody Loves Me." Harmony listened quietly to my story of the day, until I told her what Oscar said about Samuel walking away in a pinch and leaving Murray with a face full of shit. Then she murmured, "Wonder what business they're in together," but stopped as someone came clopping down the cellar steps. Lissa Belmont, carrying a plate before her like a mouse-priest with a sacrificial offering. The bouquet preceded her; my stomach growled. She laughed. "Sounds like Leo would like a cookie." She held the plate toward me. "I thought the two of you might like a nice vanilla-cinnamon cookie, fresh from the oven."

Behind her mother's back, Harmony stuck out her tongue, crossed her eyes and pulled sideways at the corners of her mouth. I quick-bit into the cookie. Mrs. Belmont set the tray on the table next to the saxophone, then looked from Harmony to me, back again. One corner of her mouth twisted upward, derisive little smile. "My, the two of you—you do look like an old married couple."

Before Harmony could go off I said, "Thanks, Mrs. Belmont. Good cookies."

"I'll leave the tray."

"You already did." Harmony's voice was as sour as her face.

Mrs. Belmont seemed not to notice. "Just don't eat too many and spoil your appetite for dinner." Then she vanished up the stairs.

Harmony's eyes followed her all the way. "We look like an old married couple, huh? Bet she baked those damn cookies just to have an excuse to come down and see if we were behaving like a young married couple."

That reminded me. I told Harmony about delivering Shannon's baby the night before. She shrugged. "Happens all the time. Girls who get pregnant go out of town to have the baby, then come back home and tell people they were away at school for a year. Leo, you are so un-hep. You're such an infant about some things."

"That's not the point. Shannon Herlihy, Harmony? Lily Fleischmann's blonde, blue-eyed niece?"

"You never heard of 'Abie's Irish Rose'?"

"All right. But the other woman, 'Aunt Nancy'. She looked as if *she* were having the baby."

Which didn't faze my little green-eyed owl. "Bet Aunt Nancy was really Shannon's mother. She was embarrassed, so she made out like she was the aunt." Harmony danced around the table, plunked into my lap, draped her arms around my neck. "What do you think my mother'd do if *I*... Leo, if you got me in the family way would you marry me?"

"Harmony..."

Already back on her feet, laughing. "Don't worry, Leo, I wouldn't let you. If I had a baby to take care of, I couldn't be an actress—a real actress, like Ethel Barrymore. Or Helen Hayes.

Not like Betty *Grable*, oh, my stupid mother! Leo, Samuel wasn't fooling, was he? About paying my way through drama school?" Sudden anguish in her voice, terrible. "He wouldn't even have to give it to me, he could lend it. I'll pay him back just as soon as I get into paying roles."

"I don't think Samuel would ever tell you that if he didn't mean it." Hope struggled to grab a foothold on her face. "I'm sure he meant it," I added.

Harmony nodded. "I think about it every minute I'm down at the Red Cross, rolling those damn bandages with those silly old women." She paused just long enough to set her jaw. "I swear, Leo, if it turns out he *was* only kidding, I'll kill him."

Dinner that night was horse steak, nonrationed, inexpensive, nutritious horse. Ramona smiled, all pride, as she served it up. "It's Heavy Belgian. Harry the butcher says that's the tastiest breed, nice and tender. He knows the man who raises them for food." Samuel smiled. I heard his thought: "If I did the shopping we'd be eating prime beefsteak." But Ramona played strictly according to Hoyle, she did our shopping, we ate horse. "Where were you all afternoon, Leo?" Ramona asked.

"Fleischmann Scrap. The junkyard."

Samuel's first forkful of Heavy Belgian stopped halfway to his mouth. "What were you doing there all afternoon?"

I told the music box story, including my stop at Hogue's Clocks and Anti-cues, but left out the part about Oscar. Samuel looked at me curiously. "You spent all afternoon fixing an old music box?"

"It's interesting," I said. "I thought I only needed to get a missing piece and put it on, but Murray showed me there's more to it than that. We took the box all apart, now I'm cleaning and polishing it. Then Murray'll help me get it back together and playing."

"I think that's lovely." Ramona smiled. "I'd like to hear it."

"Harmony said the same…thing." The look on Ramona's face was a friction brake on my tongue. According to Ramona,

Harmony was too smart for a girl, knew it, and always made sure everyone else knew it.

Samuel grinned, picked up his fork. "You're learning, Leo. Do one job, please two women. Can't argue with that." He put the neglected chunk of horsemeat into his mouth.

"I saw Oscar Fleischmann at the junkyard," I said, and now the look on Samuel's face stopped me. Fork back down, he waited for me to drop the other shoe. "Oscar told me to ask you where you got money to go to medical school. He said he paid your way, with money he put down to buy your business." I choked on the part about stealing.

Samuel launched a derisive hoot. "You believe him?"

Ramona stopped eating. We sat there, three people on alert that a bomb was scheduled to go off. A no from me would've been untrue, a yes out of the question. "I think something happened," I said. "But not exactly the way Oscar put it."

"And you'd like to hear my side?"

It was ninety degrees in that room when we started dinner, at least ten degrees hotter now. Samuel could heat a room as easily as he could light it. "If you want to tell me," I said quietly.

Samuel wiped his mouth with his napkin, glanced at Ramona. She looked like a wax statue. "Fair enough. You know how I...your mother and I came to own an appliance store in downtown Hobart?"

I knew it all right, chapter and verse. Over the years Samuel had worked his chronicle into a secular parable, always concluding with the watchword of his faith. "Count on your*self*. Trust your*self*." Shmuel Feuerstein was twelve the year an epidemic tore through his little town in northern Germany. Typhus, cholera, influenza? No idea, doesn't matter. Shmuel watched his mother, father, two sisters and a brother go below ground. "We may sorrow," the rabbi told him. "But we must bend before the inscrutable will of the Lord." Shmuel's relatives stole what money his family had, and all the property, then apprenticed the boy to a shoemaker. "Enough school," his uncle said. "This isn't America." One night, Shmuel slipped out of the shoemaker's house, ran away, somehow made his way across half of Europe, starving, stealing, but never begging. *Never.* He crossed the Channel to England, learned the language, became Samuel Firestone. Finally, he scraped together enough money for third-class passage to America. After he landed in New York, he went on a tip to Hobart, two dimes and a nickel in his pocket, talked himself into a job at Walter Shadburn's appliance store, five bucks a week, room and board. For seven years he lived with Mr. and Mrs. Shadburn and their daughter Ramona; then he and Ramona were married. Not long after, Mrs. Shadburn got sick, abdominal cancer. Doctors shrugged, said nothing to do but wait. Samuel looked after his mother-in-law, seethed over her endless vomiting, raged at her relentless pain. He went sleepless for days at a time, seemed to draw strength from his accumulating fury. "Nothing to do"? When Mrs. Shadburn finally died, he knew what he needed to do. And would do.

I nodded to Samuel. "Yes."

"All right, then. I'd taken night classes for years, finished high school, had a few college credits, top grades. But to get to med school I'd need to go to college full time. I was looking into scholarships and part-time jobs, trying to figure how Ramona and I could live, when one morning Walter didn't wake up. Now Ramona and I owned the business and the little building it was in. My chance, Leo. I took a day, drove down to New Brunswick, made my case to a dean, got admitted to Rutgers. Our state university, low tuition, great chance of a merit-and-need scholarship. I put the business up for sale, and inside a week I had a buyer, a thousand down, rest to come in a month. I figured with what I'd earn working nights and weekends, the thousand alone'd keep us going all year and then some. School opened the next week. That afternoon while Ramona and I were packing, guess who showed up, ready to buy the store. On the spot."

"Not Oscar Fleischmann," I said. Hard to imagine him as anything other than a junkman.

"The same." The memory set Samuel's face glowing. "For years he'd been telling me I was too big for my britches, a greeny-sheeny punk who thought he was going to be a doctor, ha! But now he wanted to buy my store. "It's sold," I told him. He laughed. "Yeah, sure, I heard. Guy's gonna pay you in a month...maybe. I want your place, gonna put it together with my yard, get traffic goin' both ways. You don't need to wait no month *maybe* get your dough." Arm around my shoulder. "Show you." He pulled a fist full of bills out of his pocket. "See? Cash green. Come down by my lawyer's this afternoon, walk out with this in your pocket. Then go off with the little bride there, learn how to be a doctor." I told him sorry, the store was sold. That's when he started yelling. "Ain't nothin' sold 'til the final agreement—looky here." He counted out bills, slapped them into my hand, closed my fist over them. "*Now* it's sold. There's your downpayment, in cash. This afternoon you get the rest. My lawyer's Milton Goldfarb, up in the Mainmark Building, third floor. Meet you there, four o'clock." He pointed at the cash in my hand. "See? I'm trustin' you."

I laughed out loud. Samuel chuckled. "By two o'clock Ramona and I were on the road to New Brunswick. My deal closed with the first buyer right on schedule, and a couple of weeks after that I got a letter from Mr. Goldfarb. They were going to sue me for breach of contract and I'd better return Mr. Fleischmann's eighteen hundred dollars, fast. I called Goldfarb, asked him what contract? What eighteen hundred dollars?"

"Your father and Oscar left me in the bedroom, packing, and went outside to talk," Ramona said in a colorless voice. "I didn't know the first thing about this until Mr. Goldfarb's letter came."

"So, no witnesses," Samuel said. "And nothing in writing. The son of a bitch thought he could push some greenhorn kid around. I gave him another think."

"It still wasn't an honest thing to do," Ramona said quietly.

"No. It wasn't. But I played Oscar's game by his own rules, and beat him. That's the story, Leo. Would you've done differently?"

"I think I'd've told him to take his money and shove it," I said. "Why give him the satisfaction?"

Samuel shrugged. "I'd say I walked away a hell of a lot more satisfied than Oscar. If he came here today with his deal I just might do it your way, but remember, I was twenty-two then. Old for a college student in those days, old for medical school. A little longer, I'd've had to just forget about going. Those hundred-dollar bills in my hand looked like the ticket to my future." Samuel leaned closer; little points of gold gleamed on his cheeks and chin. "You never know what you're going to do 'til you're there, Leo…and sometimes you surprise yourself."

I thought of the circus juggler, seven balls up, go for eight. "If Oscar came to you with the deal today, you'd still try to nail him," I said.

Ramona gasped, but Samuel laughed. "Maybe you're right—okay, enough. Do you think you can fit rounds into your busy schedule tomorrow morning? We'll get done in plenty of time for you to work with Murray in the afternoon. Promise."

"Sure." I smiled. He made it impossible not to.

After supper I cleared dishes from the table, started washing them in the sink. The phone rang in the living room. I heard Samuel talking but couldn't make out words. Then Ramona flew in, reached for her apron on its hook near the door. "I'll finish, Leo, go on. Samuel wants to take you to a consultation."

She looked tired. As she tied on the apron, her hands shook. "I'll do the dishes," I said. "I don't mind missing—"

She moved to the sink, pushed me aside. Eyes wide, breathing like a dray-ox under full load. One word. "Leo!"

I swiped my hands over the dishtowel, took off into the living room. Samuel was on his feet, working his collar button shut. "Go put on a white shirt, Leo, good pair of pants. And a tie. Move!"

His eyes glowed phosphorescent, unnatural. I ran up the stairs, flung my T-shirt and chino pants onto the bed, redressed myself as ordered, was back down inside a minute. Samuel nodded approval, then moved toward the front door. Ramona rushed into the room, held out a trembling hand. "Samuel," she called. "As long as you're going in, could you…"

He ran back, threw an arm around her, kissed her cheek. "Sure, don't worry."

I suddenly realized what Ramona was asking, knew why Samuel cut her off. Almost a year before, I came home from school one afternoon and found my mother on her bed, out cold, needle still in her arm, syringe in her free hand. I checked her pulse, pure reflex, slow but strong. Then I stood over her for I don't know how long, staring at the little trickle of blood from the puncture site down her arm, onto the sheet. Bathrobe open in front. I started to cover her, but then figured better not. She'd know I'd been there, that I'd seen—Noah's son, Catch-22. So I left her as I found her, picked up my books, went to Harmony's, blurted the story. We decided Ramona probably got hooked when she hemorrhaged and needed a hysterectomy after she gave birth to me. Four months in bed afterward, lot of pain. What Harmony and I couldn't figure was where Ramona got her supply, but now I could stop wondering. I can still see my mother on her bed, unconscious, undraped, as clear right this minute as the day I found her. I've never let any doctor give me a dose of narcotic, not even when I broke my arm, or had my appendix out. Some pain, you just bear. The relief's overpriced.

Chapter 6

I scrambled down the front steps after Samuel, across the lawn, into the Plymouth. "You'll learn a lot from this one," he shouted, but the way we blasted down the driveway and into the street I wasn't sure I'd live long enough to learn anything. "Buskin Brown's daughter, Rhoda. Know her?"

Rhoda Brown was fifteen, a year behind me in high school. Snotty little thing, always with her nose in the air. When it rained, boys pointed out the windows and yelled, "Hey, Rhoda, watch out you don't drown." Her father made a fortune in silk, then moved his money into a shoe chain when silk went bust. *L.* Buskin Brown, he called himself. People joked that he stuck on the L to make his name sound like a Supreme Court justice's. "I only know Rhoda a little," I told Samuel. "Which is more than enough."

Samuel laughed. "Most of that family rides pretty high horses." Then humor faded from his face. "But the girl's quite sick. Didn't feel well for a few days, then all of a sudden started running a high fever, got confused, became less and less responsive. Now it sounds as if her heart and kidneys may be failing. I've treated that family for years, but Buskin wanted a specialist. He called Art Cornwell, told him Samuel Firestone's just a G.P., all right for colds and delivering babies. Art went in, couldn't make a diagnosis, wanted to call me, but Buskin said no, if Art wasn't good enough—that's exactly what he said—then a G.P.

would only be a waste of time and money. He wanted an expert from New York. So they called the Chairman of Medicine at Columbia, Franz Beckwith. Beckwith told them, "You've got Samuel Firestone right there in Hobart, a better diagnostician than anyone in New York or anywhere else. My advice is to call him, fast."

Samuel scraped rubber on the curb as he parked in front of the hospital. "How do you know all that?" I asked.

His eyes blazed; he threw open the car door. "Art told me, when he finally called."

The scene in that hospital room was right out of a Victorian novel. Rhoda lay on her back, white face on a white pillowcase, motionless except for rapid, shallow respiration. Her mother sat in a chair next to the bed, sobbing and wringing her hands. I knew Dr. Cornwell, a neatly groomed man with a dark mustache and a professionally distinguished manner. He nodded politely at me. Buskin Brown, more than filling a nicely tailored suit colormatched to his name, looked at Samuel with a peculiar mix of resentment and hope, then noticed me. "What's *this?*" he boomed.

"This is my son Leo," Samuel said, taking care, I thought, not to echo Brown's derogatory emphasis on the first word. "Leo is my extern this summer."

Brown looked apoplectic. "But...this girl...my daughter... she's fifteen years old!" Little globules of spit flew from his mouth.

By then Samuel was flipping pages in the chart. "Rapid pulse," he murmured to me. "Falling blood pressure, falling urine output. Let's get started."

I followed him to the bedside. Brown clenched both fists, shook them at the ground, growled, "Umph! Umph!" Crimson spread up from his cheeks to his forehead, across his bald dome. Samuel studied Rhoda for a moment, then looked at me. "Otoscope."

He took the instrument, scrutinized Rhoda's ears, eyes and throat, then grabbed a stethoscope and listened to her heart and lungs. He felt her abdomen, checked reflexes, did a full examination, but quickly, almost perfunctorily. I was surprised. A girl as sick as that, where a very good doctor hadn't been able to make a diagnosis? Samuel slipped his rubber hammer back into the black bag, then said casually, "She's got diphtheria. Treat her for diphtheria, she'll probably be all right. But no time to waste."

Another surprise. I'd learned early on, a consulting doctor talks over his findings privately with the doctor who called him in, then both doctors discuss the case with patient and family. Dr. Cornwell actually gulped. "Samuel... Diphtheria's very rare past the age of ten. And there's no history of a sore throat or a cold, no pharyngeal pseudomembrane, negative throat culture—"

Samuel's face shone near-luminescent. "Unusual presentation, Art." He pointed at the pillow next to Rhoda's head. "See that little stain there? Infection's in her right middle ear."

I had to look hard, but yes, there was a small area of faint discoloration next to the girl's head. Art Cornwell looked unconvinced. "That's saliva."

Samuel shook his head, reached back, pulled the otoscope out of his bag, handed it to Cornwell. "Look in the middle ear, Art, you'll see the pseudomembrane. Diphtheria. Drum's burst, it's draining."

Cornwell's face said he'd humor Samuel. He rested a hand on Rhoda's doughy forehead, put the scope to her ear, bent to squint through it. His body stiffened. He slid out the scope, handed it to Samuel without a word.

"Fulminating case, rapid onset." Samuel spat words like a machine gun. "Must be a bacterial strain that produces a ton of toxin. Take a culture if you want, but I'd just give her fifty thousand units of antitoxin I.V. right away, another fifty I.M. Ice bag over the heart, head and neck. And sick as she is, I'd give her penicillin, soon as possible. Hundred-fifty-thousand units I.V. to start, then fifty every eight hours. She'll improve by morning."

I'd never heard such a silence, Martin. Every conscious person in the room glanced at everyone else. Poor Art Cornwell looked as if he'd been stuffed into a close-fitting hair shirt. He seemed to draw himself together by degrees, then said, "Samuel, where in *hell* are you going to get penicillin for a civilian case?"

My father smiled. "I can get penicillin." He turned to face Brown squarely. "Enough to treat your daughter. It'll cost five thousand dollars."

The previous silence was heavy but this one crushed it. Samuel glared at Brown. "Well, what do you say? Every minute we spend doing nothing makes the situation worse."

Brown looked at Dr. Cornwell, got no help.

"Do you want me to manage the case?" Samuel snapped.

Silence.

Samuel started toward the door. "I'll write a note on the chart," he said. "Good luck."

"No!"

The first word out of Mrs. Brown since we came into that room split the air. She jumped to her feet, shoved a soggy handkerchief into the top of her skirt. "Samuel, *I* want you to manage my daughter's care. If Dr. Cornwell and Dr. Beckwith both said we should call you in, then we need to take whatever advice you give us." Quick look toward Rhoda. "Especially since yours are the first hopeful words we've heard."

Buskin Brown might add an L to his name and throw his considerable weight around, but it was obvious who played the hand in that family when big chips were down. "You say if we follow your plan my daughter will recover?" Mrs. Brown asked Samuel.

Facing that woman was like standing in front of an oncoming steamroller. I wouldn't have faulted Samuel if he'd waffled, but he didn't even hesitate. "Pretty sure, Constance," he said. Quiet words, gentle but firm. "But I do know what'll happen if we don't treat her quickly."

Mrs. Brown gave her husband a look that could've withered a live oak. He answered with a timid little nod in Samuel's direction.

Samuel pulled the nurse-call string. Almost instantly, a large woman ran in, a tiny white cupcake-paper hat pinned to her beehive of white hair. "Diphtheria antitoxin, fifty I.V., fifty I.M.," Samuel said calmly. "Ice bags, head, neck, heart. I'll write orders later." The nurse ran out as quickly as she'd come in.

Samuel looked at Brown. "I need five thousand, cash. Now."

Brown spluttered, jabbed a finger toward the window at the darkening sky. "It's after eight o'clock at night," he bellowed. "Banks're all closed. Where do you think I can get—"

Before he finished his question, answer came from his furious wife, now back at the bedside. "Same place you've gotten it for a lot of other things, none as important as this. Now do what he says and hurry up about it."

Brown pursed lips, shook his head like a horse uncertain at the road his driver was directing him onto. Then he growled, "My house, fifteen minutes," at Samuel, and stomped through the doorway.

Samuel took Art Cornwell's hand, said, "Thanks for asking me to consult. She'll make it."

As we walked out into the hall, Samuel told me to go down to the car, he'd catch up with me in a minute or two. "Got to call a man about some penicillin." He held out his hand. "Bag."

I didn't ask why he needed his doctor's bag to make a phone call, just went downstairs, through the lobby, out into the car. Not five minutes later, Samuel came rushing down the walk, bag swinging from his hand as if it had no weight. He jumped in, flung the bag onto the back seat, started the car, swung a U-turn in front of an ice-cream wagon, took off uptown. He could've powered that car with his own energy. Cheeks glowing, eyes aflame, he was Hippocrates, Franklin Delano Roosevelt, Jesus Christ, and P. T. Barnum. Rhoda Brown would live because Samuel Firestone wouldn't have it otherwise. "Samuel," I said, very, very quietly. "How did you know Rhoda had diphtheria when no one else did? You hardly even examined her."

"Didn't have to," he said, eyes still on the road, speedometer moving up on forty-five. "I knew what she had, only question was where. Think back, Leo. When we walked into that room what was the first thing you noticed?"

I thought back. "All the people standing around, how concerned they were. Afraid. Rhoda looked pale, fragile—"

"That's what you saw. What did you smell? Notice a funny odor? Different from anything you'd ever smelled before."

"The hospital smell, iodine—"

Samuel cut me off again. "No, no—that, you smell every day. Didn't you notice a different smell? Sweetish, putrid? The minute I walked into the room I smelled diphtheria. Use all your five senses, Leo, all the time. Find someone unconscious and think it's diabetic coma, don't waste an hour sending urine to a lab. Put a drop on your tongue, see if it's sweet."

Samuel turned left off Roosevelt onto Ridge, then another left onto Manor. He parked in front of a house out of *Gone With the Wind*, white columns across a veranda fifty feet wide. As we pulled up, Buskin Brown stomped down the flagstone path toward us, a paper grocery bag in his hand. Samuel got out of the car, motioned Brown into the back seat, followed him. I kept my eyes forward. A minute passed, then Brown blustered, "It's all there, Samuel, I counted it three times. You don't trust me?"

Silence. Finally Samuel said, "Forty-nine, fifty. Tell you a little story, Buskin. When I was an intern, electrocardiograms were just being developed in big city hospitals, and getting one was a big deal. String galvanometer, resistors, camera with motor, light source, all touchy as hell. One day my resident showed me a cardiogram he'd done on a patient, told me to write treatment orders based on it. But the damn tracing didn't fit at all with clinical findings. So late that night I wheeled the patient into the electrocardiogram room, did another tracing, and guess what—it was normal. The resident had reversed a couple of leads. If I'd treated that patient on faith I'd've killed her. Now go on back to the hospital, Buskin. We'll be there inside half an hour."

Brown hauled himself out of the car, onto the sidewalk, stamped away to his own car in the driveway. Samuel got behind the wheel and we were off, back down Roosevelt, across Graham Avenue to Lyon, then left on Sixteenth to Jack's Pharmacy. Jack stood behind the counter, a sneer on his face. "Well, if it ain't the Angel of Mercy and his little cherub." He pointed at a brown bag on the countertop.

Samuel pulled a folded wad of money out of his shirt pocket, passed it across the counter. "Shekels for the Prostitute of Pharmacopeia."

Jack snickered, then made a show of counting bills. Twenty hundreds. He took out his wallet, slipped in the money. Forget the cash register. Samuel opened the paper bag, pulled out two little bottles, looked at them closely. "Right. Two weeks' worth. You're an honest crook, Jack."

As we squealed away from the curb, Samuel said, "Leo, you're seeing something glorious tonight." He glanced at the bag on the seat between us. "Rhoda's too sick for antitoxin alone to do much good, but this antibiotic, penicillin, knocks diphtheria bacteria cold. It's almost all going overseas for the Armed Forces, but who's going to tell me Rhoda's life is worth less than some soldier's?"

Not me. I was shaking.

"If getting penicillin for her means bending a rule, it's an easy choice." Samuel paused, sighed. "Maybe she'll take after her mother."

All the way back to the hospital I thought about rules, bending them, breaking them. I'd heard my father count Brown's money, fifty hundreds, five thousand dollars. He gave Jack two. What about the other three?

I followed Samuel inside the hospital, up to the second floor. At the door to the mens' room I called, "Be right along," then ran inside with the big black bag, charged into a stall, threw the lock behind me, sat down.

I waited half a minute, held my breath. The outside door didn't open. Carefully, quietly, as if the stalls on either side of me were occupied by spies, I clicked the latch, pulled the bag open, reached past little compartments full of tablets, capsules, bottled liquids, down into the space below. Stethoscope, reflex hammer, rubber tourniquet, ophthalmoscope, otoscope…paper crinkled against my fingers. I pulled out a bag, rummaged inside it. Couple of autoclaved syringes, several 25-gauge needles, and a glass vial of morphine sulfate, hospital stock, no prescription sticker. No hundred-dollar bills, either.

I put the narcotic back into the paper bag, stuffed it underneath the ophthalmoscope, then clicked the latch closed and walked slowly back to Rhoda Brown's hospital room. Just inside the door I stopped in my tracks. A sweetish odor, unpleasant, hint of something rotting. Faint, but definitely there. Samuel stood at the bedside, holding up a bottle of penicillin, telling the nurse exactly how and when to give it, warning her no mistake could be made, not a pinch of that precious powder could be wasted. Art Cornwell was gone. Buskin Brown seemed to be studying the progress of a fly on the far wall. But Mrs. Brown, wide-eyed, open-mouthed, gazed at Samuel with the adoration of a true believer.

As we left, Samuel told the nurse to call him for any problem. "I'll be back in the morning," he said. "By then we should see a nice turnaround."

Mrs. Brown burst into sobbing. Her husband draped an arm around her, rumbled, "You'd better be right, Samuel. I've got connections in this town."

Any boy of sixteen knew Jersey politics, but if Samuel felt concerned, he didn't show it. "Be back at nine o'clock," he said quietly. "I expect I'll see you both talking to your daughter."

Down the stairs, into the lobby, no conversation. Finally I muttered, "What a jerk."

"Brown?" Samuel slowed pace. "I don't know. Buskin's used to having his own way, and right now he's in over his head, thrashing around like a man drowning. But a few years back, when one of his machine operators got careless and lost a hand, Buskin covered all his medical expenses, then got him trained as a salesman. The man makes higher pay now than he did in the mill. You like to paint, Leo. Can you paint a man's portrait using only one color?"

As we walked up our front steps, Ramona opened the door. Eyes staring, black pupils huge, hands shaking, arms covered with gooseflesh. If I hadn't been on alert I'd have missed both the silent question in her eyes and the little nod Samuel gave in answer. He lifted his Panama, brushed hair back off his forehead, shot me a sideways glance. "Whew, long day. I could use a dish of ice cream, chocolate if possible. What say you go to Felix's, get a pint." He pulled a bill from his pocket, held it out to me.

Ramona sniffed, wiped at her nose. "Oh, that sounds wonderful on such a hot night, after such a hot day." Her voice shook as badly as her hands. Samuel told her with his eyes to let him handle this.

I took Samuel's dollar, went out to the garage, got my bike and rode up Roosevelt to Felix's Pharmacy, just below Thirty-third. Ice cream was in short supply, but white-haired old Felix Moskowitz somehow managed to always have a container or two in his soda fountain. One pint per customer, no more, and sometimes the choice was vanilla or vanilla. I waited while Felix finished filling the prescription he was working on, then sold a card of barrettes to a young woman. Finally, he trudged behind the soda fountain and struggled to scoop a pint of hard-frozen chocolate ice cream, working with the same patient thoughtfulness he gave to mixing tonics and elixirs. He molded a square of light waxed paper carefully across the top of the little white carton, shook the carton into a paper bag, rang up the sale and counted my change into my hand, one coin at a time.

By the time I pedaled home, Samuel and Ramona were sitting in the living room, talking quietly. They looked up as I came in. "Want me to dish it out?" I asked. "You bet," Samuel said. "I've worked hard enough today." Ramona's smile was almost beatific. Her face was relaxed, pupils so small I could barely see them.

After the ice cream I excused myself. "Want to read about diphtheria," I said, and went into Samuel's library. I actually did read about diphtheria, didn't want to leave myself vulnerable to a pop quiz, but when I finished, I flipped to the pages on narcotics addiction. "Withdrawal is most unpleasant," said the book. "The addict becomes agitated to the point of shivering, suffers waves of gooseflesh, gets a runny nose. As time passes, he suffers abdominal pain that can be excruciating, with bouts of watery diarrhea. When he finally secures and administers himself more narcotic, he may achieve what is called a rush, a sensation said to be equivalent to sexual satisfaction, with flushed face, evident tranquility, and reversal of all withdrawal signs and symptoms. An unmistakable sign of recent narcotic use is pinpoint narrowing of the pupils."

The next paragraph told me addiction to morphine and other narcotics is not uncommon among medical personnel because of the ease with which the susceptible personality can obtain drugs. "Unlike the usual addict, these medical addicts do not suffer complications related to impure drug or unclean apparatus of administration. They can carry on thus for years, performing their professional duties quite satisfactorily and functioning well in society, no one suspecting their addiction unless they're caught stealing narcotics."

"Stealing narcotics"! Samuel runs into the hospital, saves a girl's life by making a diagnosis no other doctor could, then steals needles, syringes and morphine to feed his wife's habit. You need more than one color to paint a man's portrait? How about black and white? I slammed the book shut, went upstairs to bed.

Chapter 7

I held up a hand to Dad, time out, then trotted down the little hallway to the men's room. Inside, I pulled out my cell phone, punched in my home number. Couple of rings. "Firestone residence."

"Helene..."

"Martin? Is something the matter?" Helene's whiskey-and-cigarette inflections, more noticeable through the phone than face-to-face.

"No. I just took a break from Dad's story, and I wanted to hear your voice."

"You're sweet, Martin, but you really don't have to check up on me. When you're done, come home. I'll be here."

"Old habits," I muttered, then quickly chirped, "Good. See you then." A New York minute later, I slid back into my seat.

Dad lifted his drink, sipped, then took my measure. "Got a time problem?"

Had he seen me on the phone? I was inside the bathroom, but I'd long ago learned to put nothing past my father. "I've got all afternoon," I said. "Go on. What happened to Rhoda Brown?"

Dad laughed, a throaty rumble, shook his head as if he still couldn't believe what he'd seen sixty years before.

Next morning, nine o'clock, Rhoda looked pale and drawn, but right on with Samuel's prediction, she was talking to her parents. She managed a weak smile as Samuel and I walked in. Mrs. Brown jumped up, embraced my father fiercely. "Thank you, Samuel, thank you." She pulled away just far enough to look up into his eyes. "I don't know how we can ever properly thank you, let alone apologize for not calling you in the first place."

"No apology needed," Samuel said. "And as for thanking me, you just did, didn't you?" He looked at L. Buskin Brown, who'd stood silent, classic hangdog face, through the entire exchange. "Maybe you'll feel better when you see my bill."

Samuel and Mrs. Brown laughed. L. Buskin smiled reluctantly. Then he lumbered forward, arm and hand out in front of him like a battering ram. He grabbed Samuel's hand. "When I'm wrong I say I'm wrong," he boomed. "From now on, whenever anyone in my family's sick, I'm calling you. If you'll come, that is."

"Any time," Samuel said lightly.

Brown let go of Samuel, extended his hand to me. "And you, young man. Whenever your father wants to bring you, you're welcome. Far be it from me to object if he wants to teach you to be the kind of doctor he is."

I said a quiet thank-you. Samuel pulled the bell cord, waited for the nurse. When she came he listened to Rhoda's heart and lungs, checked her reflexes, told her to follow his moving finger with her eyes. "Doing fine," he said over his shoulder, then turned to face the nurse. "She got the full antitoxin dose? No allergic reaction?"

"Oh, yes. And no. I mean, she got it and no problems." The nurse's little upside-down cupcake cap threatened to topple. "And Dr. Firestone…"

Samuel straightened, smiled. "What, Mrs. Rackshaw?"

"I just want you to know that when you went out for the penicillin yesterday, Dr. Cornwell did a smear and culture from the ear."

Samuel shrugged lightly. "Positive for diphtheria."

Mrs. Rackshaw nodded vigorously.

"She's getting penicillin on schedule? Fifty thousand units—"

"Every eight hours by the clock." Mrs. Rackshaw's face made it clear no earthly or supernatural power could in any way cause the slightest variation in the prescribed dose of penicillin.

"Good," Samuel looked back at Rhoda. "Great stuff, that penicillin. Two weeks, you can run for Miss America."

Rhoda simpered. "Gee, Dr. Firestone, that'd be swell."

We made a few house calls, a bad cold, an upset stomach, a nasty sprained back. Then we went to see Erskine Crosbie, in his old brown-shingled house on East Thirty-sixth Street. Erskine and his brother-in-law once had been partners in a fabric mill, but when a black-marketeer came knocking, Erskine said no, the brother-in-law, yes. So they split the business, and each man opened his own mill. Brother-in-law's nest got quickly feathered, not Erskine's. "Most honest man I've ever known," Samuel said. "That mill of his is barely getting by, but he won't let Mr. Black put a foot inside the door."

Ruth Crosbie met us at the front door, led us upstairs, past the two kids' rooms, into the master bedroom. Erskine sat propped up in bed against two pillows, surrounded by sheets of paper covered with scribbled numbers. Ruth stooped to pick up a couple of pages that had fallen to the floor, slung them back onto the bed. "He won't stop, works morning 'til night. You told him he's got to relax, Samuel, but the only difference is he's in bed instead of sitting at his desk in the office."

Erskine smiled an apology, slid his pencil behind his ear. "Now, how'n the world could I ever be more relaxed?" he drawled. "Get my meals in bed, everything else I want brought to me. If I was doin' a crossword puzzle you'd say it was fine. But then I'd be bored." His big-toothed grin made him look like the Kentucky plowboy he once was.

Ruth looked thoroughly disgusted. She was an attractive woman in her early forties, soft brown eyes and lustrous hair down to her shoulders, but right then she looked ten years older, eyes clouded, hair a mess, skin tight over her cheekbones. She lit a cigarette, blew smoke across the room. Erskine reached out to her. "Gimme a drag, Ruthie."

She pulled away as if he'd asked her to do something obscene. "Erskine, what am I going to *do* with you? You heard Samuel— no cigarettes. You haven't had one for three days now."

"An' it's killin' me. Come on, gimme a puff, just one. One li'l puff won't do any harm."

Samuel stepped between them. "She's right, Ersk. Nicotine makes blood vessels constrict, last thing we want right now. Come on, lift up your shirt." Samuel set his stethoscope against Erskine's chest, listened, then motioned me forward, handed me the earpieces. I slipped them into place. "What do you hear?" Samuel asked.

"Just regular heart sounds, lub-dup, lub-dup. Not a gallop rhythm, like I heard last time."

"He's getting better." Samuel talked to me, looked at Erskine. "Heart's stronger, no more failure, great. Any pain, Ersk?"

Erskine shook his head. "Not since right after you left yesterday, and jus' a li'l squeeze then. Went away soon's I took the nitro."

"Good." Samuel clapped Erskine's shoulder. "Keep it up. Maybe another month, six weeks, you can—"

I thought Erskine might go airborne. "A *month* more?" Erskine threw back the covers, started to get up, but Samuel stopped him cold with a finger and a word: "Don't." As Erskine settled back, Samuel said slowly, "We made a deal, Ersk. You said you wouldn't go to the hospital—"

"Not wouldn't, couldn't. You know I don't have coverage."

"*You* know I'd've fixed it."

"You know I don't approve of 'fixing' things."

Ruth stubbed her cigarette in an ashtray. Samuel smiled, then Erskine relaxed into a chuckle. "Let's see how the EKG looks," Samuel said, and started to pull the little machine toward the bed. Erskine looked sideways at him. "You 'fixed' that, didn't you? Or has Steinberg Hospital got a free loan policy on their cardiograph machines?"

"Ask me no questions, I'll tell you no lies." Samuel squirted clear jelly out of a tube onto the suction cups at the ends of the lead wires. "If I've got to treat you at home, I'm at least going to get an EKG every day. Now shut up and lie still." He slapped the first lead onto Erskine's chest; Erskine jumped. "Jee-sus, that jelly's cold."

Samuel glanced at Ruth. "Put it in the oven tomorrow, Ruthie, three hours at three-fifty. Now hold still, would you, Ersk. I've got other patients to see today."

As we drove off, Samuel didn't look happy. "Clear coronary thrombosis, mild but still… Rest, another month with no pain, he'll probably be all right. Just hope he doesn't have another attack, maybe bigger."

Samuel had a lunch meeting in the hospital, so he dropped me at home. I made myself a sandwich, ate it as I pedaled down to the junkyard. On my way through the gate, I saw two men working over the garbage heap at the far fence, could just about make them out through the smoke as George and Oscar. I parked my bike against the side of the office, then pulled the tarp off the table, sat down, started polishing pieces of brass. In my mind, I handed Harmony that music box a hundred times or more, tried to imagine how she'd look, what she'd say. When someone rumbled, "Hey, Dockie, looks like you're doing some nice work," I damn near jumped out of my chair. There were Murray and George, grinning, soot all over their faces and clothing. "Murray," I said. "I thought…"

"Yeah?"

Did I want to tell him I'd thought he was Oscar, out by the garbage fire? "Nothing, really," I said quickly. "Just thought I might have this done before you got finished out there."

George bent from the waist to study the music box parts. "Mmmm. Ain't never seen brass shine no better, looks like gold. You do nice work, boy."

"Hey, that ain't no boy, boy." Murray gave George a wicked look to go with a poke in the ribs. "That's Young Doc Firestone. You know what's good for you, you'll call him Dockie."

Junkyard talk, Martin. I knew it, just couldn't speak it. "I already met George," I said. "The other day. He calls me Leo, and that's fine with me."

George looked embarrassed, but nothing I said ever seemed to even scratch Murray's hide. "Hey, Dockie, you gotta have a little sensa humor. Don't you know how to smile?" He poked a finger into my ribs. "Cootchie-coo." I gave it my best. Murray messed my hair with a quick pass of his hand. "Gotta go down the street, meet a guy, be back later. Keep going, you're doing a jim-dandy job there."

George watched Murray ramble out of sight around the corner of the office building. "Murray don't mean no harm," he said. "Way he talks."

"I know," I said quietly.

George nodded several times, as if he weren't sure he ought to say what was on his mind. Finally he spoke. "Ain't never seen somebody fix a music box top to bottom like this—okay if I watch while I eat?"

"Glad for the company."

George went into the office, came back with a battered gray lunch pail which he opened on the edge of the worktable. He took out two fragrant hot sausage sandwiches, offered me one. I shook my head. "Already ate, thanks." I picked up the brass cylinder and a brush, started to work, but then heard Red Dexter's voice through the open window behind me. "You're doin' good, Oscar, real good. An' you can breathe easier now, too. Convenient, Jonas' ticker goin' off like that, huh? Who the hell knows when he mighta done a little talkin' outa school?"

George put down his sandwich, laid a finger seriously across his lips.

Oscar Fleischmann's harsh voice sounded mechanical. "Forty-eight, forty-nine, five-even, fifty-one, fifty-two, fifty-two fifty, fifty-two-seventy-five." He blew a long, low whistle. "More'n five grand."

"This week you eat steak," said Red. "You and Murray both." Little snicker. "More'n twenty-six and a half Cs each."

A cough, deep, phlegmy. "Guess I really am better off without Jonas, ain't I? Prob'ly be better off without Murray too. Got a nigger out there, he works like a nigger for just fifty-five bucks a week. Suppose Murray wasn't here and I hire me another nigger at fifty? Hell, hire two. Do I got to do the numbers?"

George looked like a grenade ready for pin-pull, but as I opened my mouth he shook his head and raised the shush-finger again. "Jus' listen," he whispered.

"Numbers ain't everything, Oscar." The tone of warning in Red's voice set hair standing on my arms and neck. "I don't see Samuel Firestone sittin' still if his pal Murray's health happens to all of a sudden take a turn for the worse. Especially if he thinks it was you put Murray on a permanent sick list. Don't get greedy, Os, business is only gonna get better. Be plenty dough for you *and* your son."

"My son! Shit! You think Murray's gonna take care a me when I can't work no more?" Oscar's voice became pleading, almost whining. "I'm sixty-seven years old, for Christ's sake, and when this goddamn war's over I want to have a big enough pile so I ain't ever gonna need to move into the County Home. Ain't no pensions in a junkyard, case you hadn't noticed."

"I notice more'n you think, Oscar."

"What's that supposed to mean?"

"Means if you pack away anything like half of what you guys're gonna pull in before the war's done, you won't have a thing to worry about. But go fuck with Samuel—"

"Goddamn, Red. If he's a dead corpse I can fuck with him all I want and he ain't gonna bother me or anybody else."

"Okay, Oscar. Now listen, and listen good. Lift a hand against Samuel Firestone, you'll be dealin' with me. And in case you think I'm small potatoes, you better know there's plenty big spuds at Central who'd look very unkindly on a person who's even thinkin' about sendin' off Samuel Firestone. You're smart, you'll figure there's a wall around Samuel, and Murray's right inside with him. You hear, Os?"

I went back to polishing. George drank milk from a thermos cup. A moment later, I heard, "Hey!"

I looked up. Oscar Fleischmann was barely under control, cheeks and forehead blotchy purple, mouth twisted. "Hey, nigger, what the hell you just sittin' here for?" he shouted. "I ain't payin' you good money to watch some little fairy play with his…" Oscar twisted his right arm and hand into a cutesy pose. "*Mew*-zic box."

"Lunch break," George said evenly. "Be over when Murray come back."

That did it. Oscar started jumping up and down like Yosemite Sam in those old movie cartoons. Fists in the air, up, down, up, down. *"I'm* your boss," Oscar screamed at the top of his voice. "This's my junkyard, not Murray's. Now get your black ass back to work before I start dockin' your pay. You hear?"

George didn't blink. "Who own the yard be none a my business," he said. "But Murray tell me take lunch now, an' that time ain't up yet. Don' like it, talk to Murray."

Oscar took a step toward George. George sprang to his feet. "I ain't about to hit no man sixty-seven years old," he said. "Less'n he hit me first."

Oscar stopped, narrowed his eyes. A crafty look came over his face. "How do you know I'm sixty-seven?" he said, then glanced at the office window. "How long the two a you been sittin' here?"

"You once tol' me how old you was," George said, smooth as custard. "When I first come to work here. Said you was twenty-two years older'n me and you'd outwork me any day a the week. And for you' information, we been sittin' here for almos' half an hour."

Oscar muttered something I couldn't make out, started to walk away.

"One mo' thing," George called after him.

Oscar stopped walking, looked back.

"Okay you call me nigger—but ever talk to me again like I be one, I *will* hit you, don't care about no sixty-seven years old. *You* hear?"

Oscar turned around, stomped off. Going around the corner of the building he literally bumped into Murray. "Understand you got something for me," Murray said.

Oscar sneered. "Little birdie been talkin' to you?"

"Yeah. A little red birdie."

Oscar glanced back our way, mumbled, "C'mon inside."

The two of them disappeared around the corner. George looked ready to split a gut. He and I sat as if the slightest motion on our part might set bells clanging. Finally we heard Murray's voice. "Bit short, Pop."

"What, short? You ever clear two thousand in a month before? This's the best we ever did."

"Scummy old bastard, you! We did fifty-two seventy-five, not four and a quarter. You think you're gonna screw me outa more'n five hundred bucks, think another time." Brief silence, then, "I don't give a good rat fuck who's out there hearing every word. Let 'em hear, I ain't embarrassed. Now, I'm telling you for the last time, give. Else I take. And you ever try something like this again you're gonna be Christmas dinner for buzzards."

George and I strained toward the window, but heard nothing until a booming, "What the fuck the two a you listening for?" sent us straight upward. We wheeled around.

Murray stood in front of the table, heehawing for all he was worth. I started breathing again. "You sounded just like…"

If Murray was at all put out by our eavesdropping he didn't show it. "That old cocker—he'd sell his mother to the pimps on Canal Street and throw in his granny if that's what it took to make the deal go down." Murray looked at the pile of music box parts between us. "Hey, Dockie, you're really moving. Bet you get the cleaning and polishing done today. Next time you come we'll put it all back together. Now, me'n George gotta go back to work." His face went serious. "Before you leave, cover up your work with the tarp, tie it down on all sides, and check out with me. Pop so much as puts a finger on any of it, he'll be singing soprano the rest of his life."

Later, I followed "Mean to Me" through the cellar doors into Harmony's basement. "You get better every day," I said.

She put down her sax, gave me a get-serious look.

"No, really. You sound...well, brassy and plaintive, both. Kind of like Ethel Merman with a hangover."

She laughed. Those dimples... "Are you done yet with my music box?"

"It's coming along. I spent all afternoon at the yard, working on it." Then I told her what I'd heard through the open office window, at least most of it. Before I could finish, she jumped to her feet. "I don't believe it, Leo. Samuel wouldn't—"

"Red Dexter said some big spuds at Central—that's just the way he put it—would be very upset if anyone tried to hurt Samuel. So what else can I think? Murray or Oscar or both of them must've been afraid Jonas would talk, so they fed him strychnine. Then Murray called Samuel, and Samuel signed him out as a heart attack. If it was just black market, I could handle that. But they killed a person."

She gave me a long look, then took my hand, led me across the room to a couch, sat at the end. "Lie down, Leo, come on. Put your head in my lap, that's right." She stroked my hair. "Poor baby."

At dinner that evening Ramona asked if I felt all right. I told her I was thinking, honest answer. From the Philco just around the corner in the living room, Fulton Lewis Jr. droned on about some honor Westbrook Pegler had just received. Lewis didn't think much of Pegler or the honor. "I agree," Ramona said primly.

No surprise. Ramona adored Fulton Lewis Jr., just as Samuel detested him. Lewis was an odd sort of glue in their marriage, brought them together to argue for fifteen minutes almost every evening. "We need more Peglers," Samuel said. "Lot of muck around still to be raked."

Ramona sat up straight. "If you're so fond of Westbrook Pegler, how do you explain the way he talks about Mrs. Roosevelt? According to him, she's a public nuisance."

Samuel's eyes brightened, cheeks lit. "Pegler generates so much smoke, sometimes it gets in his eyes and he hits the wrong target." Sly smile. "Nobody's perfect."

What about the man I'd seen take a five-dollar loss on a night call Down-river, then cover up a strychnine poisoning by calling it a heart attack and lying to his son?

Ramona sniffed. "In my opinion that's the only time Westbrook Pegler *is* right. Mrs. Roosevelt *is* a busybody. She'd do a lot better to stay home and look after her own house, and not make trouble for her husband."

Warning siren, loud and clear, in that last sentence. Samuel must have heard it too. He picked up his fork, shoveled a mouthful of vegetables. "Mmmm…*good* tomatoes." His smile would've charmed a wounded grizzly bear. Ramona smiled back, jerked her head toward the back yard, now almost completely transformed into a Victory Garden. "That's because they're fresh. Just two hours ago, they were still on the vine."

After dinner we sat in the living room, Samuel reading the paper, Ramona lost in that week's *Life* magazine, Roy Rogers and Trigger on the front cover. Funny, the stuff you remember. I sat on the floor with a pad, sketching them. Many fewer lines in Samuel's face than Ramona's, but his image still went onto the page darker than hers.

The phone rang. Samuel walked over, grabbed the receiver, listened for not more than a few seconds. Then he moved toward the door. "Erskine Crosbie, let's go," was all he said.

I followed him out to the Plymouth as if drawn by an energy field. "Ruthie sounded upset," Samuel said, as we turned onto Thirty-sixth Street. "Erskine's having worse chest pain, trouble breathing. Damn, I wish I had him in Steinberg."

Even the "damn" was said lightly, as if he were talking about some minor inconvenience. By the time we pulled up at the Crosbies' his face was aglow. I could barely keep pace with him, up the concrete path to the door, knock-knock.

Ruth let us in. She looked ghastly. Up the stairs, not a word, into the master bedroom, to the bedside. I lowered the big black bag to the floor, snapped the latch.

Erskine was propped up as earlier in the day, tally sheets still all over the bed, but now his face was gray, lips nearly colorless and twisted in pain. His right hand clasped his chest, fingers outstretched. Each gasping breath was a tormented effort. Ruth pointed a badly shaking finger at Erskine, finally spoke. "One minute he was fine, the next..."

Samuel patted her shoulder, then knelt to talk to Erskine. "Sorry you're hurting, Ersk, but hang on. Get you feeling better right away." He took the stethoscope from me, listened to Erskine's heart and lungs. As he straightened he motioned toward the electrocardiograph machine. "Can you set the leads, Leo? I'll give him some amyl and morphine, start strophanthin, maybe diuretics."

Which meant Erskine was in heart failure. My own heart pounded into my throat as I pulled the EKG to the bedside, squeezed jelly from a tube onto the undersurfaces of the little suction cups, began applying them to Erskine's chest as I'd seen Samuel do. Erskine groaned. I mumbled, "Sorry." My fingers shook as badly as Ruth's. I could see Samuel drawing medications into syringes, couldn't help admiring his speed and sureness. He wrapped a rubber tourniquet around Erskine's arm, swabbed the front of the elbow with an alcohol-soaked cotton swab, then quickly emptied three loaded syringes into the vein.

"Leads okay?" I asked.

He glanced, beamed me a smile. "Perfect. Start 'er up."

As I turned the switch to set the EKG running, Erskine's hand relaxed, color got better, breathing became less labored. He blew out a sigh, "Whew." He and Ruth turned identical expressions on Samuel. *Mine eyes have seen the glory...*

Samuel studied the cardiograph tracing as I switched settings from one lead to the next to the next. "Tachycardia, deep Q wave in Lead III. Ventricular premature beats." He spoke as if he were showing me an interesting bird that had just then alighted on the windowsill, but I caught his meaning. This wasn't just another attack of angina pectoris; Erskine had had a second coronary occlusion. No more home treatment. Samuel would need to get him into the hospital, and that would take some doing. When Erskine made up his mind, his mind stayed made. But what force on earth could resist Samuel Firestone?

"Feeling better?" Samuel asked.

Erskine nodded agreement. "Thanks—that was jus' awful, Samuel. I thought for sure I was going to die."

"Not now, Ersk. EKG does show some changes, though. Your heart's not getting as much oxygen as it should." Samuel looked at Ruth. "I know you don't want to do it, but no choice any more. You've got to go to the hospital. You need oxygen, regular medications, strict rest. All of which you can't get here." Samuel started for the door. "I'm going to call an ambulance."

"Oh now, wait, Samuel, wait just a minute."

Samuel turned, locked eyes with Erskine.

"I sure's hell don't need any ambulance, it's less'n a mile. I could go in your car."

"Ersk, you want that pain to come back? Try walking from here to the street. You've got to have an ambulance."

While Samuel talked, a cagey look spread over Erskine's face. "You call an ambulance now, Samuel, and I am going to get upset. Very upset. You wouldn't want that, would you?"

Ruth stepped forward. "Erskine—"

He went on, as if she'd never spoken. "Samuel, I 'preciate what you're doin' for me, I really do. But don't move quite so fast. You say I gotta go to the hospital, well, I'm takin' that recommendation seriously. I really am. Jus' gimme a li'l time."

I felt frustrated, but Samuel's smile was warm, genuine. "Sure, Ersk. Take a few minutes. You know I wouldn't do this if I didn't absolutely have to."

Erskine had pinked up nicely. His drawl was more pronounced than usual, a bit slurred from the morphine. "'Preciate it, Samuel."

Ruth lit a cigarette. Erskine looked at her with the longing of a baby for its mother's milk. "Hey, Ruthie, gimme a puff, huh? Just a li'l one." Ruth stopped him with a glance, stubbed the cigarette quickly into an ashtray.

Next came forty minutes of amiable maneuvering that would've done honor to a couple of world chess champions. Samuel zigged, Erskine zagged. Erskine was clearly feeling much better now, probably figured the longer he held out, the stronger would be his argument to remain at home. And he knew Samuel did not want him to get upset, so in this game he held the trump.

Then, just like that, the card fell from his hand. Samuel was running another EKG when Erskine stopped speaking, mid-sentence. His hand flew to his chest, then he gasped, twisted violently, threw back his head, cried out. He sat bolt-upright, astonishment covering his face. His eyes went blank and rolled upward, head lolled, hand fell away from his chest. I stared at the tracing, straight up-and-down squiggle-line, ventricular fibrillation. Disaster.

Samuel muttered, "God *damn!*" then quickly pounded Erskine over the breastbone with the heel of his hand, once, twice. Nothing. Ruth let out a little cry. Samuel dove into his bag, came out with a small bottle and a syringe. "Epinephrine." He drew some up, snapped a long needle onto the syringe, stuck the syringe between his teeth, then grabbed Erskine by the shoulders. "Take his feet, Leo," he muttered, not moving his jaw. We lifted the limp body, lowered it to the floor. Samuel ripped away Erskine's pajama shirt, felt quickly between ribs, then snatched the syringe from his mouth and plunged the needle into Erskine's chest. Dark maroon billowed into the epinephrine solution. Samuel pushed the plunger, then threw the empty syringe and needle halfway across the room, and began to pump rhythmically at Erskine's chest. "Like this, Leo," he snapped, motioning me down with his head.

I knelt, took over the pumping. Samuel edged upward, cradled Erskine's head in his hands, then applied his lips to Erskine's and puffed.

Living nightmare. I don't know how long I pumped at Erskine's chest while Samuel blew air into his mouth. Again and again Samuel felt for a pulse in Erskine's neck. "Breathe," Samuel muttered between puffs. "Erskine, breathe, you're not dead, goddamn it. Come on, *breathe.*"

Ruth pulled at Samuel's shoulder, cried, "Stop, Samuel, please stop. It's over."

Samuel didn't seem to hear, just kept blowing air into Erskine's lungs. I pumped and pumped at his chest. Ruth tugged at Samuel, called his name, yanked him this way and that, finally threw herself across his shoulders, sending him sprawling. She was beyond hysterical. "Samuel, God damn you, *stop.* Can't you see he's dead? Please. Let him go."

Samuel balanced on one hand, looked up, slackjawed.

"Let him go," Ruth sobbed. "He's dead." She clutched at her mouth, then ran out of the room. I heard her heave, then a splash. A second retch, another splash.

Samuel rose slowly from his knees, the wedding guest after his session with the Ancient Mariner. Down the hall in the bathroom, Ruth retched, coughed, choked, sobbed. Samuel gazed stupidly around the room. I ran to the bathroom, found Ruth on the floor, keening, one arm draped over the vomit-splashed toilet. Her head rested on that arm; her back heaved with each wail.

"Done throwing up?" I asked.

She lifted her head just a bit, nodded weakly. I pulled at her free elbow. "Stand up. I'll help you."

I led her, wobbling, to a little wooden stool, sat her down, then took a towel off the rack, ran water over it, started cleaning the toilet and the nearby floor. "Leo, Leo, don't," she said, tremolo. "You don't need to. I'll take care of it later."

"It's all right," I said.

I mopped. Ruth sat expressionless, hollow-eyed. When I finished I threw the towel into a hamper. "Ruth..." I faltered, pushed myself on. "I'm sorry. I can't tell you how much I'll miss him."

Slight shake of her head as if I'd wakened her. She pushed hair back off her face, then put a hand on my arm, tottered to her feet, hugged me. "We'll all miss—" She yanked away, eyes like saucers. "Oh my God, the kids. Rob and Josey. I've got to—"

"Where are they?"

"Summer camp. Near Lake Hopatcong." Big sigh. "I'll have to go up there. After we've…finished here." A cough cut in, and she started to cry again.

Then I heard another sound, somewhere behind the house. A dog baying at the moon? It got louder, then came a crash. Ruth put a hand to her mouth, stopped crying, murmured, "Oh, no." We trotted single-file into Josey's room, looked out the window into the back yard, saw a sight I couldn't have imagined. Samuel swung a red wagon against the support bars of a jungle gym. Crash, a wheel flew into the air, bounced, rolled against the picket fence. Another swing, another wheel. Through all of it, Samuel never stopped howling. A third swing collapsed the body of the wagon, bent it double. Samuel flung it away as if it were contaminated. He lifted his arms, threw back his head, let out a scream that froze my breath in my throat. Then he fell to his knees, pounded the earth, lifted his arms and head again to howl at the skies, a caveman crying bloody murder to gods below and above who'd outraged him.

"Poor Moses," Ruth murmured. "Raised his hand, but the Red Sea didn't give a good goddamn."

I couldn't watch more, turned away.

"Leo, you do know if you want to cry I won't tell on you," Ruth said quietly.

But I was the only doctor there. I went back into the bedroom, knelt over Erskine's body. The utter blankness of his face made it clear he was gone. After all his terrible chest pain, all the pumping and pounding to try to revive him… I raised one of his hands, let go. The hand fell with a thud. Every muscle, completely relaxed. I pulled the sheet off the bed, laid it over him. As I straightened, Ruth, behind me, said softly, "I'd like a few minutes with him, please, Leo."

I could still hear Samuel's dreadful howling, wondered whether a neighbor might call the police. Sometimes after my father lost a patient, he came home with eyes like flamethrowers, a landmine ready to blast the first person to step on it, but I'd never seen anything at all like this. "Sure," I said to Ruth. "I'll go downstairs, make arrangements, then see about Samuel. Do you have a preference on funeral parlors?"

I pulled down all the living-room window shades facing the back yard, told the mortuary attendants Samuel had gone to cover another emergency, and that he'd come by next day to sign the death certificate. Samuel himself was a bigger problem. After the attendants left with Erskine's body, I went out the back door into the yard, but couldn't get near Samuel, would've been killed by the bicycle he was bashing against the jungle gym. When he'd destroyed the bike and paused as if trying to decide what to go after next, I launched myself from his blind side, hit him low, knocked him to the grass, pinned his arms and lay across him. He struggled, but after a minute or so I felt him relax. Slowly, carefully, I let up pressure, then took his hand, pulled him up, walked him back through the house. Quick check on Ruth, then I put Samuel into the car and drove off. All the way home he sat silent, staring, seeing God only knows what.

One step into the house, Ramona led Samuel off upstairs, not a word. I went to the kitchen, poured myself a glass of milk and took a couple of my mother's cookies out of the cookie jar. I must've been there close to half an hour, sipping milk, nibbling cookies, thinking, when I heard an unfamiliar voice call my name. I looked up.

Samuel stood in the doorway, leaning against the frame as if he couldn't support his own weight. His gorgeous face was a wreck. Pallor accentuated the gold stippling over his cheeks and chin. He held an envelope toward me. "Leo, do me a favor."

His voice was the screak of a cracked reed. "Sure, Samuel," I said. "What is it?"

He waggled the envelope as if any further effort might exhaust him. "Take this to Lily Fleischmann."

I looked up at the kitchen clock. Nearly eleven. I almost asked, "Now?" but caught myself in time. "Sure," I said again. "I'll get my bike."

I pushed away from the table, got to my feet. "Take the car," Samuel said. "I don't want you riding a bike down there this late at night." Every word seemed to require total concentration. He gave me the envelope, then shuffled away without another word, not even thanks. I listened, heard stairs creak as he went up. The idea of my maiden solo voyage in the Plymouth pulled at me but not quite hard enough. I went to the stove, turned on the burner under the tin teakettle, waited for it to boil while I stared at the thick white envelope in my hand.

Chapter 8

Dad wiped out Drink Number Four, looked around, motioned to the waiter. The man scurried over, fired me an eyeball query. I shrugged, nodded.

"I'll get it right away, sir." Just a bit too polite.

Dad watched him all the way to the bar. As the bartender started mixing, the waiter ducked behind the counter, came up with a small tray, pulled away cellophane wrap, then stood, tray balanced on the fingers of his right hand. The instant the drink was ready, he hustled back to unload at our booth. Dad studied the tray, a nice little arrangement of cheese and crackers in circles, with some grapes and a few strawberries. Meaningful glance from the waiter. "Compliments of the management."

Dad nodded thanks, grabbed a couple of crackers and a few slices of cheese, washed them down with Manhattan, cleared his throat.

I edged the Plymouth to the curb in front of the Fleischmanns', then ran up the walk, onto the porch. Murray, in an undershirt and grimy gray pants, answered my knock. "Christ, Dockie, you know what time it is? You're as bad as your old man. Eleven at night's same to him as eleven in the morning."

I waved the envelope. "Sorry. Samuel wanted Lily to have this tonight."

Screen door opened before I finished. "Hey Dockie, ain't I *ever* gonna get to see you smile? Come on in, it's okay. Lily's still up. She's part-time over at Crystal's Coiffures on Twenty-second Street, so she don't gotta get in to work tomorra 'til ten."

Murray led me into the kitchen, where Lily sat across the table from a girl about my own age. Unlike Shannon, this one was dark, lovely black hair and eyes, clear olive skin. She looked at me with the expression of a deer surprised by a hunter. My stomach lurched.

Lily smirked. "You're here without your old man?"

I handed her the envelope. "He wanted you to have this tonight, asked me to bring it. He's exhausted. Just finished a tough case."

Lily studied the front of the envelope, turned it over, looked closely at the back, then slid it behind the top of her nightgown. I felt my face go warm, shuffled my feet. "Samuel Firestone is exhausted?" Lily murmured.

"He's very upset," I said. "One of his friends died tonight, Erskine Crosbie. Heart attack. Samuel was taking care of him."

I didn't like the way Lily and Murray looked at each other. Trying to redirect conversation, I stretched my hand toward the girl and said, "I'm Leo Firestone. My father's a doctor; I'm helping him this summer. Pleased to meet you."

Lily shook her head. "Sorry, no manners."

The girl pulled herself halfway up, leaned across the table, took my hand. Hers was warm and dry. "Likewise, I'm sure." She smiled. "My name's Teresa Baker. Your father's taking care of me. He's really peachy."

I looked down. Yes, Teresa's abdomen bulged under her light blue nightgown. "You're Lily's niece?" I asked.

Teresa looked at Lily, who flipped me a glance that said watch your step. "Just a way we've got of talking here," Lily said. "Some of the girls call me Aunt Lily so they can feel like they've got family close-by."

"Maybe I'll be here for your delivery," I said to Teresa. The poor girl went red. I backed away from the table. "Guess I'd better get along, it's late."

Lily stood up. I could see the outline of the envelope under her nightgown. "Let you out," she said.

As she pushed the screen door open, Lily pulled out the envelope and stage-whispered, "If you're gonna use a teakettle, you better learn how. Too much steam bends the paper, also leaves little water spots." She held my clumsy work under my nose.

"Thanks for the tip."

Lily refiled the envelope. "You're smart, like your old man. Maybe you'll be a good doc too, but you got a lot to learn."

I stopped halfway out. "I'm learning that in a hurry."

She smiled like Mona Lisa. "See ya."

Another rough night, drenching humidity sticking me to the sheet while I asked myself over and over what in hell was my father doing, giving Lily Fleischmann three thousand dollars? Meanwhile, from down the hall came, "Erskine! *Erskine!*" Samuel, trapped in a nightmare. Toward dawn, I finally dropped off.

Past nine-thirty when I woke. I practically leaped out of bed, ran downstairs, found Ramona in the kitchen, sitting over coffee. She looked the way I felt. "He's gone?" I asked.

She twisted her wedding ring one way, then the other. "Why, yes, dear, almost two hours ago. You know he always starts his hospital rounds at eight."

"He's all right?"

Her face asked why such silly questions? "Of course. Why shouldn't he be all right?"

"Why shouldn't he be all right? Ramona, I saw him in the Crosbies' back yard, *heard* him, after Erskine died. Screaming like a madman, smashing everything he could get his hands on. Then all night long, calling Erskine's name. Is that enough?"

Ramona spun her ring furiously, then seemed to draw herself together like a spring being wound. "He's all right," she said, as severely as I'd ever heard her speak. "This happens sometimes, not often. Don't ever talk to him about it. Understand?"

"But Ruth Crosbie was there, saw the whole thing. What about—"

"Ruth knows Samuel."

I remembered what Ruth murmured as we looked out the back window into the yard. "Poor Moses. Raised his hand but the Red Sea didn't give a good goddamn."

Ramona picked up her coffee cup, looked at me over the rim. "It's over. Do not mention it to him. And now *we're* done talking about it." She turned abruptly, flung the remainder of her coffee into the sink. Then she got up and strode out of the room.

A crack had developed in my world, and the more I peered through and saw, the more I needed to pry. Murray said Lily went in to work at ten, didn't he? I ran upstairs, put on a clean white shirt and pressed pants, brushed my hair and teeth, then went out and got my bike. I was at the Fleischmanns' by ten-thirty.

I left my bike out of sight, against the wall in the narrow alley, then strolled up the brown steps to the porch. As usual, only the front screen door was closed. I knocked, called out, "Hello?"

At first no answer, then I heard a soft, "Just a minute." I shifted from one foot to the other. Finally I saw Teresa Baker moving slowly, heavily, to the front door. She wore a white cotton maternity dress with red polka dots, black hair gathered back in a ponytail. She studied me a moment, then her face brightened. "Oh—Leo, right? Hi. Lily's out right now."

"I came to see *you*," I said, surprised at how smoothly it flowed. "Can I come in?"

"Sure." She opened the screen door, stepped back to let me pass. "You came to see me? Why?"

"Remember, last night I said I'm working with my father over the summer, and…let's go inside, sit down. Wouldn't you be more comfortable off your feet?"

Bashful smile. She worked a fold in her dress between two fingers as she led me into the kitchen and lowered herself carefully into a chair. I sat opposite her, the white table between us, chip-speckled black. "I wanted to get to know you a little," I said. "Couple of nights ago I was here, helped my father with a delivery, and I think I could've done a better job if I'd met that girl before she started her labor."

Teresa smiled, more openly now. "That was Shannon." Then I caught a break. Teresa's smile went wicked. "Yeah, Shannon said something about this cute collar-ad who helped Dr. Firestone with her delivery. Bet she'd like to see him again." She struggled to her feet, started toward the hall. "Come on."

I got up, followed. "She's still here?"

"Well, natch." Hands on hips, giving me a tough once-over. "You've got to stay in bed for a week after you have a baby, otherwise you can get real bad problems. Don't you know that?"

"Of course. Everybody knows that. I just thought she might be staying someplace else."

That got me a raucous laugh. "Like where? With her parents? If it wasn't for Dr. Firestone and Murray and Lily, the only place for us'd be the Wayward Girls Home, over on Ryerson." Her face told me exactly what she thought of that choice. She put a foot on the lowest stair. "Hey, you want to see Shannon or not?"

I went up the stairs after Teresa, timing my pace to suit hers. At the second-story landing she stopped for breath, then led me past the room Shannon delivered in, to a second flight of stairs. The higher we went, the slower Teresa moved.

From the top of the stairwell, I looked into an attic converted into a...I'd call it a dormitory, but that wouldn't really be the right word. Lightly shaded ceiling fixtures and white plasterboard walls with pink and blue trim made the room bright and cheerful. Low dividers split the space into eight cubicles so as to give the occupants privacy without isolating them. Everywhere, pictures of animals and happy children.

A low chatter stopped as Teresa and I came in. Then, three girl-heads popped up, prairie dogs in their burrows. Giggles jumped like ground lightning from a blonde girl to Teresa, who put her hand to her mouth but couldn't stop the attack of contagious embarrassment. With her other hand she took mine, then led me across the room, into Shannon's cubicle.

Shannon wasn't giggling. As we walked up to her bed she waved limply. Sad face, a question in her eyes. "Came to see how you're doing," I said.

She started to cry. "I'm all right. Just…well, you know." She swiped a soggy handkerchief across her eyes, managed a smile as unstarched as the wave she'd given me. "Thinking about my baby…"

That did it. She started to bawl. Teresa sat on the edge of the bed, put an arm around her, patted her hand. Shannon blew her nose into the handkerchief, then looked at me. "I know my baby's better off with Phil and Nancy—you met Nancy, right? Phil stayed at the hotel 'til the baby came. Then both of them sat with me the rest of the night and most of the next day. We all three of us picked his name, Alan. Alan Robert. When Phil and Nancy left with him, it was the saddest I ever felt. I'm such a dumb bunny, still crying…"

Like a stuck faucet. On and on she went about how she'd been in that attic for nearly five months, how wonderful Lily and Murray were to her, how nice Phil and Nancy were, how in another four or five days she'd be going to her aunt and uncle's in Pittsburgh. "I didn't get here 'til I was so far along, everybody on the block knew I was in the family way." She choked, wiped at her eyes. "So I can't go back home no more. I'll finish high school in Pittsburgh, then maybe go to secretary school and get a job, pay my aunt and uncle rent 'til I get married." Tears again. "If I ever *can* get married, that is."

"Why not?" I asked.

The two girls' faces scared hell out of me and broke my heart at the same time. "Would you marry damaged goods?" Shannon asked.

In those days, a real question. "Ye-e-s," I said. "If I wanted to marry you, I don't think that'd stop me. But a guy's not going to know unless you tell him."

Doubt worked its way back across Shannon's face. She chewed at her upper lip.

"Everybody's got a secret or two." The bitterness in my voice surprised me, but the girls didn't seem to notice.

Teresa smiled. "I was luckier'n her. Soon's I missed my second monthly, my boyfriend arranged for me to come here, to…" She bit the tip of her tongue.

"To what?"

"Get rid of it," she spat. "But I knew if I did, I wouldn't ever be able to take communion again. Your dad told me if I wanted to have the baby, he'd get a good couple, people with money who couldn't have their own, they'd adopt my baby and give it the right kind of life. He helped me tell my parents, and gave us a fakerino for the rest of the family and the neighbors. See, I'm supposed to be in a TB san. When I go back home, I'll have papers from Dr. Firestone sayin' I'm all cured."

"Papers?"

"Yeah. He'll make out papers for the baby too, sayin' the people who adopt it are the actual-factual parents. Right now, the lady's pretending she's preggers, and sick. Stays in her house, not supposed to have visitors. When my baby's coming, her husband'll bring her here and tell their friends they're going to the city because they need a specialist to deliver the baby. When they go back home, they'll say it worked out buttered side up, and here's our baby."

Every time I thought I'd heard it all. The Firestone and Fleischmann Baby Factory. Got an inconvenient little pregnancy? No problem. We'll take care of it one way or the other. Good couples, people with money, faked birth records, faked sanitorium clearances. Or a few swipes with a sharp curette.

I heard a creak behind me, turned to look. The woman in the cubicle across from Shannon rolled onto her side, propped her chin in the palm of her hand. Lank, tangled dark hair, cheeks pallid as cream, soft brown eyes, long lashes. Deep lines between her nose and the corners of her mouth, sharp crows'-feet running outward from her eyes. Like a piece of antique china. "If it wasn't for your father I'd be dead now," she said in a voice as anemic as her cheeks. "I'd've killed myself. My guy said maybe I had a problem, but he didn't. I went back to the doctor who did the rabbit test, and he said, well, go to Dr. Firestone, he'll help you. Your father talked to me, then he did my abortion. He said when I'm better, I should go to New York, or maybe California. He says there's more in life than being a bookkeeper for a department store in downtown Hobart." She lowered her head to the pillow, began to cry.

Teresa ran fingers through the woman's hair, across her cheek. "Take it easy, Angela. You're gonna be all reet, sweet. All of us are. You'll be outa here in a few days. Me, I'd go to California, all that sun, jivey boys—" Angela's glare silenced her, but only for a moment. "But I guess I'd be more careful. I'm gonna remember what Doc says about takin' precautions."

I felt like a new toy in that attic. The fourth girl, Susie, the giggling blonde, showed me her cubicle, decorated with pinups of Frankie-boy and Jimmy Dorsey. "Jimmy's such a dreamboat, Tommy's cold potatoes." To Jimmy's right hung a map of the world, pins in Midway, the Fijis, Guadalcanal, the Solomons, North Africa. "Green is my brother, red's my cousin, blue's my uncle. When I get a letter they tell me where they are and I put in another pin." Susie had been a cheerleader at Marblemount High, her boyfriend the star quarterback. One night when her parents were out… Same choice in the end, get rid of it now or later. She had four months to go. Lily looked after the girls, and when Lily was at work, they looked after each other. They had Lily's phone number at the beauty parlor, and Samuel's at the office and home. Lily was such an angel cake. Samuel was such a smoothie.

I finally got away, told the girls I hoped I'd see them again. As I wheeled into our driveway I was surprised to hear "Crazy Rhythm" blaring from Harmony's basement. I put away my bike, ran over, down through the cellar doors. "Why aren't you at the Red Cross?" I shouted over the music.

Harmony lowered her sax, gave me a hard look. "Day off. Why aren't you with Samuel?"

I told her about Erskine Crosbie and my morning visit to the Fleischmanns' attic. When I finished she said, "Well, that's it, then. The connection."

"Connection?"

"That's what's the connection."

"What's *what* connection?"

"Leo, you're making us sound like Abbott and Costello. The connection between the Fleischmanns and Samuel. You were saying yesterday, Jonas wouldn't play along with the scrap metal black market, and everyone was afraid he might squeal, so Oscar or Murray or both of them got some strychnine and put Jonas on ice. Then Murray called Samuel, and Samuel signed Jonas out as a heart attack. That *is* what you said, right? So think about it. If Samuel's been making out all those phony birth and health certificates, a death certificate wouldn't have been the first fake medical paper he signed. I hate saying it, but there's the connection." She put hands to her hips. "Don't you see?"

I nodded. "Makes sense. But how can we connect Murray or Oscar to the strychnine?"

She flashed that smile, gotcha. "Been thinking about that since yesterday. Where do people buy strychnine?"

"At drugstores. For rat poison, or by prescription as a stimulant. What're you getting at?"

She reached to the table behind her, came forward with a small brown bottle with a rubber dropper-top. "Here. What do you think, all I did since last time we talked was roll gauze bandages? Look at the bottle, would you."

I looked, saw the skull and bones, read, *Miss Opal Weller. Tincture Strychnos nux-vomica. Five drops in water or juice once daily. Do not exceed prescribed dosage.* I couldn't believe it. "Harmony!"

"It was easy. I just snuck one of my father's pads, and wrote for a patient named Opal Weller."

"You *forged a prescription?*"

"Leo, don't talk to me like that. Yes, I forged a prescription, so what? Then I took the Crooks Avenue bus—"

"How appropriate."

"I'm going to smack you. I went down to a drug store on Raritan Av, gave the prescription to a druggist, signed the register, 'Opal Weller'. Signed…the…poison…register. Which they keep on a shelf under the counter. So what we've got to do now is see which drug store's closest to the junkyard, then find out whether Murray or Oscar Fleischmann bought some strychnine right before Jonas died."

"We're going to walk into that drug store," I said. "Say to the pharmacist, 'Excuse us but we're investigating a murder and we'd like to see your poison register.' And the pharmacist is going to say, 'Fine, glad to help. Can I make you an ice-cream soda to drink while you're looking?'"

Matched emeralds, sparkling, perfect. "I'm a girl, Leo. I want some lipstick, a little makeup—"

"Lipstick? Makeup? You never—"

"Listen, would you. Or don't you think I can come up with a good idea? I'll say I'm just starting to buy lipstick and makeup, and I need some help. But you're a boy, you're not interested in that stuff. You'll go off and wander around the store while the druggist shows me what I ought to wear to look pretty."

Half an hour later we were on the Madison crosstown bus. Less conspicuous to check the neighborhood on foot than by bike. We got off at Sixth, started walking, and sure enough, across the railroad track and just a block from the junkyard we came to Raskin's Pharmacy. "Murray'd go right past on his way to work," I said.

Harmony answered with a smug smile. She pushed the door open; a bell tinkled. We went inside.

Cosmetics were right there, facing us, on shelf displays and free-standing carousels. All the way in the back, an old man stood behind a glass partition, probably working on a prescription. In front of him were shelves filled with cold remedies. Other display racks for vitamins and home cure-alls ran from the far left corner to the front of the shop. A hinged wooden counter interrupted the display midway. Harmony motioned with her head. "That's where it'd be," she whispered. "Right under the cash register, easy to get for customers to sign when they pay." She poked me with her elbow, then walked to the back of the shop and called out, "Mr. Raskin? Sir? Yoo-hoo?"

Raskin looked up, blinked. "Be right with you, Miss."

A minute later he was there, a gnome in a white pharmacist's jacket. Round head permanently cocked to the left, narrow fringe of white hair. His dark blue eyes were bright and friendly. "Can I help you?"

Harmony blushed, how did she do that? Maybe just thinking about the whopper she was about to tell. She dangled her little leather purse. Mr. Raskin smiled sympathy and encouragement. "I just turned sixteen," Harmony said. "So my parents say I can wear makeup now. Can you help me find, oh, some nice lipstick and rouge, maybe a little eyeshadow. I don't want to all of a sudden look…well, you know. Painted."

All the while Harmony talked, Mr. Raskin rubbed his hands together, then he punctuated her speech with a clap. "You're a sensible girl, very sensible. Makeup should enhance a girl's natural beauty, not cover it over and make her look cheap." He waggled a finger toward the cosmetics corner. "Come on over here, and I'll get you just what you need."

I rolled my eyes, strolled off toward the back of the shop. Old Raskin chuckled behind me. "Not interested—well, never mind, Miss. Cosmetics on display won't catch a young man's fancy but I dare say he'll take a great deal more notice when they're on your face."

I ambled back toward the cold remedies, scanned shelves, looked around. No one else in the store. Slowly, I worked my way through the vitamins. At the little wooden counter, I shot a quick look over my shoulder. Harmony stood facing me, which forced Mr. Raskin to look the other way—she was *so* clever. I took a deep breath, ducked down under the counter, then crab-walked the couple of yards to the shelves under the cash register, where I promptly got good and embarrassed. In 1943, what did pharmacists keep out of sight, but close at hand for customers? The two lower shelves were crammed with birth control devices, enough condoms and diaphragms to lower the birth rate in Hobart by fifty percent. But there on the top shelf sat a gray and red ledger, POISON REGISTER carefully printed in dark ink on its cover.

I dropped to the floor, grabbed the book, opened it in my lap. Entries on the first page started with January, 1943—name of poison, proposed use, date, signature of buyer. A lot of arsenic and strychnine went out of that shop, at least eighty percent supposedly to get rid of rats and other vermin. Jonas Fleischmann died early on July seventh, so I flipped pages to that day, then worked my way back through the log. July seventh, sixth, fifth, no luck. No entries for the fourth, of course. Third, second... wait a minute. I turned back to July sixth. I'd been looking for Fleischmann, but had seen another familiar name—yes, there it was, clear printed block capitals. George Templeton. Strychnine. To poison rats at the junkyard.

I closed the register, leaned forward to put it back into place, but my foot had fallen asleep under me, and I lost balance, stumbled into the shelves. Cardboard boxes went flying, packages of condoms sailed in every direction. I froze, held my breath.

"What's...?" A one-word question told me the jig was up. I scrambled to my feet. Mr. Raskin, wrathful troll, stood glaring from the other side of the counter. "What are you...?" He shook one fist in the air, gawked at the sea of condoms on the floor, then let out a shriek of pure fury. "You're stealing..." He wheeled around, couldn't bring himself to mention the unmentionable in front of the young lady.

Unfortunately, the young lady giggled, which released all Mr. Raskin's inhibitions. "Stealing rubbers—Godfrey Scissors! I'll show you a thing or two, you young hooligan!" He raised the counter on its hinges, started through.

What was I going to do, tell him I was really there to look at his poison register? Let him think I was a condom-thief. I grabbed a foil packet, stuffed it into my pocket, and in the same motion charged down the corridor behind the display racks. Mr. Raskin came hot after me. No exit ahead, just the front window. I could've turned around, thrown that little old man to the floor and run over his body to the open counter, but I didn't want to risk hurting him. As I came to the end of the waist-high rack I put up a hand, vaulted over, landed in a shower of cough drops.

Harmony was already out the door, running. We charged down Eleventh Street, ripped around the corner onto Fourth Avenue, tore along to Eighteenth Street, then turned right. Two men jumped out of our way. A leg shot into my path, and I tripped, sprawled, saw Harmony's purse sail up, then plop to the sidewalk next to me. One of the men held Harmony by the arm; she looked like a fish just hauled into a boat. I was scrambling up to help her when she launched a punch to the man's face. "Let me *go*."

"Take it easy, girlie, ain't nobody gonna get hurt." Familiar voice. Familiar face, thin red mustache. Wide snap-brim. Red Dexter, from the junkyard. He grinned at me as I got up. "Hey, young Dockie Firestone, where you goin' in such a big hurry?" He let go of Harmony; she picked up her purse, glared at him.

I forced myself not to look over my shoulder. If Mr. Raskin were to come barreling around the corner, nothing we could do about it. "Oh, hello, Mr. Dexter," I said. "Sorry, didn't mean to—"

"No sweat, Dockie. An' by the way, my friends call me Red." He turned a leer on Harmony. "Ain'tcha gonna introduce me to your friend?"

Nothing but to do it. "Harmony Belmont, Red Dexter."

"Please'a meetcha, Miss Belmont." Red took Harmony's hand, released it, then bowed ever so slightly. "Any frienda the Dockie's is a frienda mine."

"I see Red at the junkyard sometimes when I'm working on the music box," I said.

That lit Harmony's eyes. "Leo's going to give it to me when he's got it fixed," she said to Dexter.

"Oho!" Sly red fox. "Then you gotta be a real special friend."

Red's companion fixed watery eyes on Harmony in a way I didn't like. He was as ragged as Red was spiffy, a painfully thin man with greasy black hair who hadn't held a razor in some time. Red made no move to introduce him, all right with me. "I'll be at the yard later," I said. "After we're done running this errand for my father."

Red's eyes glittered under the snap-brim. "Running's the word, awright. Well, guess I better not hold you up any more, huh? See ya 'round the yard, Dockie." He tipped his hat to Harmony again, then took the raggedy lecher by the elbow and walked him around the corner onto Fourth. Harmony and I took off in the other direction.

Corner of Eighteenth and Third, vacant lot, all high weeds. We dove in, scurried toward the middle. Harmony rested her head on my shoulder. "All right, Leo. Don't say it."

"Don't say what?"

"I feel bad about what we did to that nice old man."

"Would you feel better if I told you I saw a name in that register?"

Obvious she would and did. Sparkling green gemstones, inches from my face. "You *did* find out—well, tell me. Who?"

"Not Murray or Oscar," I said, and watched disappointment and curiosity duke it out across her face. "George Templeton, their hired man. George wouldn't've killed Jonas. He probably really did just buy strychnine for the yard rats."

Harmony shook her head. "Anyone from that junkyard buying strychnine the same day Jonas died from it...what if Murray or Oscar sent George? To keep their own name off the book?"

I shrugged. "'What if' isn't proof. We're back to where we started, or close." I got to my feet. "I was going to meet Samuel after lunch, do house calls and office visits, but I think I'll get my bike and go to the yard. Work on the music box, talk to George. See what I can find out."

Mischief shot from Harmony's eyes, danced across her face. "Those *things,* Leo—did you actually take any?"

I reached automatically into my pocket, thought better of it, but too late. Harmony grabbed. "Let's see."

"Forget it."

"No." She tugged at my arm. "Come on, Leo, I want to see it. I've never seen one, have you?"

Another world then, not yet out from under Anthony Comstock's shadow. In some states it was still against the law to sell birth control devices. I shook my head. "No."

"Well, then, take it out and let's see." She squeezed my hand viciously, just below the thumb. I yelped, dropped the little foil package into her hand. She stared at it. "Hmmm. For the prevention of disease only, huh?" She ripped the foil, unrolled the rubber. "Hey, Leo, it doesn't take very much to fill this thing up." She put the open end to her mouth, blew a couple of puffs, pinched the end between two fingers. "That's more like it." She snickered, then went into a full-fledged giggle-fit, rocked, bent double.

"Not that funny," I said.

She straightened, wiped at her eyes. "Your face, Leo. The look on your face. *That's* what's so funny."

Chapter 9

I sat in the patch of shade behind the office shack, fidgeting as I polished brass. Outside the junkyard, a whistle, the two o'clock Pennsy westbound out of New York. I should've been on rounds with Samuel, but he could see patients just fine without me, I told myself. And if he wouldn't do a postmortem on Jonas Fleischmann, I would.

When I put down the last piece of shining brass, Murray wasn't there to show me reassembly. Oscar wasn't around either. The office radio played tune after tune to an empty auditorium. Halfway between the smoldering garbage fire and where I sat, George worked over an automobile body.

I threw the tarp across the table, started walking across the yard. Scrap reflected sun into my eyes. Piled refrigerator carcasses, stoves, radios, all irretrievable, beyond Murray's genius for resuscitation. Parts-machines, organ donors.

George was head-down beneath the hood of a Model-T Ford, screwdriver in one hand, pliers in the other. Muscles bulged where I didn't think I had any at all. Sweat streamed over his face, dripped onto the engine. I hesitated, then said, quietly, "George?"

He looked back at me, smiled. "Hey there, Leo. Doin' more work on that music box?"

My opening. "Yeah. Me and the rats."

"You an' the—"

"Rats. When I pulled back the tarp, one of them was underneath, big as a cat. Then while I was sitting there polishing, I felt something on my shoes, another one, even bigger. He took off soon as I moved."

"Mmm-*mmm*." George shook his head. "Can't never get rid of 'em all. Junkyard's right on the river."

"You put out poison, don't you?"

George nodded solemnly, then pointed past the entrance to the yard, beyond the pocked, scarred corrugated-metal fence. "I go down to Raskin's drugstore, over on Eleventh, buy strychnine. That's supposed to be the best, makes 'em die in turrible pain. Other ones see, they figure they better go live some other place."

"When's the last time you put poison out?"

George half-closed one eye, rubbed his chin. "Been what, five days now? Yeah, July six. I was gonna do it July fif', day after the holiday, but we were real busy all that day."

"Do you put the poison out right away, or do you sometimes leave it around for a while?" Which earned me a curious look, so I quickly added, "I sure don't want to get into it by accident."

George smiled. "Don' worry. I leaves it out on the table there in the office. Big brown bottle wit' skull and crossbones. Cain't miss it."

In other words, the bottle could've sat for hours on that table five days before. If Murray or Oscar or Red Dexter had taken out just enough to kill one man, George never would've noticed. My adventure at the drugstore was wasted time and embarrassment.

"Don't be puttin' your fingers in your mouth after you been in the yard," George said. "An' before you eat supper, wash real good." He chuckled. "Otherwise maybe I ain't never gonna hear that music box play. You be lookin' for Murray, now, right?"

I nodded.

"'Fraid not today. Him and Oscar went over to Ryerson Street, guy with a pile a stuff died." George made a face. "Widow decide to sell it all to us."

"You don't look very happy about it."

George studied me a moment, must've approved of what he saw. "Truth, I'm not. Mr. Broomall was a nice fella, did good business, but not with the right people. Man wasn't even fifty, an' best I know, he wasn't sick. But he die all of a sudden, wit' his li'l junkyard fulla scrap metal. Now his Missus sell to Murray and Oscar even before he be buried."

George's face was a picture of disgust. I thought he had more smarts than to talk that way, but then it hit me—I was Dockie, son of Dr. Samuel Firestone. A young doctor, but a doctor nonetheless, someone to be trusted implicitly. Without intending, I'd pulled a powerful extraction instrument from my father's black bag. I caught my breath, then asked, "What did he die of?"

George shook his head. "Nobody say."

At dinner that evening Samuel seemed fine, as if his behavior at the Crosbies' the night before never happened. From the radio in the living room came the voice of a newscaster, reporting on the O.P.A. crackdown on Sunday pleasure drivers. "It's beginning to look good for the Allies," the newscaster droned. "But the war is far from over, and we can't afford complacency. There's no room in this country for Optimistic Olivers."

Samuel blew a loud Bronx cheer. "Slogan time," he snapped. "Loose lips sink ships." He extended a hand toward me. "Your turn, Leo. Come on. Quick!"

"You're out of order, Mr. Hoarder," I said.

"Five points for Leo." Samuel wheeled his finger toward Ramona, her turn. She reddened, stammered. "Now, Samuel… they *are* right, you know."

"I can teach a parrot to say, 'No optimistic Olivers,'" Samuel snapped. "First, people swallow a slogan, then they grab guns. Somewhere in this world they're shouting, *'Deutschland uber alles'* and *'Heil Hitler'.*" On the edge of dark territory he clamped his jaw, reached for his fork, dropped it, grabbed again.

Ramona jumped away from the table, ran into the living room, tuned the radio through a high-pitched squeal to vibrant clarinet music. Benny Goodman, "Jersey Bounce." As she came back into the room she trailed a hand across Samuel's shoulder. "That's better," she said.

Samuel jabbed his fork into a piece of mackerel as if the fish had called him an insulting name.

By the time we washed and dried dishes, Samuel seemed himself again. Work done, we all strolled into the living room. Samuel and I sat, but Ramona stretched and said, "Such a nice evening, and I haven't been outside all day. I think I'll take a walk." She bent to kiss Samuel lightly on the forehead. He reached up to pat her cheek. "See you later."

Ramona was a lousy actress. I readied for assault.

The door barely closed behind her when Samuel said, "Sit down, Leo." He might've been inviting a new acquaintance to make himself comfortable. I sat, waited.

Samuel smiled. "I hear you made a house call this morning."

Only one thing to say. "Yes."

We sat for a few seconds, eyes locked. Samuel didn't speak, ball still in my court. "I didn't think that girl, Shannon, was really Lily Fleischmann's niece. And then last night, when you sent me with the envelope, I met another girl at the Fleischmanns', Teresa. She was pregnant too. I couldn't help wondering—"

"How many nieces Lily had, all of them pregnant and with no husbands."

We both smiled. I nodded. "Yes."

"And you couldn't very well ask me because when you came home I was asleep, then in the morning I'd already gone. Why didn't you wait 'til I came back?"

I shook my head. "Just wanted to see for myself."

Samuel's smile widened. "I'll never argue with that." He leaned forward. "Tell me what you learned."

"You and Lily Fleischmann run a kind of home for girls and women with unwanted pregnancies. You either adopt the babies out or you...uh..."

"Or I do abortions. Why is that so hard to say?"

"It's against the law," I blurted.

Samuel pursed his lips, then pounded a fist into an open palm. "Against the law of conventional morality? Sure it is. But what about the law of human decency? The law of common sense? Why isn't birth control out on drugstore shelves in plain view instead of being hidden down behind counters?"

I held my breath. Did Mr. Raskin recognize me, or find out who I was? Apparently not; Samuel went right on. "Bad enough that a girl who doesn't want to get pregnant does, but an accident shouldn't ruin the rest of her life. There are people who want a child desperately, who're more than happy to pay for a pregnant girl's obstetrical care. They come in for the delivery, take the baby home—"

"With a faked birth certificate."

Samuel's eyes widened. He laughed. "Call it faked if you like, but don't the spaces on those forms say MOTHER'S NAME and FATHER'S? What are the adopting couple going to be? And as for abortions, I hear you also met Angela Gumpert, the woman across from Shannon."

"Yes."

"She came in less than three months pregnant, terrified, and with good reason. If her crazy Neanderthal family ever found out, they might've killed her. Would you have forced her to take a chance like that?"

I tried to answer him, couldn't. He watched me struggle, then finally said, "Leo, the law just tells you what's prohibited. Only you can say whether something is wrong. Now try answering my question."

I took a huge breath, let it out slowly. "I wouldn't want to force her, no. But I don't think I could've done…what you did."

"At least say the word, Leo. Abortion."

"I don't know if I could do an abortion."

"Nothing wrong with that. Would you send a woman who needs an abortion to a doctor who *would* do it?"

"No…no, I wouldn't. That seems even worse, asking someone else to do what I wouldn't do myself. I'm sorry—"

"No reason to be sorry. You just need to know if you become a doctor, you're going to find yourself in the middle of one situation after another that can't be tied up in a pretty little package with a red ribbon. If anyone should apologize, I should, for not telling you the whole story. But I wanted to see whether you'd swallow that silly niece bit; I hoped you'd challenge me on it. Didn't think you'd go off on your own to investigate, but…" He got out of his chair, walked over, rested a hand on my shoulder. "I can't fault you for wanting to get your information firsthand. In your place, that's what I would've done. What I'm really sorry for, Leo, was my behavior last night, at Erskine's."

His voice faded. I looked up and saw something I'd never seen before. Samuel's eyes were brimming. "A better man, a better friend, never lived. I didn't save him."

I saw Erskine on the bed, writhing in ghastly pain, fatal heart attack. But after he died, not a hint of rigor mortis. Instead of the sympathy I might've felt for Samuel, rage filled my head. I was on the point of coming out with it, insisting Jonas Fleischmann died of strychnine poisoning and demanding to know why Samuel called it a heart attack. But looking at my father's grief-twisted face, all I could manage was, "You did your best."

As lame to my own ears as it must've been to his. Fury flashed in Samuel's eyes, so short a burst I wondered whether he'd really felt the emotion or I'd only seen a reflection of my own anger. He swallowed, then said, almost casually, "You're spending a lot of time at the junkyard."

No question mark but definitely a question. "That old music box I'm trying to repair—remember, I told you the other night? Murray says it's probably from about 1880, more than sixty years old! I've taken it apart, cleaned and polished it. Now Murray's going to show me how to get it back together."

Samuel seemed to hang on my every word, his face in constant change. Like wind-blown clouds and sunshine passing over a grassy hill. Easy to see why he was so good at getting information from his patients—the intensity of his attention drew words out of people that they never intended to say. I braked my tongue, held firm. Samuel waited. Finally, he said, "That junkyard's a rough place, Leo. Nasty business goes on down there. Be careful."

I let up on the brake pedal enough to say, "All right."

Samuel smiled, returned to his chair, picked up his newspaper. Interview over.

I wanted to go find Harmony, tell her what I'd learned from George Templeton that afternoon, but I couldn't, not right then. I had a pressing obligation, and it'd be dark inside an hour.

I went to my room, shook five dollars out of my bank, a buck for the condom, four bucks' penalty for stealing it and making a mess. Then I got on my bike, pedaled hard down Roosevelt. At the corner of Madison, in the middle of a cluster of little shops, a painted sign swayed in the evening breeze. HATS CLEANED AND BLOCKED, neat black letters surrounding a snap-brim that could've been Red Dexter's. I scanned the sidewalk, hoped I wouldn't run into Dexter on this trip. Enough complications already.

A few minutes later I pulled up in front of Raskin's Pharmacy, rested my bike against the front of the building, peeked around the corner of the doorway. No customers. Just Mr. Raskin behind the counter, reading a newspaper. I took a couple of deep breaths and went in.

Mr. Raskin lowered his paper, saw me. Old and round as he was, I thought he might vault over the counter and punch me. Amid a flurry of pages he jabbed a finger, spluttered about calling the police. "Mr. Raskin," I shouted. "I came to apologize."

He stopped his convulsion, stared at me. I reached into my pocket, took out the five dollars, extended them across the counter. "I'm sorry for what I did," I said. "And I'm sorry about the mess I left for you to clean up."

The old man looked at the money, then at me. He shook his head sadly. "Oy, Sonny. A nice-looking boy like you, a pretty girl like that. How old are you?"

"Sixteen."

"Her?"

"Sixteen, too."

"Sixteen. Stealing rubbers, shame on both of you. What would your mothers and fathers say?"

How could I tell him why I'd really gone behind that counter? "I'm not sure," I said. "Maybe they'd say if we were going to do it, they were glad we were careful enough to take precautions."

Mr. Raskin looked at me very strangely, then said, "Y'know what? You sound just exactly like Samuel Firestone, kind of look like him, too. You know him? Dr. Samuel Firestone?"

"He's my father."

"Your father! And you ain't afraid of what he'd do to you if I call him up and tell him?"

"No, I'm not afraid. If you think you should call him, go ahead."

Mr. Raskin shook his head again, then sat heavily on his stool. "Jeez-Christ, what the world is comin' to. What's your name, Sonny?"

"Leo."

"Leo, can you see your father goin' into a store and stealin' rubbers?"

I saw a vial of morphine tucked away in brown paper at the bottom of a doctor's bag. A caustic wave came up from my chest, blossomed into a bitter taste in my throat. "No," I said very quietly. "I told you I'm sorry, and I am." I laid my five dollar-bills in his hand.

He mistook my emotion for embarrassment, waved me off. "Put away your money, Leo. Go buy your girl a hamburger and an ice-cream soda." He narrowed his eyes. "You didn't come in here to steal rubbers, not the way you talk. If you wanted rubbers you'd'a just plain walked up and told me you were twenty-one. And I'd'a sold you your rubbers, we both of us know that. So what the hell were you doin' here behind the counter? Tell me."

"Mr. Raskin," I said, "I got bored, that's all. My friend was looking at lipstick and I decided to see what a druggist actually does hide behind the counter. When you caught me I got scared and knocked over all those damn boxes of rubbers."

The old man chuckled. "You're Samuel Firestone's son, all right. Okay, fine. I thank you for coming in here, and I accept your apology. Now, go on home and behave yourself."

Next morning on rounds, as I carried Samuel's bag I made sure to walk beside him, not a step behind. Rhoda Brown was awake, alert, feeling much better, if still weak. "A miracle," her mother said. As we walked away, down the corridor, Samuel echoed that. "Antibiotics, penicillin—amazing. Without it, they'd be at her funeral today."

"But maybe there's a funeral somewhere for a soldier who needed that penicillin and didn't get it," I said.

Samuel shrugged as if I'd made a comment about the weather. "Maybe so," he said. "But maybe is less than probably, probably's less than certainly, and Rhoda certainly would be dead without the penicillin." Short pause. "And Rhoda is under my care."

Short list of house calls that day; after the last one, Samuel checked his watch. "Eleven—let's stop by the Fleischmanns', look in on Angela Gumpert. She lost a lot of blood at her abortion."

If I felt conspicuous as we walked into the attic, Samuel and Lily very quickly took my mind off myself. They strolled down the aisle side by side, King and Queen of the Baby Mill. Samuel told Shannon she was doing fine, just another few days and she'd be on her way. He patted Teresa's big belly, said it wouldn't be much longer 'til the baby came.

As we walked up to Angela, Lily murmured, "White as a sheet," but with her dull yellowish pallor, Angela would've been a dingy bedsheet. She tried to smile, managed a soft hello. She looked weaker than the day before, eyes sunken. Samuel took her hand, slid a thumb to check her pulse. I could see him counting as he talked. "Lose any more blood yesterday?"

She shook her head vaguely. "Kind of like a heavy monthly."

Samuel passed her hand to me. "Check her pulse, Leo."

Warm in that attic, but Angela's hand was cold. I found the pulse, looked at my watch, started counting. "One thirty-three. Thready."

"Right." He pressed one of her fingernails, let go, then pressed one of mine. "See the difference?"

"Mine was red at first, then went white when you squeezed it," I said. "Hers was white to start with, and it stayed white."

"Because your hemoglobin's near fifty, and hers isn't half that. She needs red blood cells." He looked at Angela. "Your body will make back all the blood you lost, but it'll take six weeks, long time for you to feel as bad as you do. We'll give you a booster."

"Transfusion?" I asked.

Samuel nodded.

"Where's the blood?"

Samuel's eyes told me to shut up and watch.

Angela looked at the three of us in turn, then asked the universal question. "Will it hurt?"

"Little needle-stick, that's all." Samuel was already reaching into his bag; he came out with a rubber-topped bottle filled with clear fluid. "Novocain." He drew some into a small syringe, then took Angela's left hand in his, studied the inner surface of her elbow, wiped an alcohol swab over a large blue vein, slid in the needle. "Okay, now," he said, and injected. Angela squeezed her eyes shut. "Stings," she moaned.

Samuel pulled the needle out. "All you'll feel." He took a second small needle from the bag, put it onto the syringe, lowered his own left arm, swabbed, injected Novocain. "There. All set."

Back to the bag, out with two rubber tourniquets, a roll of adhesive tape, and a sealed paper autoclave bag. He tore off four strips of tape, hung them from the edge of the night table. Then he handed me the autoclave bag. "Open it, but make sure not to touch the needles."

I found myself holding about two feet of rubber tubing with the two biggest steel needles I'd ever seen at the ends. Angela's eyes flew open. "Don't worry," Samuel told her. "That's why I gave you Novocain. You won't feel a thing. Watch."

He picked up the tourniquets, used his free hand and teeth to fasten one around his upper arm, the other around Angela's.

Then he took the tubing from my hand, crimped it between his left thumb and index finger, and carefully, deliberately, plunged one of the needles into a bulging vein at his left elbow. Quickly, he released the tourniquet. "See?" Big smile. "No pain." He taped the needle secure, then took the free needle in his right hand and slowly released pressure on the tubing. A moment later, a couple of red drops fell from the needle to the floor.

Samuel pinched the tubing again, bent over Angela. "Don't move now." He worked the big needle into her vein, fastened it with tape, then smiled at her. "What'd you feel?"

She shook her head, did her best to smile back. "Little pressure, maybe. No pain."

"Good. Just remember, hold very still."

Not a sound in that room. Samuel released the tourniquet on Angela's arm, looked at his watch. The rest of us goggled, frozen, 'til Samuel said, "There," and pulled the needle out of his arm. Blood streamed down to his wrist; he grabbed an alcohol swab, pressed it onto his vein, folded his arm. As the tubing emptied, he pinched it shut again and stage-whispered, "Don't want to get air in there." Then he pressed a swab gently to Angela's arm, and slipped the needle out. Lily reached to put pressure on the puncture site.

Samuel passed me the dripping tubing. He looked at Angela. "Well?"

In the time of the transfusion her cheeks had gone from sallow to faintly pink. She smiled at Samuel in a way that under other circumstances would've been seductive. "Dr. Firestone...I don't believe it." Breathy whisper. "It feels like you actually ran life back into me."

As Samuel and I pulled away from the curb in the Plymouth he said, "In a sense I did, didn't I? Run life into her. Life, oxygen, blood. I gave her a temporary supply, tide her over 'til she can catch up."

I asked the question I'd held back since he flashed me that shut-up look. "But for a transfusion, shouldn't you use stored donor blood that's been tested to make sure it's the right type?"

"It's coming around to that, Leo. I suspect in five or ten years, blood banks will be the thing. But some professors still say direct transfusions have their advantages. Look in Kracke's *Diseases of the Blood*. For one thing, the fresher the blood, the better it works. Also, the patient doesn't need to go into a hospital, which in this case would've been a little embarrassing."

"But if your type and hers aren't the same, can't there be complications? Kidney failure, even instant death...what do they call that?"

"You've been reading, good. That's anaphylaxis, very nasty allergic reaction. You're right, that could be a risk, but not in this case. I'm Type O, Rh negative, all my antibody titers extremely low. I'm the universal donor, can give blood to anyone."

"And you feel all right now? You're not weak?"

Samuel laughed. "Do I *look* weak? No, I only gave her about a pint. Enough to build her up, not nearly enough to knock me down."

Chapter 10

After lunch I biked to the junkyard. Murray, Oscar and George were at the side of the office near the corrugated fence, making a bunch of smaller piles out of two great big heaps of metal. Oscar saw me first, pulled himself straight as I walked up. "Murray's busy," he snarled. "Go play dollies with the other girls." Nasty sneer. "Or play doctor, yeah. Go play doctor with the girlies in the sandbox."

Murray and George stopped working. All three men looked at me. I glanced at Murray, which clearly infuriated Oscar. "*I* told you Murray was busy, what you checkin' with him for? Beat it. None of us got any time today for your silly shit."

"You've got plenty of time to just stand around and be nasty," I said.

Oscar grabbed a piece of metal off the pile, a mean-look-ing steel rod. "You little fucker, I'll show you some manners." Murray and George stepped between us like a team. "Pop, quit being a schmuck," Murray growled, then took my arm and moved me a couple of steps away. George kept himself squarely in Oscar's path. "Hey, Dockie," Murray said to me. "Don't go making things tougher'n they gotta be, okay?" With his left side toward Oscar, Murray twisted the right corner of his mouth into a grin and winked his right eye. "Don't blame you," he muttered, then added aloud, "Old shithead's right, I *am* real busy right now. Why'n't you give us a hand here, we'll get the job done faster. Then I'll show you how to put that machine back together. Okay?"

"Fuckin' hell, Murray!" Oscar's face was like a ripe plum covered with fuzzy gray growth. "What's Miss Pussy here know about metal—"

"Much's you did when you were a lot older'n him. And Pop, I ain't gonna tell you again. His name's Leo, he's a good kid, and if you talk to him like that one more time, you and me are gonna have it out. Now how about let's get this goddamn work done before Red shows, huh?"

Oscar wiped the back of a filthy hand across his mouth, beamed hate at the two of us. Murray didn't seem to notice. He pointed at the two big piles of metal. "See, we got scrap here, but all mixed up together. Them little piles…" He pointed at six mounds to the right of the two big ones. "Brass, copper, iron, steel, tin, zinc, alphabetical order. Go see what they look'n feel like. Then take off pieces from the big piles, sort 'em out. You don't know what a piece is, ask me or George. Kapeesh?"

"Sure."

He worked a pair of heavy gloves out of a back pocket, flipped them to me, gave me a friendly shove, then turned back to his job. I bent over the sorted piles, one after the other; looked, hefted. Then I walked to the big pile Oscar wasn't working at, grabbed a long, heavy rod, chucked it onto the iron heap.

Good thing I was a big kid, and strong. Murray, George and Oscar tossed those steel pipes as if they were toothpicks, threw blocks of brass as if they were marshmallows. I leaned into the work, wasn't about to look anything like the name Pop called me. George caught my eye, slipped me a nod of approval. I picked up, tossed, picked up, tossed. No one said a word.

Another hour, we were done, six more or less neat piles against the wall, two large circles of brown dirt and metal bits gleaming in the sun like silver and gold. I could've wrung water out of my shirt. Murray grinned. "Good job, Dockie."

Oscar hawked, spat.

Murray gave him a hot-eye. "Got it done in less'n two hours, we were figuring three. Break time, cool off. There's Nehi, Yoo-Hoo an' Pepsi in the office, Dockie."

We hunkered against the fence, drank our sodas in silence. When Red Dexter strolled through the gate and saw the piles of metal, he blew a low whistle and rocked back on his heels as if he'd never been so surprised in his life. Then he took off, goose-stepping past the loot, singing to the tune of "Colonel Bogey," "Hitler...has only got one ball. Goering's...are teeny-tiny-small. Himmler...is very sim'lar. And Goebbels ain't got...no balls...at all." In front of the zinc by now, he turned back to us, snapped to attention, extended his right arm, shouted, *"Sieg Heil!"* Then he swept his snap-brim off his head and put his left hand to his belly to execute a full bow.

Murray nudged me. "What a character."

Dexter half-turned to scrutinize us, slyly, I thought. "My, my, my," he said. "Ikey, Jakey and Rastus eat steak this week, whatever the butcher's gettin' for it." Then he looked at me as if I were amusing him in some vague way. His thin red mustache stretched into an upcurving pencil line, dark teeth barely showing.

"Samuel Firestone's kid, remember?" Murray said. "He's—"

"Fixin' his granny's music box. So he can give it to a certain little sugar-cookie, Miss Harmony. Goin' good, is it, Leo?"

"Jeez." Murray was clearly impressed. "That's right, you were here before, when him and me...but what was that other part? Miss Harmony?"

With a flourish of his hand Red passed me the conversational ball. "My friend," I said. "Harmony's her name, she lives next door. She wants the music box after I've fixed it."

Red's face went from sly to wicked. "She and him, uh, ran into me yesterday on the sidewalk."

Murray poked a finger into my ribs. "Hey, you didn't tell me... You're a cagey one, Dockie. You sure ain't Samuel's kid for nothing." He looked back to Red. "And you. What the hell ever goes on you don't know about?"

"Not much, Murr." Dexter looked about to break into a buck-and-wing; all he needed was a walking stick. "In my business, not knowin' about stuff could be a bad thing for a person's health." He whipped the Luckies out of his pocket, shook one free, closed lips around it, flicked a match into flame with his thumbnail, lit up, took a deep drag. "Yeah!" Speaking through smoke. "Truck'll be here in the morning. Keep goin' like this, time the war's over, you guys're gonna be sittin' very pretty. Credit where credit's due."

"Fuck credit, Red," Murray growled. "It's cash and carry."

"Ho ho ho." Dexter sounded like an evil Santa Claus. "You got things just a little bit backwards, Murray. It's carry and cash, like always. Truck'll be here in the morning, I'll be here three days after that."

Dexter doffed his hat again, then turned and disappeared around the corner. Oscar sent an evil eye after him. "I don't like that son of a bitch. Acts like he knows more about our business'n we do."

Much as I hated to, I had to agree with Oscar.

Murray laughed. "He's got his ways, is all. I figure with what he's doing for us, I like him just fine." Murray put a hand to my shoulder. "Okay, come on, Dockie, deal's a deal. Get ourselves another Pepsi, then I'll show you how to put that music box back together." Another poke in the ribs. "Girls don't wait around forever for a guy."

We went out back, pulled the tarp off the table. Murray studied the array of shiny brass and steel, belched absentmindedly, then pointed with the Pepsi bottle. "First off, we gotta put all them little pieces into their right groups. Spring-barrel parts, governor, cylinder, comb. Four piles. Like we just did with the metal out there."

My opening. "Where'd all that metal come from?"

"Guy died," Murray mumbled. "Another junkman. Widow sold us the stuff."

"Old man?" I asked, trying to sound casual.

"Not as old as he coulda got." Murray aimed the Pepsi bottle at me. "Hey, you wanna fix this thing or not? I'll help you sort out what goes where, then you can make alla little pieces into four big ones. When that's done, call me."

I must've been concentrating hard on making big pieces out of little ones because when Oscar barked, "Somethin' I want to tell you," I shot to my feet, scattered music box parts all over the table. Oscar snickered. "Oh, dearie me." Gruff falsetto. "Did I frighten Little Miss Pussy? Make her drop her pretty music box?"

Blood zipped straight through my cheeks into my brain. "You want to tell me something, you can call me by my name," I snapped. "Leo."

Oscar shot out a hand, grabbed my wrist and twisted. I kicked the chair away, tried to pull free. He leaned into my face, two crooked rows of greenish-brown teeth, breath rotten enough to gag a hyena. "Far's I'm concerned, you're Pussy. Now, get that fuckin' music box done, Pussy, and get the hell outa here." He narrowed his eyes, shook my wrist. "I see you in my yard any time after that, I promise you ain't gonna like how I get you out." He turned his head to let fly a thick gob, thup, into the dirt, then wiped the corner of his greasy red neckerchief across his lips. "You think you can spend your whole life hidin' behind your brass-nuts ol' man, well, you got another think comin'. A big one."

He loosened his hold; I pulled my hand away. People like Oscar Fleischmann have a genius for drawing bad behavior out of anyone near them, then feeding on it. "That reminds me," I said. "My father asked me to tell you thanks for putting him through med school. He was still laughing the morning after I told him what you said."

Oscar's face darkened. His blubbery lips twisted, went purple. I leaned over the table, ready to clout him if he moved toward the music box. "So Sammy thought that was funny, huh?" Oscar shook his fist high over his head, calling down divine wrath on his enemy. "He's gonna be laughin' out the other side of his mouth when I start tellin' people what I know about him." The filthy old man jerked his head toward the office shack, then nodded sharply for emphasis. "I got it, all right, Chapter A to Z, and everything in between. So far I ain't said nothin' on account a Murray, but one a these days your ol' man's gonna push me a little bit too far, and he's gonna find himself sittin' in the slammer with no more medical license."

I started after him, but he held up a palm, then waggled a finger from the other hand toward the table. "Finish up that music box, then outa here." Voice like a robot's. "I don't never want to see your face or hear your voice, not one time ever again in my life." With that, he turned around and walked away. Like a hurricane, the calm at its eye more intimidating than its wind blasts.

I sat down, picked up music box pieces, tried to fit them together, but they jumped apart in my hands. I struggled for two hours before I finally finished basic reassembly, all components together, ready to go back onto the bedplate. Murray looked pleased when I showed him. He picked up the governor, eyed it critically. "Gotta be sure of that governor, Dockie. If it don't hold when you wind up the box, then wham! Teeth from the comb, pins offa the cylinder, flyin' all over the room. Put it all back together now, we'll see how it sounds."

I didn't want to use up my excuse to be in the junkyard, especially not after what Oscar said. Did he have some of Samuel's faked medical documents? Incriminating material about Jonas' death? I needed to get into that office when no one was around. "Tomorrow," I said.

Murray put down the governor, looked closely at me. "Something, Dockie?"

I told him about my wrangle with Oscar.

He shook his head, looked more sad than angry. "Pop's like a bad dog, gotta be barking every goddamn minute. Walk away, he shuts right up. But start barking back, you just might get bit." Murray shook his head again. "Him and your old man, they got a thing goes all the way back. Samuel never would take any shit, not from anybody, and every time Pop tried giving him some, Samuel shoved it right back in his face. I ain't got the faintest idea what's Pop's Chapters A and Z, but I wouldn't worry a whole lot. Guys like Pop think everybody in the world's as big a prick as them. Way he'd figure is if he ever tries nailing Samuel, Samuel'll go and spill dirt all over Hobart about some thing or other Pop might want to keep behind a closed door. Kapeesh?"

"Yes."

Murray laughed, flung one of his thick arms around me. He smelled of sweat and Vitalis, very different from Oscar's nauseating cigarette-garlic aura. "Hey, Dockie, come on, smile. Flash the pearls, grab the girls. Harmony, that's her name, right?"

I think I smiled. I tried. Murray laughed again, then disappeared back around the corner of the office. I covered my project, hopped onto my bike, rode home. Half a block away I heard the siren sax, "Mean to Me," brassy, passionate, almost wrathful. As I ducked though the cellar door Harmony lowered her horn, looked up.

"Red Cross okay today?" I asked.

She looked about to slam the saxophone to the cement floor. "Damn, Leo! When I think about what you get to do…*my* father'd drop dead before he'd take me along to see his patients. 'Being a doctah would *nawt* be a good life for a girl, brmmm…brmmmm…brmmmmmmm.' I spent the whole damn day winding gauze bandages and packing suture kits for doctors to use on soldiers. What'd *you* do?"

I tried to make it sound as unexciting as I could. "Hospital rounds with Samuel, house calls. Then I went to the junkyard."

Her face lit. "You worked on the music box?"

"Yes. But more." I told her about the heaps of metal I'd helped sort into piles, and where they came from. Surprise, she jumped to her feet. "Do you know his name? The scrap-man who died?"

I had to think. "George mentioned it yesterday…Broomall."

"Be right back."

Harmony ran upstairs into the kitchen, then I heard footsteps above my head. Living room. A couple of minutes later she was back, shoving a folded newspaper into my face. "Look at this obituary." She jabbed a finger at the paper.

"Broomall, Newton B.," I read. "Age 46. In Hobart, July 11, 1943, beloved husband of Wanda, devoted father of Lester and Sally, son of Edwina and the late Milton Broomall of Hobart. Owner of Broomall Scrapyard. I.O.O.F., Rotary, Lions Club. Services at Grunstra's Funeral Home, 3 pm, July 14."

I looked at Harmony. "That's tomorrow. So?"

"Leo, are you dense? It doesn't say what he died of, does it?"

"No."

"Obituaries always say what the person died of, like a stroke or an accident or a heart attack. Or 'a long illness' when it's cancer."

"All right. So?"

"So I'm going to his funeral. You said you thought he might've been killed. People talk at funerals, and maybe I can find out what he died of."

"But you've got to go to Red Cross."

"I'm a volunteer. If a volunteer needs to leave early to go to a funeral, no one says a word. Suppose Mr. Broomall died of strychnine poisoning? You said maybe he didn't want to sell scrap on the black market, like Jonas Fleischmann. If someone's killing junkmen for their scrap, there're going to be more. We've got to find out."

"We could tell the police."

"Oh, sure. And they'd really listen. To a couple of kids with a story but no proof. If anybody's going to dope this game, it's got to be us. You and me."

"All right," I muttered. "Guess tomorrow's going to be a big funeral day. Erskine Crosbie's is in the morning—not looking forward to that."

When I walked into our kitchen, Ramona pointed me back to the door. "Leo, get over to the Fleischmanns'. Samuel waited as long as he could. He said to tell you..." Expression on her face like she had gas, didn't want to pass it, couldn't hold it in. "Your girlfriend's going to have her baby."

"Teresa?"

"I don't know; he didn't mention a name. Go on now, Leo, or you'll miss it and he'll be upset."

I ran back outside, onto my bike, raced down Roosevelt. At the Fleischmanns', I didn't bother to knock or ring the bell, just pushed the screen door open and ran upstairs into the labor room. Teresa lay in bed, moaning softly, throwing her head one way, then the other. Lily sat at her left, gently patting her shoulder. Another woman stood like a guardian angel at Teresa's right, holding her hand. Samuel sat in a padded chair off to the side, eyes capturing every detail. He greeted me with a casual, "Oh, good, Leo, you made it. She's doing great, has her twilight sleep." He glanced toward the guardian angel. "That's Emily Ronstadt, the adopting mother. Emily, my son, Leo. My extern for the summer."

Emily was a tall angular woman with long sandy hair framing a face shaped like a pickle jar. Mild brown eyes. She smiled at me. "You're the apprentice."

Samuel moved to the edge of the bed. "Shouldn't be long— let's check her cervix." He put on a glove, slipped his hand beneath the sheet. His face brightened. "Ah! Good." He pulled a second examining glove out of his bag, gave it to me; I worked it onto my hand. Samuel raised the sheet, moved his gloved hand forward. "Cervix's all gone, head's right there. You'll feel the sagittal suture running up and down, which means the baby's head is coming out straight. Up top you'll feel something like a Y, the small fontanel at the crown of the head, so the baby's looking downward, the way it should." He pulled back his hand; blood and mucus dripped onto the sheet. "Go on, check."

As I slid in two fingers I tried to mold my face into a professional expression. Slippery, very warm. An inch and a half inside, my fingers slithered over a smooth, round object, and yes, running straight up the middle was the suture line ending at the Y-fontanel. I nodded to Samuel. "I feel it all, just the way you said."

"Good. If she were awake we'd have her push, but with twilight sleep…" He shook his head. "When the head comes a little further down, I'll pull it out with forceps."

Lily slipped a fetoscope onto her head, which made her look like a unicorn with a metal band running along her own sagittal suture. She bent to lower the bell of the instrument onto Teresa's abdomen, then tapped with an index finger, timing the fetal heart rate. "One thirty-six."

"Good." Samuel smiled at Emily Ronstadt. "Won't be long now, you'll see your baby." Emily looked like a bobbysoxer suddenly come face-to-face with Frankie.

It wasn't long, less than an hour. Curly black hair stretched, then parted the labia during contractions, receded between. Samuel and I washed our hands, put on gloves, and after Lily and Emily moved Teresa to the edge of the bed, Lily pulled open the drawer of a little night-table, took out an oblong package, unwrapped forceps into Samuel's hands. Emily gasped.

Samuel shook off her concern. "Don't worry. They're made to fit along the baby's cheeks, just like an extension of my hands."

I wondered how much money those heavy-looking forceps would bring on the steel pile at Fleischmann Scrap.

Samuel slid in the blades, locked the handles together, pulled once, and out came the baby's head, damp crop of hair, round puffy cheeks. As shoulders and body slipped through, Emily cried, "A boy!" Lily handed Samuel clamps and scissors, gave me a red rubber bulb, and as Samuel cut the cord, I sucked secretions out of the baby's nose and throat. The baby cried lustily. So did Emily. Samuel wrapped the baby in a blanket, laid the bundle in Emily's outstretched arms. She cooed into the child's face while we cleaned the bed and slid fresh sheets under Teresa. Then Emily leaned over the girl, rested the baby on her chest and whispered something I couldn't hear into her ear. In her twilight sleep, Teresa smiled.

Samuel took me down to the living room, introduced me to Joe Ronstadt, a ruddy-faced beanpole of about forty with a hook of a nose, jughandle ears, thick red mustache, and thin red hair in retreat from a tidal wave of freckles. Baggy brown suit, white shirt, yellow tie loosened at the neck. I had no trouble seeing him in striped overalls and a flannel shirt, milking a cow. Samuel put his arm around the man, herded him upstairs. Joe's eyes filled as he looked at the baby in Emily's arms. He clutched Samuel's shoulders, practically fell over his own feet trying to show gratitude. "I'll be back in the morning," Samuel said quietly. "We'll go from there."

On the way out something occurred to me. "Samuel," I said. "Everyone knowing everyone else? Couldn't that make for problems later?"

Samuel smiled like the Sphinx. He kept walking, then paused at the door of the Plymouth. "I don't think so," he said, as if choosing words from a thesaurus. "Joe and Emily know Teresa only by her first name. But why might that be a problem, anyway?"

"I was thinking the other way around," I said. "If Teresa decided she wanted—"

"Joe and Emily live out past Harrisburg," Samuel said. "But their names really aren't Joe and Emily. Or Ronstadt, for that matter. I'm the only one who knows their real names, or where they live. Which actually isn't anywhere near Harrisburg. And oh, by the way..."

Flash in his eye, I went on guard. Samuel laughed. "Leo, relax. You take everything so seriously. Teresa's not that girl's real name, either. Or Shannon, the other one's. Or Angela. Not even Lily knows any of these people by their real names. Only I do. I'll fill out the birth certificate with Joe and Emily's real names and address, file it with the county clerk, the clerk will send them a copy, and that'll be that. Nothing else in writing."

Whenever I thought I'd seen the limit, the horizon expanded. "But Samuel, that's..."

"What?"

"A crime."

"It's a crime not to help someone because of a law that doesn't allow for reasonable exceptions." Samuel was smiling now, but tightly, his I-dare-you-smile. He tossed his bag onto the back seat of the Plymouth, then climbed in behind the wheel. The motor roared, he was gone.

I walked back to the house, got my bike, rode across Twenty-second Street to Roosevelt. Pedaling seemed to take unusual effort. The air felt heavy, storm on the way.

Dinner was quick and quiet, chicken salad and Jell-O out of the refrigerator. Ramona wasn't there. "She's sleeping," Samuel told me. "I looked in on her when I got here. She probably got tired and ate earlier."

"Why does she need to take…what she does?" I asked.

Samuel took a long time to chew his mouthful. "Hasn't been easy on her nerves for years now, Leo. The Depression, this war…*me.*" He pointed at the kitchen clock over the sink. "Close to nine o'clock. Most people like some regularity to their lives, but there's none in this house. From one day to the next, nothing's ever the same. Very hard for her."

"But you love it."

I'm still not sure whether I intended that as an accusation, but Samuel didn't take it as one. "Yes," he said, and in the mounting darkness his eyes shone. "Yes, I love it."

A brilliant flash lit the sky, then a majestic boom of thunder. Samuel grinned. "Hendrick Hudson's men playing at ninepins. Better watch out you don't fall asleep right now, or you might not wake up for twenty years." Rain began to pelt the window. The room lit again; another deafening thunderbolt rattled the glass in the pane. "Good Jersey storm, clears the air," Samuel murmured. "We just might be able to sleep tonight."

He sounded as if the storm had been sent according to his order. But no electrical storm was going to clear the air between us, and the way my mind was racing, I wasn't at all sure *I'd* sleep that night.

Chapter 11

Next morning, unremitting humidity, unrelenting heat, the storm's short respite already a memory. An hour before Erskine Crosbie's funeral, Ramona and Samuel sat silent and jittery at the breakfast table, nibbling toast, sipping coffee. I prepared for a tough morning. But then they went to their bedroom to dress and came out transformed, serene. Four pinpoint pupils.

Services at the Park Avenue Episcopalian Church were brief, uninspired. Men sat quietly in black Victory Suits, no lapels, no cuffs. Women covered their low-cut blouses with black jackets, but their black skirts rode at mid-thigh. All that fabric saved so honest mill owners like Erskine could sell it low to the Armed Forces. When the minister said Erskine was not a religious man but a good man nevertheless, Samuel's body tensed, fists clenched. I couldn't keep my eyes off Daisy, Erskine's sister, sniveling in a front-row seat next to Rollie, her round, grease-haired, black-marketeer husband. "Let me have men about me that are fat; sleek-headed men, and such as sleep o' nights." Rollie didn't look at all drowsy.

Riding home in the Plymouth afterward, silence, but the closer we came, the brighter grew Samuel's eyes. His pupils widened, morphine wearing off. He stopped the car in the driveway, was out before Ramona or I had a foot on the ground. "Let's get rid of these funeral clothes." Samuel pointed at his black suit and mine. "We need to look in on Teresa, at the Fleischmanns'."

I glanced at Ramona, then looked away even more quickly.

Samuel was halfway across the front lawn to the porch. "So much for Erskine Crosbie," my mother said quietly. The acerbity in her voice appalled me. "Go on, Leo," she added. "Don't keep your father waiting."

By the time Samuel and I walked into the Fleischmanns', he was his usual self and then some. Lily, all smiles, greeted us at the door, then led us up to the labor room. Teresa held the baby in bed, one Ronstadt in a chair to her left, one to the right. As we walked in, Joe and Emily leaped to their feet as if they'd suddenly and unexpectedly caught sight of Old Glory. "Everything go all right last night?" Samuel asked.

I looked him up and down, tried to find a vestige of the savage grief he'd shown at Erskine's death, or a trace of the desolation I'd seen just a few hours before at the breakfast table. But there was none. His face was incandescent. Ramona was right—so much, no more. Samuel Firestone, M.D., was back.

Teresa rocked the baby. "He was so good all night," she said. "Hardly even cried. We took turns holding him." She inclined her head toward Emily, who smiled maternally at her. "And we talked to each other, you know, the way you told us to. I said what I hoped for him, and they said how they're going to bring him up." Teresa smiled down on her son. I swallowed hard. "I gave him his first bottle, then Emily gave him the second—I'll always remember that." A tear ran down her cheek, dropped onto the baby's face; he quivered. Teresa's smile flickered. Joe threw his arms around the girl, looked sheepishly at Samuel. "I feel like she's my daughter and he's my grandson." Not hard to understand. Teresa was sixteen, Joe easily forty.

Samuel looked like a balloon close to exploding. "Let's do a quick check," he said, and pulled a small stethoscope from his bag. He unwrapped the blanket from around the baby. I stared at the withered, browning stump of umbilical cord. The baby came to the edge of crying, but responded to the soothing of his mother's hand on his head, and a half-whispered, "It's all right."

When Samuel finished his examination he looked from Teresa to Emily to Joe. "Ready to give them your baby, Teresa?"

The girl hesitated just an instant, then nodded. "Yes." No more than a whisper. She gathered the blanket around the baby.

"Go ahead." Samuel's voice was as soft as hers, but the two words carried a force no one could've stood against. "Tell them just what you told me."

Teresa extended her arms to hold the baby out to Emily. "I came to Dr. Firestone," she said, "and asked him to…kill my baby. Because I wasn't going to be able to give it a good home. Dr. Firestone told me I could have the baby, and he'd make sure it went to people who could give it what I couldn't, and I could meet them and make sure I felt right about it." Teresa placed the baby in Emily's arms. "So I'm giving you my baby, it's of my own free will, and I'm happy doing it because you and Joe are good people, and the baby will have a good life."

Emily planted a light kiss on Teresa's cheek, which started them both crying.

Teresa's speech bothered me, thick with rehearsal, studded with wordings obviously not hers. "Of my own free will." I wondered how much free will anyone had once my father went to work. What was happening did seem to be what everyone in that room wanted, but I wondered whether Teresa would feel differently the next day, or in ten years. But how might she feel in ten years if she did keep the baby? A teen-aged single mother, in 1943? And how about the baby? What really *was* best for him?

I didn't have long to think about it. Samuel, radiant, proclaimed, "Teresa gives her baby to Emily and Joe. Who promise…"

"To raise him as our own beloved son," Joe and Emily said in unison, their voices taking turns cracking. "And to remember and be grateful for Teresa's love, which gave him life and brought him to us."

"And his name is…" Samuel intoned.

"David," Emily said. "David Franklin—" She caught herself as if she were stumbling at the edge of a cliff. "We picked the name last night, all three of us. David Franklin."

"Good." Samuel pulled a pad from his black bag, a fountain pen from his pocket, started writing. I glanced over his shoulder. Name of Baby: David Franklin. The rest of the form was already filled in, and no, the parents' names really were not Emily and Joe Ronstadt. Samuel blew on the ink, showed the paper to "Joe" and "Emily." "Birth certificate. I'll file it today, then the county clerk will send you a copy after it clears registration." He looked at Teresa. "You'll get your paper when you leave. TB'll never bother you again, will it?"

Teresa looked down. She'd caught the meaning in his words and eyes.

Samuel nodded at Emily and Joe. "I'll check Teresa, see you downstairs."

Teresa cried quietly while Samuel tapped at her chest, listened to her lungs, palpated the hard postpartum uterus just below her navel. At one point she said, "I feel strange, Dr. Firestone. I don't know whether I'm sad or happy."

Samuel rested a hand on her shoulder. "You're happy," he said. "But you feel bad about feeling happy, so you feel terrible, except you feel wonderful." Teresa couldn't seem to decide whether to keep crying or laugh.

Afterward, in the Fleischmanns' living room, Joe held a thick white envelope out to Samuel. "Here it is, Dr. Firestone, just like you said. Three thousand." Not pocket change then or now, but during the war a lot of ordinary people had money because there was nothing to spend it on. Samuel thanked him, passed the offering to Lily, who walked away with it in the direction of the kitchen. "I can't tell you how much—" Joe continued, but Emily interrupted him. "Dr. Firestone…I'm sorry. But you *are* sure it's all right?" She looked down at the baby in her arms, maternal concern all over her face. "I mean, he's only a day old."

"Don't worry," Samuel said. "Go to the address I gave you, rent a room. You had your baby unexpectedly while traveling, you're going to stay a week. Any problem at all, you and Joe have my phone number. And I'll see the little guy in my office before you head home."

Emily laid a hand on Samuel's forearm. Her eyes apologized for any doubt she might ever have harbored. Joe shook Samuel's hand. Just then Lily walked back in, waving a little black camera with a flash gun on top. Samuel laughed. "Her toy." He gathered Joe in one arm, Emily and the baby in the other, nodded to me. I stepped next to Emily. Lily studied us through the lens, then murmured, "Yes, just right," and pushed the button at the end of a cable, flash! The baby whimpered, Emily soothed him. Another round of thank-you's, then a moment later the screen door slammed. I thought about Ramona, alone in our house after the funeral, felt a terrible sadness in the pit of my stomach.

In the Plymouth, going home, I said, "That was more of a religious ceremony than the funeral."

"What?" Samuel's foot accidentally tapped the brake; the car lurched. Knowing I'd nailed him gave me courage to go on. "And you sounded more like a minister than the one in church."

Samuel chuckled, back in control. "Tell you something. Teresa needs to believe she's doing the right thing for that baby. And Joe and Emily should know what she's gone through, feel a real obligation to her. A little ceremony helps. Shows what serious business it is. Door's closed, no one ought ever open it."

"One thing to say a bunch of words, another to mean them," I said. My own boldness surprised me. "How can you be sure—"

Samuel smiled as he broke in. "Wait to be a hundred percent sure, all you'll ever do in your life is stand around watching people suffer and die. Sometimes you need to behave as if there really were certainty in this world—you know, update Pascal's wager. Put it into play where there actually might *be* something to lose."

The gospel according to St. Samuel. "Go for eight."

After lunch, Samuel went to talk to his accountant, so I biked to the junkyard. Where six piles of metal had stood the day before, now only scraps lay next to a messy heap of wrinkled tarps. I saw Murray and George off by the fence, stoking the garbage fire. Clouds of dense black smoke billowed across the river into Emerson Township. No sign of Oscar, good.

I uncovered my work, sat down, slid the music box cylinder into its brass end bearings, positioned the governor and spring assembly, then screwed them all into place. I picked up the comb, but remembered Murray's warning about the cylinder spinning around too fast and knocking out teeth. So I put the comb aside, and pulled the winding lever on the spring, once, twice. Nothing happened. I pulled a third time, no difference. When I flicked the little blades of the governor fan they barely moved, and reluctantly at that.

At least as reluctantly, I got up and walked slowly across the junkyard. Murray surprised me by laughing when I told him what was wrong. He wiped an arm across his forehead, pulled out his grimy handkerchief, blew his nose. "Sounds like maybe you got a sick patient, there, Dockie. Let's take a gander."

"I don't want to interrupt you. I mean, if—"

"You mean if Pop sees me helpin' you?" Murray rumbled.

I nodded. That was exactly what I was going to say.

"Tell you something, Dockie. All that shit about how this is Pop's junkyard—just forget about it. If my old man's got a bug up his ass about your old man, that's between the two a them, okay? Pop bothers you, I'll take care a him. Just don't *you* go messin' with him. Kapeesh?"

Back at the worktable, Murray picked up the musical mechanism, held it to the light, squinted. He flicked the fan blades with his index finger the way I had, poked at the governor gears, finally pointed at the gear-juncture of the governor and cylinder. "Look, Dockie. Bound up here, tight as a tick." He poked an elbow into my ribs. "You done a damn good job gettin' your sick patient better, but now we gotta do like your old man does sometimes. He don't do brain surgery operations, does he?"

"No. He'd call in a consultant, a neurosurgeon."

"Well, then. That's what we're gonna do now. Governor needs some adjustments, pretty delicate work. Besides..." Murray pointed at the comb, lying upside down on the table. "See them little wires underneath the teeth, curving towards the tips? They're called dampeners, and they need a ton of work, too."

I peered, shaded my eyes. "I can just about make them out. Some are bent off to one side or the other, and some aren't even there."

Murray held out his hands, hams with sausage fingers. "Can you just about see me trying to put stuff like that right? Or do some tiny little adjustment on a governor? Less'n a minute, I'd be shaking like a leaf on a tree. Put it back inside the case and take it on over to Hogue's. I'll give Chet a call, tell him what's what, and you're on your way."

Inside fifteen minutes I was there. Mrs. Hogue glared at me through the thick gray haze in the shop. Gunmetal hair drawn back hard into a bun, thin lips turned down at both corners. Someone who always got the short end of every deal, and wasn't about to let you forget it. I said hello, held up the music box in its case. "Murray Fleischmann—"

That was as far as I got. She ripped the cigarette from her lips, shouted at the top of her voice, "Chet! Kid's here from Fleischmann's." Then she jerked a hitchhiker thumb toward the back. "Listen to what he tells you, keep your mouth shut, get done, awright? He gets talkin', he'll be at it all day."

"All right," I said. "I appreciate him helping me."

Her face softened just a bit. She plugged her cigarette back in, took another drag, then half-turned in her swivel chair and blew the smoke toward the poster-picture of Roosevelt on the wall as if she were offering incense to a god.

Mr. Hogue sat at his workbench, manipulating a scatter of clock pieces through a loupe. He bulldozed a space with a hand. "Let's see what you got, Sonny."

He pulled the music-works out of its case, took off the comb, studied the governor and cylinder. "Mmmm...yeah." Then he started to work the winding lever back and forth. "Gotta take off all the power, otherwise we'll be pickin' up gear teeth all over the floor. Maybe our own teeth too." After a cackle at his joke, he unscrewed the governor, lifted it from the bedplate, peered through a hole in the side plate. "Hmmm." He pushed a thumb against the outermost gear. The fan blades balked, then started to spin, but slowly. Mr. Hogue pointed at the peephole in the governor side plate. "Look here—worm's not meshing good with the first wheel. Gonna move them two gears a hair closer. Watch."

He slipped a narrow-bladed screwdriver into the slot of a screw on the rear of the governor, advanced the screw about a quarter-turn, then peered through the brass knothole again. "Here y' go, Sonny, lookit it now."

I craned my neck to peek over his shoulder. The worm and its wheel were deeply engaged. Mr. Hogue pushed his thumb against the outer governor gear, and there went the fan blades, round and round. Picture a fox who just beat a cat to a particularly tasty bird. "Watch this, Sonny." He screwed the governor back into place on the bedplate, then pulled at the winding handle. Fan turned, cylinder rotated.

Like watching Samuel diagnose diphtheria by smell. The expression on my face set Mr. Hogue cackling again. Then from behind me came a menacing contralto growl. "Comin' along, Chet?"

If Mr. Hogue was intimidated, he didn't show it. "Goin' great, Martha. Boy's got a nice music box here, least he will when he's done." He picked up the comb, screwed it to the bedplate, then wound the spring and released the stop-finger on the side of the governor. Music played. I didn't recognize the tune but both Hogues began to sing along, "We will me-e-et in the swe-e-et by and by-y-y." Mr. Hogue shot me a look out of the corner of his eye. "Real popular tune back a few years, Sonny, back even before Martha and me. I remember my mother used to sing it."

"Mine too." Martha, never to be outdone.

The cylinder clicked to a halt. "It plays," I said. "But it sounds terrible. All those squeaky, scratchy sounds—does it need oil?"

Mr. Hogue laughed. His wife blew a mouthful of air into a disparaging sound, then pushed back a gray strand that had dared to come loose and fall across her cheek. "That's dampers, Sonny," Mr. Hogue said. "Them little wires under the teeth. If they ain't set exactly right, then the cylinder pins make a noise like hell when they hit a tooth. Gotta get every damper just so. Lemme show you."

As he picked up the comb, Mrs. Hogue said, "You can't be all the rest of the day with him, Chet. Mrs. Bishop's been drivin' me nuts, when's she gonna get her clock back?"

Mr. Hogue's eyes glittered. This was their game, no ending, no one ever declared winner. "Tell her she'll get it back when it's done. When's the last time a customer didn't get her clock back fixed? I'm gonna show Sonny here how to do dampers, then he's on his own."

Fine with me. I didn't want to spend the rest of the day in that smoky, smelly room. "I'll take it back to the yard, work on it there," I said. "Murray's really a good guy. He lets me use a table, and his tools."

The Hogues exchanged one of those looks long-married couples give each other, no need for words. Then Mrs. Hogue cocked her eyes in my direction. "Yeah, Murray's a nice guy— which is more than I can say for certain other people in that yard." Back to the lemonsucker face. "Poor Stella Fleischmann. Shoulda been snow in hell before she ever took that bastard Oscar into her house."

I felt confused, must've looked the same. Mrs. Hogue nodded viciously. "You don't know? Oscar was Stella's second husband. Sol Bromnik was her first, busted an appendix and died just like that, from one day to the next. Left Stella with a junkyard and a baby, Jonas, not even a year old. So here comes Oscar Fleischmann, that fat, stinking son of a bitch, used to pull a wagon around like an ox, selling ice. Oscar knew a good thing when he saw it, and before Solly was cold in the grave, Oscar married his wife, adopted his son, and took over his junkyard. Treated the poor woman like dirt from the first. She sure didn't want no more kids, did everything she could, but then here comes Murray, right on the same day we went into the First War. Some Good Friday *that* was. Least Murray turned out decent. But I always said Stella should've told Oscar to get lost, even if she had to starve. Didn't I, Chet?"

"Yes. You did." Mr. Hogue looked as if he'd gotten a whiff of something tainted. "But I told you then and I'll tell you now—it wasn't only her woulda starved. What about Jonas? And then Murray?"

"So Jonas and Murray were *half*-brothers," I said.

My reaction went right past Mr. Hogue, still facing down his wife from his soapbox. "We had Teddy Roosevelt then, not Franklin," Mr. Hogue shouted. "There wasn't no Social Security, no unemployment. What kind of a mother's gonna let her little kids starve? Now, if you don't mind a whole lot, Martha, I'm gonna finish showing Sonny how to do these-here dampers. Then he can go on back to the junkyard and I'll take care of Mrs. Bishop's blasted clock."

"Hmmph." Mrs. Hogue went for the Camels, made a military about-face and stomped toward the front of the shop. Mr. Hogue picked up a small pair of pliers in one hand, a spool of fine wire in the other, paused long enough to size me up. Then he reached for his loupe. "Okay, Sonny," he said. "Here's where we find out if you're a sheep or a goat." He bent over the comb, and…well, it looked so easy. In five minutes he had ten damper-wires set, cut, shaped a paper-width off the tips of the teeth. Then he gave me those little tools and sat me down to work. Fifteen minutes and probably twenty tries later, I finally got my first damper right. My hands shook as if I were freezing. Mr. Hogue patted me on the back. "Take it easy, Sonny. The tools know what to do. Your job's just to get 'em where they need to be. They'll take it from there."

Nearly a half-hour, three dampers set and shaped. Mr. Hogue held up the comb, squinted. "That's the idea." Then he opened one of the workbench drawers, pulled out another loupe and a paper bag, put the loupe into the bag, scooped in the tools and the spool of damper wire from the benchtop. "Go work in the junkyard," he said. "When you're done, bring me back my stuff."

"I can't take your tools, Mr. Hogue," I blurted.

"Y' can't? Well, how in hell you gonna put in dampers, with your teeth? It's okay, I ain't doin' no music box work right now. Bring the stuff back by next week, that's all. Now go on, would you, and let a man do his work." He glanced toward the front of his shop, cackled softly. "Before the wife gets to work on *me* again."

I thanked Mr. Hogue, then pedaled back to the yard and set myself up at the table behind the office shack. Dampering's a real pain-in-the-ass job, finicky as hell, but in a little while I got into a rhythm. Pull the pin, ream the hole, set the wire. Cut, shape, adjust. Again and again and again. After an hour I'd put in ten dampers, as many as Chester Hogue had done in five minutes. My fingers and forearms ached.

I stood up, stretched, started thinking. When Oscar told me about having Chapters A through Z on Samuel, he pointed at the office, didn't he? I shaded my eyes, scanned the yard. George was working in the Six-Six, the far corner where Sixth Street intersected Sixth Avenue. They kept dead appliances there to be stripped down for parts. George'd probably be a while.

No sign of Murray or Oscar. I walked out from behind the table, around to the front of the office and inside, just in time to hear Bill Nicholson, the Chicago Cubs' slugger, put a ball into the left field seats. A disgusting bouquet of Oscar's cigarettes, unwashed armpits, and garlic filled the room. I opened the cooler on the floor, dropped a nickel into the can, pulled out a Coke, popped the cap, swigged. Then I looked around. Below the radio on the window sill, a battered old desk with a rickety chair behind it. Another two flimsy wooden chairs between the desk and cooler. Against the wall to the left of the desk, a dented four-drawer metal file cabinet. In the back, a filthy toilet in a tiny cubicle, visible through an open doorway. I walked over, sat in the chair behind the desk, hesitated for just an instant. Then I started opening drawers.

I must've looked like a comedy-puppet, head bouncing down to look into a drawer, up to check the office doorway, then back to the next drawer. First five drawers held nothing beyond ordinary office stuff—paper, receipt books, staples, tooth-marked pencils. But in the left bottom drawer I hit paydirt. A metal strongbox.

I glanced toward the doorway, then carefully lifted the box to the desktop. Heavy. Probably a thick layer of lead under black-painted steel. O. FLEISCHMANN scratched clumsily across the top, probably with a knife point. About a foot long, foot-and-a-half deep, six inches high, held shut by a brass padlock with a thick steel bolt. Big enough to hold a ton of photographs and documents.

My heart danced a jig in my throat. The lock was a Yale, the kind you could buy at any hardware store for less than fifty cents. I pulled at it, no luck. Ride the box home on the handlebars of my bike, take a hacksaw to the lock, replace it, sneak the box back that night?

Rhetorical questions. No way to know how often Oscar opened that box. Maybe he always checked the drawer before he went home after work. George was all the way out in Six-Six but he'd probably seen me, just as I'd seen him. I'd have to come back another time, better prepared.

I put the box back, closed the drawer, stood up, started to leave...wait, file cabinet. I opened the top drawer, riffled through grimy manila folders, the story of a junkyard's day-to-day business, alphabetically arranged by customer name, accounts pending, accounts receivable. Bottom drawer, tools. Drill, hammer, screwdrivers. I kicked the drawer shut, opened the one above it. Catalogs and reference books, good place to hide documents or photographs. I grabbed a manual on radio repair, flipped it open—and right then it hit me. Motor noises, outside. I'd been hearing them but they hadn't registered; the chatter of the ball game announcer on the radio was like an anesthetic. A door slammed, then another. Murray and Oscar, back from a run in the truck.

I dropped the book into place, eased the drawer closed, heard boisterous singing. Murray. "What's the use of Goering? He never was worthwhile—so! Pack up your Goebbels in your old kit bag, *und Heil! Heil! Heil!"*

"You got that off Red Dexter." Oscar, disgusted.

"Yeah, well, so what if I did?" Louder, clearer, closer to the office. "He's a funny guy."

"Yeah, a goddamn riot. Way you're all buddy-buddy with him and Sammy Firestone, you're gonna fuck us up yet." Oscar, coarse, surly.

I slid into one of the chairs opposite the desk. Ninety-plus degrees, but the sweat on my body and arms was like ice water. Did I put the strongbox back just the way I'd found it? No chance to check, they were right outside the door. "Like I've fucked up anything so far," Murray growled. "When's the last time—"

Murray stopped in midsentence as he and Oscar came through the doorway. They looked at me, then at each other. Oscar tried to wither me with a look. "Jesus fuckin' Christ! Hey, Pussy, the hell you doin' in my private office?"

I almost said I didn't answer to Pussy, but the expression on Murray's face rerouted my line of talk. "I had to take a leak," I said. "And I was thirsty." I pointed at my almost-empty Coke bottle on the desk. "I put my nickel in the can."

"And then you just decided you'd sit your ass in *my* office, in *my* chair." Oscar stomped over, thrust his face into mine. Black hairs sprouted from his nostrils and ears. "Listen up, Pussy, last time I'm tellin' you." He aimed a bloated finger at my chest. "I'm lettin' you play with that fuckin' music box on account of it's too goddamn much trouble to fight about it with my idiot son, but from now on, you gotta piss, you go over by the fence and piss on the garbage fire. You want a drink, go down to the soda shop on Fourth Av. Keep the hell outa my private office. You got that?"

I half-turned to leave, but Oscar grabbed my shirt sleeve. "I didn't hear no answer," he snarled. "I taught my kids better manners'n that. You want, I'll teach you some, same way I taught them." He raised his free hand.

I wrenched out of his hold, felt my T-shirt rip. Smelly old son of a bitch—*he* was going to teach *me* manners. Only my promise to Murray kept me from going after him. He glared at me. I glared back. "I still don't hear no answer," he growled.

I glanced at Murray, all it took. Oscar went off like a bomb, grabbed the Coke bottle by the neck, brought it down on the edge of the desk. Glass and soda flew in every direction. He waved the jagged bottle, moved toward me. "Pussy-bastard, I'm gonna send you home to daddy in a box."

Murray rushed him from the side, grabbed his arm, twisted his wrist. The old man howled as the bottle flew across the room and shattered against the wall. I ran out, straight to the worktable. From the window above me, Oscar's and Murray's voices played a strident counterpoint, volume rising with every exchange. I slid Chester Hogue's tools into the paper bag, quickly screwed the comb back onto the bedplate, put the mechanism into the wooden case, ran for my bike at the side of the office. I'd have made it home in record time, but I stopped at the hardware store on Eleventh Avenue and spent thirty-eight cents on a brass Yale padlock with a thick steel link.

Chapter 12

Dad's voice faded. He raised his glass like an automaton, then drained it, his fifth Manhattan. I'd seen him drink that much and more, but I'd never heard him talk like this. As if the booze were throwing a bright white beam into some long-darkened no-man's-land behind his eyes. The waiter strode up, took the glass from Dad's hand, looked at me.

I nodded. "I'm driving the cab."

"Yes, sir."

The waiter marched away. Dad stood. "Got to go."

I watched for a weave or a wobble as he strode off, but he could've passed any cop's test on a straight line. Seventy-six years old, the man was a human alcohol-detoxification plant. I tried to remember a single time I'd seen him down for the count, but saw only a procession of unconscious poets, novelists, painters and musicians sprawled on our living room couch or floor, Dad standing over them, half-full glass in hand, shaking his head and muttering, "Lightweight" to Mother. But this was early in the day for Dad to drink seriously. I picked a strawberry from the tray, nibbled.

When Dad returned, his drink was waiting. He took a swallow before he was fully seated, ate a couple of crackers, coughed. "Where was I?"

"Riding home with Mr. Hogue's tools and your thirty-eight cent padlock."

Right. From a block away I heard "Ain't Misbehavin'," raucous, boisterous, one impish embellishment after another. I wheeled into the garage, jumped off my bike, tucked Mr. Hogue's tools and the music box under an arm, ran across and down into the cellar. Harmony raised her eyebrows as I came in, but kept playing. I set the music box and tools on the washing machine. Harmony went right on playing. Finally, at the end of the stanza, she ducked through the leather neckband, then slowly, carefully, laid her sax on the table. Her face was like an elf's. She chewed at her upper lip, didn't say a word.

"Cat got your tongue?" I finally asked.

She blew me a razzberry.

"All right, you've got your tongue and it works. What's up?"

Big grin. "People really do talk at funerals." She crossed her legs, looked at the ceiling, tapped fingers on the table, full measure for her every moment on stage. "I put a black dress into a paper bag, took it to work, changed in the ladies' room. Then I ran over to the church and sat in the back, next to a little old man in a cheap suit. I gave him a look like Claudette Colbert gave Clark Gable in *It Happened One Night*... Leo, damn you, stop smirking. I told him I was Linda Broomall, a niece from Connecticut, and I came by myself on the train because Daddy was overseas and Mom couldn't get anybody to stay with my little brother. I said none of us knew Uncle Newt was sick. Then I batted my eyelashes right smack in his face—"

"Just like Claudette."

Little snicker. "Yes, just exactly like Claudette, and it worked. So there, weisenheimer. 'He *wasn't* sick, honey,' the old guy said. 'Cops say some guy came lookin' to rob the place and shot your uncle, but you ask me and a whole lotta other people besides, it was something else altogether. Newt was an honest joe, you follow what I'm sayin'. Wouldn't sell scrap metal where some people wanted him to.' So what do you think of that?"

"Claudette couldn't have done better."

Whatever else I might've said went on hold because right then Harmony looked at the washing machine. Wham, hands to cheeks. "Leo, you fixed it! My music box."

"Not quite."

I don't think she heard me, just ran to the box, opened the lid, murmured, "Oh, so shiny…," then flung her arms around my neck and kissed my nose. "Play it for me."

I leaned around her to push the start lever. At the first notes, she let go of me and stood there listening with both hands over her mouth, as if she were afraid she might accidentally make a sound and shatter something fragile. Nice little tune, "Beautiful Dreamer," but squeaky as all get-out. Not as bad as before I'd done any dampering but it still had a way to go. When the music stopped, Harmony closed the lid and hugged the box. "Oh, it's wonderful, Leo. I'm going to keep it forever."

"Not 'til I finish it." I held out my hand. "Didn't you hear those noises?"

"I don't care. Come on, Leo, please. I absolutely love it."

I shook my head. "Soon."

She stamped a foot. "Leo, *damn* you anyway! Why do you have to be such a fussbudget?"

"Just a couple more days," I told her. "It'll sound a lot better, and then you can have it."

Her eyes, when she looked at that music box… "Promise?"

"Promise." I took the music box, closed the lid. "Now, listen." I told her what I'd found out from Mrs. Hogue.

She picked right up. "So Jonas was Oscar's *step*son. And just like Mr. Broomall, he wouldn't sell scrap to the 'right people'."

"Right. Oscar must have taken some of the strychnine George bought that day for rat poison, fed it to Jonas—"

"Why Oscar? Just because you don't like him, and you like Murray? Why *not* Murray? Or even both of them?"

"Because if Murray poisoned Jonas, he wouldn't have done it in his own house, with those girls in the attic. Oscar must know what goes on there—he's forever bitching about Murray being in business with Samuel. He must've seen his chance. Gave Jonas strychnine, dumped the body in Murray and Lily's living room, told them to call Samuel and get him to cover it up as a natural death. Otherwise, *he'd* call the cops, tell them there was a dead man on the floor at Murray's house, and when the cops started poking around, guess what they'd find upstairs. Maybe Oscar even waited to make sure Murray called Samuel, then went home and sat around 'til Samuel came by and told him it was all taken care of. Three birds with one stone. Oscar's rid of Jonas, has Murray tied up, and Samuel one-down."

Harmony tapped a finger on the tabletop, thinking-rhythm. "Maybe you're right, Leo, but there's one thing."

"What?"

"We really don't know for sure that Jonas died of strychnine poisoning, do we?"

Wait to be a hundred percent sure, all you'll ever do in your life is stand around watching people suffer and die. Samuel's words left my own mouth dry and sour. I ticked off reasons on my fingers. "Fresh supply of strychnine in the junkyard that day. Instant rigor mortis. A terrible expression on Jonas' face. No records in my father's office."

"Leo, I don't care what you say. You still couldn't prove in a court that Jonas died of strychnine poisoning."

"How am I supposed to get proof?" I think by this time I was shouting. "Absolute airtight proof. He's dead and bur… Oh, no. Harmony, we can't do that."

"It's the only way to get proof."

I might've known. Harmony despised wrapping bandages at the Red Cross as much as she adored Samuel, maybe more. And now that she had her teeth into an adventure, she wasn't about to let go. Jumping up and down, shouting. "We can do it, Leo, tonight. The Jewish cemetery's just across the river in Grassville. We'll go out there, find Jonas' grave, come back, stop at Samuel's office and get specimen bottles. Then go back to the cemetery at two or three in the morning. Tomorrow you can get someone at the hospital to run tests for strychnine."

"Just like that. How am I going to persuade somebody to check for strychnine without explaining why? And be sure Samuel doesn't find out?"

"Don't you know any of the pathologists well enough to say you took tissue from a neighbor's dog, you want to see if someone's leaving strychnine around? And that you'll check in later for the result?"

I sighed. "I could ask Herman Korinsky."

She clapped hands, did a little dance. Even in the dim light from the overhead bulb, her green eyes sparkled. "Come on, then. Let's go find the grave."

I shook my head. "Not now. Daytime, there're always people around. The caretaker's probably still working. We'd look funny, wandering from grave to grave, staring at tombstones. Better to go after dinner. Besides, this early, Samuel's still in his office. Little tough getting specimen bottles."

"Okay. My family gets done with dinner about eight. Meet you then to go find the grave?"

I shook my head. "That late, we may run out of light. Tell you what. Unless Samuel has an emergency, we're through eating by seven-thirty. How about if I scout the grave myself? Then I can meet you at two o'clock, to, uh, dig up the evidence."

Her brows came together, lips tightened. "It was my idea."

"Fine. Tell me how you'd like to do it."

She exploded. "Damn, Leo! Why do you always have to be so...*reasonable?*" She paused. "Wait a minute. What if Samuel comes into your room during the night to take you on a call and you aren't there? Okay, you can go find the grave by yourself. But then come back here afterward, sleep over."

Couldn't argue that. "All right."

"No chance anyone'll come in to take *me* on a call."

The venom in her voice hung in the air like a cloud. I put my arms around her, said, "I'll come in and take you on a call. Tonight."

She looked up, face suddenly smeared with tears. "I don't know what I'd ever do without you, Leo," she said. "And

Samuel." She glanced back over her shoulder at the stairs leading up to her family's kitchen. "Maybe put strychnine in my father's dinner, the puffed-up old jerk. If I did, would you get samples from *him*, Leo? Would you turn me in?"

I paused, finally managed an offhanded, "No, it'd be justifiable homicide. Just have to let you get away."

Then she really started crying. I couldn't begin to figure why. "What'd I say?"

She pulled away, wiped her eyes on her sleeve, looked up at me. I thought her face—and my heart—might crack. "What did you have to think so hard for?" I could barely hear her words. "If it was the other way around, I'd have said, 'Leo, I wouldn't *ever* turn you in, no matter what you did or why you did it.'"

She turned away, picked up her sax, started to play from where she'd left off, but now, the music was like a punch to my stomach. "Ain't Misbehavin'," played with despair, every note brimming with heartache. I walked across the room, stood in front of my easel, stared at the canvas, then started mixing paint. I painted, Harmony played the saxophone, we didn't say another word for I'm not sure how long. Finally, I put down my brush and walked across the room, heading home for dinner.

Harmony stopped playing mid-tune, threw off her saxophone, ran over, flung her arms around me. "I'm sorry." A whisper.

"No, *I'm* sorry," I muttered. "I don't know why I said what I did. I never *would* turn you in, not for anything. You know that."

Big smile. She hugged me harder. "But I wanted to hear you say it. Come back as soon as you can, Leo. I'll be waiting."

So, a quarter after two next morning, there we were, two kids on their bicycles, each with a shovel across the handlebars, riding over the Thirty-third Street Bridge into Grassville. Past the First-War Veterans' Park, up to the gates of Mt. Pisgah Cemetery. Those days, the gates were never closed, no reason. We got off our bikes, hid them in the high grass behind the stone wall, took the shovels, started up the roadway. Harmony whispered in my ear, "Got the bottles?"

I patted my pocket. "Two, just in case one breaks. And a pair of little scissors and forceps to take the samples." I swallowed hard, thinking about opening Jonas Fleischmann's coffin, finding his week-dead body, cutting into soft decomposing flesh. But if Harmony felt the least revolted at the thought of what we were up to, she didn't show it. All the way along that winding drive-way, then up the hill to the burial grounds, she never paused, never looked around. At the top of the hill I pointed left, whis-pered, "Over there, about halfway to the fence. Caretaker's house is off in the other direction. If we're quiet he'll never hear."

Half-moon, no street lamps, but my eyes had pretty well adjusted. We started down a dirt footpath, went past a huge marble mausoleum, STEINBERG inscribed above the door—as in Steinberg Memorial Hospital. Old Saul Steinberg made a fortune in the Civil War, selling uniforms to both armies. As Harmony and I passed the mausoleum I realized it'd be directly between us and the caretaker's, would hide us from view *and* muffle sound. Good. We walked past the Minkowitz plot, past Cohen, Schifrin, Walber, Meyer. I tapped Harmony's shoulder, pointed toward the next headstone.

Her glasses flashed as she moved her head to peer past me. "Bromnik?"

"Remember?" I whispered. "Oscar Fleischmann married Jonas' mother and adopted Jonas. He was born Jonas Bromnik. See, underneath Bromnik, it says Solomon, 1880-1908, and Stella, 1884-1932. Guess she didn't want to be buried with Oscar." I pointed at the fresh grave just beyond the two rectangular patches of ivy. "Jonas is next to her, no stone yet."

Harmony sighed. "Okay. Six feet deep, right?"

"That's what they say." I worked dirt with my shovel. "Pretty loose, only been a week."

We set to work facing each other, she at the foot of the grave, I at the head. I was surprised at how little sound our shovels made. Though the loose dirt came up easily, humidity was so high you could've cut the air with a butter knife. Within three minutes I was drenched. I glanced over my shoulder. Yes, the

Steinberg mausoleum was set perfectly between us and the caretaker's cottage. I pulled my T-shirt over my head, tossed it to the ground away from our dirt pile. As I bent to lift the next shovel-load, I noticed Harmony had stopped working. She shook hair back off her face, unbuttoned her shirt, shucked it off, then dropped it on top of mine. Nothing on underneath, no brassiere, nothing. Without a word, she picked up her shovel and went back to work. I tried not to look at her, thought about what would happen if we were caught. One thing for a couple of kids to explain why they were digging up a grave at two in the morning, another matter altogether that one of those kids was both a girl and bare to the waist. In 1943 a girl wouldn't take off her shirt in public if hornets had gotten in and were stinging her to death.

We'd worked for fifteen or twenty minutes, were down about three feet, when my shovel went clunk. I squatted, wiggled fingers in the dirt, found something cold and metallic. Harmony dropped her shovel, knelt beside me. "What?"

"Don't know." I ran fingers around the metal, worked it free, held it up. Rectangular container, a foot long, six inches across. I felt an irregularity on one side, peered at it. Brass plaque.

Harmony leaned forward, cheek-to-cheek with me. Her hair brushed my bare shoulder. "Jonas Fleischmann, 1907-1943…" She looked up at me. "Oh shit, Leo! They cremated him."

Harmony's face wasn't three inches from mine. One of her breasts pressed against my arm. She smelled of dirt and sweat. I dropped the box, took her by the shoulders and kissed her on the mouth. I'd never done that before—thought about it often enough, but never had the nerve. We kissed for…how do you time a kiss when you're sixteen years old? Harmony finally pulled away, smiled, patted my arm, then asked, "Can you test ashes for strychnine?"

Could've been dismissive, a pat on the arm, an on-with-business question. As if the kiss never happened. But there was an acknowledgment in her smile, like a long-married wife whose husband showed a bit of open affection at an inappropriate moment. I picked up the box, held it out to Harmony. "Feel around the edge there—nails. Must be wood, covered with sheet metal. We'd need to take it home and pry it open, but to test ashes? I don't think there could be any strychnine left, not after all that heat."

Harmony looked at the pile of dirt next to the hole, made a face. "All this for nothing."

"Not exactly nothing," I said. "One thing I learned this summer, working with Samuel, is that Jewish people don't cremate their dead. But I bet Jonas was cremated so he never could be tested. Not the proof you want, but suspicious as hell." I laid the box back in the grave, picked up my shovel. "Let's put back the dirt and get out of here."

I surprised myself at how well I slept the rest of that night. Bright light when I got up, ten o'clock. Note from Harmony on the floor just inside the door. She'd gone to the Red Cross, would be back by five, she'd see me then. Downstairs, no one home. I walked across to our house, no one home there, either. I drank some orange juice, ate a bowl of cereal, then went upstairs and took a long shower. All the while, I couldn't stop thinking of the look on Harmony's face as she listened to the music box, and her smile after I'd kissed her over Jonas Fleischmann's open grave. That music box was going to be finished by five o'clock.

Chapter 13

My cell phone buzzed. Dad looked annoyed, but stopped talking as I pushed the button and said hello.

"Martin? Martin, dear, please pretend I'm Helene. Say 'Hello, Helene.'"

"Hello, Helene," I said. "What's up?" Catching myself just in time to not say, "What's up, *Mother*?"

"Martin, you're with your dad? Just say yes or no."

"Yes. But why—"

"I'm a little worried, dear. After you called last night, he went into his den, locked the door, and didn't come out until this morning. He said nothing to me, not a word—just shaved, had some oatmeal and coffee, and went off to see you. I can't imagine what you told him, but don't say anything now. Not if he's there."

"No, of course not...Helene."

"He's drinking, isn't he? More than a little."

"You can say that again."

"Please don't let him drive home. So furious, and drunk besides, I'm really concerned."

"I'll take care of it, Helene."

Did Dad give me a bit of the fish eye there? "Nothing to worry about," I said. "I'll get the work done in plenty of time. Frank can be a pain in the ass. Just tell him to cool it, I'll talk to him later."

"You will call me later, then, dear? Let me know he's all right?"

"Absolutely. Tell Frank he can take it to the bank. Now, I've got to go—bye Helene. I love you."

"You are so sweet, dear, thank you. Goodbye."

I clicked END CALL, then slipped the phone back into its case on my hip. No question now, a clear fish eye from Dad. "Frank Riccardi, from my office," I said. "Far as he's concerned, a deadline goes down a week before it's due. He called Helene and bugged her about a program that's due from me next Friday."

"Hmmm." Dad drummed his fingers. He knew I was lying, but no way to prove it. Our old sweet song. "All taken care of," I said. "Go on. You were going to have Harmony's music box perfect by five o'clock."

Check, checkmate. Dad took a swallow, then started slowly, picking up speed as he went.

Yes, right. I could've worked on it right there at home but didn't want to miss a chance at Oscar's strongbox. I ran down to the basement, got a hacksaw and put it into a bag with the music box, Mr. Hogue's tools, and the lock I'd bought the day before. Then I hopped on my bike, pedaled off to the junkyard.

When I rode through the gate, George was negotiating with a skinny, angular man over two radios and a sewing machine. The man looked absolutely pissed, jabbing fingers in the air, stamping feet. I parked my bike against the office wall, walked toward George—and suddenly recognized the angry man. Red Dexter's raggedy friend, the one Harmony and I nearly ran down as we were trying to get away from Mr. Raskin, the druggist. "I no gotta do business with niggers," the man shouted. "Mr. Fleischmann gimme more money'n that." The man's tattered shirtsleeves fluttered like little flags as he pumped his arms.

George shrugged. "Okay. Murray 'n' Oscar be back later, talk to them." George turned, took a step away.

"Awright, awright," the man yelled. "I needa da money, I take."

"You sure?" George asked quietly.

"Gimme da money," the man shouted. "You say two-fifty, okay, I take two-fifty. My kids needa food real bad."

George reached into his pocket, peeled two bills off a small roll, then pulled out a handful of change and extracted a couple of quarters. The man took the money, stared at it as if the bills and coins themselves had insulted him, finally shoved the wad savagely into a pocket. Then he gave me a hard look, and jerked his head toward George. "Two and a half dolla' for two good radios and a sewin' machine." His red eyes were watery, hands shaking. He spat at George's feet. "Nigger and two kike-Jewmans, I lucky they don' jus' hit me over da head an' steal my stuff."

"You don't like it here, why don't you take your business someplace else?" I asked.

The man looked back at George, who smiled. "See ya, Aldo." The ragtag man nodded, shot me a withering look, then walked out the gate.

"Lucky Murray didn't hear you," George said quietly. "And Oscar...whoo. Think you had troubles with him before?"

"But what that guy said. What he was calling you—"

"Just parta the game, Leo. Hungry kids? *Aldo?*" George slapped a huge hand against his thigh, started laughing. "Ain't no kids, hungry or otherwise. What Aldo's got is the DTs comin' on. This neighborhood's fulla guys jus' like him. They call Murray or Oscar a cheap kike, say the nigger'd give better, so Murray or Os says fine, go talk to the nigger. Os'd probably even grab a piece of pipe an' start yellin' about how if the guy don't watch his mouth, there's gonna be guinea brains all over the yard. Or kraut brains, or spic brains, or Mick brains, or Polack brains. Just the way we talks around here. Nothin' personal."

"Like Miss Pussy," I said.

George went through a moment of uncertainty, then a big smile broke through. "That's *right*, Leo. Oscar calls you Miss Pussy, you're suppose' to say, 'Lookit who's talking, Mr.

Needleprick the Duckfucker.' Then you both go on wit' your business."

I looked around the yard. "They here? Murray and Oscar?"

"Went to make a pickup."

I don't think George played poker, or if he did, he didn't win much. His voice was casual but his face was dead-grim. This was no routine pickup, a refrigerator, stove, bathtub. I didn't say anything, just kept looking at George. He rubbed thumbs and forefingers together, then finally said one word. "Scrap."

"Something big?"

"Yeah." He pointed at the empty space near the fence where we'd sorted metal two days before. "That be full again this afternoon. Now stop askin' questions, go work on your music box…" Monkey business spread outward from the corners of his mouth. "Li'l Miss Pussy." He punched my arm lightly.

I knew he was waiting for me to say something like, "Okay, nigger, no ribs and beer for you today," but I couldn't, just could not force it out. I punched George's arm lightly, walked away. "Leo, why you always be such a *serious* boy?" he asked my back.

From the worktable, I could see George at the side of the office, fiddling with Aldo's radios. No way to sneak in. Later. I set myself to dampering. Pull pin, place wire, push pin back in, cut wire, shape it. After about half an hour I heard the truck, tried to ignore it, but the clattering of metal being tossed was more than I could resist.

I put down the comb and loupe, stood, stretched, then strolled around to the front of the office. Murray, Oscar and George were unloading sheets of shiny silver metal from the truck, piling them near the fence. By all rights the junkmen should've been struggling, but they picked up those giant panels easily, carried them as if they'd suddenly been endowed with superhuman strength. Oscar tossed a sheet onto the pile, turned, noticed me. A fat brown cigar dangled from his lower lip as if glued there. "Jesus fuckin' *Christ,*" he shouted.

The other men froze, then turned slowly. Oscar ripped his cigar from his mouth. "Every goddamn time I get myself in a good mood, I turn around and bingo, there's Shitface Miss Pussy. What do I gotta do to get rid of you, once and for all? Throw you the hell outa here on your little fairy ass?"

Murray moved toward Oscar. I caught the look on George's face. "*You* throw me out?" I snapped at Oscar. "Look who's talking big—Mr. Needleprick the Duckfucker. No wonder you don't know what to do with a pussy."

Murray started laughing. George's smile was for me alone. Oscar rammed the cigar back to the corner of his mouth, then growled, "You little turd, I'll mobilize you," but there was weakness in his tone, and he didn't move forward. I pointed at the cigar. "Turd yourself," I said. "What'd you do, put your clothes on upside down? I've talked to assholes before but never one that was taking a shit."

Murray and George both started yukking like Catskillers listening to Milton Berle. I felt disgusted. I'd never talked like that in my life, was horn-mad at myself for letting Oscar provoke me to it. But George was clearly right. Oscar got red as a clown's nose, spluttered, fumed, but made no move to attack. I looked at Murray. "Can I help you unload?"

Murray darted eyes in Oscar's direction. "Nah, this's easy stuff, no sweat. Go on back, do what you were doing. I'll come see how it looks when I'm done."

A few minutes after the clattering stopped, Murray waddled around the corner of the office building, head back, chugging a Coke. As he came up to the bench he lowered the bottle and let loose a monster belch, low, long, like a tuba solo. He nodded at the music mechanism, looked impressed. "You and Chet got it running, huh?"

"Yeah, me and Chet. He did it, I watched."

"Hey, Dockie—you hadn't brought it over to him and stood there, it wouldn'a ever got done, right? So you both did it. What was the matter, governor?"

I pointed to the critical screw. "Chet adjusted it here, just about a quarter-turn. To make the worm and first gear mesh right."

Murray shook his head. "I'll be go-to-hell. Guy can make any clock or music box run." He picked the comb off the table, studied it a moment, whistled. "Jeez, them dampeners—right on, every one. You do 'em, or Chet?"

"He did the first ten to show me how," I said. "I did the rest."

"God damn!" Murray held up the comb, squinted, wiggled it ever so slightly back and forth. "Can't see no difference between his and yours."

"One difference is, it took him five minutes to do ten. It's taken me four, five hours to do about forty."

Murray looked me hard in the eyes. "Dockie, gonna ask you a question. If it takes your old man a week to get a person fixed up, does anybody give a rat's ass about that week? A job takes however long it takes. Only thing matters is if it's done right. Kapeesh?"

As easily as Oscar could get my back up, Murray could put me in my place. He gave me a light smack on the back of my head. "Go on, Dockie, work on your job. I gotta do mine. Three more loads to pick up today."

"Business is good," I said.

"You ain't shittin'." Murray leaned forward, lowered his voice. "Business don't get much better'n four truckloads of aluminum..." He stopped suddenly, midsentence.

I picked up. "Aluminum—that's why you could lift it like it didn't weigh anything. And three more loads? Where's it coming from?"

Murray's high color faded. "Dockie, lemme tell you something, okay? What you just heard about aluminum is like when your old man hears something from a patient. He don't ever repeat it, not for nothing, not to nobody. So here's a very important thing—you didn't hear nothing about any aluminum, you didn't see no aluminum. You kapeesh about aluminum?"

"What aluminum?"

He looked confused but only for an instant. Then he laughed raucously. "You're okay, Dockie. Sometimes when you talk I think I'm hearing your old man."

If I didn't particularly like that—and I didn't—I had to admit there were advantages. The same way George told Dockie what he'd never say to Just Plain Leo, Murray slipped up, mentioned aluminum. And even though he caught himself instantly, the cat was still out.

I picked up the loupe, went back to work on the dampers. When I heard the truck drive off, I stood, then walked around the corner of the office to the front. George was struggling to drape a big tarp over the pile of aluminum. I ran over, took an edge. We covered the pile, weighted the corners with rocks. George looked at his watch. "Long day, three more loads coming. Be here probably 'til seven."

I thought about trying to get more information, but remembered Murray's warning. Instead, I asked George what he was going to do 'til the next load came in.

"Just donkey work." He grinned. "Nigger work. Sortin' out yesterday's stuff." He pointed at a disorderly heap of appliances, fabric, mattresses and wheels at the far side of the office. "You stay back there with your music box. Better if Os don't see you."

Kapeesh, I thought, and walked back to my worktable.

A while later, I heard the toilet flush inside the office. Not George—he was in clear view, pawing through yesterday's haul. And the truck hadn't come back, so it wasn't Murray or Oscar. Maybe they let Aldo use their bathroom. I picked up the roll of damper wire, kept working.

The truck rolled back in, motor cut out, doors slammed, one-two. Then I heard a voice I'd heard before, gravelly, strident. "Ho-ho, the Fleischmanns are prospering. Another load of metal for the Germans to make bullets out of? To fire into the bodies of your brothers?"

I turned, glanced at George. He rolled his eyes.

"Only brother I got's dead already." Murray. "Ez, get back to your *schul*, huh? Go say some nice prayers, or whatever the hell it is you do all day while honest men're tryin' to make a living."

Ez, Ezra Shnayerson. The man I heard chewing Murray out the night Samuel delivered Shannon's baby. I put down the music box comb, got up from the table, walked to the corner of the building, listened. "I heard a terrible thing," Shnayerson said. "Aluminum, what they use for building airplanes? What the Nazis and Japs can't get enough of, they'll pay a king's ransom? A carload of it vanished last night from the defense plant over on Ryle Road."

I held my breath during a brief silence. Then, "You like hearin' terrible things, Ez?" Murray again. "Well, here's one just for you." A fart, loud, fluttery. "Now I'm goin' inside, gonna use the pot, an' Ez, I swear, if you're still here when I come out, I'm gonna kick your holy ass the hell across the river into Emerson." Then I heard Murray stamp his way across the office. Slam went the door to the bathroom.

I edged my face around the corner of the building. The pile of aluminum was still covered, not a single shining piece of metal in sight. Another tarp hid the load on the pickup truck. Big, round Ezra Shnayerson, with his scraggly black beard, black suit and tie, black skullcap on his balding head, looked like one of those childrens' roly-poly knockdown toys. He jabbed a finger into Oscar Fleischmann's chest. "Oscar, you got to know the news." Bellowing like a bull at the end of a short chain with three cows in plain sight. "First from Rabbi Wise, now comes from Henry Morgenthau himself. Six thousand Jews killed every day, just in Poland alone. Death camps. They put Jews in ovens, in gas chambers. For a Jew to sell metal to the Nazis is more than treason, it's—"

"Shut the hell up, you old futz," Oscar roared back. The men looked like two angry bears, working themselves up to a pitched battle over a loaded garbage can. "Rockefeller makes a fortune in the last war and nobody says boo. Henry Kaiser, that pig, he gets fatter every day from every goddamn ship he sells, never mind half of them sink before they even get outa the harbor. You want to fuck with somebody, go fuck with Kaiser. The Jews in Germany and Poland are there, I'm here, an' that's just the way the goddamn world works. Anyway, who says we're sellin' stuff to the wrong people?"

While Oscar talked, two little girls on bicycles rode through the junkyard gate. One cut a turn a little too sharp on the hard-baked dirt. Her bike skidded sideways, she screamed, and down she went. I took off toward her, but surprise, Oscar was ahead of me. Ezra Shnayerson barked, "You want me to prove, I can prove," but he was talking to empty space.

Oscar dropped down on his knees over the little girl, crooned, "Hey, hey, honey. Don't cry, okay?" He stood her on her feet, looked over her arms and legs, then pulled off his red neckerchief and brushed dirt off her knees and elbows. "Hey, see, you're awright. Ain't even no blood." He tweaked her nose. The girl smiled tentatively. Oscar swabbed tears off her face. "Tell y' what." He put the neckerchief back on, reached into his pocket, came out with a coin. "Here's a dime. You and your friend there, go on over to Corry's, get an ice-cream cone." The girl's face lit. Her friend clapped her hands, jumped up and down. "Gee, thanks, Mister," the friend shouted. "Thank you," added the girl who'd fallen. She dropped the dime into a pocket on the front of her dress, then picked up her bicycle. "Ride them bikes careful," Oscar called after the girls. "Don't go gettin' hit by a car."

As the girls rode onto the sidewalk outside the gate, Oscar turned, saw me. "Jesus H. Christ, Miss Pussy! You really *are* a fuckin' bad penny, ain't you. Hey, you're always wantin' to learn somethin'—well, I just showed you how to get nice fresh young stuff, ain't nobody ever messed with it before an' left you a dose of clap. It'd work just as good for you with li'l boys."

I couldn't decide who was more disgusting, Oscar or Ezra Shnayerson, so wrapped up in his righteous indignation he couldn't manage to help a little girl who'd fallen off her bike. At that point, Murray strolled through the office doorway, fastening his belt buckle. He glared at Shnayerson. "God damn, Ez. You're still here."

"I'm not finished with what I have to say to you," Shnayerson rasped, but there was no wind in his sails. Oscar gave him a stern glance. Murray's expression was nothing less than dangerous. "You're done, all right," Murray growled. "You know where's the gate, the same one you came in through. Now get your fat ass out before I do what I said I was gonna, an' keep it out. I don't come fuckin' around in your synagogue, I don't want you fuckin' around in my junkyard. Kapeesh?"

Shnayerson tried to look dignified but he trudged away, a thoroughly whipped bear. "Can't stand that goddamn plaster saint," Murray muttered. "But hey, Dockie—music box comin' along okay?"

"Fine," I said. "I heard yelling, then a little girl screamed, so I came to see what was going on. I'll get back to work now."

"Yeah, us too." Murray clapped me on the shoulder. As I walked away, I heard him say to Oscar, "Maybe we oughta shut the gate, y'know? Least while we're unloading." A few seconds later the iron gate clanged.

Another three hours, two loads of aluminum later, I was finished with the music box. I could barely see straight, but not a squeak in "Sweet Bye and Bye," not a squawk in "Beautiful Dreamer," not a chirp in "Camptown Races." "Gaudeamus Igitur," clean and stately. "O Susanna," "Home Sweet Home," both perfect. I flashed back to Harmony's expression when I played the box in her basement the evening before, her smile after I kissed her over Jonas' grave. I swept Mr. Hogue's tools into the paper bag, picked up the music box, started for the gate.

Murray, Oscar and George were standing over the latest pile of aluminum, wiping their faces, drinking Cokes. Murray's eyes widened as he saw me, mouth bent into a grin. "All done, Dockie? Finished?"

I nodded. "Want to hear?

"Goddamn straight."

Oscar looked the other way, drank Coke, belched. I set the box on the ground in front of Murray, opened the lid, started music playing. Murray squatted, listened to the entire program, then stood and shook my hand gravely. "Successful operation, Young Doc Malone. Patient's alive and singing."

I thanked Murray, said goodbye to George, got onto my bike, pedaled up Wait Street. I was done with the music box, but my business at the junkyard was still unfinished. I'd need a new excuse to hang around, either that or pay the yard an off-hours visit. I thought of stopping to return the tools to Mr. Hogue, but it was already five o'clock, and Harmony's smile shone in my head like a beacon.

I rode straight home, parked my bike, followed a slow, soulful "I Can't Get Started" across the driveway and through the cellar doors, set the music box on the washing machine, turned it on. Harmony put down her sax and listened, eyes wide, lips slightly parted, barely breathing. Six tunes, not a word. When the music stopped, I asked, "Worth waiting another day for?"

"I love it." She took off her glasses, set them next to the sax, put her arms around my neck, kissed me. Briefer than the night before, but soft and on the lips, more than a thank-you. "I'll keep it in my room," she said. "Play it before I go to sleep every night. Oh, Leo…" Both arms around me again, a tight hug. "You worked on it all day?"

"All afternoon. I was hoping for a chance to sneak into the office and find out what Oscar's got in that strongbox. But someone was out front every minute."

She brushed hair away from her eyes. "Oscar? Strongbox? Leo, what're you talking about?"

"Didn't I tell you yesterday? About some sort of evidence Oscar says he's got on Samuel?"

"Not unless I forgot all about it."

She pulled free of my arms, reached for her glasses, slipped them back on, then listened like a cat at a mousehole while I told her about Oscar's threat, the strongbox in the desk drawer, and how I watched all afternoon for an opportunity that never knocked. When I held up the hacksaw and lock, she started to laugh. "Leo, you're such a dope sometimes. It's easy. We'll just go out again tonight, over the junkyard fence, into the office, take the box and maybe a few other little things so it looks like a robbery. Then we'll bring the box home and open it. Anything inside we shouldn't keep, like, say, money, we can wrap up and mail to Oscar from New York. We'll wear gloves all the time. He'll never be able to trace us."

Sounding like Nancy Drew, Girl Detective, but making a lot of sense. No razor wire on junkyard fences then, no alarm systems. Some junkyards had dogs, but Murray said dog food would cost more than they'd save on stolen merchandise, and he didn't want to be stepping in dogshit all day. It *would* be easy to go over the top, into the shack, grab the box…but wait a minute. "That strongbox is heavy. I could carry it, or pedal with it in my bike basket. But I'd never get it and me over the fence."

Didn't stop her for an instant. "Could you pitch it up and over the fence?"

I pictured myself swinging the strongbox back and forth, building momentum, finally letting go. I shook my head. "Fence's about ten feet high…hold on. At the gate, it's only eight feet, maybe a little less. I think I could manage that."

"Okay! I'll go back over first, make sure the coast is clear, and give you a whistle. You'll toss the strongbox, climb the fence, and we're on our way home to open it up. Bet we won't be at the junkyard more'n five minutes." She clutched the music box, looked lovingly at it, then at me. "You'd better sleep over…" Her lips moved, no words came, but then she managed, "Come hear how it sounds in my bedroom." Then she was gone, up the wooden stairs into the kitchen.

Back home, Ramona told me Samuel was at Steinberg, doing an emergency appendectomy. He didn't come in 'til after eight. All through dinner he went on about the stupidity of the surgical consultant who'd wanted to watch the patient overnight. "They'd have watched him straight down to the morgue," Samuel fumed. "His appendix was ready to blow. Another hour, he'd've had a belly full of pus, gone into shock." Samuel was like a bulldog with a bone who doesn't notice that no other dogs are trying to take away his prize. Finally over cake and coffee, I broke. "What if you'd been wrong?" I asked. "After a surgical specialist said wait. What if you'd gone in and operated, and it *wasn't* the appendix?"

Ramona slammed down her spoon. "Leo!"

I don't think Samuel even noticed. He was up from the table like a shot, down to his library, back within seconds carrying three books: Chambers' *Textbook of Surgery*, Martin's *Handbook of Pathology*, Adams' *Advanced Differential Diagnosis*. He set them on the table, opened them, motioned me to his side. By all three references, his forty-two-year-old patient represented a classic case of acute appendicitis, with nausea, vomiting, constipation, low-grade fever, pain gradually localizing to McBurney's point on the lower right abdomen, abdominal rigidity and rebound tenderness, and an elevated white blood cell count. Rupture of the appendix is a virtual death sentence, Dr. Chambers declared in bold italics. Therefore, a doctor is to be condemned, not congratulated, if every patient he operates on for appendicitis does in fact have the disease, because without doubt many of his unoperated patients died of appendiceal rupture.

I must have read those goddamn sentences ten times before I could make myself look up. Samuel's face was chiseled, all sharp edges, early-evening golden stubble over his chin and cheeks. "Well, Leo?"

I nodded. "But if it was so obvious, why did you call a consultant, then not listen to his advice?"

"I did listen," Samuel said. "I just didn't take it because it was wrong. And *I* didn't call him. That idiot Carlisle's the last surgeon I'd ever call into a case, but the patient's wife wanted a second opinion and her neighbor told her Carlisle talks to God every morning before he makes rounds. I told the family they could go with Carlisle's advice or mine, or they could get a third opinion, by which time it'd probably be too late to do any good. The patient finally gave the go-ahead, said he was in so much pain he'd rather die fast on the operating table than slowly in his room. He'll be fine, though. Take him a few weeks, but he'll recover."

My father was Babe Ruth, pointing his bat toward the bleachers for all to see, then hitting a home run. But the Babe did it only once, and quit while he was ahead. Samuel did it every time he came to bat, upping the ante with every pitch. *"Go for eight!'"*

"All right," I said quietly.

He gathered up the books. I was just about to excuse myself to go to Harmony's when the phone rang in the kitchen. Samuel leaped from his chair, ran inside, rushed back within a minute. "A *stat* over at County," he barked, then charged into the living room, grabbed his Panama off the back of the chair where he'd thrown it when he came in. "Come on, Leo. Move it!"

Chapter 14

"County?" I asked.

Dad nodded. "Passaic County Hospital for the Insane and Mentally Retarded—great big ugly gray stone building behind a twelve-foot iron picket fence. When I was a kid, the goddamn place always gave me creeps. Half of me wanted to run like hell, the other half had a mind to tiptoe up to the door and snoop around inside."

Dad sipped Manhattan, swallowed with a harsh "Ahh," then turned eyes on me as haunted as the old P.C.H.

I couldn't tell Samuel I had other plans for the night, certainly not the plans I happened to have. Couldn't say I was tired, sick, or anything else. I took a step toward the phone to give Harmony a quick call, but Samuel shouted, "Leo, come *on.*" He already had the front door open. "Didn't you hear me say *stat?* That's an emergency, right?"

I turned around, followed Samuel outside and into the Plymouth. We were half a block down Roosevelt before I got the car door shut. "Four-year-old with congenital hydrocephalus," Samuel shouted. "Blocked cerebrospinal fluid, head like a giant water balloon, brain crushed flat before she was ever born. Most babies like that die during birth or right after, but this one was born by Cesarean and she's still here. No higher brain function, seizures more or less controlled with phenobarb and a ketogenic diet, but she's gone into status epilepticus, one convulsion right on top of the last one. If we can't stop them, she'll die."

I took a moment to think about that. "Samuel," I said, slow as a Mississippi senator. "You said she has no higher brain function. She's a veg..." I caught myself on the brink. "She's permanently unconscious?"

"Think of it as nonconscious. Never been conscious, never will be, never can be. And what you're really asking me is—"

I wasn't going to let him put my question for me. "I'm asking why the emergency? Why we shouldn't just let her go."

"Does the Hippocratic Oath make any provision for that? Does the law of the land?"

A street lamp momentarily illuminated Samuel's face. Was that a little smile at the corner of his mouth, or a grimace of pain? Or was it just my imagination? "How about the law of human decency?" I said, very softly. "Or the law of common sense."

Samuel turned his head my way, and now, no question, he *was* smiling. "Good, Leo," he said. "I'm proud of you."

What an operator. The sincerity and respect in those six words melted my heart. "I think you're beginning to get it," he said. "Watch, when we get there. Listen."

We rode all the way out McBride Avenue, past the Veterans' Hospital. On a huge boulder out front, white letters glowed in moonlight, and if the painting job was clumsy, uneven letters with drip lines, the message was clear, V-USA. One block short of West Hobart, Samuel parked at the curb. I followed him past an iron picket gate, up a concrete walkway. Dark. A breeze came off the river, through Peterson Park, and as a towering oak tree to our left creaked and groaned, I ducked away as if from a punch.

Samuel put a hand on my shoulder. "First time at County's tough. Just don't try to pretend any of it's not real."

A guard in a gray uniform opened the front door, greeted Samuel with a deferential nod. "Doc."

Samuel pumped the man's hand. "Doin' all right, Clarence?"

Clarence was in his early seventies, thin white hair combed straight back, cheeks faux-rouged, probably a severe hypertensive. Once, he might've been a tough cookie, but a huge bay window suggested stein-lifting was the most exercise he'd taken for a long while. He stared, straight-faced, at Samuel. "Right's a person can be in this place, Doc."

Our shoes on the marble floor of the long hallway made us sound like horses. We stepped into an unstaffed elevator. Samuel pulled the inner cage-door closed, then pushed a black button with a barely visible gold *3*. The outer door slid shut. I wondered whether Samuel could hear my heart. The ancient elevator clanked and grunted. I tried to steel myself against what was coming.

As we got off the elevator I choked, gagged. Urine, stool, disinfectant, unwashed bodies—how did people work eight-hour shifts here, day after day? Samuel glanced at me, stopped just long enough to say, "Get hold of yourself." I nodded, followed him down the corridor.

From both sides of the hallway came moans, groans, cries, shrieks. Mostly inarticulate, but as we went past one room I heard, "Help me, nurse. Nurse, help me. Help me, nurse. Nurse, help me." From another room, "*Yahhhh,* they're on my face, they're on my *face!*" Rats, bugs? Hallucinations? I hoped so.

I hurried after Samuel, into a room near the end of the corridor. A round nurse with Dutch-pageboy hair stepped away from the crib, looked at Samuel as if he embodied the Second Coming. "Oh, Dr. Firestone, she just won't stop seizing."

Samuel was to the bedside. "Let's see what we can do."

I bent around him to get a clear view of the patient. Tiny body, lost in an adult-sized hospital gown, legs and arms like sticks, every bone visible beneath thin, bluish-white skin. An intravenous bottle dripped fluid into the right arm. Face shadowed below a gigantic dome, scalp stretched to the limit, hair reduced to small scattered tufts. Veins ran across the bulging forehead like long blue worms. A blood-stained tongue blade rested between colorless lips. Worst were the eyes, wandering here, there, jerking one way as the trunk and limbs tightened, then another as the body relaxed. I struggled to accept this as a human being, a little girl. Stick a needle into that head, I thought, and pop, gallons of fluid would blast in every direction. Then I noticed tiny pink and white scars and a few fresh scabs over the cranium, and realized they *did* stick needles into the head, to drain fluid. I found myself gripping the bed rail for support.

Samuel lowered the rail, then called my name, a little sharply I thought. "Leo—open the bag. Let's give her some Amytal. If it works, it'll work fast."

I threw the catch, held the big black bag out to Samuel. He took a syringe and needle, then drew fluid from a small brown vial and injected it into the intravenous tubing. Arms, legs, gigantic head kept right on jerking and twitching. He might as well have injected saline.

I scanned the room, saw no phone. Not that I could've made the call I needed to make from there. I caught the nurse's eye. "Men's room?"

An odd mixture of compassion and contempt came over her face. "Down the hall past the elevator, on your left."

"Be right back," I muttered, then rushed down the hall through stinking air. Screams, wails, howls from every direction. Past the elevator, past the mens' room, no phone anywhere. Almost ten-thirty. If I was going to call Harmony, I needed to do it then. Any later, I'd wake Dr. Belmont, who'd want to know why on earth I was calling at that hour. No time to take the elevator down to the lobby, hunt up a telephone, make my call, get back. Nurses' station...yes, there was a phone on the counter. I told the elderly nurse behind the desk I was Dr. Firestone's summer extern, asked permission to use the phone. She turned a look on me that would've stopped a train. "Only if it's official business, no personal calls. I'll be listening to every word you say." I turned away, and damned if the old gargoyle didn't get up and walk out of the station into the hallway, then stand, hands on hips, glaring. I felt her eyes on me every step back to the little hydrocephalic's room.

As I walked in, Samuel was pulling off rubber gloves. "Amytal didn't work; neither did phenobarb or a spinal tap." He dropped the gloves onto an open, used procedures tray, then raised an eyebrow at the nurse. "Better call the parents."

The nurse looked dubious. "You want them to come in?"

"Sure." Samuel looked anything but dubious.

The nurse glanced at me, left the room. The little girl's respirations slowed, deepened. Then came a massive seizure. Arms and legs flexed violently, flew outward, flexed again. The head jerked from one side to the other; eyes bounced like small boats on a heavy sea. As Samuel went for his bag, the convulsion stopped abruptly. A finger twitched, then the jaw bounced open, and the tiny figure lay still, eyes staring blindly at the ceiling. "That's it," I whispered.

Samuel's response stupefied me. "God *damn!*" He grabbed a clean syringe from his bag, a long needle, and a small rubber-capped vial. "Adrenaline." Like an invocation. He ripped away the hospital gown, plunged the needle through the child's chest. Dark red fluid swirled through the pale yellow adrenaline in the syringe. "We're in the ventricle," Samuel muttered, then emptied the contents of the syringe. He touched the side of the child's neck, shook his head. "No pulse." Then he began to pump at the chest, every now and again stopping just long enough to puff air through the gaping mouth.

The nurse walked back into the room, went instantly pale. "Leo, do what I'm doing, exactly the way I'm doing it," Samuel snapped. "Right index and middle fingers over the left, down once a second, not too sharply."

Samuel checked the neck again, shook his head, then applied his mouth to the little girl's. I brought my fingers by degrees to the chest, started pumping, one-and-two-and-three-and-four… The child's skin was cold and clammy. I told myself I was doing an exercise on a wax doll, then remembered Samuel's warning. *Don't try to pretend any of it's not real.* Every sixty seconds, Samuel signaled for me to stop so he could palpate for a jugular pulse. On the fourth cycle, his face lit. "Feel it, Leo."

I put a shaking finger to the side of the neck. Pulse, slow and thready, but definitely there. As if to put to rest any doubts, the misshapen head began to jerk side-to-side again. Limbs twitched relentlessly. "Got 'er running," Samuel said.

I couldn't say a word. What in the service of hell had we just done? That poor little wreck finally managed to escape, but Samuel Firestone, M.D., didn't like to lose, so we brought her back to shake and twitch some more. Samuel looked at the nurse. "Let's get her cleaned up, new gown, fresh blanket. Leo, put the syringes, needles and meds back in the bag. I'll autoclave them later."

The nurse and I did as he said. All the while, Samuel didn't take his fingers off the little girl's neck.

Twenty minutes later, a man and woman rushed through the doorway. The man was about forty, gaunt, with unruly black hair, hollow cheeks and a pointed chin. The woman was more generously proportioned, full face framed by a cascade of dark curls, all the more attractive for its middle-of-the-night wildness. Dark eyes broadcast concern and dread. One step into the room, the woman picked up speed, ran to the bedside, leaned to cradle the huge head against her chest. "Carlita," she murmured. "My baby." The man stood next to her. He seemed unsure of what to do with his hands.

"I'm Dr. Firestone," Samuel said quietly. "I look after the children here. I talked to you last year."

"Yes, I remember." Without letting go of the little girl, the mother nodded vigorously. "Was when Carlita got sick. She got troubles again now?"

"I'm sorry, she does." Samuel's tone was soft, solemn. "Carlita's having seizures, one on top of the other. No way to stop them."

I'd still bet today the parents and nurse heard only resignation in Samuel's voice, but I picked up on the bitterness in each of the last five words. The mother looked up at him. "She's going to…die?"

Samuel took his hand off Carlita's neck, rested it on the mother's shoulder. "This is her time."

The tenderness in his voice brought me to the edge of tears. The woman began to cry silently. Her husband bit on his lower lip. Samuel pointed toward the edge of the bed. "Sit down." He bent, lifted Carlita into her parents' laps, head cradled in the crook of her mother's arm. "My baby, my baby," the woman crooned. "Ever'thing's all right. Mommy and Daddy're here."

The young nurse's white face bloomed into a rose. She turned away. Carlita's father leaned toward the child's ear, murmured words I couldn't hear. All the while, he held the twitching stick-like legs absentmindedly in both hands. The mother went on cooing and telling Carlita she was going to be fine, nothing to worry about, but after a few minutes I noticed she was no longer convulsing. The father's face told me he knew what had happened, but the mother kept reassuring her baby, moving a loving hand back and forth across her head. Samuel touched the woman's arm, whispered, "She's gone."

The mother looked up, startled, then gazed at the still body in her lap. She relaxed her arm. Carlita's head lolled. The mother reclaimed it, then looked back at Samuel, eyes shining. "She jus' slipped away, so quiet." The woman's voice firmed. "But she knew I was here, I could tell. Don't you think she knew I was here, Doaktor?"

I held my breath. What reasonable answer could Samuel give? But he didn't hesitate. Like a natural athlete, all reflexes, getting to a ball that by every right should've been unplayable. "You're her mother, Mrs. Consuegra," he said slowly. "If you think she knew, no one can say she didn't." As he talked, he took Carlita from her parents, laid her gently on the bed, asked whether they wanted to stay longer with her. Mrs. Consuegra looked at her husband; he shook his head. "No, t'ank you." Mrs. Consuegra sounded surprisingly steady. "She gone, we go too. But we can have a funeral for her, yes?"

"Sure," Samuel said. "Quinn's, over on Eleventh Av, gives a free service for children who die here. You'll only have to pay for the cemetery plot. Want us to call them?"

The couple had a brief, silent consultation, then Mrs. Consuegra turned back to Samuel. "Yes, please. You do that."

"I'll take care of it." The nurse, back to functioning.

Mr. Consuegra said a quiet, "T'ank you, Doaktor," while his wife, crying soundlessly, worked Samuel's hand like a motorist trying to get air into a flat tire. "Yes, Doaktor, t'ank you so much. I'm so happy I got here in time to say good-bye to my Carlita. If she die' wit'out me, she'd'a been scared real bad. All my life, I remember you for this, Doaktor."

Samuel didn't say a word, just smiled and let the woman go on pumping. But the nurse spouted, "The doctor kept your little girl alive 'til you got here. When her heart stopped, he started it up again."

Mrs. Consuegra looked at Samuel the way the crowd must've regarded Jesus when Lazarus stretched his muscles. "I knew you'd want to tell her good-bye," he said, very lightly. "I'm glad it worked."

No need to blow your own horn when someone else is blowing it so brilliantly for you, and Samuel's dismissive manner seemed only to increase the intensity of the spotlight on him. He led the couple to the door, gently ushered them out, then came back inside. "All set?" he said lightly to the nurse.

"All set," she repeated, then added, "Dr. Firestone, that was wonderful. I couldn't understand why you were resuscitating that poor thing, but…"

The nurse's comments seemed to irritate Samuel. He picked up his bag, said a clipped "Thanks," then started toward the door. I followed him out of the room, down the hall, but at the next doorway he pulled up short. "Some people I want you to meet." Then he grabbed my elbow and yanked me into the room.

In the dim light, our shadows fell across two cribs. Samuel pointed at the sleeping child in the crib to the right, a boy of about three or four with coarse facial features and light spiky hair. He breathed slowly, deeply. Even in the poor light I could see how white his cheeks were. "Mongolism," Samuel whispered. "Lovable, but mentally retarded, very clumsy. Mongoloids have a high risk for congenital heart abnormalities and leukemia; this boy's got both. Won't be with us much longer." He led me to the other crib, where a child maybe a year old moved restlessly, every now and then making an odd sound like a cat's meow. Its head was small, tiny compared to Carlita's, with a sloping forehead. "Undiagnosable severe mental retardation," Samuel said. "Might live another day, a month, or twenty years."

Samuel turned, then walked out of the room. I thought we were finished, but no. We'd only just begun. I followed him from room to room, each chamber of horrors worse than the last. Damaged children, like exhibits in some ghastly museum, whimpering, wailing, throwing their arms and legs about, dreaming of what I couldn't begin to imagine. Samuel laid his hand on the troubled ones, patted them, stroked them. The smell was unbearable. "Can't be helped," Samuel said as he saw me wrinkle my nose. "Only three nurses to take care of fifty children."

"The war?"

Samuel shook his head. "That's what they'll tell you. But there weren't any more nurses here before the war. These kids don't have much influence at County Council meetings."

A little boy sitting crosslegged on his bed stared curiously at us as we walked in. "Hello, Alex," Samuel said. "Staying up late tonight?"

The boy looked like a miniature Gandhi, bald head, wizened face. He nodded slowly, as if whether to answer and how were major uncertainties. "Anything hurting?" Samuel asked.

"No. I just don't want to sleep." The weary, piping voice of a petulant geezer. I looked more closely. *Was* this a child?

"Alex, this is Dr. Leo," Samuel said. "He's learning to be a doctor."

The little man turned a weak smile on me, then slowly raised a withered arm and grasped at my hand. "Pleased to meet you," I said, and for just an instant his smile widened. As it faded, he pulled back his hand. We left him staring into the distance.

Out in the hall, Samuel said, "Alex is here because he's a bit...backward." Devastating scorn in the word. "His condition's called progeria. For some reason, all the aging processes go wild, right from the day of birth. Poor kid's only twelve, but he's got severe arthritis, coronary heart disease, all the things that are supposed to go wrong when you're seventy. He won't be around much longer, either."

In the next room, a horribly deformed dwarf, more than a hundred fractures all over his body. Didn't dare touch him; I'd break another bone. Samuel led me past him to the second crib. "This one's a little tough."

I gasped, gagged. A small baby, not much past newborn, lay on the bed. Where the navel should've been, a mass of intestines bulged and writhed through a clear, thin membrane. Wide red clefts ran up from each lip toward a single, central eye; above that eye, a tiny rudimentary proboscis of a nose. Samuel put a hand on my back. I jumped. "Cyclops monstrosity," he said. "Don't usually live past birth, but some hang on a little while. This one's three days old."

I thought I'd seen the ultimate, but Samuel wasn't through. He marched me into the next room, and as we came up to the single crib, every hair I owned stood on end. I grabbed Samuel's arm with both my hands, tried to look away, couldn't. By comparison, the cyclops was a beauty queen. This poor creature was hairless, skull indented here, protruding there. Left eye rudimentary, right eye bulging. Mouth twisted, nose an irregular blob. No hands. No left leg, a stump on the right. In all the other children I could make out an underlying order, nature's processes disturbed but still perceptible through the malformations. But this came across as random damage, as if a particularly malevolent demon had amused itself by touching the baby here, there, wherever, cackling all the while at its production of devastation and horror. "Samuel—" I began, but stopped as the child shifted, raised its right arm, extended the stump toward us, and made a ghastly groaning noise like a cry for help from the deepest pit in hell. I tried to talk, tried a second time, a third. Finally I managed a whispered, "Samuel, why are you doing this to me?"

In that dark room, his eyes blazed. He put a hand to my shoulder, moved me through the doorway, out into the corridor, against the wall. His face bent into a terrible smile. "These children, Leo—they had the bad luck to come off the production line on Friday afternoon or Monday morning. We hide them away here because they remind us too well what a God-damned bunch of long-term birth defects we all are, out of warranty from the moment we leave the factory. Our hearts fail, our livers, our kidneys. We go deaf and blind. Cancers blast through our bodies like Sherman's troops through Atlanta. We get diabetes, rheumatic fever, hypertension, lupus, cerebellar ataxia, multiple sclerosis. And doctors are God's licensed maintenance men, under contract to keep His cheesy merchandise operating. I want you to understand that. Will you remember walking through this place with me at one o'clock in the morning? Will you?"

I can still retrace that night, Martin, step by step, see every disfigured face and distorted body. "I'll remember," I said, then added, very softly, "Now, please can't we go home?"

Samuel blinked, then suddenly put his arms around me. "Sure, Leo. I'm sorry."

Not sorry he'd brought me there, that wasn't what he meant. I saw my own pain reflected in his eyes, and an overpowering wave of sympathy washed over me. In that instant I felt closer to my father than at any other time in my life. Just a flash, but if those moments lasted any longer they'd burn us to cinders.

We sat silent in the Plymouth as Samuel drove home, more slowly than usual. A thought occurred to me. "Samuel?"

"What's that?" Unusual calmness in his voice.

"Didn't you once tell me there's a lot of T.B. in county hospitals?"

"Yes, but don't worry. To catch it you need closer exposure than just walking into a room and looking at a patient."

Was he being obtuse, or playing a game? "How about mouth-to-mouth resuscitation?"

A smile took root, grew. "That would be more dangerous, yes."

A game, then, but what kind of game? Did Samuel think the contract he'd signed granted him some kind of immunity? Then it hit me—he *didn't* sign that contract. No limited license for Samuel Firestone, M.D.! I could see him reading the offer, fury mounting at every line, until he crumpled the paper, flung it into the face of the Writer, and stormed away to spend his life daring, double-daring, triple-daring. *"Go for eight."* Sure, he knew he was vulnerable, otherwise why even bother trying to get that eighth ball in the air? Now I understood how my father could do an abortion in the morning, then that same night go to the furthest extreme to keep a hydrocephalic child alive long enough for her parents to tell her goodbye.

Chapter 15

Loud crash behind us. Someone in the kitchen must've dropped a tray of dishes and glassware. Dad nearly sent our table over into my lap. He shook his head, swallowed a handful of cheese and grapes, sent the food on its way with a gulp of Manhattan, then began to speak rapidly, as if he didn't dare hesitate for fear of stopping altogether.

Past two o'clock by the time Samuel steered the Plymouth into our driveway. Lights on all over the house, something up. Ramona in her bathrobe met us two steps into the kitchen, pupils wide, hands shaking at her sides. She glanced from Samuel to me. "Leo, go upstairs."

She needed to go upstairs, was obviously late for her appointment with a needle. I held my ground. After that visit to County I was ready for anything. Samuel said, "Ramona…" in a tone that added, "Spit it out!"

Ramona's jaw twitched. She shivered like someone with a sudden high fever. "Get over, fast…" She aimed a shaking finger vaguely toward the door, then redirected it toward the Belmonts'. "Harmony's in the Steinberg E.R., someone beat her up. I tried to get you at County, but you'd left—"

Samuel and I must've looked like two soldiers, about-face! Ramona's fluttery voice came at my back. "Leo…*Leo*. You shouldn't go."

I paced Samuel to the Plymouth. We flew down Roosevelt to the Steinberg, tore out of the car, into the emergency room. A nurse led us to a treatment cubicle. As Samuel rushed in, Dr. and Mrs. Belmont caught sight of him and thanked God extravagantly. Laura, Harmony's sister, fired me a look that said, "What are *you* doing here?" I didn't answer, just stared at Harmony, motionless on a wheeled stretcher, eyes taped shut, sheets bloodstained.

At the far side of the gurney, Ernie DeNooyer, one of the senior E.N.T. men, pumped air from a black rubber bag through a trach tube in Harmony's throat. Two techs were going double-time, setting up a pulmotor…

"Martin, what's the matter?"

"Nothing." I shook my head. "Just your story. Go on."

Dad stared at me for a few seconds, popped a grape, then started talking again.

DeNooyer stepped away to let one of the techs attach the breathing machine to Harmony's trach. "Brought her in, oh, half an hour ago," DeNooyer said. "Unconscious, unresponsive. Extensive trauma, head, trunk, limbs. Collapsed right lung. We're getting total body X-rays; O.R.'s setting up."

Harmony's chest rose and fell slowly in rhythm with puffs from the pulmotor. Samuel scanned her body, head to feet. He listened to her lungs, heart, abdomen, tapped joints with his rubber hammer. Then he straightened, looked at the nurse. "Get a spinal tray."

The nurse ran from the room. Samuel rolled up his sleeves, took a step toward the sink. "Called a neurosurgeon?" he asked DeNooyer.

"Bentley. He's on his way."

Mid-scrub, Samuel half-turned, gave me a hard look. "Go on home, Leo," he said. "We left Ramona pretty upset."

I figured my mother had already calmed herself with a syringe and needle, but I couldn't say that to Samuel, certainly not in front of a room full of people. As I walked toward the door, Mrs. Belmont motioned me over, gave me a quick hug, then a pat on the arm. "Say a prayer, dear," she twittered.

I spat "Say a prayer!" all over the six blocks back home, threw the front door open, stamped into the empty living room, ran upstairs. Ramona's door was closed. I edged it ajar. My mother lay across the bed, syringe and needle still in her outstretched right hand. Now I understood—Samuel hadn't dismissed me. Stuck in the Steinberg E.R., he'd put me in charge of a second emergency. I ran to the bedside, put fingers to Ramona's wrist. Pulse slow, only fifty-two, but strong. She was breathing eight times a minute, half-normal. Call an ambulance? Not yet. Keep her airway clear, monitor vital signs. Might not have to hang out our dirty laundry for all Hobart to see.

About six o'clock, Samuel pulled into the room. He looked ravaged. "Pulse's up from fifty-two to sixty-eight," I said. "Respiratory rate, fourteen, up from eight. She's...all right." I choked on the last two words.

Samuel brightened just a bit. "Good man!" He motioned toward the door. "Let's get out of here before she wakes up."

Over breakfast he told me bad news. "Somebody just beat hell out of Harmony—fractured skull, massive intracranial hemorrhage, broken ribs, punctured lung, fractured left femur. They found her under the railroad trestle where it goes over the river near Fourth Avenue. What was she doing there after one o'clock in the morning?"

I decided to treat the question as rhetorical, shrugged casually.

Samuel struck like a snake. Hand zipped across the table, grabbed my shirt at the throat, yanked me to my feet. "That riverbank's just a few blocks away from Fleischmann Scrap! You were supposed to be there too, weren't you? But you were with me, so you couldn't make it. What were the two of you up to?" For punctuation he gave a nasty twist at my shirt collar.

Set a thief to catch a thief. Samuel knew a liar when he faced one. But after sixteen years as his son, I was pretty good myself. I stared at him for a couple of seconds, then said, very calmly, "Samuel, I've got no idea why she was down there. Please let go of my shirt."

He released his hold slowly, as if ratcheting down tension in his fingers. Then, just as slowly, he settled back into his chair. "I'm sorry, Leo. Been a long night." I could barely hear him. "I want to find out who beat up that poor girl, and I thought, close as the two of you are, you might know something."

Where intimidation fails, try stealth. But this was going to be my investigation, not his. Just as quietly as he'd spoken, I said, "I'm sorry. I don't."

Whether or not he believed me, I think he knew that was as far as he could take matters right then. He shook his head, pushed away his half-eaten bowl of cereal. "We drained intra-cranial blood, relieved pressure on her brain, then decompressed her chest, and set fractures. All we can do for now. Go get some sleep, Leo; I'm going to grab a couple of hours myself. We're in for a long haul."

When I woke out of one nightmare into a worse one, the clock on the table next to my bed said ten minutes after twelve. Five hours in the sack. I felt as if my muscles had been pounded with mallets. I got up, stood a while under a warm shower, then shaved and went downstairs. Ramona sat at the kitchen table, staring out the window. She looked composed, probably had just fortified herself again. "Any news?" I asked.

She started as if I'd shouted boo. "Oh—Leo. No, dear, noth-ing. Samuel called about an hour ago and said there's been no change. I just can't understand, neither can the Belmonts. What on earth was Harmony doing down there by the river in the middle of the night?"

Were she and my father working a tag team on me? "I don't know, Ramona," I said, and hoped the anguish in my voice came across to her as grief, not shame and guilt.

"You and she were so close—"

"Ramona, I don't *know.*"

She jumped to her feet. "Oh, Leo—I'm sorry. It's just that I'm…we're all so upset. Let me fix you an omelet."

She was cracking eggs before I could say yes or no. I wasn't hungry, but watching her whip up an omelet was better than trying to parry questions. I ate in silence, then went outside, walked up Roosevelt to the Steinberg, checked at Information. They'd moved Harmony out of the E.R., to a room on the second floor.

Dr. and Mrs. Belmont were there, talking to Samuel. Without her huge glasses, her eyes under tape, Harmony looked strange. Her only movements were still the rhythmic rise and fall of her chest in response to the pulmotor. Samuel looked surprisingly fresh but not pleased. "Touch and go, Leo," he said. "Blood pressure's low—I'm giving her ephedrine now, already tried coramine and pituitrin. Brain waves look flat, but the lung hasn't collapsed again. Just have to keep her going long enough that she's got a chance to come back."

"Thank you, Samuel." Fielding Belmont's voice was gruff. A tear rolled down his cheek. "I can't tell you—"

"You'd do the same for me," Samuel said, and though every person in the room knew that wasn't so, it seemed to settle the matter. Then Samuel went off to see a pre-op patient. He wasn't two steps around the corner before Dr. Belmont asked me The Question. "Leo, I can't for the life of me imagine what Harmony was doing down by the river at one o'clock in the morning. Do you know?"

I shook my head.

No longer a clear-cut lie. I'd begun to wonder whether Harmony really did go on her own after Oscar's strongbox. To get to the yard she'd have gone down Roosevelt, across Madison or Twenty-second, then down Fifth and under the trestle, right to the front gate. Bums slept under that trestle at night, and if one or two of them were awake, they might've tried to rob or assault her. But if so, why did they drag her all the way past the junkyard to the Fourth Avenue riverbank?

A little later, a couple of detectives took me into the hall to ask whether I could help find the person who did such a terrible thing to my friend. "Everyone says you and she were best pals," the shorter, bald, blue-suited cop said, implying that if I hadn't been with Samuel every minute the night before, I'd've been their prime suspect. I answered with a nod, then waited for what I knew was coming next.

"You got any idea what your girlfriend was doing down there at one A.M.?" This from the taller detective, a man in a brown suit, fedora to match. Scar at the left side of his mouth. His tone implied I was going to lie and he knew it. Maybe that usually worked for him, but not this time. "I'm sorry," I said. "I don't have any idea. And…"

They both leaned forward.

"She was…*is* my friend, my best friend. But she's not my girlfriend."

They exchanged a glance. The tall detective shrugged. "You *have* a girlfriend?"

"No girlfriend."

The shorter man laughed lightly. "That's good. You're not old enough to be having girlfriends. But your friend in there—"

"Harmony," I said.

"Yeah. Harmony. Miss Belmont. She didn't say anything to you, nothing at all? About why she might be going down by the river in the middle of the night?"

"No, I've told you. Not a word."

"She ever do that before?"

"Not that I know of. I don't know why she would."

"All right." Tall cop again. "You don't have a girlfriend, but maybe she had a boyfriend? Somebody she went out to meet when her parents were asleep?"

The word "impossible" ripped through my mind, but slammed right into Number Two on the Samuel Firestone List of Certainties in Life, the entry directly behind Trust Only Yourself. Nothing Is Impossible. But Harmony and I told each other *everything*. She was my friend...*no*, goddamn it, *not* just my friend. She was my...

Dad paused, looked away, squeezed his hands together, then turned back to me, face disfigured with torment.

"My soulmate, Martin. She was the only person I could ever call my soulmate."

Dad's face relaxed. For better or worse he'd finally gotten it out. No request for approval in his gaze, but I reached across the table, rested a hand on his. He jerked away, then pulled himself straight in his chair. Before he could go on, I asked, "Did you ever tell Mother about Harmony?"

"No, never. By the time I met your mother, I was long gone from Hobart, living in New York. I left it behind, left all of Hobart behind. If I'd started telling your mother about Harmony... Your mother and I have made a good life together, Martin. She's a great lady. All the shit she puts up with from me..."

Dad picked up his glass, drained Drink Six. The waiter sidled up, censure on his face thick as hasty pudding. He picked up Dad's empty glass as if it might be contaminated, then without moving his lips whispered, "Another Manhattan, sir?"

I answered. "Enough." Dad didn't object. The waiter about-faced, marched away.

Dad tapped fingers on the table. "I hoped time would let Harmony drift away, but..."

He didn't finish the thought, didn't have to.

That detective's question about whether Harmony might've been going out to meet a boyfriend hit my stomach like a shot, but they didn't seem to notice. "If she had a boyfriend I didn't know about it," I said. "If she went out at night I didn't know. I just *don't know.*"

"That's all right, son." The short detective patted my back. "I'm sure if you knew anything that'd help us find whoever did that to your friend, you'd tell us." He looked and sounded like a kindly uncle, but the tall detective watched me like a heron poised at water's-edge. Just let that fish make one wrong move.

"Yes," I said. "I would."

Toward mid-afternoon, Dr. Belmont went home to take a nap, and that triggered an idea. I asked Mrs. Belmont's permission to go to her house and get the music box. She said yes, of course, so back up Roosevelt I walked, into the Belmont house, past Laura sulking on a living room sofa, upstairs to Harmony's room, back out with the music box, back to the hospital. I set the music box on the little night-table next to Harmony's bed, pulled on the winding lever, started it playing. Not three notes into the tune, I realized—"Beautiful Dreamer." No way to stop it before the end of the tune. That's the way music boxes work. "Beautiful dreamer," that damn box played, "wake unto me. Starlight and dewdrops are waiting for thee."

Mrs. Belmont's face brightened. "Oh," she said. "I know that," and began to hum along. "Dee-duh-duh-dee-duh. Dee-duh-duh-duh—" Right there she choked, gave me a look I don't ever want to see again, let out the most horrible scream, then flew out of the chair and out of the room. I heard her high-heeled shoes clack all the way down the hall.

"Beautiful Dreamer" finished, then "Camptown Races" played, doo-dah, doo-dah, then "Gaudeamus Igitur." Not a twitch from Harmony, not the slightest sign of recognition. Strips of tape over her eyes. My hand reached out, jumped back, inched forward again. I pulled off the tape, pushed up her eyelids…and just wanted to die. Harmony wasn't there. Those dazzling green eyes were dead things now, uncoupled, drifting and jerking like fishermens' bobbers on the surface of a lake, oblivious to the music, unconscious of me.

Icy water poured through my skin, covered my arms. I managed to close Harmony's eyelids and retape them, then pushed the stop lever on the music box. It finished playing "We Will Meet in the Sweet Bye and Bye," and clicked to a halt. Thank God poor Lissa Belmont was spared that.

I picked up the music box, walked into the hall. Mrs. Belmont was nowhere to be seen. I went home, left the music box in my room, took the sandwich Ramona forced on me, ate it on my way back to the Steinberg. When I got to Harmony's room, Dr. Belmont was there. He didn't say anything about Mrs. Belmont, and I didn't ask. "No change," he murmured. "Samuel's doing a gall bladder. He'll come check her when he's done."

A few minutes later, a nurse marched into the room, pointed at me. "Someone to see you downstairs."

"Me?"

"You're Leo Firestone, aren't you?"

"Yes, but who—"

"Information Desk called up and said a man asked for Leo Firestone. He seemed to know you were here." She pointed toward the doorway. "You can see him in the lobby."

I thanked her, took the elevator down to the lobby, walked up to Information. Mrs. Stetson, an elderly volunteer, sat behind the desk. Gray cap with a big red cross set squarely atop a mound of blue hair. She looked flustered, made little clucking sounds with her tongue before she could speak. "Oh, Leo, hello. This...gentleman wants to see you."

The gentleman standing there was Aldo, the man I'd seen the morning before, arguing with George over two radios and a sewing machine. He didn't look any better, same red eyes, hollow unshaved cheeks, ragged shirt, filthy overalls. From three feet away I smelled booze, Samuel's lesson learned. In his shaking left hand, he clutched a leather purse—Harmony's. He motioned with his head toward the far corner of the room.

Mrs. Stetson's lips went crooked and stony. I thanked her, then followed Aldo through the lobby. None of the people we passed so much as looked at us; they had their own problems. At the far wall, Aldo turned his back to the room, looked over his shoulder, thrust the purse at me. "Big niggerman at da junkyard say give you dis."

I dropped into a chair, pulled the drawstring, turned the leather bag upside-down. Pencils, a couple of notepads, keys on a ring, a hacksaw blade and a greasy white envelope fell into my lap. I looked at Aldo, couldn't speak. I could barely breathe.

"I go to da junkyard, got stuff to sell," Aldo rasped. "And I hear hollerin' inside da office. Young Jewman yell, 'Dumb old fuck, you gotta get your ass outa here fast, else we're all dead. Go to New York or something.' Old Jewman yell back, 'Not 'til I get done wit' your friend Sammy, he's a coming here at six o'clock, gonna buy.' Young Jewman shout, 'Okay, but if I see you here in da morning, *I* kill *you.*' Then, young Jewman run outside an' see me. 'Hey, George,' he yell, 'Skinny guinea's here wit' some things.' Then he jump in da truck, drive away. Nigger come on out from da office, look real scared. He say lotsa bad stuff happen at da junkyard, he's a gonna scram wit' his family, back down south. He take me over by da old-radio pile, pull out dis purse, say he finded it under da desk, and I should give you it." Aldo plucked a fiver from his shirt pocket, waved it in my face. "Nigger gimme three bucks for my stuff and two more to come down here wit' da purse. I go by your house, your mamma say you're here."

I got out one word: "Aldo—"

He shook his hand back and forth. "I say I bring, I bring. Now I done." Through the lobby, zip, out the door.

I picked up the grimy envelope, reached inside, pulled out four photographs. Four crisp shots, every face clearly identifiable. Did Oscar hire a detective with a telephoto camera? Or were these snapshots Lily took with that toy of hers, the Kodak flash camera, and Oscar somehow got hold of them? There was Samuel in the attic, six pregnant girls snuggling up to him, everyone all smiles. A second shot, the Fleischmanns' labor room, Samuel talking to a girl in the bed, a well-dressed middle-aged couple standing over her. Number Three showed Murray, Samuel and Red Dexter sitting in Murray's living room, drinks in hand, laughing like the Three Musketeers. The last picture was worst. Samuel, a smile all over his face, was shaking hands with Red Dexter. Dexter was beaming. His free hand clapped Samuel's shoulder, and in Samuel's hand was a wad of bills that could've choked an elephant. "You're my man," said Dexter's face and demeanor. Or better, "You're my boy."

Everything hit me at once. Red Dexter, aluminum, what Aldo heard Murray yell at Oscar—how could I have been so witless? *Samuel* would've known Oscar Fleischmann's mind, would never have been so stupid as to plan to sneak into the junkyard the night Oscar'd be sitting on a monster stash of highjacked black-market metal. Of course the filthy old thug would've been there, guarding his treasure. And when I didn't show, Harmony went without me, must've taken a hacksaw because she knew she couldn't get the strongbox out over the fence alone. She hacksawed the strongbox, got the pictures, then either slid her purse under the desk when she heard Oscar coming after her, or it flew underneath when he caught her. Oscar didn't spot it, but George did, looked inside, wanted to get it to me because of the photos. But the negatives weren't in the envelope, were they? Aldo said Oscar was waiting for Samuel to come and buy something he had for sale. Guess what.

A red mist floated up from my chest, danced in front of my eyes. I crammed the photographs into my pocket, sprang out of the chair. Pencils flew every which way as I charged past poor bewildered Mrs. Stetson, up the stairwell, two flights to the surgical suite.

Chapter 16

I scorched into the doctors' dressing room, danced past wooden benches separating rows of metal lockers. As I wheeled around the corner to Samuel's locker, there was Samuel, getting dressed, talking to Charlie Harrison, another G.P. Samuel fastened his top shirt button, reached for his tie, then caught sight of me rushing up. "Leo, what's the matter?" Concern in his voice but not anxiety. As always, he was in control.

Or so he thought. I'd figured to take his car keys out of his pants pocket in the locker, then deal with him after I settled matters with Oscar Fleischmann, but all right, Plan B. I yanked the photographs from my pocket, sailed them past his head. As he ducked, I grabbed into the locker, came away with his trousers. "Leo, what's with you?" he shouted, but I was out of the aisle, flying toward the door. "Come back here."

No way. No more cock and bull stories. I snatched his key ring out of his pocket, charged into the corridor outside the operating suite, heaved the pants as far as I could in the opposite direction. Then I took off for the parking lot. Get the Plymouth, drive to the junkyard. Settle Oscar's hash once and for all time.

I tried to start the car, forgot the choke. On the second shot the engine caught. White smoke blanketed the lot. I threw the car into reverse, sped out of the parking space. As I turned onto the street, I caught sight of Samuel, trousers on but shoeless, running along the sidewalk in front of the hospital. He reacted as only Samuel could've—dashed directly into the street in front of an oncoming black Ford, holding up his hand like a traffic cop, stop! I thought he was a goner, but the Ford screeched to a halt inches from him. Samuel didn't even break pace.

I was onto Roosevelt, accelerating. Samuel lunged for the door handle, but I slammed the lock shut just in time. In doing that, though, I let up on the accelerator enough for him to grab the handle and leap onto the running board. If the car stalled, I'd be finished. I floored the accelerator; we took off with a roar.

Down we sailed along Roosevelt, my mind racing as fast as that car's engine, trying to figure the route with the fewest stops. Samuel banged on the window, shouted, but I couldn't make out words. He may have been trying to break the glass, but clinging to the car as he was, he couldn't generate much force. The window clattered but held.

Greens were with me all the way down Roosevelt to Eighteenth Street, where I turned right. Just thirteen blocks to Fifth, a left there, then straight to the junkyard. But as I crossed Eleventh, I saw a red light a block ahead at Tenth. If I stopped at that light, Samuel might be able to smash the window. Or run to the other side of the car—I hadn't locked the passenger door, didn't dare reach over far enough to do it. I leaned on the horn. A Cadillac going north on Tenth slammed to a stop, and I breezed through the red light. Samuel rattled the door handle.

I turned onto Fifth, clear shot now to Fleischmann Scrap. Past the railroad trestle…Harmony…to the open gate. Quick turn inside, hit the brake, cut the motor. I unlocked the door, pushed it open, jumped out. Samuel stumbled backward but kept his feet. Two people angry past reason, but one of them knowing what was happening and the other not, so any advantage was mine. Samuel took a step toward me, managed one word, "What—" before I decked him.

The last thing Samuel must've expected from his son was a sharp right, straight from the shoulder, direct to the side of his jaw. I was ready to deliver a second shot, but he went down like a poleaxed steer. Good. Save that second K.O. hit for Oscar, then call the cops. Let Oscar try to explain why he was in his junkyard at one o'clock in the morning, and why he'd beaten a girl bloody, then dumped her on the riverbank. Any whistle he wanted to blow on Samuel would be fine with me. Let the two of them squirm in chairs on the other side of a desk from a police detective.

I left Samuel in the dirt, ran to the office, looked around the yard. No one in sight, which figured. Oscar would be inside, waiting for Samuel.

I was barely through the doorway when a hulk moved from behind the door, blue and white striped overalls, red neckerchief. Flash of wild gray hair. He threw a hammerlock onto my right arm, put a blade to my throat. "Don't move, you little fucker," a growl. Voice tight, strained. Stench as if he hadn't taken a shower in thirty years. I tried ducking out of the lock, grabbed backward with my left arm, but he pulled harder, hurt like hell. He pressed the blade tight across my throat. "The hell you doin' here, Miss Pussy? Your ol' man didn't send *you* with the dough, did he?"

If I was scared, I was too angry to admit it. I wiggled again, shouted, "No money, Oscar, and you'd better let go. I've got something you need to hear."

"Oh, Miss Pussy wants to talk?" Mocking, vicious. "So, talk." He yanked my arm straight upward. I tried not to scream but couldn't hold back.

Noise at the door. Samuel, in his socks, pulled up short. Low rumble behind me, "Fuck!" Then Oscar twisted and pulled at my arm. I ducked under the knife, but Oscar slashed, blood everywhere. Oscar shoved me toward Samuel, then lumbered out the door.

I remember being on the floor, looking at my hemorrhaging wrist as though it were some strange new form of entertainment. Samuel grabbed my hand, pressed a handkerchief over the red spurts, snapped, "Hold this, Leo. Tight." As I took over from him, he pulled off one of his socks, tried to tie it around my arm, muttered, "No good," and put fingers to my left wrist. As he looked at his watch, his lips tightened. He sprang up, ran to the phone, dialed. As if from far away I heard, "Dr. Firestone—got a nasty hemorrhage, knife attack. Fleischmann Scrap, Fifth Av past Eleventh Street. Right. Just come in through the gate." He slammed down the receiver, then ran back past me toward the door. "Keep that pressed hard," he called over his shoulder.

The radio on the window ledge must've been playing all the time I was there, but I didn't hear it 'til right then. Judy Garland, "That Old Black Magic." Like listening through a sound tunnel. I don't know how much blood I'd lost to that point, but it must've been a fair amount, even as fast as Samuel got pressure on. I raised my head, looked around, saw my blood splattered halfway up the wall beside me, puddles on the dirty office floor. Fear surged into my throat, anguish over Harmony, rage at Oscar and Samuel. I retched, four or five heavy heaves, must've let go of the handkerchief. Scarlet jets from my wrist, miniature geyser. Blood slimy under my right arm.

Hazy…Samuel rushing in with the emergency bag from the Plymouth. Ninety degrees, but I was freezing. All so curious. I couldn't understand why Samuel seemed disturbed. He charged over, tossed supplies and equipment out of his bag onto the floor, came up with a tourniquet, threw it around my arm. His hand went to my neck, then I heard a faint "God *damn!*"…no, other way around, I think. Foggy, a dream…

I woke up in Steinberg Hospital, pitch-black outside, night. I.V. in my left arm, blood dripping slowly, right wrist bandaged. My head hurt, fingers throbbed, mouth felt full of cotton. I pulled the call string. A moment, then a nurse materialized just inside the doorway. Young, blonde, didn't look a whole lot older than me. "Well, you're awake…" she said. "I'll call Dr. Harrison." Then she was gone, just like that.

I scanned the room. Why weren't my father and mother there? Maybe Ramona heard about me, took a walloping slug of morphine, was sleeping it off. Samuel? He was in the operating room or the delivery room or a sickroom in a mansion facing Hamilton Park or a squalid bedroom in a coldwater shack Down-river.

Charlie Harrison was on call, available in case I happened to wake up before Samuel returned.

But when Charlie walked in a few minutes later, trouble was all over his face. He was a big man, six-four, two-fifty, ruddy, freckled, sandy hair. One of those men who always sweats, even on the coldest days. His cheeks were like beets; water poured down his forehead. He said hello, worked up a smile, felt at my neck, murmured, "Mmm. Pulse's getting slower, stronger. You're going to be all right."

"Charlie, where are Samuel and Ramona?"

His eyes filled. He cleared his throat, but didn't speak. Right then, I knew, past doubt. "You're going to have to tell me some-time," I said. "Do it now."

He made a sound somewhere between a croak and a crow, coughed violently, wiped a sleeve across his face. "You're Samuel's kid, all right." He sat on the edge of the bed. "You lost a ton of blood, Leo, would never have made it to the hospital without emergency replacement. You got a transfusion there at the junk-yard."

"A direct transfusion," I said. "Samuel."

Nod. "When the ambulance came, they found you and him hooked up vessel to vessel. You were alive. He...wasn't."

"No," I said. Automatic rejection, invalid information. I couldn't even picture Samuel disabled.

"He did that pretty often, didn't he, Leo? Gave patients direct transfusions."

"I saw him give one a few days ago."

"He may've given one or two more since, so he probably started on you with a low red cell count. The heat didn't help, or all that excitement. Maybe he had an arrhythmia, or a heart attack. Knowing Samuel, he might've put his artery to your vein, just to make sure he kept pumping as long as his heart held out."

"Ramona?"

At some point, misery becomes anesthetic. Charlie's face was near-blank. He began to mumble, monotone. "She heard about him and you, went to her room, took a dose of morphine, maybe bigger than she intended. Leo, I'm sorry."

I nodded, all I could manage.

Next few days were tough. Visitors came, everyone looking shocked, embarrassed. Murray Fleischmann sidled in, all cleaned up, white shirt and tie, incongruous. By his face you'd've thought he was afraid of spreading germs. "Hey, Dockie, you ain't looking so bad as I thought. Jeez, I'm sorry, what else can I say?" Nothing, I thought. Not after telling Oscar to run instead of turning him in. More than I could forgive, especially when Murray went on to tell me Oscar did run. A couple of people saw him charge down Fifth after he slashed me; a neighbor saw him dash into his house, then back out a couple of minutes later. The cops would catch him for sure, Murray said, but they never did. After a while, leads went cold and people began to forget. Like a rock thrown into a lake, huge splash, ripples, then finally quiet again.

One of the hospital chaplains came by to offer condolences and ask about funeral arrangements. We decided on a graveside service, light on religion. "Samuel always told Ramona if she had a preacher at his funeral he was going to stand up in the coffin and pee on him," I said. The chaplain smiled. "I'll be careful."

"Harmony?" The word flew out of my mouth.
   "Only Samuel could've kept her alive."
   "Dad..."

I had no relatives, so the Belmonts took me in. Before I left the hospital, Charlie Harrison came by to check me over. When I thanked him, he shook his head. "No way I was going to let you die, then have to face your father on Judgment Day." Anemic smile, a grimace. "He's the one who really got you through. There was only enough blood between the two of you for one, and Samuel made sure you got it. Don't ever forget that, Leo." Then slowly, reluctantly, Charlie pulled a bunch of photographs from his shirt pocket. "I picked these up the other day, in the locker room. No one's looked at them, myself included."

Fine until the last two words. Sure, Charlie looked. But he wouldn't have told anyone what was on those photos if they pulled out his fingernails with pliers. I thanked him one more time, stuffed the evidence into my own shirt pocket. That night, when the Belmonts were asleep, I tiptoed down to the kitchen, found a box of matches, burned the pictures in the sink.

Next day, the funeral. Six rows of chairs set up in front of double graves, maybe seventy seats altogether, but easily six or seven hundred people in that cemetery. A sea of black Victory Suits, cuffs and lapels gone to be made into soldiers' uniforms. Women with black skirts cut so high they'd've been considered inappropriate two years earlier at a bar, let alone a funeral. School was out for the day, flags at half-staff. Mourners craned necks, pushed, jostled, jigged and sidestepped so as not to stand on graves. The mayor and his wife were there, the entire City Council. Nearly every member of Steinberg's medical staff. Samuel's patients, the wealthy, the poor. I caught a glimpse of Lou and Lena, carefully keeping little Bub between them. Off to the left, Murray and Lily, gray-faced, formed a human barrier around four hysterically weeping girls in different stages of pregnancy. As the pastor was about to begin, a man standing near the gravesite nudged his small son. "Pay attention—this was the greatest man in the history of Hobart."

The service was short, the chaplain true to his word. Both coffins were open. I couldn't help staring at Samuel on the light blue pleated silk, determination and defiance as clear as ever in the line of his mouth and set of his jaw. Ramona looked serene, more at peace than I'd ever seen her in life. "God show mercy to their souls," said the chaplain. Attendants closed the coffins, then moved them onto cloth stretcher-straps above the open graves, and cranked them down. From everywhere in the cemetery, crying, snuffling, wailing. I kept feeling as if *I* was going to cry, but didn't. There I was at the graveside, the chaplain and I the only dry-eyed people in the cemetery.

Late that afternoon, I was sitting with a book in the little study at the front of the Belmonts' house, when Lissa Belmont walked in with Lily Fleischmann. Lily looked like the end of the world. Red eyes, skin tight over her cheekbones, thick blue veins over her temples and the backs of her hands. Hair hanging limp, unbrushed, dark roots uncamouflaged. Mrs. Belmont offered to bring a pitcher of iced tea, but Lily shook her head. "I just want to talk to him."

Poor fussy Mrs. Belmont dithered, then said, "Well, I guess I'll let you talk, then," and hurried out, making a show of closing the door. Lily didn't seem to notice or care that the poor woman was going through all kinds of hell. Just flashed me a long hot-eye, and said, "You look pretty good," as if that were more than I deserved.

"I'm getting better."

I wouldn't have thought it was possible, but she turned up the eye-heat. "I sure do wonder what in hell you and your girlfriend were up to—why she was poking around that junkyard in the middle of the night. Wasn't for the two of you little busybodies, your father'd still be alive." Lily ripped a folded brown envelope from her purse, slapped it into my lap. "Look inside," she said without moving her lips.

The envelope was full of money, hundreds, fifties, twenties. I glanced up at Lily. "What's left from the business," she snapped. "Your father's and mine."

"But this is thousands of dol—"

"A little more than six thousand. What're you looking so goddamn surprised about? You saw what was in that envelope you steamed open."

"But I thought—"

"Sure." Maybe the most savage word I've ever heard. "You thought him and me were making a bundle, right? Soaking suckers for every buck we could get? Well, every buck, every *penny*, went to the girls. To feed them, buy them medicines and clothes. Give them something for a start when they left, money to go to school or get job training, so they wouldn't have to go whoring on the street when their families didn't let them back in the house. Your father and me never took a nickel. Did he ever tell you how we got started?"

I shook my head.

"Figures. 'Cause of how it involved me. Well, *I* don't mind telling you. I got a heart condition, congenital something or other. I do all right, but if I got pregnant, fifty percent chance I'd die, least that for the baby. I always took precautions, but a few years back, I missed a monthly and the rabbit died. Would my doctor give me an abortion? Don't make me laugh. But Samuel came to the house, did the job under a local, even tied my tubes. Couple months later, he calls me, got a problem, can I help? Some young girl needs an abortion and a place to stay for a few days afterwards. I say sure, so he brings her over, does it, and tells me what I got to do for her and when I oughta call him. Everything goes jake-O.K. Then, after the girl's gone, I actually miss having the kid around. So I tell Samuel I'd do it again if he wants. But the next girl says she really ain't hot for an abortion, her boyfriend's pushing her. What she wants is to have the baby and put it up for adoption. Samuel doesn't bat an eye. Murray and I fix up the dorm in the attic..." She pointed at the envelope in my lap. "So now, I figure that belongs to you. Knowing Samuel like I did, I bet you're going to need it."

I nodded. Samuel left only a savings account with under a thousand dollars. No insurance—that would've been playing it too safe for comfort. "But it just doesn't seem right."

"Oh, *you!*" She spat contempt in my face. "'Doesn't seem right.' Your father got the money, you're going to need the money, I'm giving you the money. Murray and I are okay, thank you very much. If the money makes you feel not right, flush it down the toilet."

I put down the envelope, said, "Thank you."

"You're welcome." Still sarcastic. Then she said, very softly, "You got a goddamn long ways to go before you could ever measure up to your old man, and you know what? I think maybe you shouldn't even try." She chewed at her lip, then all of a sudden slapped me, right across the cheek. "I say you don't *deserve* to be a doctor." Before I could open my mouth, she was out the door. I never saw her again.

Then a few days later, an amazing thing happened. Money started coming in through the mail. Dollar bills, fives, tens, even hundreds. Sometimes a note saying, "Good luck," or "God bless you," but never a signature or a return address. The president of the bank that held our mortgage called me in, told me how Samuel saved his son's life after the boy had been hit by a car, then went on to say the bank directors had voted to retire Samuel's loan. So I never did have money problems. I closed up Samuel's office… Reminds me. Going through his mail one day, I found an envelope from the phone company, monthly statement for Lou and Lena Bukowski. I'd never stopped to ask myself how those two could ever have afforded a telephone? No idea why Samuel footed that tab. Maybe Bub had epilepsy, or maybe Lou knocked Lena around when he got drunk. No idea. I paid the bill, just a few dollars, and the two or three that came after. When I realized they'd stopped, I went Down-river to check, but Lou and Lena were gone. At least they cut off phone service before they left.

All that next year, I stayed with the Belmonts, awful. They were decent enough people, but I never did like them, and we rubbed each other raw. When I went away to college, I stayed away. Rented a room in town, worked summers as a waiter. Someone in New York sent payments to the registrar to cover my school expenses, every semester, every cent, so after college I could afford to go study art in London and Paris, four years. I came back to New York in 1954 and began to paint seriously. The rest is history." Jagged smile. "That's my story."

I hesitated, finally said it. "You never thought of going to medical school?"

Dad shook his head. "Hate to admit it, but I knew that bitch Lily was right." Speaking softly, slowly, as if he'd spent his allowance of words and didn't want to max out his credit. "Crazy to spend the rest of my life trying to live up to a legend. Old people in Hobart still whisper about your grandfather, but only after a quick look over their shoulders. You never had to call him back once he'd taken on a case—he knew when he was needed and there he was at the door. He once appeared in two sickrooms at the very same time, and of course saved both patients. He knew about medications no other doctor could find. Only one person, Oscar Fleischmann, was stupid enough to take on Samuel Firestone, and for that, Samuel made him disappear from the face of the earth. But only after Oscar inflicted mortal wounds on both Samuel and his son."

Dad chuckled, not with humor, then extended his right hand to show the thick, white scar across his wrist I'd never had the nerve to ask about.

"Story goes, Samuel had to choose between curing his own wound or his son's."

"Lot of truth in legends," I said. "Sometimes a truth that reality can't get itself around."

Dad's eyes narrowed. Slowly, as if I were armed and dangerous, he picked a slice of cheese off the tray, slipped it into his mouth, chewed. "What ever happened to Murray?" I asked.

"No idea. I never went back to the junkyard, didn't want to see him."

I glanced at my watch, almost four o'clock. Dad picked up. "Sorry, I didn't mean to talk so long. Should've told you this garbage years ago, but I thought—"

"You thought you might never have to. That I'd keep puttering with computers the rest of my life. That you'd get away with it."

Dad looked as if he'd swigged spoiled milk. "I used to watch you at your computers, Martin. Other kids played games, but not you. You had to *write* them, and the dicier they were, the better. Goddamn it to hell, you're going to do just what Samuel did, spit on that contract and throw it back." He wiped a finger across the corner of his mouth. "Don't go into medicine, Martin. Please."

I didn't think, just lashed back. "Just because *you* didn't have the nerve to take on your father's legend... Remember that night at dinner when Samuel first got you to be his extern, you told your mother you'd want to be a doctor if you were good enough? "

"Huh." Tight little smile. "You don't miss much, do you?"

"Runs in the family."

Dad pounded a fist, rattled dishes and silverware. His eyes bulged, mouth an ugly red gash. Fortunately, the restaurant was near-empty. Both waiter and *maitre d'* took care to look in the other direction. "I made myself a goddamn good life as a painter. You can do the same with computers."

"Painting!" I said. "And computers, for that matter. Going for eight in your own house, doors locked, no one to see or care if you drop every one of the goddamn balls."

Dad flopped back into his chair, eyed me as if I were a roach who'd had the nerve to come crawling out from between the floorboards in full daylight.

"I know what medical work is," I said. "No thanks to you. I applied to med school, I've been accepted, I'm going."

He shook his head, shoved two palms in front of my face. "All right. Fine. Go. Not the first afternoon I ever wasted, won't be the last." He slid to the edge of the seat. "Time to get on the road—" A sharp hiccup cut him off.

"Forget about that." I jumped to my feet, stood over him. "No way I'm letting you drive across Long Island, sloshed and foaming at the mouth. You can dry out at my place."

"What, leave my car overnight? Cost me more than fifty bucks! Shit, I've driven a whole lot drunker than this." Cagey eyes, challenging me. "All of a sudden you're worried about my well-being?"

"Yours and anyone's in a car within a half-mile of you. Give me your keys."

I held out a hand. He got halfway to standing; I pushed him back. He looked up, face suddenly a map of foolish questions. Great stuff, adrenaline, but in a long-distance race, alcohol wins every time. "I'm fifty years younger than you," I said. "In just as good shape, and cold-sober besides. Now are you going to give me your keys or do I have to take them?"

He reached slowly into his pocket, came out with a key ring, dropped it into my hand with an exaggerated flourish. Then he pulled two hundreds from his wallet, slipped them under his water glass, and got himself to his feet. He leaned on the table top, tried to focus on my eyes. "Be right with you, Salvation Army Annie...just want to get my note pad from my car."

"I'll go with you," I said, and took his elbow. "That extra key you keep under the hood just might be too much of a temptation."

He battled a smile, but his alcohol-disabled resolve was no match. He shook his head weakly, muttered a feeble, "God damn. Samuel *vs.* Samuel."

"Samuel by a split decision," I said. "Six drinks in less than three hours? Cab's on me. Let's go."

Second Avenue just north of Sixty-seventh is far from tenement territory, but neither is it elevator country. I wrestled Dad up three flights of narrow steps and into my apartment. Helene's face was a study, but she kissed Dad's cheek, then took his right arm and helped me lead him into our bedroom. We sat him on the edge of the bed, pulled off his shoes, dragged his pants down past his ankles, got him between the sheets. Before we were outside, he was snoring.

As she closed the door behind us, Helene asked, "Is it something you can tell me?"

Not a story I wanted to drop on her. But I remembered what Dad said, how he'd never told Mother about Harmony, and I felt a terrible sadness below my ribs, as if I'd just swallowed a cannonball. "It's all right," she said. "We all have a secret or two, don't we?"

I put an arm around her, squeezed. "I'd better call Mother—don't want her to wait up for him, or worry."

Mother sighed when I told her Dad was safe in bed, sleeping off his bender. "I don't even want to think about him like that, going eighty or ninety along the Sunrise Expressway," she said. "Thirty-five years with your father, and I've never seen him anything like he was yesterday. A madman. Martin, what on earth did you tell him?"

"Just that I've been accepted at medical school."

Silence, then a strangled, "Oh, my."

"Mother?"

"Did he tell you about...?"

"His father? Yes."

Deep sigh. "That's what I thought."

"You know the story?"

"Only that his father was a doctor, but Leo would never consider a medical career. Is it as bad as I think it was?"

"Worse."

Another sigh. "All right, then. Any more, he'll have to tell me himself. As long as I know he's safe. Thanks for calling, dear."

I hung up the phone slowly, not wanting to look at Helene. She walked over, rested her head against my back. A shaft of late afternoon sunlight found its way between buildings, through our window, cast a glow on the Leo Firestone painting next to the door. A summer meadow, grass waving gently in the breeze, each blade a sharp sawtooth flecked with red. I thought I might choke on the dry gall in my throat. "Come sit on the sofa with me," I finally managed to say. "Dad wants secrets in his house, that's up to him. I don't want them in mine."

Chapter 17

Helene and I slept on the sofa that night, curled into each other like nesting spoons. By the time we woke, Dad was gone. No note, bed rumpled, unmade. "Are you going to call home, make sure he got there?" Helene asked.

"I am home," I said. "And he's gotten home all right for seventy-six years. We did our part last night."

She clearly didn't agree, but didn't argue.

We had breakfast, then I went down, bought a copy of the four-inch-thick *New York Times*. Our usual Sunday morning routine. Helene took the first section, plopped into one of the plaid armchairs, began to read. I picked up the magazine, but couldn't get into it. I tried the financial section, entertainment, sports, but the harder I worked at diverting myself, the more my mind wandered down a path I was trying to stay off. Like Oscar Wilde, I can resist everything except temptation.

I strolled into the kitchen, washed the breakfast dishes, then walked to my study and sat a few minutes at my computer. Then I came back to the living room, tried to read the News of the Week. Pale stuff beside the churning mess in my mind. I strolled to the kitchen, dried the dishes. When I ambled back into the living room, Helene lowered her paper, stared, then said, "Martin, what's with you?"

"What do you mean?"

"What do I *mean*?" She dropped her reading to the floor. "I mean you're prowling. Into the kitchen, out to the computer, off the computer, back here, back to the kitchen, back here again. You look like a hamster running between a treadmill and a roller-ball."

"Something's bothering me."

"Your father."

"Sure."

"Well, then, call. Don't be so proud, or standoffish, or whatever. Pick up the phone and call him."

"It's not that, Helene. It's his story. It's not right."

"Like how?"

"Like how it ended. Lame. He damn near quit talking a couple of times when the story got nasty, and I think he bailed before the end. I'm supposed to believe he lived for a year with a couple of people he couldn't stand, then toddled off to college, then Europe, then back to New York, where he decided to become a painter? My *father*? Helene, Dad's a force of nature. If he'd wanted to be a doctor, he'd've been a doctor, and on his own terms. Lily Fleischmann and a Marine brigade couldn't've stopped him. Something else happened in Hobart that summer, something he didn't talk about."

She frowned. "It happened so long ago—your dad's seventy-six years old. Maybe you ought to leave well enough alone."

"Well enough's not good enough. Almost sixty years now, he's lived in pain, hasn't even been able to tell my mother. Should I just stand back and let him go on beating himself up, all the way to his grave?"

She bit at her lip. "I only hope you won't—"

"Push him over the edge? He's been at least half-over for half a century. Maybe I can pull him back. And besides..."

"There's more?"

"How about a murder that was never solved?"

"Jonas Fleischmann and the strychnine? You're going to solve that? Now? Sixty years later?"

I nodded. "Pretty sure."

She looked as if she'd just noticed what might be either a rye seed or a bug on a half-eaten piece of bread. "I guess good luck to you *and* your father."

"Your father"... The book on the coffee table, right in front of me. *Leo Fleischmann, A Fifty-Year Retrospective*, by Carla Marcuse, signed on the title page by author and subject. Dad said he'd been in Europe when? I ignored Helene's silent question, picked up the book, flipped to page 3, biography line. Born, Hobart, NJ, April 20, 1927. B.A., Rutgers University, 1950. M.A., Royal College of Art, London, 1953, Free-lance study, Paris, 1954. Four years in Europe, just as he said, but starting in 1950. If Dad went into his senior year of high school in 1943, he should've graduated from college in 1948. Simple math, but not adding up.

I hustled back to my study, sat down at the computer. Think you've got privacy? Try FindEm.com. Armed with only $29.95 and a person's date of birth or Social Security Number or state of residence present or past, you can locate *anyone*. Or so they advertise. For another $59.95 you get a background check, for $19.95 a report on criminal records. I doubt their database is anywhere near infallible, but for thirty bucks on my VISA card I figured I was playing a strong hand. Date of birth, Good Friday, the day we declared war on Germany—April 6, 1917. Last known residence, New Jersey. In just a few minutes, I learned that a Murray Fleischmann, aged eighty-six, lived at 462 Mountain Road, Verona, New Jersey. I printed the information, then disconnected from FindEm and went to GreatYellow.com. New Jersey...Hobart...Yes! Jack's Pharmacy, 247 East Sixteenth Street.

I logged off, grabbed the phone, called my office, left a message for Frank. I really do work with a Frank Riccardi.

Told him I'd be taking tomorrow off, mental health day. I didn't think he'd like it, too bad.

By nine next morning, I was in one of Mr. Avis' blue compact Hondas, going through the Lincoln Tunnel into Jersey. Route Eighty to Forty-six, across the Grassville Bridge into Hobart. A few minutes later I pulled up in front of Jack's Pharmacy. Shabby little place, brown shingle siding faded and warped. Whole neighborhood looked down at the heels, sagging roofs, peeling paint, grass all scruffy, untrimmed. I got out of the car, walked to the screen door, pushed against the seventy-year-old metal Nehi ad. A bell tinkled. Behind the counter a man looked up.

Watery blue eyes framed by wire-rimmed spectacles followed me across the shop. I walked by wooden shelves crammed with over-the-counter remedies and health-related appliances, strolled past an honest-to-God soda fountain. Clocks do run faster in New York, but here they seemed to have stopped some time before the New Deal.

"Help you?" the druggist asked.

"Hope so. You the proprietor?"

"Yes."

The man looked like an old-time schoolteacher, florid cheeks, narrow nose, thin tight lips, sparse gray hair combed over his dome. He began to work his thumbs rapidly against his index fingers. I flashed ivories. "My name's Martin Firestone; I'm a student at N.Y.U. Med School, doing a study." I pulled my wallet, flipped it open.

He studied the picture on my driver's license. "Firestone... Firestone..."

"Samuel Firestone was my grandfather. He did a lot of business with Jack."

Lips tighter, face redder. "Yes, Jack did talk about him." Thumbs going sixteen to the dozen, I hoped he wouldn't set the counter on fire. "Jack was my father-in-law, died twenty-two years ago. Now, please, Dr., uh, Mr. Firestone. What's this all about?"

"I'd like to look in your poison log from July, 1943," I said. "If it's still around. See about one of my grandfather's patients."

He started to laugh, then looked closely at me. "God damn, you're serious. From 'forty-three? Yeah, sure, what do I care? There's a ton of old stuff, prescriptions, ledgers, down in the basement. You want to go look, be my guest. Gonna get your hands a little dirty, though."

"Won't be the first time," I said quietly—and thought, or the last.

Verona's an upscale town west of Montclair, about half an hour from Hobart. I drove slowly, rehearsed my lines, just a bit twitchy at the prospect of gambling big-time with Dad's chips. But that's what doctors do every day, gamble with other peoples' chips.

I wound my way past one small palace after another, finally pulled up in front of a huge black wooden sign with gold letters: The Wapping Ridge Residence for Seniors, Number 462 Mountain Road. Behind the sign, a long hill, grass manicured neat as the eighteenth fairway on a championship golf course. A narrow asphalt drive wandered through the green to a great stone building, brown crossbeams below each window.

I turned into the drive, tooled to the front of the building, pulled into a visitor's space. A geezer in a striped shirt and screaming red and yellow plaid pants sat strapped into a wheelchair on the porch. He watched me get out of the car, eyed me all the way up the steps. Then he waved a shaky hand in my face. "Marty! Get over here!"

That threw me and it must've shown. "His son's named Marty," said a man in a deck chair next to the old guy. Crisp white shirt, narrow gold tie, full head of brown hair neatly combed, super-thin Duke Ellington mustache. "He calls every young man he sees Marty." The dandy's speech was Bostonian, each word veneered with patrician precision. "I've not seen you before. Are you looking us over for your parents?"

"Marty!" Phlegmy old-man's voice. "Come over here! Can't you even say hello to your father?"

Now fighting a full-blown case of fidgets I patted the man's shoulder. "Sure, Dad, I'm always glad to see you, but right now I've got some business inside. I'll be back a little later, all right?" I bent, planted a light kiss on his forehead.

"Always busy, always running places," the man groused, but there was no longer bite to his words. I wondered how often the real Marty kissed his old man. "My name actually *is* Martin," I said to Wapping Ridge's Brahmin-in-Residence. "Martin Firestone."

The man extended his hand, gave mine a tentative press. "Paul Conklin."

"I'm here to visit Murray Fleischmann," I said. "Do you know him?"

The expression on Conklin's face suggested I'd just turned over a rock and sent something brownish-black with a thousand legs scurrying for new cover. "Yes, I'm afraid I do know Mr. Fleischmann." He pointed at the doorway. "You'll probably find him in the billiards room. Take a right as you enter, then four doors down on your left. But perhaps you should check in at the office—on the right, directly inside."

I thanked Mr. Conklin and went in, to the office. A young woman with a round face and frizzy permanent curls beamed a professional smile at me from behind her desk, then got to her feet. She wore a light blue summer dress, cut low across the front. A name tag pinned precariously on the left identified her as Shirley. When I gave my name, told her why I was there, she opened a gorgeous pair of violet eyes to the limit. "Oh, Mr. *Fleischmann*." Her voice was like her manner, all bouncy gaiety, hallmark of a person who spends every day dealing with young children or old people. "Except for his daughter I don't think he's had a visitor as long as I've worked here, and that's almost five years now. Are you a friend?"

"He and my father were friends," I said. "Years ago, in Hobart."

"Hobart?" The woman looked as if I'd tried to force a square piece into a round hole in a jigsaw puzzle. "I thought Mr. Fleischmann came to us from a private home in Verona."

I warned myself not to say Murray was once a junkman. "This was a long time ago, almost sixty years. Lot of people who lived in Hobart then live somewhere else now." Mostly under ground, I added privately.

Shirley moved past me toward the door, moon face shining with good will. "Well, you just follow me, Mr. Firestone. Mr. Fleischmann always plays billiards in the morning."

Four doors down, on the left. Old men and women walked ahead of us, passed us going the other way. "The people here look in pretty good shape," I said. "Except for that poor old man on the porch, who—"

Shirley's expression stopped me midsentence. "Oh, dear, Mr. Wagner again. I'll go attend to him after I've gotten you together with Mr. Fleischmann. The incapacitated residents are in another wing." She waved vaguely toward the far end of the building. "But sometimes Mr. Wagner wheels himself out to the main entrance and sits there to wait for...did he—?"

"He thought I was his son, called me Marty. I played along. No problem."

Shirley looked stricken. "His son died last year, very suddenly, a heart attack. Mr. Wagner sits out on the porch every chance he gets, and waits for Marty."

A lump rose out of my chest, settled into my throat. That kiss I gave Mr. Wagner was the best story I could've told him. If it cheered him up only for a while, fine. What's forever?

I followed Shirley into the billiards room, all dark wood paneling. On the far wall, floor-to-ceiling glass doors, open to let in a soft late-spring breeze. Racks with cues flanked the doors. Three tables neatly aligned front to back, plenty of space between them to take any shot. At the near table, a gaunt, angular coot of about eighty, with rimless glasses and the hollowest cheeks I'd ever seen, chalked his cue methodically. His companion stood hand to chin, studying the balls on the table like a chessmaster planning his next move. Red suspenders crossed over a rumpled white shirt to hold up a pair of brown worsted pants that might've been pressed about the time Nixon left office. Not much hair on top, gray swirls down his neck and over his ears. Intense brown eyes, thick lips, beak of a nose, skin like creased and pebbled leather. Big chest, big belly, big ass, big everything. My man, no doubt. A wave of chills flew up my back, across my arms, over my face. The old junkman scratched at his head, nodded, then bent to line up his shot.

"Mr. Fleischmann..."

He jumped as if goosed, wheeled around. "Shirley—Jesus Christ!" He seemed about to say more, but when he noticed me he made a gurgling sound in his throat, and all his high ruddiness drained. He leaned against the billiards table as if for support. Shirley put a hand on his arm. "Mr. Fleischmann, are you all right? I'm sorry, I didn't mean—"

"Nah, nah, nah. Just thought for a minute..." He pulled away, a little roughly, worked his heavy lips into a twisted grin. "Can't get rid a me that easy, Shirley."

Shirley didn't seem put off by his speech and manner. "You've got a visitor," she said, with a wave of her arm grand enough to suggest I might be royalty.

The old man squinted, studied me for a moment. Not quite the face I'd expected, no hint of that ebullient grin Dad saw so often. Instead, a map of deep lines and folds, all roads leading to the downturned corners of his mouth. His gaze wavered, shoulders sagged. He still hadn't recovered his color. "Mr. Firestone told me you and his father were friends, years ago," Shirley said. "In Hobart."

The sun came up like thunder out of China 'cross the bay. Murray's eyes looked like dinner plates. "Jesus H. Christ in thermal underwear! No wonder I thought...you gotta be Leo Firestone's kid."

"The same," I said, and extended my hand.

He stood his cue against the table, gripped me with a trembling hand. Skin on that hand like cigarette paper, brown-spotted, veins bulging, but nothing wrong with the man's muscle power. Murray peered into my face. Clumps of thick black hairs in his nose quivered, reeds in wind. "Leo ain't...you didn't come here to tell me—"

"No, he's fine."

"Sheesh, I'm glad to hear that. Practically all I ever get now is this one's sick and that one's dead."

"Dad's seventy-six, still painting, having exhibitions."

"He is, huh?" Hollow laugh. "Well, good, good for him. I wish him the best. Hope he's still doin' his thing right up 'til the day he dies."

"Like his father."

Lightly spoken, but the message hit home. Murray's face drew taut by degrees.

"Talk to me?" I asked.

"Yeah, yeah, sure." Mumbled. The jig was up and the speaker knew it. He seemed to struggle to look me in the eye. "Yeah, I'll talk to you." He turned to his playing partner. "You mind, Ben?"

Ben waved a bony hand. "Naw, 'course not, go visit. Tomorrow."

Murray gestured toward the glass doors. "There's a little trail, runs through the woods out back. We can walk, talk."

I nodded to Shirley. "Thank you."

"You're very welcome. Have a nice visit." Her face said she'd give a month's pay to come with us.

Murray led me outside, then along a flagstoned path across a wide lawn. He moved with an old man's shambling gait, leaned left, then right. A man rode a mower past us. Fresh-cut grass on a warm spring afternoon, better than pot. I inhaled deeply, instant transport back thirty years to my caddy days, Lakeside Hills Country Club, ten bucks a bag for eighteen holes. We passed four old men and women playing croquet; Murray snorted dismissal. Croquet definitely was not his game.

As we approached the woods, flagstones gave way to a clearcut path, wide enough for us to walk side by side. Murray slowed to a stroll. I followed pace. "You didn't say what was your first name," he said. "Else I didn't hear."

"Martin. Martin Firestone."

"*Doctor* Firestone?" The old junkman seemed to be sizing me up as a possible buy. "You a doctor?"

"Not yet. I'm going to start med school this fall."

"How's your old man feel about that?"

"He doesn't seem too fond of the idea."

"Oh yeah?" Murray cackled. "Well, I ain't heard from Leo for close-on sixty years now. How the hell'd you ever find me?"

"Internet. No big trick these days."

He stopped walking, turned a five-alarm dogeye on me. "Next question's *why*? What do you want from me?"

"Dad told me a story Saturday, about himself and you. And Oscar. George Templeton. Chester Hogue, a girl named Harmony..."

Murray's face went slack. He looked around as if for something to hold on to. I reached a hand toward him, he shifted away. "Your old man just yesterday told you that stuff for the first time? You never heard nothing before?"

I shook my head. "All I ever knew was what my mother told me, that my grandfather died young, and he was a very good doctor."

"'A very good doctor'? Christ on a rubber crutch! Samuel Firestone was a one of a kind. Didn't anybody ever tell you—"

"About selling metal and babies on the black market? No."

Murray staggered as if I'd hit him. His thick lips blubbered, eyes begged for clemency. "Take it easy," I said. "I'm not here to hassle you. It's just that parts of my dad's story go clunk, and I need to find out what really happened. For his sake."

Murray sighed, deep, long. "*Vay iz mir.* Hey, listen, I'm an *alte cocker* now, eighty-six years—"

"I won't make any problems for you, promise. Just answer a few questions. It'd make a big difference for my father."

He looked like a junkman being offered highly questionable merchandise. "I helped your old man plenty, and did he ever so much as say thank you?" Murray's forehead went dark, his eyebrows set sail on an apparent collision course, but then his gaze softened. He turned his head, hawked, spat ferociously, like someone trying to get rid of a foul taste. "Not that I can really blame him, though, tell the truth."

"He's still got that music box..." Tossing out a lie, just to keep talk flowing, but suddenly blown away by the realization it was no lie at all. "He wouldn't get rid of it for anything," I babbled. "Keeps it in his den."

Murray gave me the fish eye, then laughed into his sleeve. "Christ Almighty, that music box..." He waggled his hand, motioned me down the path. "There's a bench just a little farther. We'll go sit, you can ask your questions."

The bench stood at a turn in the path, on the edge of a crag. Murray settled heavily into place. I parked beside him, looked down into the deep ravine. A stream gurgled through luxuriant ferns and mosses. Murray turned toward me, tapped fingers on the top back slat. "Okay, Dockie, shoot. What kinda questions you got?"

Dockie.

"Start with Oscar and Samuel. Why'd they have such a case on each other?"

Murray chuckled, but the sadness in his eyes was almost a palpable weight. "Way it was, that's all. Like putting a wildcat in a room with a giant bulldog and shutting the door. Samuel had this silver tongue—I mean, imagine, a kid on his own, lost his whole family, he walked and talked his way all across Europe, finally got himself over to America. At Shadburn's appliance store, he talked his customers into trading in their old stuff 'stead of selling it for junk. Then of course he fixed it and sold it used for ten times what Pop or any junkman woulda given for it. Really got to Pop. Once when I was a little kid, seven years old..."

Murray chuckled again, now with genuine amusement.

"Pop's having lunch, left a full-loaded wagon parked outside the tavern, and when he comes out and says giddyup to the horse, wham! There he is on his ass, junk all over the street. We couldn't even eat supper that night, way Pop carried on. 'It was Sammy Firestone who done it, that snotnose greeny fucker, took the bolt right offa one of the wheels.' Pop was gonna kill him, we should just wait and see. So first thing next morning, I hustle on down to the appliance store, gonna get a look for myself at this Sammy character, maybe he's got horns on his head. But all I see is this nice looking young guy with Mr. Shadburn, they're taking new line cords outa a box and putting them on their appliances. All of a sudden Mr S. jumps up, grabs me by the shirt, yells at me to get out of there, and if I even go close to a refrigerator he's gonna cut off my dick and balls. He waves one of the cords. 'And tell your old man if I ever see *his* face one step inside my door, your mother's gonna take him home in a box.' Scares living crap outa me,

I don't have a clue what the hell's going on. But Samuel comes over, walks me outside, got a look on his face like somebody's telling him a joke. He asks, real nice, what it is I wanted. I say I was only hanging around, and why's Mr. S. so sore at me? Then Samuel tells me how Pop came in the day before when him and Mr. Shadburn were with customers, and afterwards Samuel saw all the appliance cords were cut off right at the plug. That's how it went with your grandpa and Pop—do to me, I do double to you. I think for Samuel it was just fun and games, but Pop, no. If he coulda, he'd'a got somebody to blow Samuel away. But find a person anywhere near Hobart to lay a hand on Samuel Firestone? Maybe the sun wouldn't come up next morning."

"What about Oscar paying Samuel's way through med school?"

Big shrug. "Sorry, Dockie, never did hear Samuel's story. I was still a kid when it happened. By the time him and me got to be friends, it was all water way gone to hell under the bridge. But did Pop ever carry on, not a peaceful supper for over a week. Sammy Firestone robbed him! Sammy Firestone swiped his scratch! Sammy Firestone double-crossed him and ran off with his dough! Yelling, screaming, spit flying outa his yap, fists waving all around—"

"Sounds like Oscar shot first, asked questions later."

"Huh!" Ten pounds of contempt in a one-ounce expletive. "Smelly old bastard never stopped shooting off his mouth. Swung his hands a lot, too. I still got scars from where he hit me when I was a kid. Never gave me a chance to tell him maybe I didn't do what he thought."

"So when Oscar stayed in the yard overnight to keep an eye on a stash of aluminum and caught a girl in the office, I'll bet he didn't give her a big smile and say, 'Excuse me, Miss, but what are doing here, hacksawing my strongbox at one o'clock in the morning?'"

Murray on ready-alert. He nodded, waited.

"I'll bet he hauled off and beat her within an inch of her life without even thinking about it. Then what? Did he realize what he'd done, drag her a few blocks away, drop her under the trestle?"

All through my speech Murray nodded like an automaton. But I jammed his mechanism by saying, "That doesn't fit."

"What don't fit?"

"Oscar leaving Harmony alive. He was a loudmouth, a bully, a thug, but street-stupid? I don't think so. Oscar would've known where that girl's finger would point if she ever woke up, and he would have finished the job. I'm betting someone else dragged Harmony to the riverbank, someone decent enough to call an ambulance afterward and say they'd seen a young girl lying under the Fourth Av trestle. Someone who wouldn't care a bit if she did wake up and finger Oscar, because by then, the aluminum would be safely out of the yard. Let the old bastard go to jail. Let him go to hell."

Murray couldn't hold back a quiet snicker.

"But that would mean someone else was in the yard with Oscar. *And* that Oscar would've let him take Harmony away alive."

Murray's whole body tensed. He looked like a relic dug up by an archeologist and exposed to the light of day for the first time in centuries.

"There's another problem," I said. "Oscar sounds like the meanest son of a bitch ever to draw breath. Never mind he wouldn't've let the girl get away alive, he had a knife to the throat of a kid whose father happened to be the man he hated most in the world. No way he'd've just cut a wrist. He'd've slit my father's throat from ear to ear. That wasn't Oscar there, was it?"

Murray hung his ancient head, kicked absently at a leaf.

"It was someone who'd set the kid up but wouldn't't've killed him for anything, even when the setup went sour. I know who. What I want to hear is why and how."

"You done pretty good so far," Murray mumbled.

"Take me the rest of the way."

Chapter 18

Murray looked like a spaniel silently pleading not to be whipped. "We try and do what's right... Yeah, Pop was crackers over that aluminum, said two of us were gonna stay all night and take turns keeping an eye open every minute, right up to when the stuff was rolling away in Red's truck. I told him we got the aluminum under wraps, nobody's gonna bother it, let's lock up and go home, but it was like talking to a wall. 'That fuckin' Ezra Shnayerson—he wants to play games with me, he's gonna find out I play pretty goddamn rough.' So, finally we draw straws. I get the long one, I go home. Little before one in the morning the phone rings. George, he's hysterical. He was sleeping, wakes up hearing a girl scream and Pop yelling at the top of his lungs, so he runs inside the office and there's Pop holding the girl by her hair, pounding shit outa her with a lead pipe."

I closed my eyes.

"Hey, you asked for it. You want I should go on?"

"I'm listening."

"George tries to get Pop to quit, pulls at him, grabs him, slugs him. But the old shitheel's out of his mind, just goes right on bashing the girl with the pipe. When the girl stops screaming and Pop don't even slow down, George gets really scared. He picks up a hammer offa the desk..."

"Which took care of Oscar."

Nod. "I'm down at the yard inside a five minutes, what a scene. Pop stone cold dead in the market, girl next to him, she's still breathing. Blood all over the place, purse and a hacksaw and Pop's strongbox laying between the girl and Pop. She musta climbed the fence away from where he was sitting, got past him into the office, but when she turned on the light, or when Pop heard a hacksaw... I try waking her up but she's limp like a dishrag, bruises from that pipe all over her head and face. I look at Pop, that filthy scum, wish I could kill him all over again. For what he did to that poor girl he didn't deserve to die so easy.

"But what the hell were George and me gonna do? Call an ambulance, have cops coming two steps behind? With all that aluminum piled right inside the gate? Tell the cops this colored guy killed his white boss? In 1943? George woulda been a goner. So while George starts cleaning up blood, I put the girl over my shoulder, take her down by the trestle. When I come back, *then* I call the ambulance. After that, George'n me get done cleaning up. We finish the hacksaw job on Pop's strongbox—wanna guess what we find?"

"Pictures."

"Bingo, Dockie, but not what you're thinking. Nothing to do with your grandpa. Kinda pictures you'd buy from a gink in Times Square. Also some dough, ten hundreds. I take half, give George half. Then we stand there looking at each other, what the hell we gonna do about Pop's body? All of a sudden I get an idea. Red Dexter'll be there first thing in the morning with a truck, right? Maybe he can take away more'n aluminum. Wouldn't be anything new and different for those guys, and besides, Red and me, we go back a long ways. Better give him a heads-up, though. I pick up the phone, call him."

The old junkman stopped talking, chewed at his lip. His face seemed to melt. Thick jowls hung from his jaws, a wattle developed at his throat. "Soon as Red hears what's up, he says sure he'll help, we gotta stick together. He'll be right down and scope the situation, don't want to show up cold in the morning with a coupla truckmen. Not twenty minutes, he's there, looks fresh as a daisy. He gives Pop the once-over, then he laughs. 'Lemme get this straight, Murray,' he says. 'Oscar catches a girl in here hacksawin' his strongbox, starts beatin' her up. George there bops him with a hammer. You drag the girl over to the Fourth Av trestle and call an ambulance. That's it?' I tell him yeah. 'Okay,' he says. 'Then we gotta move fast, can't wait 'til morning. Girl wakes up, there'll be cops all over this place in nothin' flat. We'll bury Oscar under your dump back by the fence, then I'll call for a truck, get the aluminum outa here. Then *we'll* get the hell out. Cops come lookin' for Oscar, they sure as hell won't think he's hidin' underneath a burnt-garbage pile.'

"I look at George, he looks at me. Makes sense. Meanwhile, Red's over by the desk where I left the girl's purse while me and George cleaned up. Red's hand's on his chin; he gives the purse a hard squint. 'Something...' He pulls white gloves outa his pocket, puts 'em on, picks up the purse, opens it. Keys, pencils, girl stuff, then out comes a little wallet. Red flips the catch, looks inside. 'Harmony Belmont, 286 Roosevelt...son of a bitch! That sugar-cookie Oscar laid out? She's Samuel Firestone's son's girlfriend.'

"I think, shit, this's getting more terrible every minute. 'Leo?'

"'Yeah, Leo the Dockie. I ran into the two a them a few days ago, she was carryin' this purse. Thought I recognized it.'

"Now I know what the girl was doing there. 'Pop told Leo he had some kinda goods on Samuel, kept 'em here in the office,' I say to Red. 'Leo musta told the girl.'

"Red puts the purse back on the desk, takes off the gloves. 'Then we really gotta move.' He gives Pop a little kick on the ass, gives me a shove. 'Let's go.'

"Me and George pick up Pop, schlep him outa the office, all the way out back. Red takes the strongbox and pictures. We pull a bunch a stuff off the pile, dig a hole good and deep, make sure nothing'll show. Then we shove in Pop. 'Uh-oh,' Red says. 'Probably got some I.D. in his wallet, maybe even dough.' He gives George a nudge. George goes down in the hole, bends over, and all of a sudden, Red's holdin' a rod, silencer on the end. Little noise like a pin stuck in a balloon, then George falls over on top a Pop."

The last seven words were so soft I could barely hear them. Murray turned a desolate face on me. "Next thing, Red's down in the hole, gun in one hand, and quick with his other, he pulls George's key ring off his belt, slips it into his own pocket. Then he grabs Pop's wallet *and* George's, climbs up on George's back, jumps outa the hole, puts the wallets in his pocket, slips the gun back inside his jacket. Then he gives me the eye. 'What the hell you waitin' for?' he says. 'C'mon, we gotta fill up the hole.' I tell him, 'Go ahead, shoot me too, get it done.' He laughs. 'Stop being stupid, and shovel, hey? Get the hole filled, garbage over it. Then we'll talk.' He throws the strongbox and pictures on the pile, just another little bit a trash.

"Back in the office, Red grabs the phone, tells somebody he needs a truck over at Fleischmann Scrap an hour ago. Then he takes a rag, mops up a coupla bloodsmears from where Pop was lying. 'Sorry, Murray,' he tells me. 'The nigger hadda go. If the girl got a look at him and she ever wakes up...but even if she don't wake up. Let the cops go askin' him questions—'

"George wouldn'a said Word One."

"Red shakes his head, taps out a Lucky, lights up. 'Murray, Murray—hey, listen, pal, I know how you feel. He was a damn good nigger. But you can't count on a nigger to act like a white man when cops start in on him.'"

Flash of fire in the old junkman's eyes. "I take a step, gonna put out his lights, but I'm all of a sudden looking at the wrong end of that Quiet Betsy. Red waves it sideways. 'Murray, stop bein' a schmuck. Sit down...yeah, that's right. Good.' He puts the rod back away, sits himself down in the other chair. 'Listen, Murray—be pretty dumb-ass business for me to kill a goose, lays gold eggs like you do. And with no more partners you're gonna be one rich goose, startin' with a great big load of aluminum, all yours now. We just gotta make sure nobody comes 'round looking for Oscar or the nigger. Nigger's easy. Come morning, his wife and kids'll be missin' too. Anyone asks you, he said he was gonna go take his family back down south. Happens alla time.'

"I hear a motor outside. Red runs, opens the gate, closes it behind the truck. Great big moving van, coulda held Fort Knox and the U.S. Capitol at the same time. Couple gorillas jump out, grab off the tarps, start tossin' aluminum like it was foam rubber. Not twenty minutes, all the aluminum's on the truck and the truck's on its way.

"Red and me go back in the office. 'Meet you here about nine,' he says. 'We gotta close the door on Oscar. Make the cops and everybody else think he beat up that girl, then took a powder. So nobody ever gets it into their head to dig around under the garbage. And Murray, mum to Lily for right now, huh? 'Cause if you ain't worried about your own health, you oughta be about hers...oh, hey, wait a minute.' He takes out Pop's and George's wallets, looks in Pop's, shakes his head. 'Mother Hubbard's.' Then he peeks in George's, whistles, pulls out a handful of bills, does a quick count. 'Well, looky here, Murray. Nothin' in Oscar's wallet, but five hundred in the nigger's. Where's a nigger get five hundred bucks, huh? Guess we know what he was doing while you were *schleppin'* the girl over to the trestle.' Red tries to put the scratch in my hand, but I pull away like it's on fire. 'I don't want it,' I tell him.

"He gives me a funny look. 'Murray, whaddaya think? You walk away from the dough, the nigger's gonna wake up? Or you're fixed so good you don't need a fast and easy five? Come on, pal, you don't want me thinkin' you're a bad businessman, now, do you?' He slaps the dough in my hand, then smacks me on the arm. 'See you back here, nine o'clock.' Then he puts on his white gloves and picks up the purse.

Murray shifted his weight to the other buttock, hawked, wiped at his eyes. "That's when I knew, Dockie. Up to then, I figured I could play in the dirt and just go wash off my hands afterwards. Trust a guy like Red Dexter 'cause I thought we were pals? Talk about being a schmuck. I wanted to go straight to the cops, but I knew damn well a lot a them had their hands in Red's pocket. I was scared for what could happen to Lily. Red's boys would've done worse than just killin' her.

"So quarter to nine, I'm back there, and nine sharp, here comes Red, looking like he had a good ten hours in the sack. He's wearing his gloves, carrying that leather purse. 'Girl's still out,' he says. 'Prob'ly ain't never gonna wake up.' He waves the purse under my nose. 'Good thing you didn't get rid a this before I got here.' Then he tells me his idea. We're gonna set up Leo, get him down to the yard and make him think he spotted Pop hauling ass to New York. I ask him ain't there some way we could do it without Lily, but he shakes his head. 'She'll go along. If she don't understand, tell her how the gun that killed your nigger friend a few hours ago just might turn up registered to Murray Fleischmann, and a couple bodies might just be dug up in Murray's junkyard.' He holds up the purse. 'And this might turn up in the wrong place, with Murray's fingerprints all over it. *And* a bum might walk into the cop shop downtown, tell 'em he was under the Fourth Av trestle last night and saw a guy dump a girl... Hey, nothing personal, Murray. Just business, is all.'"

Murray spat a gob into the underbrush. "I couldn't believe it, Dockie. You try and do what's right for everybody but one thing always leads to another, and sometimes that ain't the thing you wanted. I didn't ever mean for nobody to get hurt."

"I believe you."

He worked me over with his junkman's eyes. "Red and me lock up the yard, then I go stop by Pop's house, get some a his clothes, smelliest ones I could find. From there I head on home, talk to Lily. She ain't the least bit hot on Red's idea, don't want to take a chance on getting Samuel in trouble, but I ask her what are we supposed to do, and besides, why should Samuel get in any trouble except maybe with his son, which he oughta be able to handle. She still ain't happy, but finally goes and gets her album with the pictures of all the girls ever stayed with us, and their babies." Murray's face twisted into a grim mask of torment. "That attic was her whole life—mothers, babies, they were alla them her kids. Samuel wasn't crazy about her taking pictures, but she said please, she'd keep the album where absolutely nobody'd ever find it. And Samuel—"

"Figured if someone ever did find the pictures, he could talk his way around anything. Even a handful of money and Red Dexter's hand on his shoulder. But Samuel wasn't in on the junkyard operation, was he?"

"Course not. With your grandpa it was only people. Why do you think he died broke? See, Dexter and his wife wanted kids, but she once had this bad infection, blocked up her tubes, which of course is something Samuel knows. So he makes a deal with Red. Him and the Missus'll get the first baby off the line—"

"If Red gives Samuel and Lily enough money to get the operation rolling."

"Bingo, Dockie. Our upstairs in the attic, that was the Red Dexter Dormitory for Girls Had Noplace Else to Go. Plus, enough scratch to buy medical equipment, supplies, medicines, everything Samuel needed. Lily took a picture of Red and Samuel and me yukkin' it up, then one of Red giving Samuel the dough. 'Get both a them shots,' Red tells me. 'We want to make good and goddamn sure that kid is so lathered he don't stop an' think, just comes runnin' down here all set to put out Oscar's lights.' So I take them and a couple others. Meanwhile, Lily gets a wig, dyes it gray and cuts it so it's like Pop's hair. Then I go back to the yard, open up, business as usual 'til three o'clock. Longest day I ever spent in my life. Three o'clock, I lock up, go on back home, and Lily turns me into Pop. Makeup, wig—was she good or what? 'Course it don't hurt I'm built just like him. With his stinkin' clothes, I'm a goddamn ringer."

Murray's words quavered with disgust. "I sneak out the back way, run down to the yard, go in, lock the gate behind me, sit in the office. Few minutes later, here comes White-Gloves Red, opens up with George's key, walks in like he owns the place. I give him the pictures, he puts them in an envelope, puts the envelope in the girl's purse. 'I got that bum Aldo out in the car,' he says. 'Girl's still in Dreamland, kid's glued to her bedside. Samuel's got an emergency gall bladder operation scheduled for four—'

"'How the hell you know all this?' I say to him. He grins, taps out a Lucky, lights up, blows smoke at me. 'Murray, how many times I got to tell you, it's business? We're everyplace. I know a nurse...hey, it's almost five. Gotta get Aldo over to the Steinberg. That kid's gonna be down here before half an hour, keep a good eye out.'

"Red goes, leaves the gate open. I wait in the office, door locked, watch out the corner of the window. Anyone except your old man comes, I'll lay low like nobody's home right now. Just about half an hour, Samuel's car flies in through the gate, pulls up in front. Out jumps Leo, runs around to the other side. I hear a noise but don't see nothing. Next thing, Leo's tear-assin' straight for the office, ready to blow Pop away. I unlock the door, let him come in, grab him from behind so he can't get a good look at me. I'm gonna give him a couple cuts, knock him around enough to put cotton in his head and rubber in his legs, then run out the gate, duck down by the river, head on home the back way and get changed back to Murray. But I didn't count on Samuel..."

The old man choked on the name, put his hand to his mouth. His eyes filled but he fought it off. "Here comes Samuel through the door, shit! What the hell *happened*? He gets any kinda look at me, the whole plan's dead as a mackerel and me along with it, never mind Lily. Quick slash on the kid's wrist, blood all over the place, I pitch him across the room and take off. Out the gate, down Fifth, over to Pop's, in, out, just so maybe someone'll see me. Then I sneak back home through the alley. I figure Samuel'll take care a your old man, he can take care of anything. But then I hear what happened and I'm sick, Dockie, sick at my heart, sick to death. Whole next day I can't even get outa my bed. And Lily..."

Murray paused, as if to let a painful cramp in his belly pass. "She tells me *I* deserve to die, then won't talk to me, won't set a foot in our bedroom. She goes and lives up in the attic with the girls. Last one there was the little blonde, Susie. A couple from Maryland was gonna take her baby but Lily calls 'em, tells 'em Samuel died and the deal's off. Then she goes and talks to Doc Charlie Harrison and Phil Jurgens, our lawyer. When Susie goes into her labor, Charlie comes, does the delivery, and Lily's finally got her own baby, names her Clara. Lily quits work at the beauty shop, stays home with Clara, cooks our food, cleans house, but won't come anywhere near me. Won't let me hug her, won't let me *touch* her. She buys twin beds, moves 'em into our room, puts Clara right next door. Ten, eleven years later,

Lily's heart starts to go. 'Promise me, Murray,' she says. 'When my heart gives out, you'll take good care of Clara.' 'Well, sure,' I tell her. 'What else would I do? I love Clara, she's my kid too.' Look Lily gives me woulda froze a chili pepper. I figure maybe moving to Verona might help, big house, real nice neighborhood , but nah, no dice. We go on just like before, only I got a longer ride to work. When Lily's laying in her bed dying, every time she looks at me I can see it in her eyes. *For what happened to Samuel I won't ever forgive you.*"

Murray's eyes clouded. "V-J Day, I figure I'm out, but no. Enlist with a guy like Red Dexter, you're in for the duration—*his* duration. Red comes by one morning, says now there's gonna be a big building boom, all the soldiers coming home, and The Business needs a right guy to run a wholesale-retail hardware store. So I go to a certain lawyer, he writes up a power of attorney, says I got full authority to manage Pop's affairs, dates the thing from some time in 1942, and turns around his chair so he's looking out the window while I sign Pop's name. Notary seal and bingo, Murray Fleischmann can do whatever he wants with Fleischmann Scrap. I sell it to Wyslinki, dumb fucking Polack, and inside of just a couple years he runs the place into the ground."

"Into the ground is right," I said. "That's where they put up those municipal housing projects in the sixties. Oscar's under fifteen stories of brick and concrete."

Murray nodded grimly. "I'd laugh except George's there with him. Anyway, I open up my...*their* hardware store, out Route Four in Grassville. I buy from who they tell me, sell to who they tell me, look in the other direction while money gets to be cleaner than when it came in through the door. When Lily dies, couple days after the funeral, I buy me a rod, sit in my living room with it a whole night long. Only thing stops me pullin' the trigger is I remember what I promised to Lily. Clara's seventeen now. Lose her mother, then have her old man blow away the top of his head? Nah. In the morning I go off to work, pitch the rod in the river on my way. Clara keeps telling me I should find a nice woman, get married again, but truth is...aw hell, Dockie. Truth is, I tried a few times with a woman but couldn't never, you know. So I just go on at the hardware store, that's my whole life. Every morning I wake up and think, shit, I'm still alive, another day. Finally I hit sixty-five and they let me retire."

"Honorable discharge," I said.

A laugh burst from the old man's mouth. "You're something else, you know that? When I saw you back there in the pool room I damn near had a heart attack, thought I was seeing ghosts. Goddamn crime your grandpa never got to lay his lamps on you."

"Dexter end up under concrete too?"

Another laugh, this one muted in thick sarcasm. "Red? Not on your life. Big car, jewelry for the wife and girlfriends, mansion in Atlantic Highlands, bodyguards, died in his bed maybe five years ago, eighty-nine years old. But you know something? I think maybe he was as much of a prisoner as me." Wistfulness drifted across Murray's face like cloud cover rolling in late on a summer afternoon. "Sixty years now, I been saying, Why? Why wasn't it *me* drew George's straw, or even better, Pop's? That poor girl...George, his wife, kids...Samuel..." Murray swallowed hard, couldn't hold back a sob. "All of 'em wiped out because of what a schmuck I was. Murray Fleischmann and one goddamn little straw fucked up how many lives?"

The old junkman put me in mind of a bear at the zoo, tormented by cruel children, desperately trying to paw his way through the bars of his cage. "I figured I owe Leo, owe him big. Whole summer long, I go down to see him at the Steinberg, he's practically camping out next to that girl's bed. Hospital visiting hours those days're two to four in the afternoon, that's it, period, but him only sixteen and he gets them to look the other way. I tell him, let me help a little, huh? And he says, 'I'm okay, Murray,' or 'Thanks, Murray, I'll let you know if I need anything.' Lily says to me, he don't *want* help, how many times he gotta tell you? But..." Murray pounded his big right fist into the palm of his left hand. "*I'm gonna give!* I put money in envelopes, no return address, however much I can manage. Mail 'em from different post offices, so he thinks it's from all different people. Then, when he cracks up, I go see a lawyer in New York... Hey, Dockie, I'm tellin' you news?"

I nodded. "Dad cracked up? I never knew—"

"Yeah. Happened right before school started. One day he doesn't come outa his room, and them people he's stayin' with, doctor and his wife, they go inside, but no Leo. Finally, one of them checks under the bed, and bingo, two eyes. He's curled up in a little ball, back against the wall, won't talk, won't move. They get Doc Harrison, he calls a shrink, they take the kid to this high-class bughouse in Clifton, Crestview Rest Home. Almost two years, he's there."

Why he didn't graduate from college until 1950.

"So like I was sayin', I go to New York, get a lawyer, pay what I can, nobody knows who the dough's comin' from. They sell his house for him, which pays the rest of his bills at Crestview. By the time he's out, I've got that hardware store, a cow with gold tits, so I get my lawyer to send money straight to your old man's college, tuition, room, board, the works, every single semester. Then, the whole four years he's in Europe, my mouthpiece sends him jack to live on. Let him say no to *that*."

For a moment I saw Murray as he must've looked to Dad, shoulders square, eyes flashing, his right hand pumping high above his head. He let loose a raucous crow, the old Hobart buyer and seller's victory cry. "Runs in our families, see? Pop put Samuel through school, I put Leo through."

"But that's not the whole story," I said.

As if I'd splashed cold water in his face. "What the hell you mean, not the whole story?"

"Oscar lived his life on autopilot—push his button, then watch him yell and scream and wave his fists. Did he ever once plan anything even a minute ahead? When Samuel told him the appliance store was sold, all he could think to do was push money into my grandfather's hand, there! Now it's sold to *me*. I can't begin to see Oscar working out a complicated scheme to poison Jonas, drag him over to your house, dump him in your living room, and then hold you, Lily and Samuel for ransom."

"Yeah?" Canny eyes, sizing me up. Was I holding four aces or bluffing off a ten-high?

"You told Samuel and my dad that Jonas loved the ladies, but never the same one long enough to get married. Even if he happened to get one of them pregnant, right?"

Murray's face swung sharply away, as if I'd slapped him. I kept myself talking, faster. "I'll bet especially if he got one of them pregnant. Remember Jack's Pharmacy, down on Sixteenth, closest drugstore to your old house? Jack's son-in-law runs it now. On my way out here I stopped to look over their poison log from July, 'forty-three."

Murray turned back, stared at me. "Shit," said his face. "Four A's."

"Do I have to show you the page Angela Gumpert signed? 'Strychnine, to poison a rat.' A rat who got her pregnant and wouldn't do what in 1943 was the only decent thing *to* do?"

"All these years..." I could hardly make out the words. "But what the hell difference does it make now? Except for me and Leo, they're dead, every one of them. You're good, Dockie, damn good at putting together two and two. Yeah, it was Jonas, all right. He was some piece a work, my brother, had Mama's looks and a twenty-four carat gift of gab. Girls were nuts over him from the time he was ten years old. Most honest businessman you ever saw, wouldn't touch black market metal, but he'd shtup a different girl every night and tell her she was his one and only. Like a game for him.

"Then the war. Worst thing a guy could do was put horns on a serviceman. My dumb-ass brother actually kept score. He was up to sixteen when he got holda Angela, that poor broad, she'd married a sailor, had a quick baby, then the guy got himself blown up someplace in the Pacific. Jonas hears a couple guys in the junkyard talking about it, and sees his big chance. Already got sixteen Silver Star Shtups, now he can get a Gold Star. Guy could talk like an angel while he's screwing like the devil, and he's in Angela's pants before she knows they're offa her. Naturally, he couldn't take time to put on a rubber, so next thing she knows she's in the family way, with a battleax mother-in-law and two very nasty brothers-in-law who ain't gonna like her news one bit.

"So she goes to Jonas, and Jonas drops her on Lily and Samuel. This poor Italian Catholic girl, she can't even look Samuel in the face when he talks about abortion, but what else is she supposed to do? She can't live seven months in that attic with the baby she's already got, and besides, what's she gonna tell her family and her husband's family? Her own mother's dead, so Samuel goes to the mother-in-law, tells her Angela's got very serious nerve problems 'counta what happened to her husband, and Samuel's got her in a special hospital in New York, no visitors. Can Mother-in-law keep the baby for a week, maybe two, then look after Angela for a month or so after that? What's the old bag gonna say except yes?

"Now it's all set—we think. But the night before the abortion, Angela calls up Jonas, says she wants to talk to him. He comes over, she takes him in the kitchen, and the rest we only find out later. Angela makes one last pitch for a walk down the aisle, and of course Jonas says no way. Okay, she says, it's jake by her as long as he covers alla the costs, and while they're talking about that, she gives him coffee, strychnine's already in the cup. Lily and me hear this terrible screeching, we run in, and there's Jonas down on the floor, going like a jackknife, open-shut-open-shut. Angela's standing over him, screaming about how he ain't ever gonna mess up any more women. He's just plain screaming, then he goes blue in the face an' stops breathing. Angela doesn't even notice, just goes on hollering about how that'll fix *you*, you son of a bitch.

"I look at Lily, she looks at me. Cops get a foot inside the door, our whole operation's straight down the tube, and Lily and me *and* Samuel are in for heavy time. So I schlep Jonas into the living room, Lily gets Angela upstairs, then she calls up Samuel. No ans...uh...your old man told you about his mother? Your grandma?"

"That she was addicted? Yes."

"Okay then. Your grandfather was the first doc in Hobart had an answering service, knew he needed it. Lily calls, tells the operator it's an emergency, operator gives Lily the number where Samuel's at. Lily calls there, tells him what happened. 'Heart attack, huh?' Samuel says. 'Be right over.' The rest you know. Samuel went to Pop's afterwards to make sure Pop swallowed the heart attack story. Then we cremated Jonas so no one could ever check and find out what he really died of." Murray blew a low whistle between his teeth. "Loose ends we got dangling around our lives...all these years, that poison-book, just sitting there at Jack's, waiting for you to come around and look at it."

"I didn't exactly say I looked at it—"

"Hell you didn't. You said—"

"That I stopped to look over their poison log from July, 'forty-three. Druggists usually don't destroy old poison logs, just stash them in the attic or basement and forget about them. The stuff in Jack's basement goes back to 1924, piles higher than my head. Filthiest damn place I've ever seen. I quit looking for that log after the third time I had to clean rat shit off my hands. But I'll bet anything it's there. If you'd made me dig it out, I would've."

Murray looked stricken; then he snickered. "Oh, man! I don't believe in that reincarnation stuff, but if anybody could ever come back to life it'd be Samuel Firestone. All you need's a Panama."

"Glad to finally tell your story?"

Little wave. "Six one, half dozen the other." The old junkman rested a hand on my shoulder, sized me up. "Tell you, Dockie. What I really wish is I could one more time see Samuel and Lily and George, look 'em in the eye, tell 'em I'm sorry. But that ain't never gonna happen." If Murray looked like a frightened spaniel before, now he looked like a mournful overweight beagle, liquid brown eyes endlessly sad above puffy folds of skin. "Only one left for me to talk to is your old man, and yeah, I did pay his way through school, but that ain't enough. Before one of us croaks, I'd like to at least look *him* in the eye an' tell him there ain't been one minute the whole last sixty years I didn't feel sorry for what I done."

"I'll see what I can do," I said.

Murray narrowed his eyes. "Bet you figure he's a real tough nut, your old man."

I smiled. "Bingo yourself."

"Yeah. Well. He *is* tough, hadda be. What-all he went through that summer woulda stopped most people cold. His father, his mother, then afterwards the girl. I never in my life saw a person suffer like your old man suffered for that girl, whole summer long he was absolutely devoted to her, heart and soul and kidneys. You only know one parta him, just like you only know the one parta *his* old man he picked out to tell you."

I took Route Twenty-three, Pompton Turnpike, out of Verona, drove Charlie Barnet's once-upon-a-time musical inspiration into Great Notch, where I stopped at a diner and chewed Murray's request along with a turkey sandwich. I'd carried more junk away from Verona than I'd bargained for. "Me and your old man, we're more alike than you probably think," Murray once told Dad, and how right he was. With the best intentions, the Sorcerer and the Junkman paved twin freeways to hell. Helene probably would tell me if I couldn't get to well enough, just leave bad enough alone. Quit now, go back to New York, let the story lie.

But stories should never lie, nor end unfinished.

I threw money on the table, ran out to the car, got back on the road, twenty minutes into downtown Hobart. Found a meter on Market Street, hoofed a block to the big white granite Hobart City Hall. Pigeons scurried around my feet. I sprinted past the towering statue of Alexander Hamilton, prime target for the Pigeon Bomb Brigade, took the worn graystone steps two at a time into the building, rode the creaking elevator to the fourth floor, zipped into the Office of Vital Statistics. A dark-haired woman slowly sneaking up on middle age sat behind a counter, framed by frosted glass panels. She asked how she might help me.

"I need to see a couple of death certificates," I said.

She reached to a pile of forms. "Fill out one of these for each certificate you wish. You can leave them here or mail them in. Allow four to six weeks..."

Her canned speech tailed off as she saw the green paper rectangle I pushed toward her, Ben Franklin giving her a steady double-O. "It's a family matter," I said. "Urgent."

She looked around. Another clerk, busy talking to another customer. No one else in the room. "I see..." the woman said, then pulled in the money with a hand like the claw on an arcade machine. "We're not terribly busy right now. I think we can accommodate you."

On the road again, Hobart to Peconic Bay, early rush hour. Plenty of time to think. Tempting, so tempting, to drive only as far as Manhattan, give Mr. Avis back his car, pick up

Helene and go somewhere for dinner, definitely a couple of drinks. But I knew I'd hate myself in the morning, and probably every morning after that.

As I turned into my parents' driveway, the late-afternoon sun splashed flame over the stucco house. Fierce glare off windows, I threw up a hand to shade my eyes. Only one other car there, Dad's gray Jag, good. No need for Plan B, the one that took Mother into account.

I used my front-door key, stood, listened. Silence. I started through the vestibule, walked slowly into the living room, stopped in front of Mother's piano just long enough to glance at her portrait. Then I took off down the left hallway. Dad's den was at the end of that hall, as far as a person could go and still be inside the house. His painting studio was all the way in the other direction, past the kitchen. I walked the length of the hall, stopped in front of the door, raised a fist—and froze.

Dad's den, *his* room. Over the years, I'd managed a few peeks when he came out for dinner or to go back to his studio, but I never saw anything remarkable. Big rolltop desk, wooden chair, a leather sofa, books, paintings, a table radio. Every so often, I heard soft music behind that door, figured it came from the radio.

I looked at my fist, willed it forward, couple of knocks. No answer. I tried the knob. Locked.

Without thinking, I drew back a foot and kicked in the door.

I wrenched splintered fragments out of my way, ducked through the frame, charged across the room to a small music box on an ebony table at the far side of the sofa. The colorful card inside the opened lid featured hovering angels, children at play, and a man turning the crank of a street organ. On a central panel, six tune titles in flowing script—"Sweet Bye and Bye," "Beautiful Dreamer," "Camptown Races," "Gaudeamus Igitur," "O Susanna," "Home Sweet Home."

Like a sandbag to the ribs. I wiped at my eyes, then looked up at the wall, at a painting I *had* seen before, but only in glimpses, and not many of those. A girl blowing a saxophone, sandy hair flying every which way, dimples you could disappear into. Brilliant green eyes glowed behind huge lenses. Dad never did portraits, *never*, but there was his tiny black LEO in the lower right corner. Not a particularly large canvas, just about the right size to sit on a portable easel in a basement, under an unshaded light bulb. I couldn't recognize my own mother from the face in the painting over the piano, but I could've counted Harmony's freckles.

I walked back through the smashed door panel, leaned against the wall, just let the waterworks run. How do you get your mind around sixty years and counting in purgatory?

I gave myself a couple of minutes, then swabbed my sleeve across my face and pulled myself upright. Work to do, not going to be easy.

Still no sounds other than my own. In his studio, all the way at the other end of the house, Dad wouldn't have heard my break-and-enter. I walked back through the kitchen, then down the hall to the open studio doorway.

He stood at the far end of the room, next to the window, brush in hand. I tiptoed in. My shadow fell across his canvas.

He wheeled, turned a face on me ragged with anguish. Lips bloodless and contorted, skin loose under hollow eyes, jaw full-open on its hinges. I backed away.

"Martin! God damn it to hell, you startled me."

Was he trying to position himself between his work and me? "Saturday, you wanted to talk to me," I said. "Today, other way 'round." I pointed at the wet paintbrush in his hand. "I can go out if you want, wait 'til you're done."

He shot a glance at his watch, then shook his head. "No. Your mother's over visiting Millie Hartog, won't be back for another hour. Just let me clean up." He grabbed palette and brushes, walked to the sink.

Something about the painting... I looked more closely. A little boy, right arm splinted, lay on a mattress on the floor of a dimly lit room. Over him stood a hefty woman in a short, sheer nightgown, shoulders hunched, head bowed. Opposite the woman, a dark, unkempt man leaned against the wall, black hair falling over his piggy eyes. Anger, humiliation—the misery of the couple took my breath away. Two other figures were incomplete, faces blurred, attitudes unclear. A man wearing a Panama hat stood in profile, arm extended, seemingly talking to the couple; at his side, a tall boy held a big black bag that looked too heavy for him. I reached a finger. Paint on most of the canvas was long dry, but scrapes and irregularities in the wet paint over the man and boy attested to Dad's frustration. One thing was clear. What light there was in that squalid room emanated from the man in the Panama.

Voice from over my shoulder. "See anyone you know?"

Dad set his palette and brushes onto a small wooden table, lowered himself into a straightbacked chair, motioned me toward another one across a little worktable. As I sat, he stretched his long legs, then fixed that look on me guaranteed to turn my trousers into short pants. "All right," he said. "What's up? Cut to the chase."

Did he know what was coming? Couldn't tell, but he was taking great care to look anywhere except at his painting. I swallowed, moistened my tongue against the roof of my mouth. "Your story the other day... I've been thinking." I tried to launch a graceful dive into treacherous conversational currents. "I was out to Verona this morning—spent a little time at the Wapping Ridge Residence for Seniors of Highly Independent Means."

Dad stared, flummoxed.

"I talked to one of the inmates...Murray Fleischmann."

Now Dad barely managed to stay seated. "Murray Fleischmann? I didn't think...wouldn't have thought he was still alive."

"Eighty-six," I said. "With all his marbles bright and shiny."

Dad shook his head. "I'll be goddamned."

"Not necessarily," I said.

"All right, Martin." Fighting to get back into control. "Why did you go to see Murray, and what did he tell you?"

"Got a little time, Dad?"

"I already told you. Your mother'll be back in an hour."

Chapter 19

Dad listened carefully, not a word while I told him how Jonas Fleischmann really died, what happened to Oscar and George, how Red Dexter's coverup scheme led to Samuel's death, and what Murray's life had been since that summer. I finished into silence. Finally Dad spoke through his teeth. "Always knew I blew it, just never how badly."

I leaned across the worktable. "Dad, it was wartime. You played in the majors at sixteen, with some pretty savvy vets." Lips tight, jaw set, he looked ready to go off, but I went first. "You're every bit as arrogant as Samuel ever was."

Flash of shock in Dad's eyes.

"You think you earned the whole rap for that disaster? Goddamn it, give Oscar Fleischmann the credit he deserves—people like him spread rottenness like cancer. Give Dr. and Mrs. Belmont credit for being so stupid with Harmony. Give Harmony some credit herself for running off alone to the junkyard instead of figuring there must've been a good reason why you didn't show. Most of all, give Samuel credit. Getting a sixteen-year-old kid to put eight balls in the air when he was still—"

"Enough."

Could've meant "Shut up," but it sounded more like "My turn." I waited.

Dad sighed. No Manhattans under his belt now; words were not going to come without a battle. "Bending rules for a sick person's benefit, sure. But before you can bend a rule, you've got to know the fucking thing even *exists*, and Samuel wouldn't have recognized a rule hung in front of his face in neon lights. He was law unto himself, unrestricted license. When he finally lost his footing he had nothing to grab hold of, and a whole world came crashing down around him."

"Crushing his wife and Harmony. George, George's family. Mangling Lily and Murray. Crippling his own son. He earned his credit, Dad."

No response.

If I needed to drag it out of him, I would. "Did you say Harmony died right after Samuel?"

Wary nod. "Not long."

"While you were still in the hospital yourself? You never got to see her again? Like you never saw Murray after Samuel's funeral?"

"Martin..."

I pulled two papers out of my pocket, laid them on the table in front of my father. "Photocopies, death certificates. Samuel Firestone, July 17, 1943. Harmony Joy Belmont, August 27, 1943. Dad, that's a month and a half later."

He looked slowly from the papers to me, eyes weighted with nearly six decades of suffering.

"Murray said you practically pitched a tent at Harmony's bedside that summer. When he wanted to see you to offer help, he went to the hospital. Early morning, late at night, didn't matter. Why didn't you tell me that?"

No answer.

"Sorry Dad. But you really did get a contract offer yourself, didn't you?."

Past the point of no return. Dad's eyes were those of a man waiting for the trap to be sprung, an instant of exquisite pain, then eternal peace. He sat straight in his chair, voice loud, clear. "All summer in that hospital room... Harmony, cheeks gaunt, more sallow every day. Her hair went to tangled greasy knots on the pillow, so I learned to give bed-shampoos. I brushed her hair, put it in barrettes. Every two hours I turned her so her skin wouldn't break down. Her pulse and blood pressure stabilized, she started breathing on her own, but never moved a muscle, every brain wave study flat as a ruler-line. One afternoon, Charlie Harrison came to talk to the Belmonts and me, told us what I knew was coming. Beds were tight at Steinberg—war casualties—and Harmony might stay the way she was for months or years. She could get nursing care at County.

"Poor Mrs. Belmont went completely to pieces. Dr. Belmont took her home, gave her a sedative, stayed with her. I sat with Harmony a while longer, held her hand. Finally I got up, went home, picked up the music box..."

We both glanced toward the den.

"And took it to the hospital, up to Harmony's room, put it on the night-table, turned it on, watched. Nothing, not a twitch. I pushed her eyelids open...oh, Martin. Like the eyes on a fish after you whack its head with a club."

I didn't know how he was getting through this, wasn't sure how much more I could handle. I pictured Helene, eyes closed, motionless, tubes in every orifice, dripping, draining. Hair framing her face on the pillow, an angel with a black halo.

"I closed Harmony's eyes, stood there a minute, maybe two, thought of her at the Passaic County Hospital for the Insane and Mentally Retarded. Feeding tube in one end, catheter in the other, lying in her excrement, becoming a leather-covered skeleton with bedsores. 'God *damn* you, Samuel!' I think I actually shouted it out loud. 'How could you leave her like this?' Weeping, bawling... I glanced back toward the doorway, then I pinched Harmony's nose with one hand, covered her mouth with the other. She didn't struggle, didn't even move. I counted to a hundred, then felt at her neck. No pulse."

"Dad..."

"'There, Samuel, I said. 'I've cleaned up your mess.' I shut off the music box, sat for a few minutes, then went out to the nurse and told her Harmony died. She said, 'Thank God.'"

And a few days later, you...broke down."

Eyes like pie dishes. "How—"

"Murray."

"Should've known. Christ!" He pounded one fist into the other, twice, three times, then looked hard at me. "Six weeks in that hospital room with nurses, doctors, techs, *everyone*, looking at Harmony and murmuring, 'If only Samuel were here.' Like prayer, past any logic, but they believed, every goddamn one of them, Samuel would've saved her. After she died, I couldn't sleep, three whole nights, just lay in the bed listening to Lily shout at me, over and over and over, *You don't deserve to be a doctor.* The morning of Harmony's funeral, I...." He set his chin. "I'm not going to tell you I'm sorry, Martin. If I had to, I'd do it again."

Sixty years of wrath and fury in paint, each canvas a crumpled license fired back to the Writer. Dad's face was terrible, but I couldn't stop, not after coming this far. "One thing to bend a rule to benefit a patient..."

Eyes narrowed, corners of his mouth pulled tight. He looked away, then back to me, spoke so softly I could barely hear. "Poor Charlie Harrison couldn't pronounce death, but Harmony really *was* dead, wasn't she?" He tapped a finger on the arm of his chair, slowly took my measure. "What would you have done?"

I could almost hear my grandfather's voice. "You never know what you're going to do 'til you're there—and sometimes you surprise yourself." *Would* I have pinched that girl's nose and covered her mouth? Decided she was better off under ground than at the Passaic County Hospital for the Insane and Mentally Retarded? My mind's eye saw Helene, strapped for the rest of her life into a wheelchair, making incoherent sounds, purposeless movements, and something in my throat cut loose. Words poured out, I couldn't have stopped them to save my life. "Dad, I didn't meet Helene at a party. I met her at Bellevue. They brought her in unconscious, intubated, boyfriend babbling sixteen to the dozen, terrified she'd die. He'd slipped angel dust into her drink, a little love potion. I was the aide on the ward that shift. Seizures, coma, brain activity so abnormal... About four A.M., we got her stabilized. I was cleaning up, went into the bathroom, and when I came out, there was her father, bending over, just about to pull the plug on the respirator. I hit him with a flying tackle. He started shouting about how he didn't want a vegetable on his hands for the rest of his life. I pulled him away, chased him the hell out, and then stayed in that room almost five days, called in sick to work. I made sure Helene got every medication, right on schedule. I washed her, dried her, brushed her hair, changed her catheter. Cleaned her up when she... Nurses brought me food. I used the bathroom right there, even left the door open while I was inside. Didn't put a foot out of that room 'til Helene woke up and got completely off life support." I paused, as short of breath as if I'd run a mile. "Afterward, of course, I still spent all the time I could there, and when she was discharged, she came home with me. Call it continuing care. Any time I was away from her more than a few hours, I had to call, check up. A little fatigue, some stress at work, she'd be screaming, no control, then afterward, depressed as hell. Mother wondered why we wanted such a small wedding? That's why."

I thought Dad's smile might break my heart. "Well, tit-tat, boyo. I tell my secret, you tell yours. So you'd have let Harmony go to County?"

What had he just said, a few minutes before? "She really *was* dead, wasn't she?" Professor Skeptikos, he used to call me, and those two words, "wasn't she?" invoked the one commandment a skeptic is bound to obey, his faith grounded in the inexplicable. When nothing's taken on faith, everything is possible.

"Unconscious patient gets the benefit of my doubt, Dad. With just maintenance treatment, no heroics, Harmony probably would've gotten pneumonia...."

Fierce scorn on Dad's face ground me to a stop. Oscar Wilde, who could resist anything except temptation, also said that all men kill the thing they love. "The coward does it with a kiss," Wilde wrote. "The brave man with a sword."

"Go on," Dad said.

Quick-step from Wilde to Waller, cue from Fats. I think I smiled. "One never knows, Dad, does one?"

He looked as if I'd offered him a week-old chunk of liverwurst. "Martin, Martin... What if Helene never did wake up?"

I came within a hair of saying, "I always *knew* she would," caught myself, but it didn't matter. The look in Dad's eyes said he'd gotten my king into a corner square, absolutely nowhere to go.

"Twenty-five years, I've been waiting." Dad's voice was like far-off thunder, rumbling behind a distant hilltop. "Knew this was going to happen. *He'd* have heard that story I told you Saturday, then gone meddling with Murray Fleischmann—and all for *my* good, of course." Dad pounded his chest so hard I was afraid I'd hear bones crack. "So Sleeping Beauty was going to wake up because *you* said she would. And now you think your contract's signed and sealed—well, think again, kid. You didn't even *know* her. What would you have lost if Helene's old man did pull that plug? A dream? Every goddamn night we go to sleep, and have another dream." Most wicked chuckle I've ever heard. "Those five days in her room were just your teaser, the old come-on. God's little lead card. Sucker-bait. There'll be more Helenes, and one day, I promise, a worse-than-Helene. God help you, son, if she—or *he*—doesn't make it."

He'd never called me son. Our eyes met. Black double-wall opened, an instant. Dad was right. If those moments lasted longer they'd burn us to cinders.

I cleared my throat. "Dad, you pleaded guilty nearly sixty years ago, got life without pardon from the sternest judge in the courthouse. But now you're up for parole, time off for good behavior. Take it. Tell Mother—"

Bang! The little worktable cracked and fell apart under the blow from Dad's fist. On his feet, standing over me. "Your mother and I have been married almost thirty years, Martin, been together close to thirty-five. I'm warning you, don't go meddling there. Don't even think about it."

I tried to sound calm. "She can take it, Dad."

"'She can take it.' Oh, Martin, you mooncalf. You fucking gold-plated double-dog-damn idiot." Again, he pounded his breastbone, enraged penitent. "I know good and god-damned well *she* can take it. It's *me* who couldn't. Let me just start talking to your mother about Harmony... Martin, I have all the respect in the world for your mother, a ton of affection—don't look at me like that. It's worked for thirty-five years. We have a good thing going." He laughed, hollow; Dad faked humor about as well as he faked any-thing. "I've never lifted a hand to your mother."

"I've never seen you lift a hand to any woman."

"I haven't been married to any of them." Another chuckle, this one real. "You mean well, Martin," he said, gruff, but almost a whisper. "At least *I* didn't have to bleed myself dry for *you*. But stay the hell out of what's none of your business and all of mine." He paused, chewed his lip, then his face relaxed ever so slightly. "I shouldn't have tried to keep you away from medicine. Wrong for Samuel to try to push me into it, just as wrong for me to push you the other way." He saw me about to speak, held up a hand. "I'll give you that. No more."

I jerked a thumb back over my shoulder. "Dad, at least finish that damn painting before it finishes you."

He stretched his hands high over his head, rocked back on his heels. By degrees, his face arranged itself into an expression of mild amusement. Fleshy lips curved ever so slightly at the corners, black eyes gleamed like polished ebony. Then he jumped to his feet, shot over to his easel, lifted the canvas, pushed it into my hands. "Here, Martin. I can't finish it, but I'm finished *with* it. Take it home."

I opened my mouth to object, but Dad, pokerfaced, slipped me a sucker punch. "Play your cards right, some day it'll be worth a chunk of change."

Under ordinary conditions I'd've laughed. Sun streamed through the window across Dad's face, highlighting his pebbly cheek. "Murray Fleischmann..." As if the words were being dragged forcefully from his throat. "You said he's at Wapping Ridge..."

"Residence for Seniors."

"I'd like to go see him. Thank him for helping me through my tough times. If he hadn't paid my way..." Dad paused, then added, "You want to do something for me, Martin? How about you run a little interference? Ask Murray whether he'd mind if I come?"

"Sure. Even go with you, if you'd like."

Dad's face brightened. "Would you?"

Would I miss the chance to see the Junkman and the Sorcerer's Apprentice face to face? Not for anything. "Sure."

Grim smile. "Thanks. Appreciate it."

I lifted the painting, took a step toward the door, then remembered. "Dad..."

Picture a man just through a root canal, who sees the dentist staring at another tooth. "*What*, Martin? What the fuck is it now?"

I pointed toward the hall. "Dad, I'm sorry. I...kicked it in. The door."

"Kicked in the *door*? What in holy hell are you talking about, Martin? You forgot your key? You don't believe in doorbells, they're against your religion?"

Hands on hips, wide-eyed as a buzzard on a tree limb, watching a bit of roadkill wriggle. I pulled myself to full height, eyes level with his. "Not the front door." I willed evenness to my voice, no shouting, no cracking. "The door to your den."

"The door to my... Jesus, Mary and Joseph!" Out of the studio as if shot from a cannon. I followed him at full pace, trying not to bang his painting against walls. Through the kitchen, down the hall, to the splintered door at the end. Dad wheeled around to face me. Not a sound, but his three-letter question was clear.

"I knocked. You didn't answer."

He dueled with a smile, back and forth across his face. "You knocked, I didn't answer. So you kicked in the door?"

I nodded.

The smile overran all disputed territory.

"I didn't want Mother to come home and find it." I pointed into the room, at Harmony. "Your basement project that summer?"

Smile suddenly in full retreat. "Only one I kept."

He ducked through the smashed door panel, and in an instant had Harmony off the wall, into the closet, closet door closed. Then over to the desk, opening a drawer. A moment later he was back, holding a small piece of paper, which he waved toward his shattered door. "Don't worry—your mother's come home to a lot worse than this," he growled. "Go on home, Sleeping Beauty's waiting." He put the paper into my free hand. "Here's something else, goes with your painting."

All the way back to New York, those two death certificates were like a bonfire in my shirt pocket. When the young copy-machine girl at the Hobart Vital Statistics Office saw the name on the first certificate, she sucked in a sharp mouthful of air. "Oh—do you *know* about him?" Rhetorical question, she ripped right on, told me how Dr. Samuel Firestone once cured her gramma who was *that far* from dying, knew just what was the matter and gave Gramma some special medicine that only he knew about. The copy machine spat out its work; the girl laid the warm sheet of paper in my hand. "But y'know, it's like..." Red cheeks, embarrassed giggle. "Well, kinda dumb. Gramma sometimes says she thinks Dr. Firestone didn't *really* die, he just, like went into hiding or something. 'He knew what to do for everybody in Hobart,' Gramma says. 'How could he not know for himself?'"

Near-dark by the time I got home, apartment pot roast-fragrant. Helene dogeyed me, stared at the painting under my arm. "Martin..."

I put my arms around her, hugged her long, hard. As we moved apart, she said, "Martin, something's the matter. Your dad...?"

"He's fine."

"Something's not fine. Or someone." She motioned toward the table, sit down. "I'll pour you a glass of wine, and you can tell me."

Bad hearing it, worse knowing I had to tell it, especially to Helene. But I'd learned at Bellevue, the longer you wait to drain an abscess, the worse it gets, and at some point it's just too late. Thirty or more years of my father's good thing, *I* didn't want.

Helene couldn't take her eyes off the painting. "Your dad's work is weird, but this? No faces at all?"

"Makes sense, trust me."

By the time I finished my story, Helene's thin, delicate skin looked painted with chalk, Harlequin gone cheerless and tragic. She drummed a spoon on the table top, chewed her lip. Finally, she managed one word. "Heartbreaking."

I looked across the room at the Firestone on the wall, jagged, blood-tinged blades of grass.

Helene pointed the spoon at the faceless painting. "Are you going to hang it?"

"If you don't mind."

"Well, no..." She rallied. "Of course not." Then she paused, just a moment. "Don't you feel at least a little sorry you never knew your grandpa? He sounds so... I think I wish *I* could've met him, maybe once."

I fumbled in my pocket, pulled out the photograph Dad gave me before I left, handed it to Helene. "Next best thing."

She studied the picture, then me, back to the photo, back to me. Her hand crept up, covered her mouth. "My God," a whisper. "Except for the hair—"

My silver mane. "From Mother's side."

"Only thing you got from her." Helene made a little noise, the half-choked gasp you might hear from a person sitting next to you in a movie theater, as the killer, unseen behind his victim, draws up just close enough to raise his weapon. Her face went dead-grim, lips drained. "Oh, Martin, I'm scared—because I don't think *you* are."

I wiped at a bead of sweat running down my cheek. "Why should I be—"

"You didn't call me today, why not? You're *always* calling to make sure I'm all right. You called Saturday from the restaurant, why didn't you call *today*? To tell me you were going out to see your father? That you'd be so late."

I didn't answer, couldn't.

Which infuriated her. "You *knew* how late you'd be." Up on her feet. "Didn't you think I'd be concerned? Worried? *Scared*?" Fists balled over her head, slim body rigid, shuddering. "Martin, *why didn't you call*?"

Because I never even thought of calling.

Against my will, I saw my sixteen-year-old father, sitting in the kitchen with Samuel, storm about to break, Samuel's face aglow. "Yes," Samuel said. "Yes. I love it."

"I'm sorry, Helene," I murmured. "Sorry. Really, *really* sorry."

After I got Helene cooled off and under the covers, I put our uneaten dinner into the fridge, dragged myself into the living room, flopped on my back on the couch. That was hours ago. I doze, come around, doze again. A Mobius-strip movie runs on the ceiling above my head, story without end. There's my young father, Murray Fleischmann, Lily. Oscar, George, Harmony. Ramona and Samuel...or is that me? I snap awake, pull the photo from my pocket, play stare-down with my grinning mirror-image. Don't ask who blinks.

I try not to imagine what my wife might be dreaming.

I stretch, swing my feet to the floor, take Harmony's death certificate from my pocket, tear the paper into tiny bits, watch them flutter into the wastebasket next to the couch. Then I pull out my grandfather's certificate, and tuck it with his photo between the back of Dad's painting and the wooden stretcher-frame. Carefully, quietly, I hang the painting on the front wall of the living room, eye-level, where I can't help but see it every time I reach for the doorknob. "He knew what to do for everybody in Hobart—how could he not know for himself?" Good question. Goddamned good question.

To receive a free catalog of Poisoned Pen Press titles, please contact us in one of the following ways:

Phone: 1-800-421-3976
Facsimile: 1-480-949-1707
Email: info@poisonedpenpress.com
Website: www.poisonedpenpress.com

Poisoned Pen Press
6962 E. First Ave. Ste. 103
Scottsdale, AZ 85251